When the Heart Sings

MUSIC OF HOPE SERIES

Book Two

When the Heart Sings

MUSIC OF HOPE SERIES
Book Two

A WWII Women's Fiction Novel

LIZ TOLSMA

GILEAD PUBLISHING

When the Heart Sings, book #2 in the Music of Hope series

Copyright © 2018 by Christine Cain
Published by Gilead Publishing, LLC
Wheaton, Illinois, USA.
www.gileadpublishing.com

gp GILEAD PUBLISHING

Scripture quotations are from the King James Version of the Bible.

ISBN: 978-1-68370-042-5 (printed softcover)
ISBN: 978-1-68370-043-2 (ebook)

Cover direction by Larry Taylor
Cover design by John Wollinka
Interior design by Amy Shock
Ebook production by Book Genesis, Inc.

Printed in the United States of America.
18 19 20 21 22 23 24 / 5 4 3 2 1

To Lisa,
the sister of my heart.

Your innumerable kindnesses and your
overwhelming generosity have sustained me during
many difficult times in my life. May you truly find the joy
that comes in the morning.

The Pole listening to Chopin listens to the voice of his whole race.

—Ignace Paderewski, prime minister of Poland from January–December 1919 and a world-renowned musician

To be defeated and not submit, is victory; to be victorious and rest on one's laurels, is defeat.

—Józef Pilsudski, Polish revolutionary and statesman

And now shall mine head be lifted up above mine enemies round about me: therefore will I offer in his tabernacle sacrifices of joy; I will sing, yea, I will sing praises unto the LORD.

Psalm 27:6

♪♫♪

Glossary of Foreign Words

Polish words
Babka – an older, respected woman who would help with births
Dzień dobry – good day
Do widzenia – good-bye
Dzięki – thank you (informally)
Dziękuję Ci – thank you (formally)
Jestem w domu – I'm home
Karpatka – cream cake
Kołaczki – Polish cookie filled with fruit, poppy seeds, or almond
   paste
Moja miłość – my love
Moje serce – my heart
Moje słońce – my sunshine
Nie – no
Pani – Mrs.
Pan – Mr.
Tak – yes
Tata – dad
Złoty – Polish currency

German words
Achtung – attention
Bitte – please
Danke – thank you
Essen – eat
Frau – Mrs.

Guten abend – good afternoon
Guten tag – good day
Halten sie – stop
Hauptmann – Wehrmacht rank equivalent to captain
Hauptscharführer – the highest enlisted rank in the SS
Herr – Mr.
Ja – yes
Jude – Jew (singular)
Komme – come
Lebensraum – literally "living space." Hitler's plan to have what he considered the racially superior Germans colonize Poland and enslave the Slavs living there.
Liebchen – sweetheart
Mutti – mother
Nein – no
Oberführer – senior colonel in the SS
Obersturmführer – first lieutenant in the SS
Schnell – hurry
Sehr gut – very good
Untersturmführer – second lieutenant in the SS
Volksdeutsche – someone who is considered German regardless of their nationality. The Poles could avoid some persecution by signing a piece of paper renouncing their Polish citizenship and becoming *Volksdeutsche*.
Vater – father

Chapter One

Central Poland, Early Spring 1943

*P*ain ripped through Natia Palinska's midsection. She grasped the bedcovers as another contraction gripped her and stole her breath. "*Nie, nie.*"

Her husband, Teodor, smoothed her hair from her damp forehead, his fingers calloused. "*Moje słońce*, it will be all right, my sunshine. Just hang on. Please, let me fetch a doctor."

She released the sheet and grasped him by the elbow. "Don't leave me. Our baby ..." Her heart pounded. She had failed him again.

"Hush now."

"It's too soon. Not another one gone." The pain in her heart was greater than that in her abdomen. This time, she'd held on to the pregnancy longer. This time, their child had moved within her.

The contraction ended. She sucked in a deep breath.

"You need a doctor. You're bleeding so much." His voice cracked.

She did this to him. Caused him this sorrow. Tears blurred her vision. "What doctor? The Germans took them all."

"Then the *babka* at least. She'll know what to do. This delivery is different." He gripped her hand until he almost crushed it.

"Don't go. Please. What if I need you? I'll be alone." The back of her throat burned. If only Mama were here.

He caressed her cheek. "*Pani* Nowakowa is right down the road. I'll be back in less than five minutes."

Another pain racked her body. She returned Teodor's crushing grasp. If only the Lord would make it stop. The agony in her body. The agony in her soul.

She focused on breathing until the physical anguish passed. "Go, go. Before another pain comes."

Teodor kissed her brow and hurried from the small bedroom, the scent of the fresh outdoors lingering behind him. She stared at the small crucifix on the wall at the foot of the bed as she smoothed down the soft cotton sheet, hot tears racing down her face. "It's not fair, Lord. Do you hear me? It's not fair." The words tore from her, and she wrenched the sheets. "Why are you ripping this child from me? From us? Teodor hasn't done anything wrong. He doesn't deserve such a terrible thing. And neither do I. Please, please, just make it stop. Save our little one. That's all I want. All I have ever wanted."

Sobs consumed her, every bit as breath stealing as the labor pains. She fought for control as her abdomen tightened. Where were they? She needed her husband. She couldn't do this without him. Only his presence would give her the strength to continue.

The click of the door announced Teodor and *Pani* Nowakowa's arrival as another full-blown contraction hit. The floor creaked, and the two of them stood on the bedroom's threshold.

The stooped and wrinkled *babka* shooed Teodor from the room. "You stay outside."

"*Nie.* I want him here."

"The birth room is no place for a man." *Pani* Nowakowa lumbered to the bedside, turning sideways in the narrow passage between the bed and the wall. "There now, my dear, remember God is in control. He is the one you want."

Natia nodded. That was the truth, her head told her. But her heart, her soul, said something different. How could God have ordained this for them, all the hardships of these last few years?

Once the pain passed, *Pani* Nowakowa examined her. "You're almost there. Soon, you will remember your discomfort no more."

Nie, this agony would stay with her for the rest of her life. Just like twice before. Her heart hadn't healed then. This wouldn't be different. "Ah!" How could something so small hurt so much?

The tiny life slipped from her body.

No wriggling.

No crying.

At least not from the child.

"It's a boy. Too young to survive." *Pani* Nowakowa wrapped Natia's son in a towel and rubbed him. He didn't respond. Didn't squall. Oh, what Natia would give for even one tiny cry from him.

"All right, dear, let's finish up. You've had a rough go of it. You need your rest."

A short while later, with the bleeding stopped, fresh sheets, and a soft, clean nightgown, *Pani* Nowakowa handed Natia her child. A wisp of light hair, like his father's. Fists curled, fingers complete with the littlest of nails. She stroked his fragile, cold skin. If not for his blue tinge, she would think him just sleeping. So very, very small. Yet so very, very perfect.

Why did she have to lose him?

The *babka* opened the door and motioned for Teodor to enter before she slipped away.

"See our son." Natia held him out to her husband. "He's perfect."

Teodor's hands shook as he cradled the stillborn. "Beautiful. He looks so much like you."

"*Nie.* Like you." The lump in her throat swelled until it all but cut off her breath. "I'm sorry. I can't give you a child."

He leaned over and whispered in her hair, "At least I have you and we're together. That's all that matters." Yet his voice was husky, and moisture gathered in his eyes.

❧

Teodor sat on their bed beside Natia, who held the body of their son. A thin, colorful quilt covered her skinny legs. Light streamed into the bedroom window, over Reverend Jankowski's shoulder, and illuminated the baby's face. The once-retired pastor sprinkled water over the child's forehead. "In the name of the Father, and the Son, and the Holy Ghost, I baptize you Andrzej Ludwik Palinski."

Teodor's heart clenched at the words. At the stillness of his son. His hands shook as he wiped the moisture from Andrzej's eyes with a handkerchief and then dabbed Natia's tears.

"He is in heaven. His suffering is over." Pastor Jankowski rubbed Teodor's shoulder.

Natia gave a small, single nod.

Teodor swallowed hard. "Thank you, Reverend. We cling to the Lord's goodness in such times as these." The right words to say, but did he believe them? They'd had so much pain and suffering. This would be their third little mound on the hill.

What if the Germans hadn't killed their village doctor at the beginning of the war? Would this child have survived if he had medical care? Teodor fisted his hands.

With trembling, age-spotted fingers, the good reverend capped the bottle of baptismal water with a *clink*. "Such faith like that will sustain you. It's all we have these days. Let me know if there is anything I can do. The church is always open for prayer, and I would be happy to share words of comfort."

Natia kissed their son's damp forehead. "You have been good to us, Pastor. We're in your debt."

"Nonsense. That is what the Lord has called me to do." He made the sign of the cross and then showed himself to the door.

"Let me take him now." Teodor held out his hands, and Natia placed the tiny, lightweight child in his arms. If not for the Nazis, this child might have lived.

She was pale, her green eyes shimmering with unshed tears. "What might he have grown up to be? What would his life have looked like?"

Teodor closed his eyes, trying to imagine this little, still boy bursting with life and exuberance. "He would have climbed every tree in the village, come home wet every evening after playing in the creek, and would have snatched every *kołaczki* cookie you baked."

Natia sniffed. "He would have followed you everywhere. He would have helped you in the fields and would have milked the cow. With him around, you wouldn't have to work so hard."

He opened his eyes and rubbed his wife's soft hand, his eyes burning. "You work hard too. Maybe God will grant us a girl to help you in the kitchen and around the house."

"I can't go through this again. Three times we've lost a child. Two little markers in the field, and soon another one. My heart can't endure another loss." She stroked her still-swollen belly.

His heart couldn't take much more either. Her soft eyes, the downturn of her mouth almost undid him. How could he have prevented this? She did work too much. He should have helped her more around the house and lightened her load.

Natia bit her full, red lips. "And I'm about to suffer another loss when that German family comes from Ukraine and takes over *Tata's* farm."

Lebensraum. Living space for the Germans, colonists who would push out and enslave the native Slavs.

By all outward appearances, the Lord had forsaken them. Taken their children and their food. They had to produce more and more to stay alive. Made it impossible for him to care for his family. Now they were about to take their farm. Their livelihood. The letter from the Germans lay unopened on the cracked and faded kitchen counter. He didn't have to read the contents to know what it said. But he couldn't tell her.

"Teodor?" She touched the back of his hand, and a tingle raced up his arm.

"What?"

"You grew so quiet. What's wrong?"

"Nothing." Everything. He stared at his son's flawless, tiny face. Soon, they would have to leave this child and their others behind. But how did he tell her?

Now was not the time. That much he knew. She would need to prepare to leave their home, the only place they'd ever known, but first, she needed to heal, both in body and spirit.

He scrubbed his face as heat built in his chest.

When the Nazis forced them out, would they ever come home?

❧

The rolling hills spread out in front of Teodor, the expansive sky blue above him, a tree line in the distance. From across the adjoining farm fields, Teodor's father-in-law, Filip Gorecki, waved at him as he picked his way over rough clumps of dirt, sturdy work boots on his feet, a gray cap covering his dark, curly hair.

Teodor waved back and trod over the furrows, the stubble of last year's rye crop rubbing against his brown wool pants. Though the weather had warmed and tiny green sprouts burst from the soil, he hadn't plowed under his fields. There was no point. A weight pressed on his chest. He shook his head to clear away his thoughts and met Filip halfway between their small houses. "Good morning to you."

"Good morning, Teodor." Filip clapped him on the shoulder. "How are you and Natia doing?" He glanced at the three crosses on the hill. His grandchildren. He held up a basket covered with a white napkin. "Helena made some sausage and cabbage soup to help Natia regain her strength."

Teodor took the rustic woven basket, the spice of the sausage tickling his nose. "*Dzięki*. Natia will like to taste it and see how her sister is coming along as a cook."

"How is she holding up?"

"For two days now, she just lies in bed and stares at the wall."

"Natia's a strong woman, just like my Berta." Filip stared beyond Teodor and into the past. "We lost two children between Natia and Helena. Each time, Berta pulled herself from bed and returned to her life. God was her strength. Even when the cancer ravaged her body, she was the strongest woman I knew. Natia is much like her." Filip shook his head. "What about you?"

"It never gets easier. I thought maybe this time ..." Teodor sucked in a steadying breath and rubbed his rough cheek. How long had it been since he shaved?

The older man stroked his graying mustache. "You look like the horse trampled you."

"I haven't slept much. My mind replays what I could have done differently."

"Don't blame yourself. You're still young. You never know what the Lord has in store."

"Especially these days. How are the preparations for your departure going?"

Filip's features sank, as if he grew a year older with each passing second. "How are we supposed to pack up and leave everything we know and love? I was born on this farm. I brought my new bride here, and she gave birth to our children here. And here I buried her. Now, because the Nazis don't like us, they force us from our homes and into camps."

"I understand." Teodor glanced at the cemetery at the end of the field. "We got our notices the day the baby came. We leave with you."

"Oh, Teodor. How awful. This surely isn't helping Natia."

"I haven't told her."

"You can't put it off."

"How can I deal her this blow when she is in mourning? Right now, she can't handle the news." Right now, he can't handle it. Loss piled on top of loss and threatened to rip him open. How could he walk away from the land that cradled his children?

"The German settlers will arrive no matter what. Give her time to say good-bye."

"I'm worried about her fragile nerves." If he couldn't sleep, couldn't eat, what about his wife? She would shatter, and he wouldn't be able to pick up the pieces. She'd never survive the camp.

"I understand. You'll have to be gentle, but you must tell her. Either you go peacefully, or they force you out. That would be much worse."

"The trauma of not being able to say her farewells might be her undoing. But why now? Why not after she's healed?" As if the wounds from the loss of each child would ever scab over for either of them.

"It's never convenient to leave the only life you've ever known."

Teodor forced himself to breathe in and out. Their tiny blue stucco house lay behind him. In front of him stretched their few acres of farmland where they grew potatoes, beets, and cabbage. The small, red barn stood empty to his left. Not much, but it was theirs.

"If I can do anything, let me know." Filip's voice was husky.

How much worse for him to leave, an old man with two younger children at home. "If only I could stay on my farm." He would go to any lengths to spare Natia the pain of leaving.

"You could if you signed the *Volksdeutsche* paper stating you're willing to denounce your Polish roots and become Germanized."

"Never. That equals betrayal of our nation, the highest form of treason. I love Poland and would give my life to protect her. I cannot turn my back on her."

"Not even for your wife?"

Teodor strode in a circle, kicking at stones. Could he do that to shield Natia and save their home? "It goes against all I've ever believed. And everyone in Piosenka would hate me. In doing so, I would make myself and my wife outcasts."

"I'm not sure there will be many Poles left here soon."

"And I doubt the ethnic Germans would accept us. In the end, we would lose all we've worked for anyway. Not even for Natia could I sign that paper. We must be willing to suffer to remain loyal to Poland."

Filip stared at the brown earth for a long while and then sighed. "I'll send Helena over later to sit with Natia. Heart wrenching as it is, she'll come out on the other side."

A small smile tugged at Teodor's lips. "And as stubborn as the winter's snows. But two blows in quick succession could be too much for her."

"I'll pray the Lord will give you the right words to say at the right time."

The men parted, and Teodor carried the basket with the soup back to the house. He entered the cool interior and pulled off his heavy dark-brown wool coat, his eyes needing several seconds to adjust to the dimness. "Natia, look what Helena made for us. Some cabbage soup, according to your father. It smells delicious. She didn't burn it this time." At the enticing aroma, his stomach rumbled.

After a few moments, Natia shuffled from the bedroom, still in her housecoat, her brown hair disheveled, a curl over one eye. "Do you want me to heat it for your lunch?" Dark half-moons underscored her green eyes.

"*Nie*, you sit down. I'll warm it." He moved about the kitchen, so small that a few steps took him from the door to the little stove on the far side of the room. Within moments, heat bathed them, and the sweet aroma of sausage filled the air. Teodor sat beside her while they waited for it to warm. "I'm glad to see you up."

"I want to stay in bed forever. But I can't. There are chores to be done. You'll be planting soon."

"You're remarkable." He rubbed her shoulder.

"Like Mama. Life hit her hard, but until her final illness, she always got back up. I also know there is something you are keeping from me."

He shook his head, probably more than necessary.

"You're not sleeping. In the middle of the night, I hear you pacing. You tread on that squeaky floorboard in front of the sink."

"If Poland ever needs spies, I'll give them your name."

A brief flash of amusement lit her eyes and then faded like the sunset. "What is it?"

"There is time. Right now, you concentrate on getting your health back, and let me do the worrying."

"So whatever you have to tell me isn't good?"

He should have his tongue cut from his mouth for not watching his words. "Don't press me." He rose and stirred the thick soup.

She came behind him and wrapped him in an embrace. Her touch was warm. He should be comforting her, but instead, she did the soothing. "Please, tell me. Don't leave me to wonder."

His stomach fluttered, and not from hunger. "Your family is almost ready to leave. *Tata* told me they have packed what they could and given away what they couldn't." He was a coward for not saying the words, but maybe she would catch his meaning and he wouldn't have to utter them.

Though they had only been married three years, they understood each other's thoughts as well as couples married for decades.

Natia gasped. "We got our notices."

Cold surged through his midsection. He nodded.

She slipped to the floor.

♩♫♩♪

Chapter Two

*N*ie, Teodor, *nie*." His words about the Germans' orders to leave shattered the small piece of Natia's heart that remained. How could she endure it?

He knelt beside her on the uneven wood floor and pulled her close, his wool sweater rough against her cheek. "I know." His words were soft.

"How can we leave? We just buried Andrzej." Every muscle in her body clenched. She couldn't do it. She wouldn't.

"The Germans don't know our pain."

"Even if they did, they wouldn't care. They hate us. They want to be rid of us."

He stiffened. See, her words hit a nerve, for they were true. The Nazis had almost as much disdain for the Poles as for the Jews. They would stop at nothing to Germanize this part of the world. Including ripping apart families.

"We'll make do. At least we have each other. We'll go together, be together, along with your father and Helena and Zygmunt."

She sat up straight and grabbed his arm. How could he even think of leaving this place? Their children? Even if it meant being with her family, she would refuse to go. "We'll ignore their order. What does one couple more or less mean to them? Let's run away, hide in the forests like the partisans. There we can be free. If we do what they command, they will win."

"How long before they discover us? Days, maybe weeks if we're lucky. And then winter will come, not for a while, but it will come. We can't survive the cold without a roof over our heads.

Nie, we'll pray for God's protection and go to the labor camp. I'm not afraid of hard work."

Couldn't the man see reason? What had turned him so compliant? "It's not the hard work I fear but the living conditions, the disease, and the hunger. All the unknowns." They had heard about the horror of these places. Only crazy people wanted to go. Was that what happened? Had the loss of their child addled his brain?

"If we hid, those things would be no better than in the camp. Maybe worse."

"And most of all, I'm afraid of being separated from you." He gathered her close. She nestled into his sweater that carried his unique, fresh smell of outdoors and laundry soap. If only she could stay in his embrace forever. Safe. Sheltered. Secure.

They sat together until the shadows on the floor lengthened. At last, much too soon, he released her. He touched her chest. "Here, Natia, in here is where I'll be. Always in your heart. I don't know if we'll be allowed to live together or even see each other. But we are married. A part of each other. One flesh. That will never change."

She kissed his work-roughened fingers. He was right, of course. Very few choices presented themselves. They were at the mercy of the Germans. Men who showed no mercy. "Can we do this?"

"There is no other way. We have to obey. So we will. Each day, we will get up, get dressed, and do what is required. We'll carry on, always looking forward to that day when we can return here and resume our life together."

"We'll be back?"

"I promise."

"I'll be with my babies again?"

"You will. I'll do whatever I must to make that happen."

"Knowing that gives me a reason to keep moving forward."

"You will survive, Natia. I have every faith in you. You're a stronger woman than you realize."

"With you by my side, I am."

"With or without me. When you need it, you have a reserve of fortitude you can only imagine."

What was it Mama always quoted from the Bible? *"Strength and honor are her clothing; and she shall rejoice in time to come."* But Natia wasn't like Mama. "I'm still scared. Aren't you?"

He kissed the top of her head and then rose to his feet, reaching out to help her stand. "Are you ready to start packing?"

It wasn't until she lay in bed that night, the darkness falling heavy on her, the wind moaning outside of the window, Teodor snoring beside her, that it hit her. He had never answered her question.

He was afraid.

And she should be too.

✺

Teodor's slow footsteps carried him into the only town he had ever known, the only place he had ever lived. One street ran east and west and boasted most of the businesses. He strolled by the little tailor shop and clothing store his father's friend had owned. Both men now lay cold in their graves, *Tata* for twenty years, since Teodor was five, leaving him and Mama alone.

No sweet, enticing scents rose from the bakery. Since the arrival of the Nazis and rationing, the business had been shuttered. There was no flour or sugar.

He approached the first of several north- and south-running streets. He turned to his right and could just make out the gentle curve of his aunt's tiled roof. Or of what had been his aunt's home, the place he'd spent his summers playing with his cousins. More than ten years had gone by since they emigrated to Australia. Did any of them fight for their adopted country?

For several more blocks, he wandered down the street, hearing the voices and seeing the scenes of his childhood. Playing *serso*, a toss-and-catch game with sticks and a ring, with his cousins. Acting as Joseph in the Christmas play at church. Stealing kisses from Natia underneath the willow. His vision blurred. How could he leave this place, the one thing he loved only a little less than God and his wife? The timbre of well-known voices, the sweet recognition of friendly faces, the soft darkness of familiar soil.

This place that held the graves of his three children and both of his parents.

For the last time, he turned the cool metal knob on the door into the small grocery store and entered. *"Dzień dobry."*

The middle-aged woman, gray streaking her braided hair, came to the counter, a reproduction of the Black Madonna of Częstochowa behind her. Most of the shelves surrounding her bore nothing more than dust. *"Dzień dobry,* Teodor. What brings you in? I thought you'd be preparing to leave. How is Natia faring? We are sorry for your loss."

Which of her questions did he answer first? Perhaps it was best to steer clear of the more emotional topics. Take care of business and walk out before he broke down. He focused his gaze on the Madonna's golden halo. "I've come to settle my account. I don't know when, if, we'll be back to pay."

Pani Lisowa nodded and shuffled to the far end of the well-worn wood counter, bent over, and produced the account book. She flipped the pages until she came across Teodor's name. "It's not much."

"I'll feel better leaving no balance."

"That's why we'll miss you. The Palinskis were always the most honest, hardest working among us. I have a difficult time imagining that, once you leave, there will be no more of you here. I've missed your mother so much in the four years she's been gone."

He nodded, unable to force any words through the narrowing in his throat. Maybe if he had helped Mama with the heavy chores, made sure she ate more, provided for her better, her heart wouldn't have given out when the Nazis entered their village. So many maybes in this life. Unable to choke out any words, he pushed the *złoty* across the counter and paid his bill.

As he did so, *Pani* Lisowa grasped him, her hand warm, her grip firm. "Your parents would be proud of you. Your mother was. She always talked about you and how much she loved you. Don't let those Nazis rob you of who you are."

Again, all he could manage was a single nod.

"You take care of that wife of yours, you hear?"

"I will." Teodor croaked out the words. Pressure built in his chest.

She leaned across the counter and pecked him on both cheeks. "God go with you."

"And with you."

Before he lost control, he spun and sprinted from the store. He raced down the street until he left the town far in the distance. By the time he slowed, he was almost back to the farm. He stumbled from the dirt road and ambled over the one soft part of the field he'd plowed under in the fall.

With a shudder, he fell to the ground. The loamy scent of the earth surrounded him. He picked up a clod and rubbed it in his hands, staining them with dirt. Maybe in this way, he could have his farm with him. He and this ground were connected. He had slaved and saved to buy the small plot he called home. But it was his. His and Natia's. Together, they sweated to plant the crops and to harvest them. To store a bit away for the winter's food and for the spring's planting.

What loomed in front of them? What awaited them?

Even if they returned, could they ever recapture their peace and happiness?

Could he keep his promise to his wife?

❧

Natia bent over the yellow and white daffodils that bobbed their heads in time to the music of the wind. With her scissors, she cut a handful and divided them into three small bouquets. She wiped her hands on her apron, set her chin, and climbed the low hill at the edge of the cabbage field. Teodor hadn't turned the land over last fall, hadn't done anything to it this year. He'd known they were leaving.

Before she arrived at the top of the rise, she turned to survey this place she'd called home since their marriage. It wasn't much, but enough. Enough to fill their bellies for the winter and enough to keep the driving rains and swirling snows off their heads. She'd planted roses along one side of the cottage and daises along the back. This year, she wouldn't see them bloom or smell their sweet scent.

She swallowed the rising tide of salty tears. *Nie*, she would be strong, like Mama. Teodor hadn't let her see his fear. Each day, he greeted her with a soft kiss and a gentle smile. Each night, their tears mingled, but with each morning came new resolve.

Once she had drawn in a deep breath and let it out little by little, she finished her trek to the place where Teodor had planted three small, white crosses. Where their children rested until Judgment Day.

A fresh mound of dirt marked the most recent grave.

She placed a bouquet in front of each cross. Her little ones. The children who would never laugh, never cry, never sing. So she did the laughing, the crying, and the singing for them.

Today she sat on the ground near them. The sun warmed her shoulders, and she pulled the black embroidered scarf from her head, the breeze on her face as if her little ones caressed her cheek. "I'll miss you, *moje miłości*. But you will never be far from my thoughts. I'll carry you with me always. Your father has promised we'll be back. If I can, I will be."

She kissed her fingertips and then touched each cross. "Beata, Szymon, Andrzej. Don't forget I love you and always will." Numbness overtook her.

A tune rose in her chest, one sung by generations of Polish women to their fussy infants. She had sung it to her younger siblings after Mama died. Now, one last time, she would sing it for her children. She cleared her throat. The lilting, rocking melody floated over the countryside.

> *Go to sleep, my little doll*
> *Time for you to go to bed*
> *I'll be rocking you*
> *And you'll close your eyes.*
> *Luli luli luli luli luli luli lu,*
> *Luli luli luli luli, a ty oczka zmruż.*

A deep voice chimed in with hers. Teodor had come up behind her without making a noise, so she never heard him until he sang the lullaby with her. As they ended, his voice cracked and he dropped to the ground beside her.

She peered at him, his blue eyes glistening with unshed tears. The numbness fell away, and her own tears gathered. She stroked the side of his face and swallowed hard. "My grandmother always sang that song. Only once or twice through, and I'd fall asleep."

"One day, you'll sing it to our children and grandchildren." His own tears slid down his wind-burned cheeks.

"You don't have to wrap the truth in cotton. I wish I could take this pain from you." But she could only accomplish that by giving him a child.

And she had failed.

"Having you with me helps."

She cupped his cheek. "You always try to protect me, and I love you for it. But this, you can't shield me from. Trouble is coming." She shivered.

The jangle of a horse's harness broke the stillness of the moment. Old *Pan* Majewski sat on his ramshackle cart, whistling to his swayback mare as she plodded down the rutted road. His wagon bumped along. By the time they got to the train station in Śpiewka, they would all have backaches.

Teodor took her by the hand. "It's time."

From where she stood, she studied the doorway of her childhood home. *Tata*, Helena, and Zygmunt appeared, each carrying a suitcase. Helena was only nine, Zygmunt but seven. Natia sighed. What would happen to them?

She squeezed Teodor's calloused fingers. "I'm ready." For the last time, she gazed on her children's graves. So small. So alone. The wind whipped her black wool skirt and cut through her embroidered blouse and vest. "Good-bye, my loves." The words caught on a sob. With every bit of strength she had, Natia turned her back on them, held her husband's hand, and they picked their way across the field.

❦

Teodor, Natia, and her family sat in the back of the crude wagon, long ago having exhausted all conversation with their kind neighbor and each other. The kilometers rolled by, greening fields on either side of them, the vast plains stretching before them. For her entire life, Natia had lived in the same area, near the small village of Piosenka, worked the same land, worshipped in the same church. Family had always surrounded her.

Across from her, Zygmunt and Helena huddled close to *Tata*, their eyes large in their small faces. Each of them, including the children, wore a diamond-shaped yellow patch with a purple edge and a purple *P* in the middle. What fate did the Nazis reserve for ones so small? For each of them?

Natia's head bobbed as she fought off sleep. Teodor rubbed her aching back. "Go to sleep if you want. You need your rest, so you can heal."

She squared her shoulders to keep him from worrying. "*Nie*, I'm fine. This is an adventure, everything new and different. Our first ride on the train." She had to keep Zygmunt and Helena from becoming too frightened.

Zygmunt's green eyes, so much like her own, lit up. "I can't wait. We'll get to see the world. Or at least Poland. This is going to be fun." The breeze ruffled his fair hair, so opposite of hers.

The naïveté of a young boy. Teodor whispered in Natia's ear, "I know your heart is breaking."

"Would you rather that I cried? That wouldn't make anything different. Poles are used to change. How many countries have we been part of in our lifetimes? It's another storm to weather, that's all." Her voice shook, just the tiniest of bits.

Tata gathered his younger children close to himself. "We'll be fine. All of us. God will take care of us. We'll rest and trust in him. And enjoy the train ride." He chuckled, the sound of his laugh as melodic as any song.

If they could remain together where she could watch over the children, her husband and father at her side, they would be fine. Still, she drew her shawl around herself as if it might protect her from the future. They had heard about the labor camps. The hard work. The disease. The death.

Farmer Majewski turned around but pointed ahead of them. "See that?"

A cluster of buildings rose from the undulating hills, silhouetted against the horizon. Most were sturdy brick. Several smokestacks rose from factories, dwarfing the buildings below them.

"There's Śpiewka. We should be there soon."

Helena bit her lip. She hadn't said two words since they'd left. Natia stretched across the cart and squeezed her sister's fragile hand. "Think how exciting this will be and how much you'll have to tell your friends when we go home."

"Will you stay with me?"

"I won't let go of you. I promise. And *Tata* will be with us too."

Zygmunt, every inch a boy, sat forward in the cart. "Look at that. What a huge town."

Teodor whistled. "It must be three times the size of ours. Maybe more."

"That's about right." Farmer Majewski nodded.

"Wow." Zygmunt widened his eyes until they almost popped from his head. "It's like a city."

Tata laughed again. "Nowhere near the size of Kraków or Warsaw."

"I've never seen anything so big. Can we stay here?"

Natia relaxed against Teodor, who drew her close. "And miss out on riding on the train?"

"Never."

"Sit down." Natia caught Zygmunt by the hem of his brown tweed jacket and pulled him to the seat beside her, a light-colored curl falling over his eye. She pushed it back. "You'll fall out of the cart and miss the entire adventure."

Śpiewka filled up more of the horizon as they approached. Several other wagons shared the road with them. A horn sounded, and a green canvas-covered German transport truck whipped by. Then another came, and another, followed by a Nazi in a dark uniform on a motorcycle. All the while, Zygmunt knelt in the wagon bed and leaned over, taking in the sights.

Her palms damp, Natia held fast to her brother. They entered the town, crowded with homes, businesses, hotels, and taverns. The tang of vinegar and cabbage floated on the air. Before too long, *Pan* Majewski reined the horse to a halt in front of the red-brick train station.

Zygmunt scrambled from the cart first, hopping from foot to foot. Teodor climbed down and helped Natia and the rest of the family disembark. In keeping with her promise, Natia clung to Helena.

Teodor passed the farmer a few *złoty*. "*Dziękuję Ci* for taking us. We appreciate it."

The farmer returned the money. "It's the least I could do. Your family has done mine many kindnesses over the years."

Tata clapped *Pan* Majewski on the back. "God go with you."

"And with you."

Natia kissed the man on his wrinkled, whiskery cheek. "God bless you."

"And you." Within a heartbeat, *Pan* Majewski climbed into the seat and disappeared down the road.

Zygmunt skipped ahead of the group while Helena matched Natia's steps as they made their way toward the tracks.

People crowded the tiny station and spilled onto the cobblestone street. The sweetness of ladies' perfume mingled with the sourness of unwashed farmers. German soldiers patrolled the area with rifles over their shoulders and dogs straining on leashes.

"You there." One with dark eyes and a downturned mouth hollered at them. "Papers."

The group stopped and produced what the man demanded. Natia pressed against Teodor.

The Nazi stared at the triangular patch on their coats. "Get in the station. *Schnell, schnell.* There isn't time to waste."

A train whistle bellowed. Teodor jumped, and Natia sucked in a breath. He squeezed her shoulder.

"I've never seen so many people in one place at a time." The chaos of voices filled her head. Women and children cried. Men shouted. Their captors yelled louder. *Schnell* was the only word she could decipher. *Hurry.*

To what? An uncertain fate?

"This is great." Zygmunt attempted to wriggle through the crowd, but *Tata* caught him by the collar.

"You need to stay with us."

Natia reached into her small bag and withdrew four squares of fabric. "I couldn't sleep last night, so I made each of you a gift." She presented her husband, father, and siblings with handkerchiefs embroidered around the edges, each with their initials in one corner.

Zygmunt stuffed his into his pocket. "I don't see why I need a fancy handkerchief. I can use my sleeve."

Natia tsked. "May our tears of sadness soon be turned to tears of joy."

The others folded their gifts and tucked them away.

"*Dzięki*, Natia." Helena sniffled.

The crowd surged forward. Every farmer and villager from fifty kilometers in each direction must be here. Their small group had no choice but to shuffle along. Their only other option was to be trampled.

The train hissed. Up ahead, the Nazis herded their prisoners into large, windowless boxcars. Natia's heart slammed against her ribs. Her steps faltered.

Dear Lord, this couldn't be.

They wouldn't ride to the camp in a passenger car.

Instead, they would travel to their destiny crammed into a cattle car.

Like animals.

Chapter Three

*T*eodor held to Natia as if she would disappear if her fingers slipped from his grasp. The crowd in the train station pressed forward, carrying them, Filip, and the children as a wave carried a grain of sand. Their fellow Poles pressed in on every side until taking a breath was almost impossible.

He stared at her profile, her high cheekbones, her long, thin face, her dark-brown hair that fell in soft waves and bounced on her shoulders when she walked. Something deep inside drove him to memorize the shape of her nose, the curve of her mouth, the tilt of her head. He painted a picture of her, one to hold close to his heart in case the worst happened.

Nie, he had promised to take care of her. To not let anything separate them. That's the vow he needed to concentrate on. He couldn't let her down. Couldn't bear a repeat of what happened to Mama.

Their German captors shouted at the throng, forcing more and more of his fellow countrymen into the already-stuffed cattle car. With a rattle and a bang, they shut and bolted the door, then worked to fill another car.

That clanging reverberated in Teodor's head. His breaths came in short, irregular gasps. Beside him, Natia trembled. "What are they doing to us? Cows and pigs travel better than this."

"Don't worry. I'm not going to let you go. We'll be fine." Saying the words was one thing. Believing them was quite another.

"How will any of us survive?" She gazed at her family.

That was the point. The Nazis didn't want them to live. They wouldn't rest until they wiped every Pole off the face of the earth. Jew or Christian.

But didn't the Lord promise to save a remnant? *Tak*, that was of Israel, but surely he would spare some of the Polish people. And maybe, just maybe, Teodor and Natia and her family would be among them. "I'll take care of you. All of you." And he would. No matter what it took.

Already, just here on the platform, the odor of unwashed bodies pressed together threatened to bring up his small breakfast. What would it be like on the train?

They inched forward, and Helena whimpered. "What is going to happen to us?"

Natia smoothed back the girl's dark, curly hair. "Don't worry. We'll be fine as long as we stay together. Isn't that right, *Tata*?"

Her father nodded but pinched his mouth shut. He couldn't lie to his daughters.

"We'll have an adventure." Zygmunt bounced on his toes. "I just wish I could see the train."

Better that he was too short.

"Teodor?" Natia leaned against him.

He gazed at the top of her head, her black-and-red embroidered scarf around her shoulders. "Yes, *moje słońce*?"

"I love you."

"And I love you."

With a soft touch to his lips, she hushed him. She nestled into him, her small body against his. Her heart pounded against his chest. His answered the irregular beat.

Life without her would be gray, silent, and meaningless.

His Natia. His love. His life.

And then, much too soon, they reached the edge of the platform. The crowd jostled and pushed against them. A soldier rammed through, right between Natia and Helena. His wife lost hold of her sister. "Helena. *Nie*! Come back!"

"Natia! Natia!" Helena's cries answered, but Teodor couldn't spy any of them.

"*Tata*! Helena! Zygmunt!" Each name expelled as a tortured shriek from his wife's lips.

"We'll see you there." At her father's shouted reassurance, she relaxed.

The soldier shoved Teodor and Natia forward. No steps made boarding easy for her. An armed soldier stood next to the door. "*Schnell, schnell.*"

Teodor lifted her by the waist as the crowd crushed against them. Someone inside grabbed her and pulled her into the mass. He hopped up behind her, straining to keep her in sight. She had already lost her family. She would not lose him. He wound his way among their fellow passengers until he stood beside her.

Person upon person squeezed inside until Teodor couldn't move his arms. Men. Women. Small children. And the Germans forced in even more. Oh, for just a lungful of fresh air.

The soldiers shut the door and extinguished the light. Only a sliver of brightness eked through the cracks around the door. He rubbed his thumb over the back of Natia's warm hand. "How are you doing?"

"Nauseous. And worried about my family."

The temperature inside rose until sweat rolled down Teodor's back. "Think about something else, and your upset stomach will pass."

With a creak the train groaned forward. On the other side of the car, a woman screeched. "Let me out. I can't take this. Get me off!" Her screaming filled Teodor's ears.

Natia nestled against him. "What should I think about?" She almost had to shriek herself to be heard over the hysterical woman.

"Remember last summer, when we took a picnic by the creek?"

"The sun played on the water. The weather couldn't have been more perfect."

"And the delicious cookies you made. How you sang to me. Sweeter than any of the birds in the trees."

"A day when we forgot our troubles. A good memory."

"One to relish." He stroked her hand with his thumb.

The kilometers clacked away under the train's metal wheels, the car swaying in time to their rhythm. The occupants quieted, their voices low. Even the panicked lady's tone softened, though she murmured under her breath. The tang of urine filled the air. In the back, someone retched. The stench worsened until Teodor gagged. His stomach heaved, but he bit back the foul bile.

The train rumbled under their feet, each turn of the wheel taking them farther from the home they loved. He strove to hang on to that memory he had shared with Natia, but already it faded like a winter's sunset. How could he think of something beautiful when all around him was ugly?

And then, in the suffering and confusion that surrounded them, a song broke through the quiet din. Sung by not just any voice.

His Natia's sweet soprano.

God, my Lord, my strength,
My place of hiding, and confiding,
In all needs by night and day;
Though foes surround me,
And Satan mark his prey,
God shall have his way.

Her voice, though weak, carried a force behind it. Like a soft tap on the shoulder, but one that demanded attention. As the haunting melody wound its way through the packed car and over their heads, their fellow occupants quieted until only the crazy woman's mumblings remained.

Christ in me, and I am freed
For living and forgiving,
Heart of flesh for lifeless stone,
Now bold to serve him,
Now cheered his love to own,

Never more alone.

Even the mad lady stilled by the end of the verse. As Natia sang the last one, more and more voices joined the chorus until the words of the Polish warrior hymn echoed off the metal walls, rose above the train, beyond the sky, as a prayer to heaven.

Up, weak knees and spirit bowed in sorrow!
No tomorrow shall arise to beat you down;
God goes before you and angels all around;
On your head a crown.

As the last notes of the song died away, a reverent quiet filled the space. They traveled several kilometers, the steady click of the metal wheels against the steel tracks fading into the background.

Teodor held his breath. If he exhaled, the moment might pass. Instead, the words and melody of the hymn he'd sung a hundred times penetrated to his very marrow. A song for him to carry deep within no matter what lay in front of him.

And then, a child wailed. Like a dropped mirror, the holiness of that place in time shattered. The din of voices resumed.

"Watch out for that one. Watch out for her." The insane woman's screams sliced through whatever peace may have pervaded the train car.

Natia stiffened. "Is she talking about me?"

"I doubt it."

"What does she mean?"

"Don't pay attention to her. She's out of her mind."

"Everyone here is out of their minds. Everyone in the world, maybe." Her voice trembled.

He chuckled, more to bolster her than from humor. "*Nie*, you heard how the people sang with you. There is sanity left. Maybe not much, but a little."

"Mama always crooned that hymn as she worked in the kitchen or in the fields. Always it was her expression of joy. Even when she was dying, the cancer ravaging her body, she croaked out the words. I sang it with her, over and over, until she couldn't sing anymore. That's when her song became mine." Natia sighed and relaxed against him.

"Go to sleep, my love." He kissed the top of her head. Perspiration dampened her silky hair. The mass of bodies warmed the air, but not that hot. Her brow shouldn't singe his lips when he kissed her.

Something was wrong.

She shivered.

Very wrong.

Eons later, and the train still moved toward their unknown destination. A few voices rose and fell, but most of the boxcar's occupants allowed their conversations to die. With each passing moment, the pungent stench of human waste increased until Teodor's eyes watered. His dry tongue stuck to the roof of his mouth.

For many long hours, the train chugged and snaked its way through the Polish countryside. At least, Teodor assumed they were still in Poland. He'd heard stories about trains racing across the land. His friend in Warsaw, who had ridden in one, wrote and told him that the trees and farm fields whipped past the window, so fast the trains moved.

But this one creaked along, in no hurry to reach its destination. In one way that was good. The unknowns of the labor camp ate away at his middle. How would they be treated? If the Nazis' prior actions were any indication, not well. From the way they stuffed the passengers on this train, they had no intentions of kindness.

Yet another part of him wanted to shout at the engineer to push harder. He willed the wheels to turn faster. Natia slumped against him. If not for the crush of people, she might have slid to the ground. He supported her the best he could.

She was ill. Weak from childbirth. All the standing took its toll. They needed to get off this train, somewhere she could put her feet up and rest, lie down and regain her strength.

What if it was childbed fever?

Nie. He shut the possibility from his mind. The *babka* had been careful to keep the bedroom clean. She'd washed her hands more than once. Women didn't die from that anymore. Natia couldn't have the fever. Just couldn't.

Someone in the back passed around dippers full of water. By the time they reached Teodor near the front, they were empty. At last, one came to them about a quarter full. "Natia, wake up, *moje slońce.* Here's some water. You need to have a drink."

She stirred and peered at him with glassy eyes. "What?"

"Water. Sip and see how good it tastes." He put the dipper to his mouth but didn't drink. She needed it much more. With a smile, he nodded. "Refreshing."

Like a little bird, she opened her mouth. With great care not to spill a single drop, he trickled some down her throat. She swallowed. "*Tak*, that is good."

"That's it. Keep drinking." He poured more of the precious liquid over her tongue. Little by little, she drank.

"Save some for the rest of us. You can't have it all."

Teodor turned to locate the source of the deep voice.

"I haven't had any yet. And I'm bigger than anyone."

Teodor didn't have any trouble picking out the man from the crowd. He towered over everyone by at least a head. With his broad shoulders and ample stomach, he took up enough room for three people. "My wife is ill. She has a fever."

The crowd leaned away from them. He grabbed Natia under her arm and strained to keep her upright. Some of the water sloshed over the side of the dipper.

"We don't want any diseases." The burly man's voice bounced off the car's steel walls.

"She doesn't have a disease. She just gave birth to a child. Can't you see she's ill?"

If there were more room, the hulk of a man might have pushed his way through the crowd, picking up those in his path and throwing them to the side. "You don't know she doesn't have something else. And where is the baby? You're lying."

A man behind Teodor grabbed him by the collar.

The dipper slipped from his hand, wedging between him and his wife, the water splashing on his shoe. He clung to Natia with one hand. "I'm not."

The man behind him twisted the neck of Teodor's shirt, lessening his ability to breathe. He gasped.

"I don't see a child. You're spreading disease."

"Lech, stop it. Let go of that man." A woman's call rang from the back.

The world dimmed.

Teodor fisted his free hand. With all his strength, he swung and connected with Lech's left temple.

The grip on Teodor's shirt loosened, and he inhaled. Lech swatted at the air and missed Teodor. Too high.

Natia pushed away from him. "Don't fight."

He nodded in the direction of the woman beside his wife. "Hold her for me."

As soon as he had both hands free, he wriggled around and rained punches on Lech's head.

Lech returned the volley, catching Teodor in the ear.

"Lech!"

"Teodor." Natia's soft voice pierced him.

He held up his hands. "Truce. Fighting among ourselves doesn't serve any purpose. Hours ago we sang a hymn together. Our child was stillborn. That's why we don't have a baby."

"Leave them be, Lech. And you too, Borys. They've been through enough." The woman who called must be married to one of them.

Teodor picked up the dipper and handed it to Lech. "My apologies."

Lech blinked once, twice, three times, his green eyes wide, his red hair a mess. "She can have two extra sips." He bowed his head.

Borys nodded. "I'm sorry for your loss."

Natia fell against Teodor, her voice thin. "Please, *moje serce*, my heart, don't fight with him. Or anyone else. I shouldn't be entitled to more. If I take water from them, we'll all be sick. You worry too much." Her cheeks burned red.

"My job is to worry about you, the responsibility I took on the day we married, and my privilege."

She stroked his stubble-covered chin. "You are too good to me."

His wife dozed as the train progressed to their destination. Her chest rose and fell in a steady rhythm. At least her sleep was peaceful. The best thing she could do now was to rest.

The whistle blew, ringing out from the front of the train as it slowed, rousing the occupants from their stupor. The brakes squealed, and the car jerked to a stop. He kissed Natia's forehead. "We're here."

She straightened, though she leaned on him more than he would have liked. "We'll see *Tata*, Helena, and Zygmunt."

From outside came a commotion. Dogs barked. Voices rose both from beyond the door and inside the car.

"Where are we?"

"What's going to happen now?"

These questions swirled in Teodor's mind too.

Natia stroked his chest, her hand shaking. "I love you, Teodor. For all you've done for me, for who you are. You'll forever be with me, no matter what happens in the next minutes and days."

"Sing our song again. The one you've sung for me a hundred times like you did by the creek last year. Please, for me, if you have the strength while we wait."

So she did, while he bathed himself in her lilting Polka music.

Memories are precious to me dear,
for time is all I fear
The days, the years, the hours,
swiftly are fleeting by.
The days, the years, the hours,

swiftly are fleeting by.
Then looking back on the years dear,
our eyes may fill with tears.
For joys, and thrills, and sorrows,
may never return tomorrow.

The bolt clanged in the lock, and the train car's doors slid open. Teodor blinked in the sunshine.

The black-clad soldiers, the lightning-bolt SS symbol on their lapels, yelled at the prisoners, motioning with their rifles. *"Schnell, schnell!"*

Always hurry up with them. Didn't they ever slow down?

The crowd surged forward, pushing Teodor and Natia along. They came to the door. He jumped down and reached back for her. She all but fell into his arms, then smiled at him, warm as the sunshine. They moved toward the small two-story brick station, unable to do anything less. And beside him, though he held tight to her hand, she stumbled.

And fell.

♪♫♪

Chapter Four

$\mathscr{T}$he bright spring sunshine warmed Elfriede Fromm's face as she swung her egg basket on her arm. A small giggle bubbled inside her. Imagine that. When Erich brought her to this little Polish town earlier this year, she'd been afraid she wouldn't like it here. But Pieśń Nabożna was a very nice place. Different from Bremen and the rest of Germany, but still pleasant.

She meandered through the town square lined with shops, three-story buildings crammed shoulder to shoulder, rising above the heart of the village. In the middle stood a statue of the famous Polish composer Frédéric Chopin, lean and elegant in a long frock coat. The Poles treated the musician almost as a god. Years of exposure to the weather had turned the statue green. His right hand was missing, sheared off, perhaps during the German invasion.

A long, low whistle in the distance heralded the arrival of the train. An image of her husband's stern face flashed in front of her eyes, his Hitleresque mustache twitching. He had told her to stay far away from the station. She was too delicate to witness the arrival of those detestable Poles, those barbarians, as he called them. He pampered her.

"Good morning, Frau Fromm. How are you today?" Frau Rzeźnikowa waved from the butcher shop's steps as she swept the front walk. She had come from Germany years ago and married one of the local men. Good for Elfriede, as Frau Rzeźnikowa was one of the few people in town who spoke German.

Elfriede closed the small distance between them, a smile curving her lips. "I'm very well. And you?"

"With a day like this, I couldn't be better."

"Is the spring weather always this glorious?"

"We get rain, but this brilliant sunshine makes up for what we suffer in the winter. Some beef came on the train yesterday. I saved you the best cuts. Come in, and I'll get it."

Elfriede entered the shop and leaned on the wooden counter while Frau Rzeźnikowa hustled to the back for the meat. The almost-homey smell of sausage spices filled the air. The butcher's wife hurried through the door and returned to the counter, her round cheeks rosy. "Here you are, my dear." She patted Elfriede's hand.

"Do you know anything about the trains that come from all over the country?"

The smile on Frau Rzeźnikowa's face vanished, and she stepped backward. "Why do you ask?"

What should she say? "I'm curious. *Vater* loved trains, and when he went from Bremen to Berlin on business, he took me with him. At the station, I'd watch the trains coming from all over Europe and going to exciting places. I loved it. The hustle and bustle, the smoke and dust, the rich and poor, all mingled together. The clanging of the bells and the belching of the engines were the best parts. I'd like to go to this station and see for myself."

"No need. Our little stop in this nothing town will pale in comparison to Berlin. *Nein*, you hurry home and get that meat in the icebox."

"I suppose you're right." Elfriede huffed out the words. But once outside again, the call of the locomotive's whistle tugged at her. Why did Erich and Frau Rzeźnikowa think she shouldn't greet the train?

She set her shoulders and headed in the station's direction. The only time she'd been there was when she and Erich arrived from their temporary duty station in Berlin for his new job overseeing the factory. They didn't linger when they disembarked, but now she followed the call of the whistle and found the station in short order.

The nondescript red-brick two-story building squatted near the single set of train tracks. She entered and made her way through the large waiting room and out to the back of the building. A covered porch provided protection from the elements.

Elfriede sat on the wood bench worn smooth by many years of patient people awaiting arrivals or those anticipating a trip to Warsaw or Kraków or some other large city. She set her basket beside her. As the sun hid behind a cloud, she drew her white cardigan around her shoulders.

The train tooted its horn and chugged down the track. She peered at it as it approached. The engine led the way, followed by a few coaches and many boxcars. But Erich said they were bringing workers to the factory today. Maybe there was more than one train. She settled back. Watching for the arrival of the passengers might be a pleasant way to spend a few hours instead of holed up at home alone.

If only she had her child. He would keep her company. He would love her. She bit the inside of her cheek to keep away the threatening tears.

The black behemoth chugged into the station, gave one last gasp, and stilled. German officers with dark uniforms like her husband's, carrying rifles on their shoulders, spilled out of the coaches. Several of them clung to the leashes of snarling, growling German shepherds. They strode to the boxcars and slid open the locks.

"Let's get going. Out, out, all of you. *Schnell*. Move it, move it."

Elfriede slid forward on the bench. What was going on?

And then dazed men, women, and children, their eyes large, tumbled from the cars. Had they installed seats or benches in the cattle cars? They poured out, a steady stream of them. How had they all fit in there? And the gagging odor of human excrement that followed them overtook her. Perhaps the Poles were as filthy as Erich had told her.

As the passengers disembarked, a group of young boys called out insults in German and pantomimed slashing their throats.

She shivered. Had her son lived, he would never have behaved in such a barbaric manner.

As she rose, she pressed her lavender-perfumed handkerchief to her nose and wandered down the track toward the last car. The back of the officer's head, his blond hair shaved close to his skull, struck a chord of familiarity. Erich.

She slunk into the crowd so he wouldn't catch her here. No need to earn his ire.

He slid the bolt away with a clang and pulled the creaking door open. "*Schnell, schnell*. Let's go."

More Poles stumbled out, peering around. One man, average in height but broad in build, jumped down. He reached back and caught a small woman who just about fell into his arms. With the greatest of care, he set her down and kissed the top of her head. He whispered something into her ear. Maybe words of love.

Elfriede's heart twinged. Erich could be like this. And other times . . .

The man led the woman forward as the mass overflowed from the train car to the ground. And then, as they moved across the platform, the woman's foot caught. She tottered and fell. Elfriede froze, gooseflesh breaking out on her arms.

"Men to the left, women and children to the right." A soldier separated husbands and wives, fathers and children, sisters and brothers. One couple refused to be parted. With two bullets, the soldier sent them to their deaths together.

Her stomach rolled, and she squeezed her eyes shut. The image remained seared into her brain.

After steadying herself, Elfriede dared to open her eyes. Erich marched toward the young couple she'd seen before. He nudged the woman with his gun's butt. "Get moving. If you can't work, we don't need you. You are disposable."

Elfriede dug her fingernails into her palms. Her husband, that cruel? *Nein*, she must have heard him wrong. She tightened her grasp on her handkerchief.

He prodded the woman again. She glanced around. Her survey stopped at Elfriede, who hugged herself. Something familiar flickered in the woman's green eyes. The droop of them, the half-closed lids, the flash of light spoke of pain and suffering.

The woman gathered herself and gave a weak shout. "*Tata*, Helena, Zygmunt."

The man at her side held her upright and spoke to her.

Elfriede clasped her abdomen. She moved forward.

Erich jabbed the woman again. What would he do to them? Shoot them? Elfriede picked up her pace and reached the threesome in a few strides. She took hold of her husband by his arm. "Stop it. Don't hurt her."

He spun around, his mouth agape. He shook her off. "Get out of here." His words were tight, his blond mustache twitched, and his face reddened.

Her heart raced faster than a hummingbird's wings. "She's ill. Let me deal with her. I need help around the house. Imagine how nice it will be to have good meals instead of what I make. And someone to do the shopping who understands the language. Maybe with rest, I'll conceive."

"*Nein*. She's needed in the factory. We don't want a Pole in our home. They're filth. Not a toy or a pet for your pleasure. And you're capable of conceiving. You just don't want to do your duty."

"Look at her." Elfriede pointed at the woman now doubled over, her jaw clenched. "You won't get any work out of her in her condition. We'll bring her home and give her a trial. Let her get better and cook and clean for us. If she doesn't do a good job, you can take her away."

"Meanwhile, I'm down a woman. *Nein*. You shouldn't even be here."

"I was curious. You can't keep me locked in the house."

Erich raised his angular chin a tiny bit. "We will not have an argument in public. I've said my piece."

"And I've said mine. The woman is coming with me." Where

had that gumption come from? She gritted her teeth and pulled the woman from the man Elfriede assumed to be her husband.

He lunged forward and cried out. She didn't understand his words, but his tone was pure anguish. He clung to his wife.

Didn't he see she was trying to help? Keep them from being shot? Yet her stomach twisted as she tugged away the woman. "I'll take care of her and help her get better. She'll work for me."

Of course, neither the man nor the woman understood her. So she yanked again on the woman and motioned that she should follow.

A stream of tears rolled down the couple's sunken cheeks. The woman covered her face and sobbed.

What was Elfriede doing to them? Shaking away the thought, she squared her shoulders. She needed help. And this woman, for whatever reason, needed her.

Erich gripped his rifle, his knuckles white. "See the commotion you caused? Can't you mind your own business? You should be learning how to run a proper home instead of interfering here."

She straightened. Never in their short marriage had she talked back to him. But something deep inside drove her. She couldn't identify it or label it. This was one fight she had to win. "She will come with me. I want her for my own. That is the end of the discussion."

❧

Little by little, Natia lost her grip on Teodor. This blonde-haired woman pulled her from her husband. Her one lifeline in this crazy world. The soldier shoved Teodor forward. She clutched her middle with one hand and her heart with the other.

Then her husband, her song, her everything, disappeared into the crowd.

"*Nie, nie.*" She screeched as much as the mad woman on the train. Who cared when she was losing everything? "Teodor, come back. Come back to me." Her knees buckled, and she fell to the ground.

The German woman reached down and brought her to her feet. She said something Natia couldn't understand but spoke the words in a gentle, river-like manner.

By the time she peered up, Teodor was nowhere to be found. He might as well have ripped her heart out and carried it with him. The ache of losing him couldn't be any worse.

What was she going to do without him? Without any of her family?

Would she ever see them again?

Her legs trembled and threatened to give way. She was as weak as a cup of her grandmother's tea. Only dehydration lessened her tears. But sobs wracked her body as she struggled to catch her breath. Without Teodor, what was the point?

The German woman with the thin eyebrows and full lips steadied her. Why? What did she want?

She handed Natia a handkerchief embroidered with an *EF* in blue. Natia wiped her eyes.

"*Komme.*"

That, Natia understood. She had to come with the woman. For whatever reason, she'd fought with the Nazi officer and won the right to Natia.

The woman grabbed a basket sitting on the bench on the platform and led them into the empty waiting room. Natia stumbled. Would the woman beat her? Already, her side was bruised from the gun butts.

Nie, the German woman smiled, just a slight upturn of her mouth. Could she be sympathetic to Natia? Kind, even? None of the Nazis she'd had the misfortune of encountering in Piosenka were nice. They spoke in harsh tones and forced the villagers to walk in the muddy street. Neither was there kindness from any of those who invaded their town and stole their farms. Natia had made a point of steering clear of them.

The woman pointed to herself. "Elfriede Fromm."

So that was her name. "Elfriede." Natia pointed at herself. "Natia Palinska."

Elfriede tried it out. She giggled at her own attempt to pronounce the foreign name. Then she motioned for Natia to sit on one of the benches. They settled down. Very little was happening inside. All the commotion went on outside. The shouting of the guards. The cries of her countrymen being driven who knew where. Perhaps she could catch a glimpse of Teodor or the rest of her family through the window. One last look at them, a memory to carry with her until they were reunited. If they were.

Then a gunshot reverberated in the air.

Natia's pulse pounded in her ears. Her stomach plummeted like the mercury in the thermometer in January, and she jumped up. "Teodor!"

Elfriede pulled her down and shook her head. She pointed at the thin gold band on Natia's right hand. "Teodor?"

"*Tak*. Teodor is my husband." Had he been among those shot? What was happening out there?

Elfriede tried the Polish word. "Husband."

Natia nodded.

"Husband Erich." She motioned outside, scrunched her eyebrows, and pursed her lips.

That was the man on the platform? Natia's trembling didn't cease. If she went with Elfriede, she would encounter him again. Cold shot through her body.

They rested for a while before Elfriede took her by the hand and led the way out of the station. Away from Teodor, away from her family. Were any of them still alive? She hadn't been able to say good-bye to them.

Together, Natia and Elfriede walked several blocks, stopping a few times for Natia to catch her breath. Elfriede chattered away in German, but Natia didn't understand a word. And she didn't care to.

Just when she didn't think she'd be able to take another step, they arrived at a pleasant cottage, very Polish in its construction with a pink stucco exterior, a red-tiled roof, and curved dormers. Elfriede led the way into the bright interior. Soft-blue walls echoed the blue of the sky overhead, with white ceilings reminiscent of clouds. The ocher-colored tile floor might have been the road outside. If her heart wasn't breaking, she would think it charming.

Elfriede brought her to the living room and motioned for her to sit on a dark-blue couch in front of an elaborate blue-and-white-tiled stove. With all gentleness, Elfriede situated Natia, placing a colorful embroidered pillow under her feet and a downy yellow blanket over her shoulders. Who would have thought just an hour ago that a German woman would be waiting on her?

Within moments, Elfriede brought a warm cup of real coffee. Natia gulped it and burned her tongue.

But Elfriede didn't laugh. She took the delicate flower-sprigged cup from Natia and set it on the rough-hewn end table. She pointed at Natia's belly, still a might distended, and then made a rocking motion.

Natia nodded, then glanced at the ceiling. Her breath came in ragged gasps. She had no one left. Her parents and siblings were gone. Her children were gone. Teodor was gone. Maybe not even alive.

Then Elfriede rubbed her own stomach, rocked an invisible baby, and gazed at the heavens.

Perhaps, just perhaps, she understood Natia's pain. But a sympathetic captor didn't lessen the knife ripping open her middle.

♪♫♪

Chapter Five

$\mathcal{E}$ach time Teodor attempted to turn to catch one last glimpse of Natia as the German woman led her away, the soldier who split them up barked at him and poked him with the business end of his rifle.

Natia's hollow wail ripped Teodor to shreds, her beautiful, hopeful song replaced with mourning. She should only ever make joyful music, a melody that spoke of peace and happiness.

As the Nazi pushed him along, Teodor lost even the noise of her cries in the din of people around him.

He was alone. Without her. Torn from her without so much as a good-bye.

He had failed her.

His dry throat stung. He hadn't had anything to drink since they left the house yesterday morning. Was it only twenty-four hours ago that they bade farewell to their home? Their children? When would they get a drink? Even a few drops of water? But none was forthcoming.

The Nazi soldiers had separated the men from the women and children. More husbands without their wives. More fathers without their children. Helena and Zygmunt would be alone. But he didn't spot them anywhere. Not even Filip. What had happened to them?

After a long roll call, during which Teodor didn't hear Filip's name, the Germans led this motley band of farmers and shopkeepers down the cobblestone street, away from the Pieśń Nabożna train station. At least they remained on Polish soil.

No one peeked from any of the brick and stucco buildings. Why? Was there no one left here? Anyone who cared?

Not too long into their hike, his legs cramped and so did his stomach. A piece of bread, a few sips of milk. That's all he needed. All he wanted, besides his wife.

Shooting pains started in his ankles and bolted up his calves and thighs. Still, the hike continued. They bypassed the heart of the town. All the better for the Germans to hide their dirty little secret.

And then a sprawling industrial complex came into view. The sandstone buildings weren't any great feat of architecture but long, low places with rows upon rows of windows watching the new arrivals. Dual smokestacks rose three times as high as the three-story factory.

Screams and cries filled the air once more. Were Filip's and Helena's and Zygmunt's among them? Teodor closed his ears to the sounds.

The Nazis shaved everyone's heads. To get rid of the vermin they brought along, or so they said. Teodor caught a whisper of Russian prisoners coming here a few months earlier after one camp was closed due to typhus. The razor touched his head, his already short, fair hair floating to the ground.

Maybe the Lord took Natia from him to protect her. So she could heal in body and soul. So she wouldn't have to experience this treatment. Yet shouldn't he be the one looking out for her? Wasn't that his job?

The soldiers handed them each navy-blue, long-sleeved coveralls and herded the clutch of men who were left into a large room crammed with three-tiered bunks and prisoners' belongings. Turning around was next to impossible. Where were they all going to fit?

The officer from the train station, the one with the perfect nose like the slope of the Alps, stood on a crate and gave a shrill whistle. All talking halted. Each of the new arrivals turned to him.

"I am *Untersturmführer* Fromm. This is to be your new home. Each day, you will work in the factory producing parts vital to Germany for her success in her defense of the fatherland. You will be assigned tasks throughout the complex. You are expected to work hard, doing your part to bring glory to Germany.

"No talking will be allowed on the floor. You will be expected to work as many hours each day as we need you. You will be given lunch and dinner. Work hard, and life will go well. Disobedience will be met with swift and sure retribution.

"You may find a place for yourself. Work begins in one hour."

One hour? They expected them to start labor without food or drink? The guards strode out of the room, and a mad scramble ensued for the thin mattresses on the rough plank beds. Just a few square meters for each man. With the rest of the group, Teodor rushed forward. He was fast enough to snag a middle bunk near one of the many arched windows set into the brick wall. He dropped his case on the narrow pallet and pulled out a blanket.

And his picture of Natia on their wedding day. The only photo he owned of her. For several minutes he gazed at her as the film captured her in that moment. Eyes shining, shoulders relaxed, laughter on her lips. So young. So carefree. So innocent. Before the troubles of the world pressed on her and wore her down.

He shuddered. Where was she? What were they doing to her? *Lord, please help me to figure out a way to take care of her. May the woman who took her from me treat her with kindness.*

He stroked the picture, touching her cheek. "Be well, *moje słońce.*" He set the precious photograph under his pillow.

"I was here first. You can't have it. I've claimed it for myself." The shout rang out from across the room.

"You weren't here before me. I already had my hand on it when you strode up and shoved me out of the way." This man had a deeper voice than the first.

Teodor turned to see two men matched in height and weight facing each other.

"Shoved you out of the way? I did no such thing. You pushed me when you got here so you could say you had the bunk."

"Do you want to see pushing? I can give it to you. Don't underestimate me. I wanted to be an Olympic boxer."

"Wanting something doesn't make it so. I wanted to be king of the world. You don't see that happening."

"You're acting like it by taking others' belongings."

Teodor moved forward for a closer look. Most of the men in the room had the same idea.

Smack. One man's fist connected with the other's cheek.

"Umph." The second man landed a punch in his opponent's stomach.

The crowd got in on the action. "Get him. Don't let him get away with that. Take him down."

Teodor threaded his way through the gathered throng. He burst through the circle around the men. The fairer one had the other in a choke hold. "Stop it. What are you doing?" He pried the one man's hold loose and forced his way between the two of them.

"Stay out of it." The blond one reached around Teodor and cuffed his opponent's ear.

Teodor chopped him across the arm. "Leave him alone. Both of you, quit it."

"Make us." The darker man kicked his foe between Teodor's spread legs.

"If I need to, I will. You're behaving like naughty schoolkids. Like them." He nodded in the direction of the door.

That sucked the fight out of the prisoners. Another man came forward and pulled the blond man away.

"This is what they want." Teodor raised his voice so all the men in the dorm heard him. "They want to divide us, to demoralize us, so we turn on each other. That makes us weaker and easier victims. If we expect to survive, we must stand together. To fight for ourselves and for each other against the Nazis. How will we come out alive if we attack each other rather than the enemy?"

The question hung in the air. The words soaked into each man. "He's right." The voice was familiar to Teodor. Jerzy Skala. Tall. Skinny. They went to the village school with each other. "If we stick together, it will be harder for them to break us. A herd of cows is more difficult to control than a single one."

A murmuring buzz filled the room. One by one, the men peeled from the crowd and returned to their tiny living spaces.

Teodor approached Jerzy and clapped him on the shoulder. "*Dzięki* for your help. It's good to see you." A familiar face. A touch of home.

"I couldn't let an old chum stand by himself. Especially when he's right." Jerzy walked alongside Teodor as he found his way to his little spot in the world. "How have you been?"

"Not too bad. I moved to the next village over after school and got an apprenticeship with the local cabinetmaker. He taught me the trade, and I took over for him when he died. Married Zofia, and we have two children. How about you?"

"I married Natia, and we have a small farm. We've had three children, but all of them passed away." Pain sliced through him. "I'm blessed to have a devoted, loving wife."

A shrill whistle pierced the air. An officer in an olive-drab uniform and a red-and-black swastika armband stood in the doorway. "Time to work. *Schnell, schnell.* Let's go."

The men hustled out of the room. Jerzy and Teodor brought up the rear. The officer from the station leaned over and whispered to him as he passed. "I'll be watching you. Every minute of every day. And remember, I have your wife."

A shiver raced down Teodor's spine.

❦

For most of the day, Natia rested on the couch, sleeping away the hours. When she did wake, the German woman left her embroidery on the flowered wing chair near the sunny window and brought some broth from the kitchen.

"*Essen, essen.*" She held the fine silver spoon to Natia's lips.

She sipped the warm soup that contained several pieces of beef. And soon her stomach rebelled. She hadn't been hungry since before her baby's birth. Even though Teodor had urged her, she hadn't eaten much.

But she had to regain her strength. If she couldn't work, they wouldn't let her live. Each time Elfriede encouraged her to eat, she did, no matter how hard she had to fight to keep the food in her stomach.

By midafternoon, the dizziness and weakness that had overwhelmed her lessened to where she managed to sit up for a while. Elfriede joined her on the couch. With a shy glance to the side, she showed Natia her work.

With tiny, intricate stitches Elfriede had embroidered a mountain valley scene. Snow capped the tops of the purple peaks, while yellow and red flowers bloomed in the meadow. A half-finished chalet filled one corner of the piece. "It's beautiful." Natia smiled and pointed at the work. "Beautiful."

Elfriede nodded. "*Danke.*" She jabbered on. If only Natia could understand. Then she might ask Elfriede what she wanted from her and where Teodor was. When they might be reunited. But for now, gestures would have to do.

Elfriede made progress on the little chalet as the shadows lengthened across the tile floors. Before the lamps needed to be lit, she got up and went to the kitchen. She banged pots and pans together. The stove's heavy door scraped back. The shovel clanged against the coal bin as she fed fuel into the oven. Then a moment of silence.

"Ouch, ouch."

That word was universal. Natia slung back the blanket and rose to help, the world tilting as she did. As she stood and fought to regain her balance, the rear door clicked open and banged shut. A man's deep, rough voice filled the small cottage. A moment later, the soldier from the train station trooped into the room, his jaw clenched, his hands fisted, his dark-blue eyes narrowed.

He marched to her and slapped her. She staggered, her heart thumping as fast as a polka's beat.

"What are you doing? You are to help my wife."

"She didn't tell me anything."

"What? You thought you were here on holiday?" He struck her again and stared down at her. "You are going to have a baby?"

She shook her head.

"Then you have no excuse for lounging. You're a fat toad. My wife is delicate. Fragile. You are a Polish workhorse. You will take over the duties here. Immediately. The cooking, cleaning, and laundry. Do I make myself clear?"

"*Tak*, I will." Still wobbly on her feet, she scurried by him to the kitchen. A knife and a pile of potatoes sat on the table.

Pan Fromm moved by her and crouched beside his wife, who perched on a nearby chair, blood seeping through a towel.

The way he stroked Elfriede's hair intensified Natia's longing for Teodor.

"Hurry up and tend to my wife."

Though every part of her shook, Natia steadied herself against the chair and unwrapped Elfriede's finger.

Thank goodness, it had almost stopped bleeding. Natia cleaned the wound and, with Elfriede pointing her in the right direction, found more dressings in the lavatory. She bandaged her up. "Good."

"*Ja, sehr gut.*" At least they understood each other about that.

By the time she served Elfriede and her husband the potatoes and sausage she prepared, blackness edged at Natia's consciousness. The food and the chair invited her to rest and replenish herself.

Elfriede motioned for her to sit. She pulled out the seat to join them. *Pan* Fromm pounded his fist on the table and shouted at his wife in German. She slouched in her chair, a single tear trickling down her cheek.

Pan Fromm turned to Natia. "You are here to work, not to fraternize with my wife. She is far your superior. Do I make myself clear?"

"Very."

"Tomorrow, I'll have a pallet brought for you from the factory. The floor is good enough for tonight. That should teach you your place."

Her cheek stung and her face burned. Mama's wise words rang in her head. *"He prays but has the devil under his skin."*

Oh, Teodor, Teodor. How was she ever going to survive?

♪♫♪

Chapter Six

awel Bosco finger-combed his thinning gray hair and tapped his pencil on his scarred desk. Papers littered the top of it, notes on various patients he had treated over the years. Many of them had already succumbed to the Nazis. Many of his intellectual peers had disappeared as well.

Including Józef.

A deep ache, one that penetrated his bones, spread throughout him, and he bit back the sob that arose at the thought of his son.

How many more would die before this madness ended?

Another trainload of prisoners arrived last week. The factory sprawled on the outskirts of the village and dwarfed the modest homes around it, but how many could even that large building hold? He shuddered. How many of the newcomers brought the fleas that spread typhus?

An epidemic of some sort was a real possibility.

Antonina knocked at the open door and entered. After thirty years of marriage, she knew him inside and out. "I brought you a cup of tea, such as it is."

He stood and pushed his glasses up his nose, then worked the kink from his back. "*Dzięki.*" He took the cup, the earthy fragrance of dandelions breaking more of his tension.

"You work too hard." She gazed at him, her eyes as green as the summer's grass.

"I'm going to get busier, I'm afraid. The dysentery and severed fingers I'm seeing from prisoners at the camp may only be the beginning."

A soft knock sounded at the front door, and Antonina scurried away to answer it. What would he do without her?

She returned a moment later with *Pani* Fromm trailing her. "I told her you only have a minute."

"Nonsense. I have plenty of time." He switched to the German he learned while studying in Cologne many years ago. "Come in, Frau Fromm, and have a seat. *Dzięki*, Antonina."

As she left the room, his wife closed the door.

He leaned forward and studied the perfect Aryan woman in front of him, skin unblemished, blonde hair rolled in the latest fashion, her blue silk dress not showing any signs of wear. "What can I do for you today?" He asked the question, though he knew the answer. Elfriede Fromm paid him a visit just about every month.

She rubbed her hands together, as if washing them. "It's the same. No baby again this month." She pulled a handkerchief from her black patent leather pocketbook.

He rubbed his jaw. What could he do for her? And if he didn't come up with a cure for her, what would happen to him? Too many of his colleagues had disappeared in the early days of the war when the Nazis sought to wipe out the Polish intelligentsia. He wiped the sweat from his upper lip. "I'm terribly sorry. As I've told you, I don't see a reason why you aren't conceiving. Not a physical malady, anyway. But you are worried and emotional."

"I carried a child once before, a little boy that I lost. What is wrong with me that it isn't happening again?"

"Stress takes a toll on your body. If you relax, I'm sure you will conceive."

She nodded and stroked a strand of blonde hair back into place. "I long for a son to carry on my husband's family name and to bring honor to the fatherland. To have as many boys as possible to fulfill Germany's destiny. That's the duty of every good German woman."

Pawel leaned back and studied the Nazi's wife. So young. Her blue eyes shimmering with naïveté. And she came to him, a hated

Pole, one targeted by powerful men like her husband, seeking to further the pure race the Germans sought.

Yet there was something about her. Fresh. Innocent.

Part of him reached out to help her.

Part of him retched at the thought of another Nazi roaming the earth.

"Rest as much as you can. Take it easy and allow your husband to pamper you. I'm sure that in no time, you'll cradle your child." If he kept giving her assurances, hope, perhaps her husband would not find a reason to be rid of him.

He pushed up from his creaky wooden desk chair and showed *Pani* Fromm out. He leaned against the door frame as she ambled down the street and out of sight. His wife approached and embraced him from behind. "You're troubled."

He turned and kissed the top of her head. "Aren't we all?"

"But you're worried about something you aren't sharing with me."

"It's confidential."

"I don't know why she comes to you all the time."

"She needs my help."

"It's dangerous, Pawel." She kissed the inside of his hand. "I've already lost Józef. I can't lose you."

"Don't fret." But it was treacherous business he was about.

⁓

The days lengthened as Natia's strength returned. In a way, the hard work *Pani* Fromm demanded of her was good. She didn't have the time or energy to mourn the loss of her son. Or to dwell on the ache in her heart that came from missing her family. And Teodor.

Because without him, she wasn't whole. She was as empty as the coal bin in the morning.

She tried to sing to fill the void in her heart. Always before, it helped. The melodies soothed her spirit at the loss of her children. The tunes celebrated each new day with Teodor. The songs spoke of better times amid hardship. Sweet memories of Mama and the rest of her family.

But now her mouth and vocal chords refused to cooperate. Each time she attempted to voice a melody, the notes choked out rough and scratchy. Not her usual smooth soprano, the voice Teodor compared to a bird.

She hummed a few bars, but even that bit of music was hollow.

Pani Fromm wanted apple strudel for dessert tonight. She told Natia where to find the recipe, but she knew how to make it by heart. Both the Germans and the Poles shared a love for this dessert.

She set out the flour and the butter, but she scraped the bottom of the crock that held the sugar. No sweets without it.

If Elfriede wanted more, she'd have to get it. Natia brought the container into the main room where the woman reclined on the sofa with her needlework.

"No sugar." Natia pointed to the almost-empty jar.

Elfriede motioned to her pocketbook and said something. Natia fetched Elfriede's purse from the table across the room and grabbed her shoes from the back entry.

"*Nein, nein.*" Elfriede took the handbag but swatted away the shoes. Instead, she pulled out her wallet and peeled off several *złoty.* "You go."

"Me?" Natia pointed at herself, sure Elfriede must have used the wrong Polish word.

"*Ja.* You go."

"*Nie.* You must."

"*Nein.*" Elfriede settled back among the cushions. Her behavior had been odd the past several days. She'd gone out, came back an hour later, and planted herself on the sofa. From there, she directed Natia's work. *Pan* Fromm told her that Elfriede wasn't to get up and wasn't to do any work whatsoever.

Was she expecting?

"No strudel."

"You go."

"*Pani* Fromm?"

"You go." She set her full lips in a firm line.

Elfriede must feel that her husband wouldn't object to Natia shopping. They didn't keep her locked in a room, but they had never let her out of the house either. Then again, they knew Teodor was a prisoner. Even if she escaped, she wouldn't go anywhere without him. If he was here, she would stay.

Maybe the fresh air would release her song.

She grasped the money Elfriede handed her, grabbed the straw marketing basket, and headed down the street. The village wasn't large enough for her to get lost.

The sun illuminated the little town, and its warmth penetrated her white blouse. She'd been too ill and distraught when she arrived to notice its charm. Tile-roofed cottages lined the old, narrow streets. One stooped woman whistled as she swept her front porch. She stopped and waved at Natia as if all were right with the world.

Up ahead, a massive compound of buildings spread across the road, two smokestacks towering overhead.

Could this be the place where Teodor was, if he was alive? As she scrubbed the kitchen floor a week or so ago, she'd overhead a conversation Elfriede had with her husband. While she hadn't understood most of it, she caught her husband's name and something about a factory.

Could he be here? Almost right in front of her? Did she dare even dream the possibility? So close he was, and yet so far. Just out of her grasp.

And if he was here, were the others too?

She wiped her sweaty hands on her simple black wool skirt lined with petticoats. Her heart pattered inside of her. *Oh, Teodor, if only I might communicate with you somehow. Speak to you. Let you know I am fine.*

And that I love you.

She gazed at the long lines of windows. Three stories of them. Which one might be closest to where he worked?

Glancing around to make sure *Pan* Fromm and his underlings weren't around, she set down the basket. She would have to start at this end and sing all the way down the line to be sure he heard.

If her voice would work.

She tucked a strand of hair behind her ear. For the first time since they arrived, she let the music take control.

> *When for a moment thou dost speak, my darling,*
> *'Tis like the music of angel voices calling,*
> *Mute is my joy that I may be so near thee,*
> *Hark'ning, and hoping that thou mayst persevere,*
> *Naught else desiring, forever, forever, but so to hear thee.*

Chopin's words, those of a Polish hero, poured from her with very little thought. Not scratchy or hoarse, but clear and true. She closed her eyes, and the melody transported her to a better time, when she worked the fields beside her husband. When he loved her through the night.

The song spoke for her.

The music cried with her as she told Teodor of her loneliness. It held her up as she reassured him that she had recovered and was well. It soared with her as she poured her love out to him.

She meandered along the side of the building, singing the soft, tender melody over and over, with as much volume as she could muster. Would he hear?

Dare she hope that he would answer?

Silence echoed in the void.

No movement from the windows. No sign that anyone inside heard her over the noisy machines.

Of course. How silly to think her song would reach him. And especially crazy to believe he might sing back to her.

❧

The hum and whine of machinery filled Teodor's head as he

reached the top step for the hundredth time during his shift and picked up another crate to be loaded for shipment to Germany. The Nazis hadn't enlightened the men what the pieces his fellow prisoners manufactured were for. He rubbed his lower back. After several weeks on the job, his muscles still cramped after many long hours hefting the heavy boxes.

He wiped the sweat from his forehead before it dripped into his eyes. Their captors forbade them from opening the windows. What were they afraid of? Someone jumping out? Then again, a couple of broken legs might be preferable to working in this miserable place. At least he got to taste the fresh air each time he descended to the first floor. And had the chance to search for Natia's family. So far, without success.

Oh, but he missed his land. The warm breezes in his hair, the kiss of the sun on his cheek, the taste of the earth in his mouth. He missed the familiar sight of the crosses on the hill, though it brought fresh pain. *Tak*, he worked hard for little, but what he did was for himself and Natia. Here, the walls confined him, stifled him. If only he had a few moments to roam free.

As he pulled the next box to be carried so he could lift it, the container slipped from his hand and clanged to the concrete floor. In two long strides their supervisor, *Untersturmführer* Fromm, reached him. He bent over Teodor, Fromm's face mere centimeters from his, the pungent, vinegary odor of sauerkraut almost overwhelming. "What are you doing, you careless dog? For that, you won't have anything to eat when your shift ends. Maybe that will teach you not to be so sloppy. Just like your wife."

Once Fromm turned his back, Jerzy shot him a glance. Teodor shrugged. The paper-thin, dry piece of brown bread and the watery soup with only the promise of a rotten potato was no great loss. Let some other poor soul choke it down. Tomorrow, Fromm might turn his ire on one of the other workers, and he'd get more to eat.

But Natia. Was that hound depriving her of food? She needed to keep up her strength. What was he doing to her? Teodor dug his fingernails into his palms. If only he had a way to know she was safe and well. But if he ever found out that dog did anything to his beautiful wife ...

Their shift ended many long hours later. The men from his department shuffled back to the barracks on the building's top floor. Too tired to even be hungry, Teodor flopped onto the middle of the three-tiered bunk. He didn't have the energy to scratch at the fleas that bit him.

Jerzy sat beside him. "I'm sorry you had to miss the meal. Though, as usual, there wasn't much."

"I figured so."

"I saved this for you." Jerzy slipped him a crumbly piece of bread.

Teodor sat up, almost banging his head on the bunk above him. "You didn't have to. I don't want you in trouble on my account."

"Don't worry. I've had my fill of Fromm. Anything I can do to lessen his bite, I will. It's a small rebellion, but one nonetheless."

"I'm grateful."

"You have to keep up your strength. You proved the other day you can prevent us from getting to each other. We need you. And Natia needs you."

The bite of bread stuck in his throat. Dwelling on his wife only increased his desire for her. His chest burned at the thought of Fromm with his hands on her.

"You long for her as I long for my family."

Teodor wiped the crumbs from his hands. "At least you know where your wife is." He shuddered.

"Maybe. They picked me off the street at random one day, and it would be just like them if they shipped her and my children to a different camp. But what can we do?"

That was the question. "Something. Anything to end this war as soon as possible. To rid our land of the Germans the way they want to rid the land of us. We can't allow them to run over our people like they've done for almost four years. When they invaded, we fought the best we could, but it was over so fast, I didn't have time to join the battle. And who could stand against the blitzkrieg, especially when Britain and France turned a blind eye to our plight? But now, we've given up. Stopped fighting. That isn't right."

"Look at us." Jerzy gestured wide, taking in all the dirty, overworked, tired men. "They have us caged. What can we do?"

"I don't know. But there has to be something." Teodor massaged his temples. Something to get back at them for what they'd done to his mother. And something to get back at them for what they were doing to Natia and countless others like them.

This time of day, a quietness covered the room. The day shift workers settled into their bunks. Men from the night shift left to work. No one had the energy to speak.

Just as Teodor lay back on his almost-flat pillow and gazed at his picture of Natia, a sound cut through the calm. A beautiful, haunting sound.

A sound he would recognize anywhere.

Natia's song.

Her voice, so pure, so clear, so perfect.

He hustled to the window. Despite the warnings, he flung it wide. There, three stories down, his beloved.

His breath hitched.

The music floated to him, enveloped him. Heartache. Love. And, in a strange way, peace. Her melody spoke to him.

Should he shout to let her know he heard? That he was alive and well?

Nie. That might put her at risk. And him.

The sweet, lilting melody was one he'd heard before. And the words captured him. She longed for him as much as he did for her. He answered her with the rest of the song, his voice rough.

> *But when the love light in thine eye is glowing,*
> *And on thy cheek the roses red are blowing,*
> *With fonder yearning follow thee my gazes,*
> *Ah, then! Ah, then! Ah, then, my darling,*

Ah, then, my darling,
I long to draw near thee, sweet though thy lips,
I no longer will hear thee,
Will seal them with kisses.

And then a uniformed German came along. He gestured to Natia and pushed her forward.

Teodor caught her green-eyed glance before she scurried away. Oh, Natia.

♩♫♪

Chapter Seven

*I*f only the German soldier hadn't come and pushed Natia along. For just a few more precious seconds with Teodor. He'd heard. He'd answered. *Tak*, she should be satisfied. But she couldn't get enough.

At least he was alive. But when would be the next time she would hear from him?

As she headed to the Fromms' house, she swung the grocery bag filled with sugar, vegetables, a jug of milk, and a loaf of bread. The song she'd sung resonated in her heart. In the depths of her being, she held a piece of him. A place where the Nazis couldn't steal him from her.

She examined every home she wandered by, some painted peach, others blue, still others mint green. Who lived in each of the cottages? What were their lives like under the occupation? Had they lost anyone they had loved?

That was the worst part about not being in the factory. She couldn't search for her family. Perhaps she could find a way to ask Teodor. Maybe he knew. Zygmunt and Helena must be so afraid. If only Natia could comfort them.

As she strolled on, a mewling sound emanated from the alley to her left and drew her from her reverie. A kitten? Perhaps the orange tabby she fed a few scraps to every night had given birth to a litter. The animal was scrawny, but weren't they all these days?

She peeked down the dark alley, not able to distinguish much. There it came again. Once she had glanced over her shoulder to make sure no one watched, she followed the sound into the darkness.

Something ahead of her shuffled. A weak shaft of light dispelled the gloom. Natia moved deeper into the alley and almost tripped over something. She gazed down.

Nie, not something.

Someone.

A haggard woman crouched in the shadows, a faded blue kerchief on her head, a scrappy baby with dark, matted curls clutched to her breast. She stared at Natia with large brown eyes.

Natia knelt beside her and stroked the child's head. Her son might have had hair like this, might have held on to her like this child clung to his mother. She closed her eyes, then opened them and straightened her shoulders. "What are you doing here? Can I help you?"

The woman shook her head.

"Please, let me do something."

The infant moved just enough for Natia to spy a spot of yellow on the lapel of the woman's coat. A Star of David.

She was Jewish.

Natia's mouth went dry. How had she survived all these years? Had she been in hiding? Most of the ghettos had been filled and some emptied. Despite the chill in the air, Natia shrugged off her sweater and wrapped it around the woman and child.

"Don't turn us in." The woman's voice was low and scratchy.

"I would never do that." Never. Life was too precious. Too fragile. "But you can't live in the alley. When did you last eat?"

"I don't know."

What could she do? Bringing the woman to the Fromms' was out of the question. And Natia knew no one else here. Not anyone she could trust. She hugged herself. The alley was dirty and garbage filled. Not good conditions for a young child, his life threatened by innumerable diseases. But if the baby remained quiet, the shadows hid them. No easy task for the woman.

"I'm Natia. I'll help as much as I can." She drew the bread and milk from her bag along with a bunch of carrots. "For you." She held out the offering.

"You would give this to us?"

"They hate me almost as much as they hate you." She pointed to the diamond-shaped scrap sewn to her dress, the large *P* proclaiming her status. "But you have to keep your baby from crying. That's what led me to you." She rubbed the child's bony hand, and he grasped at her finger. If only …

The woman nodded. "He's hungry."

The banter of a couple of German soldiers drifted into the hiding spot. Natia shrank back, her breath coming in short gasps. If they found her here, giving aid to a Jewish woman and child, they would send her to a camp worse than Teodor's. Natia had heard the rumors about them. Everyone had. About how women and children were murdered upon their arrivals. The three of them must be still. Silent.

The child whimpered. Natia covered his mouth and glared at his mother who jiggled the boy in her lap.

Eternal moments passed. The soldiers moved on. Even after their words faded in the distance, Natia kept her voice at a whisper. "This will help the baby. He won't cry if he's been fed." How she would explain the double purchase on the Fromms' account, she had no idea. But one thing at a time. She couldn't leave the woman and infant to starve.

"I'm Rachel. This is Solomon. *Dziękuję Ci.* Thank you from the bottom of our hearts."

"I'll come as often as I can. If I can sneak a blanket from the house, I'll bring that."

"You've done enough."

Nie, it wasn't enough. It never could be enough. Not for the mother, and especially not for the little one. She had to save them. She couldn't watch another child die. For now, this would have to do. Helpless as she was herself, she could aid another human.

"I have to go before I'm missed. If you need anything, I live in the cottage at the end of this street. The pink one with the roses blooming in the front. Come there but go to the back."

Rachel nodded. "Again, *dziękuję Ci.*"

Natia stood and hurried toward the street and then glanced both ways, holding her breath. No Nazis. She blew out the air in a single puff. Her pulse hammered in her neck. She would do what she could for Rachel and Solomon.

Especially for him.

❧

The long days stretched in front of Elfriede. Here she sat with nothing to do. She had followed the doctor's recommendations. Natia had taken over the household duties. She did the marketing, the cleaning and scrubbing, the cooking, even the laundry. Elfriede did nothing.

For a few hours, she enjoyed the pampering. But that changed by the first afternoon. She could only embroider for so long before her fingers cramped. A breath of fresh air might do her good. Dr. Bosco said to rest and relax, not become a hermit.

Erich and *Vater* both treated her as a china doll, especially after she had become pregnant. They had agreed she would make a fine wife for an SS officer. Even *Vater's* usual frown at her bumbling ways had turned upside down. So the wedding had taken place. Followed a few months later by her miscarriage.

She left Natia up to her elbows in flour, kneading rye dough for bread, and headed toward the center of the village.

After a while she found herself in front of the butcher shop. By this time of day, the line of women waiting to purchase their ration of meat had dissipated. She entered the shop to the jangle of a bell.

Frau Rzeźnikowa entered from a back room, her white apron stained with blood. "Frau Fromm, how good to see you. Your girl was in here earlier and purchased a fine cut of beef for your goulash. Is there something else I can help you with?"

Elfriede glanced around the small room dominated by the counter. She shifted her weight. "I, um, I . . ." Her hands sweated. Erich would be furious if he found out her mission. But she could trust Frau Rzeźnikowa to be discreet, couldn't she?

"Yes, dear?"

"Do you have some time?"

The plump, middle-aged woman, her graying hair pulled into a severe bun, smiled. "For you, always. You remind me so much of my own daughter, now in Kraków. Shall I put the kettle on? I only have ersatz coffee, but I'll pour us each a cup." She motioned for Elfriede to follow her behind the counter and into the small back room.

A plain white ceramic stove took up one corner of the space, reaching from the floor to the ceiling. Frau Rzeźnikowa pulled out a chair next to the table covered with a cheery yellow cloth. She poured coffee into a pair of stained white china cups and set one in front of Elfriede before she dropped into the seat across from her.

"What can I do for you, my dear? You were hesitant to ask, but you shouldn't be. I'm happy to help with whatever I can."

Elfriede fingered the tablecloth's hem. "*Danke*. Not all the townspeople would be as accommodating. They don't appreciate us Germans."

Frau Rzeźnikowa took a slow sip of coffee. "I've been here a long time, and I don't judge people by their nationality. I make my judgments on a case-by-case basis. I prefer to look at the individual rather than the people as a whole."

Hitler would disagree, but Elfriede didn't. Frau Rzeźnikowa had a point. "That's a good way of saying it. I came to ask a favor."

"If it's in my power to do it, I will."

"Is your husband around?"

"He's gone upstairs to take a nap. His heart isn't too good, and he tires by this time. We're usually out of meat by now, so that frees him to rest. Is it something womanly?"

"*Nein*." She spit the word out. "I mean, not really." She couldn't share that part of her life. "You see, Natia only speaks Polish, and I only speak German. We've learned a few words from each other, just enough to get by, but I'd like another woman to chat with."

"I see." Frau Rzeźnikowa's wrinkled face softened.

"Not that I don't enjoy a talk with you. But she's my age. It's different."

Frau Rzeźnikowa patted her hand. "I understand, I really do. How can I help?"

"Will you teach me Polish?"

Her mouth dropped open. "You want me to teach you the language?"

"*Ja.*"

"What does your husband think?"

"He speaks Polish." True, he learned it as a child from their housekeeper, but he did know the language. "Why shouldn't I learn?"

"Because the Nazis want to destroy Poland and everything Polish. Including the language." As soon as she uttered the words, she covered her mouth.

"I'm sure that's an exaggeration." Was it really? An image of the workers stumbling from the train's cattle cars, the murders of the couple who refused to be parted, flashed in front of her. "Besides, I'm not telling Erich. He's working. I need something to do all day."

"You don't know what you're asking of me." The older woman scrunched her forehead, deep lines etching her skin.

"I will pay you well."

"You don't have to pay me at all. I'll do it."

Elfriede resisted the urge to clap her hands. "*Danke, danke.*"

"That's *dziękuję Ci* if you're being formal, *dzięki* if you're not."

"*Dziękuję Ci.*" Elfriede laughed at the strange word. "It's very different from German."

"That it is. But you'll pick it up with little trouble. You're young, as I was when I first learned."

"What else?"

They spent another thirty minutes practicing various Polish phrases, things that would be most helpful in communicating with Natia. By the time she bade Frau Rzeźnikowa *do widzenia*, or good-bye, she could ask for something she wanted and request a drink of coffee and a plate of schnitzel.

She hummed a tune, one Natia sang all the time, as she strolled down the streets lined with quaint cottages. The sun melted away what little tension remained in her shoulders. This was good for her.

Up ahead, the smokestacks of the factory rose, casting a shadow over the landscape. What were the people doing inside? What about Natia's husband? Erich had mentioned that he worked there.

She skirted the factory and came to her own home at the village's edge. Roses climbed up the wall, and bright yellow and orange flowers nodded in the breeze.

"*Dzień dobry*," she called to Natia as she stepped over the threshold. "*Jestem w domu*. I'm home."

Erich stormed around the corner. He narrowed his stormy blue eyes. "What did you just say?"

"I greeted Natia."

"Frau Palinska is busy ironing the sheets." His nostrils flared. "Why do you speak Polish?"

"You do."

"Unfortunately." He stepped closer, towering over her. "But I don't want to hear that language crossing your lips again. Not one word. Do you understand me? Speaking like them makes you no better than them."

She cowered in the corner. "Erich, you're frightening me."

He huffed and turned in a circle before kneeling in front of her, softening his voice. "I'm sorry. I didn't mean to shout. It's what happens after dealing with those vile Poles all day. Listen to me, though. They and their language are barbaric. Don't sully yourself. For me, please." He stroked her cheek and kissed her, his mustache tickling her lips.

But in this, she might have to disobey him. She just could never allow him to overhear her.

e~o

For the past several months, a beautiful song drifted through the window as Teodor started his long factory day. He may not have food or a soft bed or warm clothes, but he had all he needed.

Natia.

While her first visit came late in the day, she now arrived at the same time every morning. If he started to look forward to it, that might jinx it. But he couldn't help himself. Her music brought a sweet beginning to his days.

This morning, as she passed under his window, she sang a happy, upbeat tune. One a little girl might skip rope to.

Here we go to market,
To buy my love a locket,
To keep in every secret,
And hold it in my pocket.

So that must be where Fromm allowed her to go. Her excuse for getting out of the house and coming to within wishing distance of him. He didn't dare go to the window to stare at her, though he could drink in the sight of her for hours upon hours.

He chuckled to himself at the ditty. So good it was to hear her cheery song. Her heart was healing. The heaviness, the pressing ache over their baby's death, lifted.

He answered with a silly tune of his own.

Here we go to labor,
To buy my love a fish,
Never more so happy,
Than when it's on the dish.

Okay, he didn't have her sweet voice or even her talent for

singing on key, but he let the melody flow from his lips. To let her know he heard her. Thought about her. Loved her.

Mostly, to let her know he was fine and that she didn't have to worry about him.

> *When I want for mother,*
> *For sister and for brother,*
> *You'll tell me they are near you,*
> *To see you and to hear you.*

Of course, she wanted to know about her family. But he didn't have good news for her. Not bad, but not the best.

> *You lack the tender care of mother,*
> *The joy of sister and of brother,*
> *Oh, but that I might find them,*
> *That once more you might mind them.*

A slap on his back broke his reverie. "You're rather chipper for the start of a dull working day." Jerzy chuckled.

"She puts me in a happy mood." He cocked his head in the direction of the window.

"If only we all had wives who sang like doves."

"I wouldn't give her up for anything. And to know she's alive and well, stronger than when we arrived, makes this place bearable." How much better it would be if he could touch her or talk to her. But most of the men didn't get the thinnest shred of information about their wives. He shouldn't complain. Only, to have her so close, within a whisper, and not be able to be with her was its own form of torture.

"I anticipate her morning songs, and she's not even my wife." Jerzy bent to tie his heavy work boot.

"It's amazing what a little uplifting like that can do for a person."

Off in the corner, one man retched. The sharp, putrid odor permeated the stifling room. Jerzy scrunched up his nose. "*Tak,* but we need more of it. Months have gone by with no relief. The men get weaker and sicker by the day."

They moved to the floor of the factory. Each week, their captors raised the quota of pieces that needed to be produced and readied for shipment.

Today, Teodor worked on a drill press. On the floor below, the women produced needle bearings. On this floor, the men manufactured other pieces. Like what he worked on now. He had no idea what they were for, but over and over he drilled six holes into a rounded slab of metal. Over and over he dropped the finished parts into the box beside him. Still more parts came.

He inhaled, long and slow, imagining the fresh smell of the rain on his crops, the low of the cow in the barn, the softness of the dirt under his feet. And in his mind's eye, he saw the cemetery on the rise. His throat constricted. Too much loss. He sighed. Best not to dwell on his faraway home.

As he pulled down the lever on the drill press, he sang Natia's song in his head. A place where the Nazis couldn't hear him and couldn't order him to stop.

Fromm made his way to Teodor's machine and kicked over the box that held his work. "You don't have much done for so late in the day." He scooped up all Teodor had finished and placed it in Jerzy's box. "See, he has completed double what you have. You will stay at your station until you meet the quota." With that, he marched away.

Teodor wilted.

Jerzy leaned over. "We must do something. We can't allow him to get away with this."

"What? Retaliate?"

Fromm thundered from across the room. "Quiet on the floor."

"I don't know. But we have to come up with a plan."

Teodor lowered the drill press. The bit screeched as it ate into the metal. His head throbbed. But he picked up another undrilled piece and repeated the process. Five, ten, fifteen times.

What could they, mere prisoners, do? He lined up the template, making sure it was on just right, as their overseers had taught them.

Wait a minute.

What would happen if he didn't drill the holes in the exact place they were supposed to go? What if he moved the template over just a few millimeters?

Perhaps these parts wouldn't fit whatever they were supposed to fit. They wouldn't be usable. The prisoners might slow down the production of whatever equipment these pieces belonged to.

His hands trembled. Wouldn't that be something?

He resumed his task with renewed fervor. Every few pieces, he placed the template in the wrong position. Just a little bit off and not every piece, so the supervisor would never suspect.

He flew through the quota Fromm set for him and returned to the barracks as Jerzy settled in for the night.

Teodor leaned over his friend's bunk. "Hey, wake up. I have a plan."

"Hmm? A plan for what?" Jerzy opened one eye.

"Shh, keep your voice down."

"What are you up to?"

"You said we had to find a way to exact our revenge on the Germans. Well, I believe I've come up with something."

Jerzy opened the other eye and sat. "You did? What is it?"

"Shh, I don't want anyone else to hear." He shared with his bunkmate what he had done. "What do you think?"

"You're brilliantly out of your mind. What happens if we get caught?"

"That's why we have to do this just right. Too much, and the Nazis will catch on. Too little, and our sabotage will be ineffective."

"It might work. But are you willing to suffer the consequences if we're found out?"

A chill raced up Teodor's spine. But whatever it was, the risk was worth it. They needed to defend their country however they could. Restore Poland to its former glory. They needed to get back to their lives and their families as soon as possible. This was one thing that he could do on the inside to take care of his wife.

Bringing the war to a swifter close meant one less day Natia had to be subjected to Fromm.

Teodor could do his part.

Great risk? Yes. Worth it? It had better be.

Chapter Eight

Fall 1943

A hollow, empty ache overwhelmed Natia as she worked in the kitchen frying pork and cabbage for Elfriede's dinner. *Pan* Fromm informed her yesterday that he would be out tonight.

Teodor's last song to her spoke of hunger. Hunger for her. Hunger for God. And probably physical hunger. At least she had a small meal in her stomach. What was he enduring? How did he manage to stay alive? The tunes they sang each other were wonderful, but never quite enough. More. That's what she needed. More time with him. More words from him.

My, how she missed Teodor. Not even a child to remind her of him. And what if he died in there? And how were *Tata*, Zygmunt, and Helena doing? If Teodor suffered, they must be also. *God, protect them all.* Or she would be left with nothing?

Like always, she bit back her cries, then scooped a spoonful of the pork onto a saucer and blew on it until it cooled. Each evening, the tabby pawed at the back door, so Natia fed her a tablespoon or so of whatever they had. The scrawny feline gobbled it up.

She opened the door. Her breath hung in the air, her own little cloud. Any day now, winter would come. Had they really been here six months? And yet, the time without Teodor stretched out forever.

A sprinkling of stars glittered in the dark velvet sky. She chuckled. Teodor tried once to teach her the constellations. How had he seen a bear and a goat and a dipper in the shimmering lights? *Nie.* They were jewels at the Lord's feet.

From the ground came a groan. The kitty? Cats didn't make noises like that. Noises wringing with misery. She glanced at the tiny yard. Another groan and a feeble cry. And two dark lumps in front of her. Natia took three steps and bent down. A thin, frail woman and an emaciated child.

Rachel and Solomon.

She had found them in the alley once after their first encounter, but then they were gone. Disappeared. She had guessed on a train much like the one that brought Teodor and her to this place.

But *nie*, they weren't taken away. They were here.

She touched Rachel. Burning with fever. No coat, no star anywhere to identify her as Jewish.

Blood whooshed in Natia's ears. What was she supposed to do?

"Help me."

Natia almost didn't hear Rachel's faint plea.

"*Tak*, I will get you help. Don't move. Stay right here." Not that she was in any shape to go anywhere. Natia turned and stumbled into the house. "Elfriede! Elfriede! Come. Help." Her mistress's Polish had improved to the point they could communicate their basic needs to each other.

Elfriede scurried into the kitchen. "What? Food not good?"

Natia shook her head as she pulled the frying pan from the fire. "*Nie.* Outside. There is a woman and a child who need our help. Come with me." She scurried from the home again. Elfriede followed, her oxford heels clicking on the tile floor.

Elfriede stepped outside and gasped. "Who are they?"

"I don't know. I found them when I came to feed the cat." Elfriede probably didn't understand half of what she said.

Elfriede bent beside Rachel and touched her forehead, much the same as Natia had done. "Woman sick."

The baby cried. Shaking from head to toe, Natia picked up

the little one. A child in her arms once more. A warmth rushed through her. "Hush now, hush. Everything will be fine. We'll take good care of your mother." She made a move toward the kitchen door.

"*Nein*."

Elfriede's sharp word halted Natia in her steps. "What?" Elfriede answered.

Natia crinkled her forehead, not understanding the German word. Elfriede pointed to the bug bites and the rash, touched her forehead, and clutched her head.

Ah, typhus. A deadly disease. And often, epidemic inducing. "*Nie*. We will help her."

Elfriede grasped at her arm, but Natia wrenched away and hustled into the house. She set the baby on the davenport in the living room, tucked embroidered throw pillows around him so he wouldn't roll off, and went back for the mother. She motioned for Elfriede to help.

"*Nie*. I can't."

Her refrain these days. Natia grabbed Rachel under her armpits and dragged her into the cheery blue kitchen.

The glow of the light inside highlighted the condition of the two. Red bite marks covered Rachel's arms and legs. Natia opened the top two buttons of her dirty blouse. A red rash covered her chest. Her collarbone jutted out under paper-thin skin. The baby wailed.

"My child. Please. Give me him. All I have left."

Natia picked up Solomon and brought him to his mother. Rachel smoothed back her baby's dark, curly hair and kissed his olive, dirt-streaked cheek. "My little one. *Moja miłość*. My love."

Natia's chest constricted so she had a difficult time drawing a breath. How many times had she crooned those words to her children? Always at the point when they were about to be separated forever.

Elfriede sat hard on the chair at the table. A sparkle of a tear tracked down her face.

Natia knelt beside Rachel. "Where are you from? Are there relatives to watch over the child?"

"None of that matters." Her breath rattled in her chest. "Take care of my son, my Solomon. Please help him. You can save him."

Natia bit her tongue to keep from speaking the child's Jewish name. Wherever they came from, whatever happened to them, they were Jewish. No wonder there were no other family members. She glanced at Elfriede. She didn't flinch, didn't show any emotion. Good. Maybe she didn't hear or maybe she didn't know.

"Promise me."

"What? Promise you what?"

"You take care of him."

"You'll recover and take care of him yourself."

"*Nie*, I won't. He needs a home. Please."

Natia wasn't the one to give it. She didn't have one of her own. Not one she was in control of. How could she take care of a Jewish child when she was a prisoner? What about the risk if *Pan* Fromm discovered Solomon's race? She would join Teodor in the camp. Or worse. Her ears rang.

The baby whimpered and stroked his mother's sunken cheek. The woman kissed her child's forehead and whispered something into his ear Natia didn't understand. Yiddish, perhaps.

All her love in those few gestures.

"I love you, my little one." With one more raspy intake of air, Rachel stilled and then went limp.

"She's dead. She's dead." Elfriede screeched. She jumped up and strode a tight circle. She said some other things Natia didn't understand.

What should they do? They couldn't have her lying in the middle of the floor when *Pan* Fromm returned. They had to get rid of the body. How? Where?

Natia scanned the room. A sheet. That was the first thing they needed. She pulled a clean one from the hall closet.

"*Nie.* Not that." Elfriede tugged the linen away from Natia, but she held fast.

"*Tak.* We use this." She yanked it free of Elfriede's grip, picked up Solomon, laid the sheet over the woman's lifeless body, and tucked the ends underneath her.

Now what? If only Teodor were here. He would know what to do. She needed his direction right now. *Nie*, she needed God's direction.

Please, Lord, help us.

An idea struck her. "Doctor?"

Elfriede gave her a frightened-child look, eyes wide, mouth open.

"Doctor. Where is the doctor?" Natia clasped her hands together to keep from striking Elfriede.

She pointed to the right. "Green house. Big. Flowers. Two minutes."

The infant wailed again, no doubt hungry, wet, and afraid. Natia held him out to Elfriede who shook her head.

Natia choked back a scream. *Pan* Fromm could return any time. She had no choice. She bounced the child. His damp curls clung to his forehead. Natia crooned a children's lullaby. *"Go to sleep, my little doll. Time for you to go to bed. I'll be rocking you, and you'll close your eyes."*

The little boy blinked three times and drifted to sleep.

Natia didn't waste a moment but dashed out the door and raced down the street to the doctor's home.

❧

Pawel and Antonina sat at the small, round table in their kitchen's alcove, the green-tiled stove bringing welcome warmth. Tonight, she had cooked him sausage, pickled beets, and sauerkraut.

Though meat was scarce, she'd managed to come up with some and even a few herbs and spices to make his favorite meal.

No sooner had he taken his first bite when a knock came at the door, a rapid pounding. Even more than four years after the SS had carted away Józef, his heart stopped beating for a moment whenever anyone banged like that. The shouts of Nazi voices from that night still rang in his head.

He could never silence them.

He dug his fingernails into the soft wood of the chair's seat. Antonina stood, but he motioned her to sit. "I'll see who it is. By the sound of it, I'll need my medical bag." And hopefully nothing more. He kissed her on his way by.

He opened the door to a young woman clutching a sleeping child. She panted.

"Come in. How can I help you?"

She stumbled over the threshold. "I'm Natia Palinska. I—I work for the Fromms. You know them?"

He could guess her story. She wasn't in their employ in the usual manner. "*Tak*, I do."

"A woman … She came with this baby … And then … And I don't know what to do."

"Please, come sit and have a cup of tea."

"There isn't time. The dead woman is in the middle of the kitchen."

He stepped backward. "She died? The child's mother?"

"*Tak*. And I suspect typhus."

"Where did she come from?"

"I have no idea. I stepped outside to feed the cat, and there she was. We brought her in, but she didn't live long. She made me promise to care for her child."

He finger-combed his few remaining strands of hair and sighed. No telling where she'd picked up the disease. Or if she brought along the fleas that carried it. If he wasn't careful, he could be looking at an epidemic. "There isn't much I can do. Scrub the child to kill any vermin he might be carrying. And dispose of the body."

"We can't let *Pan* Fromm find her. Or the child."

"Why not?" A pain started behind his left eye.

"You can see the child is starving. So was the mother. Her name was Rachel, and the child's is Solomon."

"Jewish." He whispered the word.

"*Tak*. I met them twice before and gave them a little food."

He made a circuit of the room. He'd helped some Jews, but never anyone living under a German's nose. "I suppose you want to keep him?"

"I made a vow I intend to fulfill."

"How will you prevent *Pan* Fromm or his wife from discovering his racial heritage?" One look at the circumcised child during a diaper change or a bath, and there would be no hiding his secret.

"Come. Help us with the body. While we work, I'll tell you the idea buzzing in my head." She shifted the child on her shoulder.

"I can bring her here and arrange for her burial. Does she have papers?"

"I didn't look. My guess would be she doesn't."

He grabbed his gray felt fedora and his black wool coat from the hook by the door. He turned to his wife. "I have to go out. I'll be back soon." He'd done some crazy things during the war, took some risks to help people, but this might be the craziest. He hadn't been able to help his Józef, but he gave assistance to those he could, in honor of his son, who had been a promising lawyer, and those intelligentsia who weren't spared. To make him proud of his father.

His wife stopped him on his way out. "Take care." Her usual admonition. Tonight, it took on special significance.

He followed Natia through the darkened streets to the Fromm residence on the edge of town. Before the war, it belonged to the local school's headmaster. He disappeared in the early days of the occupation, along with both the village's priests.

God, why so many and not me? Why my son?

He shuddered as he entered the home. Elfriede reclined on the couch with her feet curled underneath her, whimpering. Above her, a Bavarian cuckoo clock ticked. Pictures of her and *Pan* Fromm sat on the end table and on the piano in the corner.

He and *Pani* Palinska moved to the kitchen. In the center of the room was the body covered with a sheet.

A chill raced through him when he examined the dead woman. Her ribs and pelvic bones protruded. An angry, red rash covered her neck, chest, and upper back. Bug bites spotted her extremities. Typhus. No doubt about it.

"I'll take care of her."

"You can't tell anyone. You have to keep it quiet."

"I know a man with the utmost discretion. But what about the child?"

She pulled him deeper into the kitchen, beyond the small table and near the door. "Frau Fromm has been distraught since the woman arrived. I'm not sure she caught the child's name, and I don't want her to start piecing together the puzzle. You fill out birth certificates. Can't you falsify one? Give him a nice Gentile name? Maybe even a more German-sounding one?"

"That's illegal."

"Everything right these days is illegal. To do good, we are forced to break the law. I know it's a risk, but I'm begging you to help. It's the only way to save the child's life. If *Pan* Fromm finds out his ethnicity …"

He patted her work-roughened hand. It wouldn't be just the child's life. *Pani* Palinska's was also at stake.

"I lost three children of my own." Her voice was little more than a whisper. "The last one just days before we arrived here. Please, don't send this child to his death."

As if he could. This woman understood what it was like to bury her own flesh and blood. He rubbed the back of his neck, the pain behind his eye intensifying. "If your employer discovers what we've done, it will bring dire consequences for us both."

"There is nothing more precious than a child. Every little one born into this world deserves a chance at life. Give this one his chance." *Pani* Palinska's voice was thick and husky.

How could he say no to this woman? How could he turn his back on a human being created in God's image? When he took the Hippocratic Oath, he swore to protect all who came to him.

He steeled his midsection. "I'll do it. What name do you want for him?"

♩♩♩

Chapter Nine

When the older doctor asked her to name the child, Natia released a breath she didn't realize she'd been holding. He was going to help them.

What to call him? She and Teodor had a long list of boy's names they liked. And they'd used two of them so far. Two boys for Teodor to go fishing with, to play chess with, to work on the farm with.

But this one? He needed a special name. A meaningful one. One Teodor would like. "Dominik. 'Belongs to the Lord.'"

The older man gave three small nods and touched the baby's head. "*Tak*, that's very beautiful. He belongs to no one else. And for a last name?"

"Palinski."

"*Nie*. You can't use yours. That would tip off *Pan* Fromm in an instant. You couldn't explain the sudden arrival of the child."

"But I want him to be mine."

"Natia, I need you." Elfriede wandered in from the living room. "You talk. Why?" She looked from Natia to the doctor and back again.

"What do you need?"

"Dinner. When?"

"Soon." Natia balanced the baby on her hip and moved the pork and cabbage to the warm part of the stove. She focused on the doctor and spoke fast so Elfriede wouldn't understand. "Give him any name you like but get those papers to me right away."

"Kedzierski."

Natia pinched her lips closed to keep from bursting out in laughter. The doctor wanted to name him curly hair? She smoothed back one springy lock from the child's forehead. It did fit. She nodded.

"I'll return in a while with the cart to take his mother away. Scrub him well to kill any fleas. I'll bring delouser when I return." He made a move to leave.

"Wait. How old is the baby? What do I feed him?"

The doctor bit the inside of his cheek. "Maybe about six months. He's malnourished, so it's difficult to tell. Feed him some bread sopped in milk. I'll return soon." He placed his fedora on his graying head and shuffled out the door into the chilly night.

Natia turned to Elfriede. "*Pan* Fromm. What time?"

"Ten or eleven."

Good. That gave them several hours. Elfriede sat on a white ladder-back chair and held Dominik while Natia put a large pot of water on the stove to warm and finished dinner preparations. Once Elfriede had her meal and the water came to as hot as Natia dared put a child in, she stripped the little one, threw his clothes in the fire, and dunked him in the water. At first he squealed, and not in delight.

But worse than that, the child was circumcised. If Elfriede or *Pan* Fromm ever saw, they would know right away this one was Jewish.

Natia couldn't let that happen. Ever. She moved to block Elfriede's view of the baby. So far, no reaction. She must not have noticed.

Natia poured water over the boy's head, and he sputtered, coughed, and cried. His mournful wail cut Natia's heart. For him, she ached. And for herself. If only her own children had cried.

She cleared her throat and sang a silly little song, one Zygmunt and Helena had loved when they were small. "*Splash, splash, we'll take a bath. Shiny clean and smelling sweet. Wrap him in a towel and hug him tight.*"

Dominik stopped crying and stared at Natia, his dark eyes large in his thin face.

She scrubbed him with disinfectant soap until his skin reddened. Then she deloused him with the nasty-smelling medicine the doctor brought.

He had taken Dominik's mother away.

Natia kissed the baby's head. When Dominik grew up, what would she tell him about the woman who had given him life? She knew nothing about her. Where was she from? Did she have any family? Probably not, but Natia couldn't be positive.

Elfriede's fork clinked on the plate. "What's his name?"

Good, she hadn't caught the mother's answer. "Dominik. 'Belongs to the Lord.'" Her back to Elfriede to block her view of the child's naked body, Natia lifted the little boy from the water. She wrapped him in a towel and gave him a vigorous rub to keep him warm.

"That's a good name. I like it. Your babies. You cry?"

Every day. And every night. "*Tak*."

"Me too." The light in Elfriede's pale-blue eyes dimmed. "My baby is gone."

With a thump Natia sat in the chair across from Elfriede. "Boy or girl?"

"Boy. Frederich."

For a moment, they both sat in silence. Across the cultural divide and differences in station, they shared a commonality. Sometimes Natia had believed only she and Teodor understood the pain of losing a child. But it happened every day, all around the world. She wasn't alone. And she'd found a tie with Elfriede Fromm.

Dominik stirred. Natia pushed back her chair. What to clothe him in?

Elfriede tapped her arm before disappearing into the main bedroom. A room Natia wasn't allowed to enter. The only one she didn't have to clean.

A moment later, Elfriede emerged with an armload of clothes.

Baby clothes. Had they been for the child she'd lost? Natia nodded. What a great sacrifice Elfriede made. Natia had never been able to give away the tiny clothes in the dresser at home.

With a shaking hand, Elfriede passed Natia a stack of diapers. "Small." She motioned to the pristine-white nappies. "Big." She gestured in Dominik's direction.

But they might be able to make it work. Natia got out her needle and thread and stitched two diapers together to make a larger one before pinning it on Dominik, careful to be sure Elfriede was out of the room. Some of the clothes were larger, like Elfriede's baby would be this age at this time of year. Natia slipped a long nightshirt on the child. Though meant for a younger infant, it fit the skinny little one, and it would keep him warm.

As Natia cleaned the kitchen, Elfriede fed him bits of bread. "He likes."

In fact, he devoured piece after piece. Natia gripped the dish-cloth tight. What if Elfriede decided she wanted to keep Dominik? What could she do about that? Natia had no claim on him. She was little more than a slave. Elfriede could do whatever she pleased.

But if that's what she decided, it would mean Dominik's death. Natia couldn't allow that. No matter what, she would protect this child. She wouldn't lose him. Not ever.

She picked up her dish towel to dry a plate. The baby giggled. Love flooded her.

Later she tucked Dominik in her bed for the night. How could she not fall in love with a child who slept beside her? She crawled under the covers and rubbed his cheek. "Oh, little one, sleep well. Dream about happy things. I'll try to do the same."

She'd just dozed off when Dominik cried, a pitiful mewl. Though she walked the floor with him, he didn't settle down. "Are you hungry again?" She went to the kitchen and pulled out the loaf of bread.

The front door clicked open and then shut. Heavy footsteps approached.

Pan Fromm.

"What is a child doing in my house?"

✑

Teodor sat sweating over the drill press despite the chilly temperatures in the unheated factory. So far, their sabotage scheme had worked to perfection. The holes they drilled were off enough so the supervisors didn't catch on. To the naked eye, you couldn't tell anything was wrong.

And it sped up production not to have to be quite so precise with the template location or drilling. Even Fromm hadn't bothered Teodor for a few weeks.

And that suited him just fine.

Plunk. He dropped another piece into the box beside his work station and picked up the next hunk of metal. He leaned over to Jerzy as he pulled on the lever to lower the drill. "It's time."

Jerzy furrowed his brow. "For what?"

"To let the rest of the men in on our scheme."

Jerzy glanced around the room.

"Stop it." Teodor jabbed him in the side. "You look guilty."

"Because I am."

"They haven't caught on so far."

"So far. Those are two big words."

"We can't fight. The invasion was over so quickly, I never joined the military and defended my country." He swallowed as his mind replayed the day the Nazis invaded their town, when life changed forever. A day he would always regret. "Here is my chance. And I'd like to give everyone that same chance."

"Can we trust them?"

"Quiet." Fromm's bellow echoed in the room.

Teodor drilled a few more pieces. After several minutes, Fromm turned his back to them. "Why not?"

"The Germans might have planted a spy among us."

A huge guffaw built in Teodor's chest, but he suppressed it.

"Who on earth would want to live and work and try to survive in these conditions? You're paranoid."

"Cautious is more like it. I have a wife and children. You have a family too."

That's all that occupied his brain these days. And that's what drove him. He needed to be with his bride as soon as possible.

"Just getting through each day, trying to make it to the end, is hard enough. You've heard the rumblings about Kiev the same as I have."

Rumblings that the Russians had recaptured the city and pushed the Germans west. "How much can we be sure of? Kiev is far away. A year or more might pass before the Soviets arrive. We could all be dead." Not a cheery picture to paint, but the truth.

When they returned to the barracks at the end of the day, darkness had already enveloped them. The soldiers didn't bother them in here. Too much disease. Too many vermin. Too much suffering, even for the hardened Nazis.

Still Teodor waited until long after their shift to gather the men around him. They didn't turn on the lights, in part to avoid drawing the guards' attention, and in part because the moonbeam streaming through the window illuminated the room.

"What is this all about?" A man coughed.

Another took up the cry. "Yeah, I don't remember appointing you king." Sounded like Lech.

Teodor held up his hand for silence. "Just hear me out. What we've been slaving away manufacturing in this place has something to do with the German war machine. We're supplying parts for their tanks or airplanes or ships. Whatever it might be, we're one of the cogs that keeps them turning. Those who keep them moving forward, oppressing our people, stealing our homes and land. Killing us."

A buzz shot through the crowd, though they kept their voices quiet. Now Teodor had their attention. "We're partly responsible."

One bear of a man with greasy hair stepped forward. "Watch

it now, Palinski. You'll find no greater patriot than me. I'd die for my country. How about you?"

Jerzy spun around and stood shoulder-to-nose with the much larger man. "Hear Teodor out. Palinski is in here because he refused to sign the *Volksdeutsche*. Just like the rest of us, he's lost everything. Listen to him."

Teodor hid his grimace. Jerzy didn't need to fight his battles for him. But the near-giant backed down.

"What I'm proposing has everything to do with patriotism. About how, even though we're slaves in this prison, we can do our share to defeat our enemy and return our country to its former glory."

A few men nodded.

Teodor drew in a deep breath. "Jerzy and I have been testing this plan for the past several weeks. And so far, it's gone without a hitch. Now we're ready to offer it as an option for anyone who wants to join us."

A light bobbed outside the door, visible through the window in the entry. Teodor hushed the men. As a group, they held stock-still, not daring to breathe until the guard's shoes creaked away from them and the light disappeared.

Teodor kept his voice as low as possible. "If we make mistakes on these parts, the Nazis won't be able to use them in their application. That will slow their production and hinder them in battle."

A man hiding in the shadows spoke up. "How do we do that?"

"Make an error. A small one. Don't set the template in the exact position. Move it over. Even a few millimeters works. My guess is the design is precise enough that even a tiny variation from the plan will render the part useless."

The bear stood again. "And what if they catch us?"

Teodor outlined the same procedure he and Jerzy used. "Of course, there is risk. No battle is without it. But there is also no reward without risk. Look around you. How much longer can you endure? Isn't it worth the chance to end the war even a day or two sooner? That small amount of time might be the difference between life and death for you. Or for your family."

Murmurs rippled through the group.

"Not everyone needs to participate. Even a few of us will make a difference. Who is with me?"

♪♪♪

Chapter Ten

Natia stood in the middle of the living room and stared at *Pan* Fromm, his mouth pinched, his nostrils flaring. She pulled Dominik tighter against herself, her knees weak.

"I'll repeat my earlier question. Why is there a child in my house?"

"I–I ..." She drew in a deep breath. If she continued to stammer, he would get suspicious. "This is my sister's child. She passed away not long ago and sent her baby here. The woman who brought him can't care for him anymore."

He stepped closer. She pulled the thin gray blanket around Dominik's head to keep *Pan* Fromm from spotting the flea bites. He would never let the baby stay if there was any possibility of typhus. "And what do you propose doing with this infant?"

Natia locked her knees to keep from slumping to the floor. "His name is Dominik. And he won't be any bother, I promise. He won't affect my work. Your wife enjoyed playing with him this evening. Perhaps having him around will cheer her."

"Or the child might tire her and cause her untold grief and heartache. Have you thought about that?"

"This little one is a good tonic. He brings a joy that's been missing from this home. Ask *Pani* Fromm. She'll tell you."

Pan Fromm moved toward her until he stood close enough for her to smell the foul beer on his breath. He narrowed his eyes and pointed at her. "The child may stay on two conditions. One, that he never, never, *never* interrupts me, either day or night. If I can't enjoy my evening or if I can't get a good night's sleep, I will remove him from my home. Along with you. Two, that he not upset my wife. If I find Elfriede struggling with having a child here, I will take care of the problem myself. Is that clear?"

A knot formed in Natia's stomach. She nodded. How she would keep Dominik from crying, she had no idea. But she would try everything she could.

"I'm going to bed. And I'd better sleep through the night."

Natia dragged on her way to the market the next morning, Dominik tied to her in a sling that she'd formed from an old bed-sheet. Within a few steps of the house, the baby fell asleep.

If only she could shut her eyes for a little while. To keep Dominik from crying, she had walked the floor and fed him bread at regular intervals throughout the night. He hadn't uttered a peep. But now Natia had a difficult time staying awake. She blinked her gritty eyes.

As she approached the factory, she perked up. She would get to tell Teodor about the baby. Already, she had a connection with the child. Both had lost their mothers. Both had no home to call their own. Both were hated and hunted by the Nazis.

Large, gray clouds loomed overhead. The wind bit through Natia's coat. She gazed at the rows and rows of windows on each of the three floors of the factory. Now she knew which one Teodor was near. Each day, he answered her with little songs of his own. Most of the time, she laughed at his feeble attempts at a melody. Her husband bore many good qualities.

Singing was not among them.

Still, his replies kept her going until the following day.

She approached the window about three-quarters of the way down the row. Today she would sing a special song.

Go to sleep, my little doll
Time for you to go to bed

I'll be rocking you
And you'll close your eyes.
Luli luli luli luli luli luli lu,
Luli luli luli luli.

The song for her children. The song for this one, whom she now counted among her own. The first one who had responded to her voice.

A shadow passed in front of the window and paused. Teodor never lingered. She never caught more than a glimpse of his sketchy outline.

She reached into the sling and pulled Dominik into her arms. The little one protested the interruption to his nap. Natia turned him around and kissed him on the cheek.

Teodor stayed. So did she.

She sang the lullaby again. My little doll. Her doll. Their doll. With each word, she poured out her love for Dominik. Her love for Teodor. Her love for their family. The music filled the air and warmed the chilly day.

❧

Pawel sat at his paper-covered desk, slipped off his wire-rimmed glasses, and rubbed his temples. This wasn't his first time forging papers. He'd done more than his fair share. Birth certificates. Baptism certificates. Passports.

But something struck him about this job. Maybe it was the fact that it was for a Jewish child living in a German house with a Polish prisoner. Or because of the woman's close association with *Pan* Fromm, who required his services at the factory from time to time. Whatever the reason, his hand shook as he drew his pen from the middle top desk drawer. He dipped the nib into the ink and focused on the job in front of him.

He didn't hear his wife enter the room until she set a cup of tea in front of him. "You're concentrating very hard."

He stared into her light-green eyes, the feature he'd first fallen in love with three decades ago. To this day, she had the capacity to steal his breath. "Hmm?"

"What is that?"

He whipped the paper into the drawer, then slammed it shut. "Nothing."

"Pawel."

He picked up the old, chipped cup, his favorite mug, and lifted it to his lips. "You know there are things I can't answer."

"I don't want anything to happen to you. Not like Józef."

He stroked her cheek. "I miss him too."

"The pain hasn't gone away."

The gash in his own heart continued to bleed. "Maybe it never will. But don't you see? I couldn't help him." He closed his eyes until the burning in his throat subsided. He would never forget Józef's look as the soldiers murdered him. Pawel shook away the image and opened his eyes. That's why he did this.

"My dear, these are dangerous times." She clasped her hands together. Deep lines etched her forehead.

"Walking down the street can be risky these days. I've managed to survive so far, even though many of my colleagues haven't. I can't do nothing. Perhaps God saved me for a reason. To live the life Józef couldn't."

"But I have a feeling this is different." She reached out and grasped him by the shoulder. "Please tell me it's nothing you can get into trouble for."

He touched her hand. "You worry too much. I've escaped the Nazis' clutches because I'm important to them. Without me, they wouldn't have a doctor at the factory. And they need one there."

"They could always bring in one of their own."

"Stretched too thin would be my guess, especially with the massive casualties on the Eastern front." He stood and pecked her lips. "I'm not going anywhere."

She grabbed him around the waist and pulled him to her. "Don't leave me."

He whispered in her jasmine-scented hair, "I won't."

The ringing of the telephone interrupted the moment. Antonina stepped from his embrace. "I'll let you get back to work." With a soft click of the door, she left.

He answered the call. A muffled voice came through the line. "We have a problem, Bosco."

Pain throbbed behind his right eye. Stanislaw, his contact in Warsaw. "What is it?"

"The dog ran away."

Sweat covered Pawel's hands, and he thumped into his chair. Code for someone in their network being arrested.

"Apparently just took off, no leash, no collar, no nothing. Just left incriminating evidence." Stanislaw gave a wry laugh.

But this was no joking matter. The man needed to watch his tongue in case an operator was listening on the line. Especially if they could be implicated in whatever the arrested compatriot had left behind. "That's not good news."

"I'm sorry to tell you. Why don't you do something to cheer yourself up? Go on holiday. Take a trip. Get out and see Poland."

Pawel harrumphed. "You make it sound like an adventure." Antonina had had a bad feeling. He opened the desk drawer and stared at the false birth certificate.

"Of course it would be."

"I told you I didn't want a dog." Pawel's part in the resistance was supposed to be between Stanislaw and him. No one else.

"I'm sure the animal will return, and everything will be fine. But it wouldn't hurt for you to take a trip. Imagine how good it would be for your health. I worry about you."

What kind of incriminating evidence was Stanislaw talking about? How much did the Gestapo know about him? "I'm sure you have nothing to be concerned about."

"Maybe, maybe not."

Pawel ended the call, then paced the small room lined with book-filled and medicine bottle-covered shelves. He couldn't leave his patients. He was the only medical professional for a wide area. For himself, he'd have to take the chance.

But Antonina ... "Darling, can you come in here?"

Within moments she returned, wiping her hands on her apron. "You don't have to go out?"

"The call was someone warning me about a possible threat. It's probably nothing, but I would feel better if you weren't here. We have a little savings, and you've always wanted to visit the Black Sea. Why don't you go?"

"In the winter?" She raised her eyebrows.

"It won't be so crowded."

She bit the corner of her lip. "Not without you."

He came around the side of his desk and pulled her close, closer than before, closer than ever. "Please, do this for me."

"*Nie*, I refuse to go alone. You must come with me. I've already lost one piece of my heart. I couldn't stand it if I lost the rest."

"The people here need my help."

"And if you're arrested, they will truly have no one to care for them."

"I don't think it's anything. In a few weeks you can return. Just for my peace of mind. Please."

She soaked his shirt with her tears. But she would do whatever he asked. And that's why he loved her.

❧

Teodor pressed his forehead against the icy window overlooking the road in front of the factory. Why did Natia choose to sing that lullaby? She only ever crooned it to their children. Each of whom rested on a hillside in their hometown, far from here.

Every time she sang it, sadness and pain laced each note. Often she broke down in the middle of the song, too great was her sorrow.

The tune pierced him and twisted his heart. The ache grew until it threatened to consume him. He had so looked forward to having a son or two by his side, working the fields with him, playing ball with him, teaching him everything he needed to know. That song not only spoke of Natia's pain, but of his own. In Andrzej's perfect face, he'd glimpsed the possibilities.

Only to have his dreams torn from him for a third time.

Why did God keep stealing their children from them? It wasn't right; it wasn't fair. They were good people. Look at these Germans giving birth to child after child. Why would God give those monsters offspring, but not those faithful to him?

And why did Natia choose to sing these words today? Each of her songs conveyed a message. That she was well. That she worked hard. That she missed him. What was she trying to tell him with this selection?

And then she stopped and drew a bundle from the sling around her shoulders. He squinted. A sack of flour? A bag of straw?

She turned it around.

Nie. A baby.

Her face glowed. That smile, he hadn't seen that smile in almost two years.

Gooseflesh prickled his arms.

A baby.

He leaned against the windowsill. She lost the child just days before they arrived here. She was recovering from the birth. They hadn't . . .

There was no way this was his child.

He clenched his fists.

Fromm.

Teodor shuddered.

Wait. They hadn't been here long enough for Natia to give birth. What was going on?

Jerzy slapped him on the back. He winced.

"What's wrong? Is it something with Natia?"

"I don't know. She, she has a baby."

"You lucky man. You didn't tell me."

"Because I don't understand. She couldn't. It's not mine. Hers. Ours."

"You aren't making sense. Why would she have a child if it didn't belong to either one of you?"

"Perhaps it's the Fromms'. That must be it. For whatever reason, Natia has the baby with her today. She sang the song to give me hope that one day we'll be free and can have the family we've longed for." Teodor spoke more to himself than to Jerzy.

"It's time to get to work."

"I'll be right there." In a low voice, Teodor sang the lullaby back to Natia and the child. Just so long as she didn't get her heart broken, whatever her connection to the infant. Today, for the first time in a long time, she was happy. *God, don't let anything happen to wipe that smile from her face.*

He spun around, the barracks already empty. How long had he stood by the window? He scurried across the room and out the door.

Straight into Fromm.

He slapped his crop against his hand. "Ah, Palinski. Running a bit late today, I see."

Teodor stared at the floor and lunged forward.

"Not so fast." Fromm pushed on his chest to stop him. "Tardiness is not tolerated. I must come up with an appropriate punishment for you. Hmm, let me see. I already have your wife. Sweet little thing she is."

Teodor bit his tongue until he tasted blood.

"She does a pretty good job of keeping me happy."

If he chomped down any harder, he might sever his tongue.

"Don't worry. I'm keeping her warm. But today, I think I shall have you shovel coal. We go through quite a good deal of it, especially in such chilly weather."

Teodor spun around. "I'll get my coat."

Fromm blocked his way. "No need. You'll get plenty warm without it. In fact, leave your shoes here. You won't need those either."

Teodor peered at Fromm. The man sneered, a cold glint in his blue eyes. At no time did you take your shoes off and leave them unattended. Not even to sleep. Footwear left lying around had this curious habit of disappearing. He opened his mouth to protest but clamped it shut.

He wouldn't talk back. Wouldn't complain or grovel. Fromm wanted nothing more than that. Well, he would wait a very long time before Teodor did any such thing. He slipped off his heavy work boots, tucked them underneath his thin, lumpy pillow, and followed Fromm to the factory yard.

The wind screeched a welcome. The cold ground burned the bottoms of his feet, but he didn't cry out. Fromm would never break him.

The pile of coal that needed to be shoveled into the furnace room loomed larger than Teodor himself. Likely this job would take all day. He picked up the shovel and got to work. The work kept his body warm. His feet were another matter. Not long passed before pain shot through them. Then they went numb. Every now and again, after scanning the yard to make sure no guards watched him, he stopped and rubbed the feeling back into his toes. Sharp, shooting pins-and-needles pain, but feeling nonetheless. That, at least, meant blood flowed through his feet. Meant he wouldn't lose them.

Overnight it had rained, then frozen. Ice formed the coal into one giant lump. He scrambled up the pile and chipped at it until it broke into smaller pieces. He stood on top of the mound as a woman carrying a bag made her way down the street in front of the factory.

Not any woman.

Natia.

His breath caught. Here, with no window separating them, he got his first good look at her in over six months. She rubbed her hollow cheek. Wasn't Fromm feeding her enough? Thin hands peeked out from underneath her heavy, brown wool shawl. At least he allowed her to wear that.

She glanced up and caught sight of him. A slow grin spread across her oval face. Oh, she was as beautiful as all the dreams he'd had of her throughout these long, agonizing months.

"Teodor."

"Natia, *moje słońce*." He spun in a circle to make sure no one watched them. A group of guards stood at the far end of the yard on a cigarette break.

She, too, glanced around, then approached the fence. The smile evaporated from her lips. "Where are your shoes? What are they doing to you?"

"That's not important. What about you? And this baby?" He pointed to the sling around her middle.

"His mother showed up on the Fromms' doorstep last night. She passed away, but not before making me promise to care for her child. This is Dominik. He's pure joy."

Yet dark half-moons hung under her eyes. "Are you sure? Are you well?"

"Very well, now that I've seen you. But you. Oh, Teodor ..."

He must look a sight. His coveralls hung on him. And he hadn't had a shave or a bath in about as long as he could remember.

"Hey, you. Who are you talking to?" One of the guards approached.

Nie, not already. They'd had such a short time together. *God, why tease me?* But she had to get out of here. Before they found her. Before they put her in this horrid place. "Go, Natia, go. Stay well and strong. Keep singing to me. I love you."

"I love you too."

Before he blinked twice, she disappeared.

Had she been real or just a hallucination?

♪♫♪

Chapter Eleven

ominik slumbered on the mattress in Natia's attic room, and Elfriede touched the baby's head, the dark curls soft under her fingers. Careful not to wake the sleeping child, Elfriede picked him up, hugged him close, and inhaled the fresh, unique baby scent of soap and talcum. "You are a sweet little one. Such a good, good baby. If only you were mine. If I could produce babies for the Führer, maybe then Erich would love me." *Vater* had told her that was what good German women did. That was how you earned the respect and admiration of your husband. It was her duty.

One she'd failed.

Much as she'd failed *Vater* because she couldn't cook, couldn't keep house. She could never take *Mutti*'s place after she died giving birth to a son. Like Erich, *Vater* yelled and sometimes hit her. And this baby's arrival only underscored her shortcoming. Just like *Mutti*'s.

Dominik nestled against her, his little body warm and soft. Oh, to be a mother. What would her child be doing now? Sitting up, rolling over, crawling? Maybe pulling himself to a standing position holding on to the furniture?

Would another child ever fill the empty place in her soul?

While Natia worked in the kitchen, she rocked Dominik and kissed his forehead. If only she could be good enough to bear many children for the Führer.

A picture sat beside the bed. Elfriede picked it up. The man from the rail station and Natia. She wore a white dress embroidered with flowers. A wreath of flowers adorned her hair. This must have been their wedding day. Teodor also wore white with a white embroidered cape over the top. How very handsome he was. And strong. No wonder Natia fell in love with him.

"What are you doing?"

Elfriede startled and Dominik cried. Natia hurried over and tried to rip Dominik from her arms.

"Don't. I can do it."

"What are you doing?" Natia pointed to the picture in Elfriede's hand.

"Your husband nice man?"

"*Tak*. My husband." She emphasized the word *my*.

What had she thought Elfriede might do? "You love him."

"Very much." Her voice took on an air of wistfulness, and her shoulders slumped. The tilt of her head, the shimmer in her eyes told the story.

"Why you sad?"

"I miss him." She pointed to her heart. "Here."

"I talk to him. Tell him. You see your husband." It was only right that a married couple be together.

"I did."

"You see him?"

"*Tak*. Two weeks ago." A few of the tears splashed onto her cheeks.

"Then why you cry?"

Natia wiped away the moisture. Her eyes glittered, steely and hard. "It is cold. Very cold." She said something else Elfriede didn't understand.

"What?"

Natia went to the window and threw it open. "Outside." She pointed beyond the window. "Cold." She rubbed her arms and shivered.

"Your husband outside in cold?"

Natia's mouth tightened even as she nodded.

Why would that make her sad? That was part of life in this

corner of the world. It got cold. Sometimes, from what Frau Rzeźnikowa told her, it even snowed. And this year, so far, she said it was warmer than usual. "So, why sad?"

"No coat. No shoes."

Elfriede must have misunderstood. That didn't make sense that a man was outside without his coat and shoes. "I don't understand."

"No coat." Natia mimicked pulling on a jacket. "No shoes." She mimed tying shoes.

"*Nie.*" If she knew how to tell Natia she was wrong, she would say it. "*Nie.*"

"*Tak. Tak.*" Natia stomped her boot-clad foot.

Maybe just for a minute. To run outside for some reason. Perhaps even men being men. Didn't they do that sort of silly stuff? Her cousins did. "Why?"

Natia motioned like she was digging. Working.

But that couldn't be. If so, it was because of some rogue guard not following the rules. Getting out of control. "I tell Erich. He fix."

"He knows."

Then the matter was settled. No need for Natia to be sad. Elfriede wiped her hands to be rid of the topic. "Erich fix. All done."

Natia grabbed her by the wrist. She rattled off a sentence that went by much too fast for Elfriede to catch. But she heard *Erich, make, husband, outside, no coat, no shoes.*

Her insides turned as cold as the December weather. She wrenched free from Natia's grasp. "*Nein. Nein. Nein.*" She plopped Dominik on the mattress and rushed from the room, covering her ears.

❧

Teodor sat on his bunk and rubbed his painful feet. Ever since his coal-shoveling stint, they throbbed when it got cold. As he had feared, during the time he worked out of doors, his good boots disappeared. He had an older pair he'd brought from home, but the soles had already worn through. He wore his heaviest socks, but how long they would last was anyone's guess.

Darkness enveloped the prisoners' dormitory. The few industrial light fixtures strung from the ceiling didn't penetrate the far reaches of the room.

Or his heart.

Nie, only Natia's songs brought any light. The pureness of her voice, the perfectness of her pitch, the loveliness of her words, only that pierced his soul. He tucked each of her songs deep inside, recalling them at varying times throughout the day. Each time he misplaced a template, her music filled his ears. For her, he did this. Walked on the edge of danger, the threat of getting caught always hanging above him.

At night, her haunting melodies massaged his aching heart and lulled him to sleep. Only her songs soothed him enough from the worries of the day so he could manage a few hours' rest.

Without her, he couldn't endure this. The endless hours at a machine or hauling boxes. The empty bowls at dinnertime. The shooting pains in his feet.

Just as the room fell silent for the night, four guards burst into the dormitory and flipped on the lights. Teodor blinked as his eyes worked to adjust. They wore knee-high boots, black belts, and metal helmets. "Up, up."

The prisoners tumbled from their bunks as the guards cased the room. They pulled five men from the group. The tallest, brawniest among them swung his rifle around, as if he might shoot everyone in the room. "This is what happens to Polish pigs who dare to cross us, breaking their drill bits on purpose to slow production. And the same fate awaits whoever else would try it."

Teodor's heart skipped several beats as the guards switched off the lights. Long after the men were gone, the sound of their cries echoed in Teodor's head. Some had tried their own version of sabotage.

In the darkness, Jerzy hissed at him. "That could have been us."

"I know." What were they doing? Teodor picked at the pilling on his blanket. Then again, best not to do that. He might wear a hole in it. Already, the cold seeped through the bricks and into the room. The one minuscule coal stove in the middle of the barracks did nothing to provide heat.

"Someone was watching out for us."

Teodor rubbed his temples. "I try to believe God is here. Every day, I truly do. But look around. Is he really caring for us? *Nie*, he isn't. That is my job. How can I take care of my wife when I'm stuck in this miserable place? When we married, I promised to be there for her. And I'm not." Just as he hadn't been there to take care of Mama when she needed him the most. And that proved to be a fatal mistake. "Now this child comes along. I must protect them both. But how?"

Jerzy lay back on his mattress with a creak of the board.

Teodor stretched the crick in his neck. "There has to be something I can do. If I could get out of here."

"Don't even think about it. Getting yourself killed is one way to be sure you won't be there for Natia and the child."

"I know. I know. But there has to be more."

"Aren't we doing enough? Maybe even too much? Our lives hang by a thread."

"That's just it. I don't know. We're already making the pieces wrong."

"At great risk to ourselves."

"*Nie*, we're doing it right. A little bit here and there." He stiffened as the kernel of an idea struck. "What if the machines didn't run? What would happen then?"

Jerzy sighed. "I suppose work would stop until they could be fixed."

Teodor grinned. "That carries a double bonus. It slows the rate at which we deliver parts to Germany. They won't be able to make as many weapons without them. And it gives the laborers something other than our Sunday break."

"Are you out of your mind? You saw what happened to the men tonight who got caught."

Teodor slid under the blanket and pulled the sheet to his chin. "Maybe. Maybe this place has made me crazy. But what other choice do we have?"

"We work for these people and pray for the end of the war." Jerzy coughed, a dry hack.

"That's not good enough. We have to do our part." Was no one else willing to defend Poland, to work to free their families from this oppression?

"We're doing all we can. I, for one, would like to survive to see my wife and children."

"If you don't do something to speed that along, you might not make it out of here alive."

Phlegmy cough answered phlegmy cough in a circuit around the room. Jerzy added his to the rest.

"Disease is only going to worsen. And if the German losses continue, our overseers will grow desperate. They'll demand more of us and demand it be done faster. They'll march off more of us like they just did."

"I don't like the idea of risking my life, but I see your point. What is it you propose?"

"I'm a farmer by trade, not a factory laborer."

Jerzy lay silent for several minutes before he cleared his throat. "The mayor's motorcar once got sand in it and refused to run. Sat for two weeks until a mechanic fixed it."

"Sand. Or something to gum up the machine's inner workings. *Tak*, that just might do the job."

"And where are you going to get sand?"

"Maybe not sand, but dirt. From outside."

"You want to shovel more coal?"

"Of course not. But what if I sneak outside at night when there is no moon? It might work."

"Success has many fathers. A failure is an orphan."

"*Dzięki*. I realize I'm alone in this."

Another sigh from Jerzy. "*Nie*. If I can't talk you out of this insanity, I might as well join you. Together, we'll topple the Nazi regime."

"Or die trying."

♩♫♪

Chapter Twelve

A light mist fell as Natia scurried to the village center. She drew her black wool shawl around her shoulders. She'd much rather have snow than this miserable, cold, raw rain. How nice to see the fields covered in white, stretching out in the distance, sparkling in the sun.

She didn't dare bring Dominik out in such foul weather but left him home with Elfriede. Right now, the baby slept, so Natia had to hurry before he woke up and required a clean nappie.

Today she would have to sing a short song. This one, another tune by Chopin. Their church's organist had a phonograph and often let Natia listen to her records. She loved those days, when they would sit and sip tea and listen to the beautiful music. The woman had played Chopin so often that Natia knew many of his songs by heart. The words skipped along with the tune.

Were I a sun, so high in heav'n outbeaming
Only on one should be radiance by streaming,
Not upon forest, not upon meadow
Would I dispel the shadow,
Into thy window brightly gleaming
Only for one all day I'll be beaming.

Teodor didn't wait long to respond. He had learned the songs as she sang them around the house.

Were I a birdling, blithsomely winging,
Only for one would I ever be singing,
Not for the forest, not for the meadow,

Sporting in sun and shadow,
Under thy window, thy window swinging,
Only for one my song I'd be singing.

She reached up and blew him a kiss. He remembered the tune, the one they had sung as they sat under the tree where their children were now buried. Her heart twisted a little more. "Only for you," she whispered as she rushed away, keeping her head down to try to stay as dry as possible.

By the time she reached the town square, the deluge had drenched her shawl and her clothes. She shivered. How nice it would be to sit in her kitchen at home, the fire in the small ceramic stove brightening the dark interior.

And then she peered up, gagging at the sight in front of her. In front of Chopin's statue lay the bodies of five men, their sightless eyes peering into the gray heavens. Their blood mingled with the rain and flowed over the ancient cobblestones, their faces so disfigured by the gunshots they little resembled men. Adding to the horror, even Chopin had been riddled by bullets.

She covered her eyes and pressed hard, willing the images in her brain to fade. They refused but replayed many times. Slipping on the wet pavement, she ran at top speed to the butcher's shop. As she entered, the old wood floors creaked under her feet.

Pani Rzeźnikowa came from the back room to the counter, a wide smile gracing her wrinkled face. "Good day, *Pani* Palinska. The rain is coming down, isn't it? You look like you're soaked to the bone."

Natia pointed outside, her fingers shaking, her entire body trembling. "Wh-wh-what happened?"

"Come sit down. You've had a fright."

"*Nie*, I won't. Tell me, how did those men die?" Natia gasped for breath.

Pani Rzeźnikowa rubbed her forehead. "The soldiers brought them from the factory, lined them up, shot them, and then left them there. No one in Pieśń Nabożna is brave enough to take the bodies away for burial. They're too afraid of what the Nazis will do. My people are cruel."

"Teodor?" The fleeting thought froze Natia to the spot. *Nie*, he had answered her song this morning. "Why? Do you know why they executed them?" She couldn't control the shivering that rattled her.

"You're going to get ill. Come in the back. I'll get you a towel and a warm drink. Then we can talk."

"I need to get back to Dominik."

Natia followed *Pani* Rzeźnikowa behind the counter and into a small sitting room just large enough to hold a table, two chairs, and a stove. Natia shook out her coat and used the towel the butcher's wife brought to dry her hair. In short order, they settled at the table covered in a yellow cloth.

"*Pani* Fromm doesn't have a lick of sense in her head, sending you out in such weather."

"What do you know?"

Pani Rzeźnikowa clutched her mug until her knuckles whitened. "Because I speak German, I understood them. I listened at the door. Those they murdered had been sabotaging the work at the factory. What you see by the statue is their punishment. And the bodies have been left to teach us a lesson. Before they went, the guards called out and told us they wouldn't hesitate to do the same to anyone who got in their way."

Numbness enveloped Natia. Teodor had always been a true patriot, upset he couldn't fight the Germans in 1939 because the battle only lasted a short time. Could he be involved with anything like this? *God, don't let anything happen to him. Or to the rest of my family.*

Pani Rzeźnikowa patted Natia's hand. "This is a close-knit village. We aren't blind to what's happening. We know the rumors about the camps, those awful places where the Nazis exterminate those they don't like, where women and children don't stand a chance at survival. Whispers of words such as Auschwitz and Mauthausen. But what can we do?" She shook her head. "So instead, I offer you a cup of coffee and a listening ear."

"And teach *Pani* Fromm some Polish."

"She asked, and I didn't see the harm. You must be lonely. If you can communicate with her, it will make your life easier."

"You did that for me?"

"For you. And for her. She is young and naive and here without a mother to lead her."

"That is true." Natia sipped the bitter brew, its warmth spreading throughout her.

"Maybe if I can guide her, she will grow up."

A small pain pinched Natia's heart. "You remind me of my mother. She died when I was fifteen, but she possessed so much wisdom." If her mother were here, things would be different. "Every day, she taught me something. I keep those little nuggets with me and remember them when I wish I could speak with her and ask her advice."

"That makes you wiser. Good for you. I'm sorry you don't have her anymore."

"She was an extraordinary woman."

"And what about your husband?" *Pani* Rzeźnikowa nodded at Natia's right hand and the gold band around her finger.

"We came here together. He's at the factory."

"How difficult to be so close and not to communicate with him."

Natia swirled the dark liquid in her cup. The woman had been nothing but kind. And even helped Elfriede in order to help her. Perhaps she could be trusted. Natia sucked in a breath. "I–I do. That's why I don't mind being out in the rain. I walk by the building where he works and sing. He answers me with a song. The music is how we keep in touch, how we know we're doing well."

"What a wonderful gift. The Lord has blessed you. Not many couples in forced labor get to see each other. Look at the men at the factory. How many hear from their wives?"

"I don't know."

"Well, I can tell you." *Pani* Rzeźnikowa shifted in her seat. "None. In that, you are fortunate."

Natia resisted the urge to snort. Fortunate? *Nie*, not at all. "My father and brother and sister are here too. At least, I believe they are. Of them, I have heard nothing since I arrived. Teodor hasn't either. I–I don't know what's happened to them or if they're even alive. Especially after that." She tipped her head in the direction of the statue.

"Oh, that is unfortunate. Perhaps your husband will get word of the rest of your family. Don't give up hope. The Lord can do great things."

Could he? Did he even care anymore?

"So, tell me about Dominik. How is he doing?"

At the change of topic, Natia inhaled and relaxed her shoulders. "Very well. He's growing and gaining weight. Dr. Bosco has been helpful."

"I'm glad. But there is more to the story."

There was, of course, but not anything Natia would share. Not even with a friendly woman. "The story is that I love the boy and want to raise him as my own. Mine and Teodor's."

"You don't have any idea who his mother was?"

"*Nie*. I'm sure he's not this war's first orphan."

"And not the last." *Pani* Rzeźnikowa tsked and shook her graying head, her hair pulled back in a severe bun. "Such a shame." She leaned in. "But be careful. *Pan* Fromm is a calloused man. And demanding."

"That, I already know."

"There is steel in his eyes and hardness in his features. Watch your step."

"I do."

"Good, because I fear for you. That is the one thing that worries me about your situation. And your husband's. If you cross that man, you stand to lose everything."

Natia hugged herself. Judging by the scene on the street, *Pani* Rzeźnikowa was right.

❧

The weather had cleared since the day before, and the moon broke from behind the clouds and lit Pawel's way as he donned his felt fedora and left the Nowak residence. A new baby, praise the Lord. But to be born into such a world. What did the future hold for that little one? For all of them?

Lord, may it not be a future like Józef's.

Pawel shook off the melancholy. No use in dwelling on the past. Or the future. They had enough problems to deal with in the here and now. He rubbed the back of his neck and yawned. Sleep would be top priority when he returned home.

His empty, quiet, lonely home since Antonina had left. Before this, they had never spent a night apart. At least not one when he wasn't working. How he missed her beside him, her thoughtful, loving ways.

He'd heard nothing from Stanislaw and, so far, no SS had paid him a visit. If they were going to arrest him, they would have done so by now. Perhaps today he would be able to sleep with both eyes closed.

He came to the Fromm residence, the cheery pink exterior welcoming and inviting to all except *Pani* Palinska. Though it looked nothing like a prison, that's what it was for her.

And that baby. Already, *Pani* Palinska was in danger, under the control of that man. Now, more so than ever. Pawel would check on them. See how they were doing. He was only going home to a cold house.

He rapped at the door. Inside, Dominik wailed at the top of his lungs. That sounded almost like colic. As a baby, Józef had such a scream. The nights Antonina walked the floor with that one, just so Pawel could sleep.

He banged on the door. "*Pani* Fromm, *Pani* Palinska? It's Dr. Bosco."

The baby cried all the harder. Pawel glanced around. He tried the knob. It turned. He pushed in the door and stepped over the threshold.

An angelic voice floated down the stairs. *"Luli luli luli luli luli luli lu. Luli luli luli luli."* Ah, a lullaby. If anything would get the baby to stop screeching, that would.

But it didn't. Dominik refused to be consoled. Pawel jiggled his black doctor's bag. Some castor oil might do the trick. He made his way toward the stairs.

"I told you to keep that child quiet at all times."

Pawel stopped. That was *Pan* Fromm, his voice cold. Hard. Demanding.

"I'm sorry." *Pani* Palinska spoke, a quaver in her words. "He doesn't ever cry so. I don't know what's wrong. He might be ill."

"I don't care what the reason is. When he first arrived, I gave you the conditions under which he could stay. One was that he wouldn't cry and disturb me. Ever."

"Erich, be reasonable." *Pani* Fromm's soft, innocent voice.

"Be reasonable? What is there to be reasonable about? After overseeing a horde of filthy Poles all day, I expect to return to a peaceful home. Not to this pandemonium."

"Really, Erich, our child—"

Smack. The sharp slap propelled Pawel up the stairs to the small, chilly attic bedroom. He stood at the door since there was little room for him to enter.

Dominik wailed. *Pani* Fromm touched her red cheek and winced. *Pani* Palinska cowered in the corner and jiggled the screaming infant. *Pan* Fromm, unable to stand upright in the cramped space, raised his hand.

Pawel burst in and grabbed Fromm by his upraised arm. "Stop it. Stop it right now."

Fromm spun around, wrenching himself from Pawel's grasp.

"How dare you come uninvited into my house?" He stood mere inches from Pawel, a bead of sweat on his forehead, his breath hot. "You leave my family alone, or I'll have you taken care of like should have been done in '39 with the other high and mighties."

Like the Nazis had done with his son. Pawel's pulse throbbed in his neck. His tongue stuck to the roof of his mouth. "You can do with me what you wish but leave the women and the child alone." The Gestapo would visit him for sure.

"What right do you, a Pole, have to come into my residence and speak to me in such a manner?"

"I'm the only doctor in the village or the surrounding area. You need me."

"I need you?" Fromm scoffed. "I need you like a boat needs a hole."

"What would you do if I wasn't around and you had an epidemic? You couldn't have all of your workers sick, could you?"

Without warning, Fromm landed a punch in Pawel's midsection. He doubled over. Fromm chopped him on the back of his neck. Pain shot down his back. He fell to his knees, his glasses slipping to the floor. A woman screamed. So did the baby.

"I'll show you how much I need you."

"Erich, don't." Tears laced *Pani* Fromm's words.

Fromm hauled Pawel to his feet. "You disgust me. You deserve what's coming to you."

Pawel's stomach clenched. What did he have in mind? Had his time finally come?

Father, protect me.

Chapter Thirteen

The night Teodor and Jerzy had waited for arrived. Cloudy. Chilly. Moonless. Jerzy fell asleep in the bunk below Teodor. But he didn't dare close his eyes, despite their heaviness. If he allowed himself to slumber, they would miss their chance.

For a long while he sat on his bed as straight as possible. Snores and coughs rumbled throughout the room. Beds creaked as their residents shifted to search for a more comfortable position. There wasn't one to be had. But you slept because you worked so hard for so many hours.

Once the night deepened to its darkest and quietest, Teodor reached down and shook Jerzy awake. Neither man said a word. They slipped off their boots, tied the laces together, and slung them around their necks. On stocking feet, they tiptoed toward the door.

Teodor crouched and duckwalked closer to the room's entrance, his pulse pounding in his ears. Just as he expected from several nights of observation, the guard had left his post. Teodor peeked around the door frame. Light emanated from a room farther down the hall. A few laughs too.

He tapped Jerzy's arm and motioned for him to follow. They slunk down the hall, toward the room where the soldiers congregated. It was the only way out. If they weren't on the third floor, they might jump from a window.

A floorboard squeaked under Teodor's foot. He stopped, stock-still. Held his breath.

The Nazis in the room ceased laughing. Spoke in low voices.

He couldn't understand their words, but they must be asking each other if anyone heard that noise. He grabbed Jerzy by the arm and pulled him into an empty office.

Sure enough, the light from the room increased. A large guard stepped into the hall. He shone a flashlight down the passage and into the dark corners.

Teodor couldn't breathe. His heart slowed, then sped up like a sprinter striving to win a race.

With a click, the guard opened a door down the hall. With another click, he shut it. Teodor and Jerzy moved farther into the room, under a desk.

Click, open. *Click*, closed. The German repeated this process, moving ever closer.

Would he never get here? Just get it over with?

Oh, Natia, I'm so sorry.

The officer entered the room and swung the beam around. Teodor closed his eyes and remained as motionless as possible.

The front of the desk faced the German. And hid Teodor and Jerzy.

Click. The door shut.

Teodor expelled his pent-up breath.

A few more rounds of doors opening and shutting followed before the officer returned to his comrades, that pesky board creaking.

Jerzy leaned forward and scooted out of their hiding place. Teodor pulled him back. "Wait."

"What if the guard goes back on duty?"

"We have to time it right."

They waited.

A song ran through Teodor's head. The one Natia sang on the train.

> *God, my Lord, my strength,*
> *My place of hiding, and confiding,*
> *In all needs by night and day;*

> *Though foes surround me,*
> *And Satan mark his prey,*
> *God shall have his way.*

But why this way, Lord? Why not at our little farmhouse, surrounded by children?

Beside him, Jerzy shifted positions.

The Lord answered in another verse.

> *Up, weak knees and spirit bowed in sorrow!*
> *No tomorrow shall arise to beat you down;*
> *God goes before you and angels all around;*
> *On your head a crown.*

The time came to move. Teodor elbowed Jerzy and crawled from their hiding place. His friend followed. They resumed their creep down the hall. With each step, they approached the light, the room where the Nazis entertained themselves. Inside, one of them slapped a table. Teodor jumped and skidded to a halt. Jerzy bumped into him.

The Germans roared with laughter. A chair scraped back. The cadence of the voices changed.

Break time must be over.

Jerzy grasped Teodor's shoulder, his fingers digging into his flesh.

A drop of sweat trickled down Teodor's back.

The door swung open.

⌒

Natia huddled in the far corner of her attic bedroom as *Pan* Fromm chopped Dr. Bosco on the back of the neck. The older man slumped to the floor. Her heart thrummed in her ears.

"Erich, *nein, nein.*" Elfriede's face reddened as she screamed at her husband.

He spun from his evil deed and unleashed a torrent of words at his wife.

Dominik screeched at the top of his lungs. Natia patted his

sweaty back and smoothed his damp curls. She should sing. Music always calmed the baby. But Elfriede's shrieks and Dr. Bosco's moans drove the song from her heart and her lips.

In one long stride, *Pan* Fromm hovered over her, then reached down and yanked her to her feet. "I told you there would be consequences if the baby cried. And so there will be. I never wanted you in the first place." As she clutched Dominik, *Pan* Fromm dragged her across the floor by the arm.

"Where are you taking me?" Would she end up like those men in the square? She couldn't breathe. And what about the baby?

"Where you've deserved to go since the beginning." They moved closer to the door. Natia had to step over Dr. Bosco.

Elfriede leapt into the doorway. "Erich." She said more to him, her tone pleading.

Pan Fromm gestured, swinging wide while still grasping Natia, his grip crushing her upper arm. He answered his wife, his words controlled and cold.

Elfriede shook her head and raised her voice. "*Nein. Nein.*" She tugged at Natia, much as she had at the train station that first day.

He screamed at her, a vein bulging in his neck, and then pushed his wife.

She stumbled but didn't fall. She alternately pleaded and yelled. Each of them pulled on Natia like they were trying to tear her into pieces. Her head rang.

After several minutes, with a torrent of angry words, *Pan* Fromm released his hold on Natia and she stumbled into the corner.

"You get that baby to shut up. Right now. Or I will strangle it. I swear, I will." He leaned forward. A strange light passed through his steely blue eyes. Just a brief flash of something. Regret? Grief? And just that fast, it disappeared. "My son should have lived, not this boy." He clenched and unclenched his fists.

Her breath fluttered in ragged gasps. She rocked Dominik and whispered into the little one's ear. "Please, sweet baby, please stop crying. You'll be fine. You'll see. I know you miss your mama, but she wanted you to live. That won't be possible unless you stop crying. We can't let him take you away. We can't let him part us. Never will I allow that."

Pan Fromm marched from the room, every inch the Nazi officer. The front door slammed shut. But Natia couldn't stop shaking. Neither could Dominik.

Dr. Bosco struggled to a sitting position. "Get my bag." He pointed to the bed.

Natia came to her feet and, jiggling Dominik, brought him his battered black doctor's case. "Are you hurt? How can I help?"

"I'm fine." His face, the same color gray as his hair, told a different story. "There are some drops in a glass vial for the baby. Give them to him every time he eats. They should help."

"Oh, *dziękuję Ci*." She resisted the urge to kiss the man on the top of his almost-bald head. Instead, she touched his upper arm. "You saved our lives."

"I didn't. *Pani* Fromm did. He was ready to take you to the factory. Only because of her intercession are you still here."

"And Dominik?"

Dr. Bosco shook his head, the skin underneath his hazel eyes sagging. "You don't want to know."

Her throat constricted, and she patted the baby's bottom.

"After tonight, are you sure you want to keep Dominik?"

"Of course." *Pani* Rzeźnikowa was right, though. *Pan* Fromm was a dangerous man, one who expected his rules to be obeyed. "I could never let him go. Please understand. My heart would break to lose another child." Not a fourth one. One she had come to love as much as any mother could.

"*Tak*, we keep him." Elfriede straightened. "My husband never hurt a baby. I make sure."

"You can't control him. He brought me, a grown man, to my knees. With one strike, he could kill." He said something to Elfriede.

She shrugged. But her jaw tightened, and she squared her shoulders.

Natia shifted Dominik from one arm to the other, then back again. Her stomach clenched as she turned to the doctor. "She would have you arrested. And Dominik doesn't go anywhere without me. No matter what."

Dr. Bosco glanced at Elfriede. "Are you sure she doesn't understand?"

Natia nodded.

"If I can save a child, even just one, then the risk is worth it." He would be worthy of his son.

She kissed Dominik's hand. The baby's cries quieted. "You wouldn't save him. She wants this child. If you take him from this house, Frau Fromm will send her husband after both the baby and you."

Elfriede helped him from the floor to a half-standing position. He kept his attention on Natia. "It's a dangerous game. Be very careful. I'm just down the street. If you need anything, any time of the day or night, please let me know."

"You're in danger too. Don't you fear *Pan* Fromm? He'll arrest you, surely."

"That's possible, though I've evaded that fate for a while. If it comes, it comes. That's the Lord's will. I'll not stop doing my work and protecting the innocent." He sighed, almost knowing, almost understanding.

This time, Natia kissed him on both cheeks, the squirming baby between them. "God bless you and go with you."

"And with you." He squeezed her arm. "You are in worse danger than I am."

❧

Elfriede closed the door behind the doctor, blocking out the chilly wind that tore down the street. She leaned against the jamb, trembling from head to toe. What had just happened? What had Erich done?

All fell quiet upstairs. Thank God. It wouldn't do for Erich to return and have the baby crying. She didn't want a repeat of the drama. Didn't want him to harm Dominik. Didn't want him to take the little one away. He almost had. For a while she didn't think she'd be able to stop him, not until she threatened to tell *Vater* how Erich had hurt her. That made him think twice. To lose *Vater*'s approval would mean losing any chance at a promotion.

Her chest squeezed, pinching her heart. Maybe one day she would be able to give Erich the son he demanded. The son he deserved. To carry on the family name. To propagate the Aryan race. To make the fatherland proud. That was her duty, one *Vater* taught her to believe in.

Until then, she would love Dominik. Instead of breaking her heart, having a baby in the house soothed her, calmed her spirit, and healed her soul. Lessened her loss. Dominik did the same for Natia. That, they shared.

She moved to the window and pushed the blackout drapes to the side. What did it matter that a sliver of light eked onto the street? The Russians wouldn't bomb this little nothing town. She searched for the stars, but clouds covered the sky.

The front door creaked. A burst of cold blew in. She gasped and turned. "Erich. You're home."

"Is that brat sleeping?"

"Why do you call him a brat? You wouldn't say that about our child."

Color flooded his face. "Our child? The one you've been unable to produce? You and your father duped me into marrying you. Were you even pregnant at the time? Were you?"

She backed up a step. "*Ja.* I wouldn't lie. And *Vater* isn't upset. He paid for this position for you."

"You're a failure. Look at Frau Eisinger. Expecting her eighth child, I believe. Five sons so far. Not like you, who can't bear a single child. And the one you lost is one less for the perfect Aryan race."

Erich slipped off his coat but hung on to it and narrowed his eyes. "Not only that, but you stepped into my business. You hollered at me in front of these Polish pigs. Why?"

She took two steps backward, her mouth dry. "You frightened me. I didn't want you to hurt anyone."

"What happens to the Poles is not your concern. They aren't worthy of breathing the same air as you. You are pure. They are filthy. Polluted."

"Natia is kind."

His nostrils flared. "Don't make friends with her. With anyone here. They are beneath us, only good to serve us for a little while."

His words chilled her to the bone. "What do you mean?" She willed her shaking hands to still. This wasn't the sweet, attentive man she'd married.

He pressed his hands together in a prayer position and touched his nose, his face returning to its usual pallor. "I'm sorry. I didn't mean to upset you. You're too delicate for such things. You shouldn't have to see any of this. Perhaps I should send you back to Berlin." He stroked her cheek, the same cheek he had slapped.

"*Nein.* I want to stay with you." How would she conceive a child if they were separated?

"It's too much for you."

"I will do better, I promise. Just keep me here with you. What would I do without you?" A lone tear escaped from the corner of her eye.

He relaxed his shoulders and gathered her in his arms. "Very well. You know I can't deny you anything."

He kissed her, firm and sure as always. He tasted of cigarettes and alcohol. But she didn't mind.

As long as he didn't abandon her.

Chapter Fourteen

The door to the Nazi's break room swung open. Teodor froze. The big bear of a guard stumbled into the hall. Right in front of Teodor and Jerzy. Teodor took three tiny, hesitant steps farther into the shadows and hunched over. If only he could keep his knees from trembling. The German didn't bother to turn on his flashlight. He walked right by Teodor and Jerzy.

As soon as he took his post, Teodor and Jerzy finished their slow, careful trek to the door. Little by little, holding his breath, Teodor turned the knob. "Don't squeak, don't squeak." He moved his lips but didn't allow any sound to escape.

The Lord answered. The door opened without making a noise, and they slipped outside. As soon as they closed the door, once more with complete silence, Teodor dared to breathe. "That was close."

They stuffed their pockets with the loamy soil. Perfect. This should clog up the machines and shut down production for a good while.

Not much time passed before their pockets overflowed with the soft earth. His coveralls sagged. He nodded in the door's direction. Jerzy slapped his forehead. "The guards." Of course, they had returned to duty, keeping watch over the dormitory door. A problem Teodor hadn't planned for.

"No way in. No way out." Jerzy pointed to the guard monitoring the grounds' perimeter.

Escaping wasn't an option. Especially not when Fromm held Natia hostage. It would bring dire consequences for his wife. He paced in small circles before leaning in to whisper to Jerzy. "Shift change."

"How long?"

Teodor shrugged "Two hours?"

"But it's freezing." Jerzy coughed.

The guard spun around and swept the yard with his flashlight. Jerzy and Teodor flattened themselves on their stomachs on the cold, hard ground. Teodor tensed his muscles to keep from losing control of his bodily functions.

After a few minutes, the guard turned his attention in the opposite direction. Teodor gasped and drew in a lungful of oxygen.

Being in the chilly, damp night air for any length of time wasn't good for Jerzy. They needed a different plan. But what? He gazed into the distance, toward the town. To where Natia was.

What was she doing? Was she safe? If only they could get to her. They could escape, leave this miserable place, find somewhere to hide until the end of the war. It had to come soon.

But how would they get out of here? There were too many guards. Too many searching lights.

Natia remained just out of his grasp.

He shook himself to clear his head. That was it. "A diversion."

"How?"

How, indeed. They had nothing at their disposal except rocks, dirt, and coal.

The coal shovel. Was it still out here? Teodor, his eyes now adjusted to the dark night, motioned for Jerzy to stay put, then crawled to the coal pile, watching the guard. Was that it? He reached out and touched the hard steel. *Tak.* He picked it up and hurried back to Jerzy.

Three minutes later they slunk inside again and up the stairs. Teodor peeked around the corner of the stairwell into the hall. The break-room door was shut, a sliver of light shining at the bottom. This time, no voices or noises came from within. The guard at the dormitory's door turned his head. Teodor nodded to Jerzy.

In their stocking feet, they scurried to the first doorway. They repeated the process, moving to the next room each time the guard turned away.

After a few rounds, they came to the room where they had hidden on the way out. Teodor turned the desk so the opening faced neither the doorway nor the window. Jerzy tucked himself underneath it.

"Ready?"

Jerzy nodded.

With all his might, Teodor flung the shovel through the window. The glass shattered with a terrific crash. He scampered toward the desk and slid underneath it just as the door opened. Though his muscles strained, ready to dart out of the room, Teodor held himself in check.

And for good reason. Maybe half a minute later, several soldiers rushed into the room. They questioned each other, their words fast and furious.

At best, Teodor and Jerzy had a couple of seconds to get out and back to their beds.

He pushed Jerzy from underneath the desk and followed him. Holding his shoes against his chest, he slipped and slid across the smooth wood floors.

The diversion had drawn away the guard. They sprinted across the hall and entered the barracks. Hundreds of men sat up in their bunks and stared at Teodor and Jerzy.

"What are you up to?" The question came from several sources.

"Hush." Teodor's heart pounded in his throat. He and Jerzy bounded for their bunks.

They made it just as the guard returned to the room. He flicked on the light. "Who broke that window?"

Teodor pulled his blanket over his face. Would the other men turn them in?

A heavy, insistent, demanding knock sounded at Pawel's front door. A chill raced through his body. *Pan* Fromm must have come to pay him a visit. It had only been a matter of time. And now what would happen?

The knocking at the door rang in his head much as it had the night the Germans came for his son. So did Antonina's screams. At least this time, she wasn't here.

Was this what Józef felt as the Nazis stole his life? Did his stomach churn the same way, did his hands shake this much?

Pawel rose from his desk chair and made his way to the door. His wife would never know what happened to him. That was the worst. She would always wonder. If only he could tell her good-bye.

He wiped his sweaty hands on his pants. Whatever happened, at the end of the line, a better place awaited him. *Lord, may that thought have given Józef peace.*

He opened the door.

Fromm grabbed Pawel by the arm and pulled him into the living room. "I will not tolerate a dirty Pole pig interfering in my family."

"I didn't want anyone to get hurt."

"What happens in my home is not your business." Fromm shoved Pawel against the ceramic stove.

In a burst of light, pain raced through Pawel's head. He touched the back of his skull. Sticky blood covered his fingers.

Fromm kicked him in the stomach. He doubled over, the air whooshing from his lungs.

"Stay away from my family. That includes Natia and the little brat. Don't ever come near them again or I will kill you. And I won't need my gun."

Pawel's mouth went dry. Fromm was certainly capable of making good on his threat. But that wouldn't stop Pawel from protecting the women and the child should the need arise.

Fromm marched toward him and pinned him against the smooth tile. Pawel's head pounded and buzzed so much he had difficulty hearing Fromm's next words. "An interesting bit of information crossed my desk this week. I'm sure you know what it's about."

Pawel didn't move.

"Does the name Stanislaw Rosinski mean anything to you?"

Once again, Pawel remained still and forced himself to keep his breathing steady and even.

"I asked you a question. I expect an answer."

But Pawel remained silent, the only sound in the room the incessant ticking of the schoolhouse clock on the wall.

Fromm punched him in the temple. Thousands of bright lights burst in front of his eyes. He would have stumbled backward, but the stove and Fromm's pressure on his shoulders kept him upright.

"Answer me, or I will track down your wife and make her pay for your silence."

If it had only been his life, Pawel would have sealed his lips and welcomed whatever Fromm meted out. But his wife. His heart constricted. He wouldn't allow any harm to come to her. "I don't know the man." His words carried confidence, a confidence he prayed Fromm would believe.

Fromm again punched him in the stomach. Pawel coughed, and the metallic taste of blood soured his tongue. His legs wobbled.

"You have been working with Stanislaw, forging papers for Jews, haven't you? I want the truth."

"That's what I told you. I've never heard of the man. I do not forge papers."

"And what would I discover if I searched this house?"

"Go ahead. You will find nothing incriminating." Of that, he was certain. Antonina accused him of being too meticulous. This was one case where that was a good thing.

Fromm released him, and Pawel slumped to the floor. The Nazi stomped away to the office. A racket sounded as Fromm ransacked it. Pawel raised himself on all fours and crawled to his office.

Fromm held up a handful of papers, a wide smile crossing his face, a brightness in his icy blue eyes. "What do we have here?"

"Blank birth certificates."

"Ones that you fill out with false names and information to hide people's Jewishness."

Tak, including Dominik's. "Ones that I use to record births in the town. Nothing else. You're looking for something that is not here. Every doctor in Poland has a stack of blank birth certificates."

Fromm tossed the papers in the air, and they fluttered to the ground. He strode from behind the desk, his fists clenched, his eyes narrowed. "Don't get mouthy." He kicked Pawel underneath his chin, snapping his head backward.

Pawel fought against the darkness that threatened to consume him. Fromm's boots pounded on the wood floor as he moved around the house. More bumps and bangs. Expletives.

The fog closed in on Pawel. He pushed it away.

The floors creaked as Fromm returned to the room. "I know you're involved. Believe me, I will watch your every move. At some point, you will make a mistake. When you do, I will be there to make you pay."

Fromm stomped from the room and slammed the front door.

Pawel gave in to the darkness.

❧

Teodor clutched the blanket that covered his face and squeezed his eyes shut. *Lord, don't let them hear my heart pounding.* Not a man in the barracks stirred.

"Since none of you are that smart, I'll repeat the question. Who broke the window?"

Teodor's heart stopped, raced, and stopped again.

Silence filled the room. A palpable, ear-splitting silence.

Multiple boot falls echoed in the quietness. Multiple guards. The sound of them came from different spots in the barracks as they fanned out. Probably with their hands behind their backs, scrutinizing each prisoner.

The sharp thuds approached ever closer. Then stopped in front of him. The Nazi flung back his blanket. "Ah, Palinski. You've been nothing but trouble since you arrived. Was it you? Did you cause this commotion?"

Another guard piped up from across the room. "We recovered the item used to break the window, sir."

"What was it?"

"A coal shovel."

How could he have been so careless? Of course, he'd been the one shoveling coal in the yard. He knew it was there. The evidence pointed straight to him.

Natia. Alone in the world. He dug his fingernails into his palms.

"You, up." *Hauptscharführer* Krug yanked him from the bed.

"I didn't do it." Somehow, he kept the quiver from his voice.

Krug stooped and glowered at Teodor. "Of course you did. You were in the yard. Knew a shovel was there. How long have you been hiding it? Or did you somehow sneak out tonight?"

Teodor clutched his shoes to his chest. Another piece of evidence staring them straight in the face.

"Why are you holding your shoes?"

"It's more comfortable to sleep with them off, but I don't want them stolen, so I hang on to them. Like my ragged old blanket when I was a child."

A round of titters swept across the room.

Krug struck Teodor. His eyes watered. With his free hand, he touched his cheek.

"I don't enjoy being made a fool of."

"You asked. I answered."

A slap stung his other cheek.

"I will not tolerate impertinence. Is that clear?" The guard locked his jaw. "Let me see the boots."

"Pardon me?"

The officer screamed in his ear, "Are you deaf? The boots."

As he handed them to Krug, Teodor managed to swipe them across his chest. Maybe that would dry them and knock off some of the dirt.

"These are damp."

What did he say to that? "*Tak.*"

"Why?"

Teodor might go deaf if the man insisted on shouting. "I spilled my water at dinner. They haven't dried yet. It's a damp evening."

Krug grunted and handed Teodor's boots to him, then turned to the rest of the men. "Has he been in the room all night?"

A murmur rippled through the prisoners. All yeses, as far as Teodor could tell.

A smart aleck piped up. "How would we know? We were sleeping."

The guard drew in a deep breath, a muscle jumping in his cheek. "That is enough. You will have double duty tomorrow." He returned his attention to Teodor. "And you are coming with me."

Teodor slumped against the bunk. What awaited him?

♪♪♪

Chapter Fifteen

ominik, still weary from his middle-of-the-night screaming session, slept late the following morning. So did Elfriede. When she did make an appearance in the kitchen, red rimmed her eyes and her always-tidy and rolled blonde hair hung in disheveled waves around her face and shoulders.

"What do you want for breakfast?" Natia bent to stir the fire in the stove.

"Coffee."

"More? Eggs?"

"*Nie.* Just coffee."

Natia poured the brew into one of Elfriede's fine Dresden china cups and motioned for her to sit. Even though Elfriede said she didn't want anything else, Natia cut slices from a loaf of brown bread and slathered them with butter and marmalade, foodstuffs no ordinary Pole would have access to. She presented the plate to Elfriede and sat across the table from her.

Elfriede sipped the coffee and nibbled on the bread. Natia let her be until the dark half-moons under her eyes faded.

"Last night? Your husband?" How did she convey to Elfriede what tore at her soul? "Why?"

"Angry."

"Why did he hurt the doctor?" Natia mimicked *Pan* Fromm's chopping motion.

"He is not bad."

"He hurt the doctor."

"The baby cry." Elfriede studied the steam rising from her cup.

"He was going to take me to the factory. And probably kill Dominik."

"I do not know why. He is good man."

"*Nie.* Look at what he did."

Elfriede peered up, her brows furrowed.

Natia blew out a breath. "Your husband is bad."

"*Nie.* Bad day at work? I don't know."

"Can't you see? Are you that blind that you don't know the kind of man your husband is? What is going on in this town? Even in this house? Wake up." She banged on the table.

Elfriede startled. "I don't know what you say. But Erich is good man."

"Why? Why last night?"

"Our baby never cry." A tear shimmered on Elfriede's pale lashes. "Our baby die. In here." She pointed to her abdomen.

"My baby too. Three never cried. My husband doesn't hurt people."

"Erich is sad. Angry at God. Why God do that?"

And that was one of the questions for which Natia had no answer. *Why, Lord? Why so much hardship and trouble and grief in this life? And why take it out on the innocent?*

"But he shouldn't hurt people. Not the doctor. Not Dominik."

"He not hurt the doctor."

"He did." Elfriede had stood in the same room, watched the same things as Natia. Saw what her husband did. Why did she refuse to admit it? Why did she cling to this idea that her husband was good and honorable? "He punched the doctor. And hit him." Natia again pantomimed *Pan* Fromm's actions. "He hurt me." She rolled up the sleeves of her white blouse to reveal the bruises.

Elfriede bit her lower lip. She stared at Natia, her pale-blue eyes blank. Empty. Like she was trying to push last night's images from her mind.

"*Nie.* You can't deny it. I won't let you. It's time you faced it. He made my husband go outside. He hit the doctor. He hurt me.

You understand me, I know you do. Listen to me." She grabbed Elfriede by the hands. "Listen to me."

"I love him." The words came out little more than a whisper.

"He's evil."

Elfriede yanked free of Natia's hold and covered her ears. "*Nein, nein.*" She continued in German for a long while.

A little child who refused to see the truth. Who refused to open her eyes to what was going on.

Natia pulled her hands away so she had to listen. "He is bad." She enunciated every word.

Elfriede gazed up. For half a second, the world stood still. No one moved. No one breathed. No one's heart beat.

In the next instant, her eyes and mouth softened. Tears streamed down her face. Sobs wracked her slender body.

And Natia went to her and comforted her.

◦◦◦

Led by *Hauptscharführer* Krug, Teodor wound his way down the musty staircase. Nothing had turned out how he planned it.

They suspected him. *Stupid, stupid, stupid.* He should have never thrown that shovel. Of course, it pointed the finger straight at him. No one else would have known about it. Would they?

Nie, he couldn't sacrifice someone else, lie about them, to save himself. He would never be able to live with himself.

Even if it meant leaving Natia alone.

Hauptscharführer Krug shoved Teodor into a cold, metal chair, went around his large desk, and lit a cigarette, blowing smoke rings into the air. His hat, an eagle on the front of it, sat on the desk beside him, and his light-brown hair stuck up in the back. "So, we have a situation here."

Teodor tapped the edge of the seat.

"You see, I know you were the one who tossed that shovel through the window last night. Who else could it be? You knew where it was. And you're strong. I watched you from the window the day you were in the yard. Like an ox, you work."

Teodor stared at Krug, right into his deep-green eyes, and didn't blink.

"What I can't figure is why you were outside. You didn't hide that shovel in your room for so many weeks. It was there yesterday when I walked by. That leaves me to conclude you left the building, retrieved the shovel, and then, under the guards' noses, hefted it through the glass."

Teodor's stomach rumbled.

"Do you care to enlighten me?"

"About what?"

"Why you went out. Your boots were wet, and not from your water at dinner. From the damp ground. Why did you do it?" Krug cracked his already-gnarled knuckles.

"I didn't. I never left the barracks."

Krug leaned forward in his chair, resting against the desk. "That is a lie."

Teodor didn't cower. "It is not. I've already tasted the German methods of discipline. I have no desire to become subject to them again."

"And that's why you aren't telling me the truth. What if I question the other men?"

"You would hear it wasn't me." He stilled his trembling knees.

Krug slithered around the desk and stood over Teodor. "Is that so?" He stroked his clean-shaven, pointed chin. "I'm not convinced. I have a feeling a few hours outside shoveling coal would have them singing like caged birds."

Teodor grabbed the edge of the chair with all his might to keep his expression neutral. "They cannot testify to what isn't the truth. No matter what, they won't implicate me, because they can't."

"Is that so? Shall we test that theory?"

"Do what you want, but you will not get information either from me or from them."

"You and your Polish pig friends are lucky. Berlin is sending some of its best and brightest here to inspect the plant. We don't have time to go down the line one by one until we find a man whose mouth will run like a faucet. *Nie*, we need to increase our production in the next week to make our best impression. In fact, that's what I'm going to do. Double quotas for everyone."

"You can't be serious."

Krug returned to his seat. "Oh, I am."

"The men are exhausted and starving. Already, you push them to their limits. You will kill them if you demand more. What will you do without workers?"

"There are plenty where you came from. And for your insubordination, I'm going to triple the quotas. Is that all, or would you like to go for quadruple?"

Teodor bit his tongue until the metallic flavor of blood filled his mouth.

"Very good. Get to work. And by the way, you yourself will work twenty-four hours for the next five days until the inspectors arrive. If you fall asleep, I will shoot you myself."

No sleep? Could a man survive that long? Already he'd gone almost twenty-four hours without rest, and his mind was foggy.

"Get to work."

Teodor scraped back his chair and dallied up the stairs and down the hall to the factory floor. Look what his hasty words had gotten them, not just himself, but all the prisoners. Not double the work but triple it. He hadn't exaggerated to Krug. The men wouldn't survive.

And he doubted he would himself.

He tuned out the hum of machines and the grating of drills as he sat on the stool in front of his press. He picked up a piece, set it up, drilled it, and plopped it into the box beside him, his actions automatic. Maybe he could do this in his sleep.

A few machines away from him, a man swayed and fell from his stool. Krug marched over and kicked the man in the side. "Get up, you worthless swine."

The man didn't move. Under his breath, Teodor willed him to get to his feet.

Krug's face reddened. "I told you to get up."

After a moment, the man came to his knees, trembling all over.

Krug pulled his pistol from its holster and shot the man in the head.

Teodor gasped.

Krug marched to his side and pressed the firearm against Teodor's temple. "Do you want to be next?"

Teodor held his breath, not able to think or move.

"Get to work. You have a long time until your shift is over."

The day dragged on. Making mistakes on pieces didn't require concentration anymore. And his ordeal had just begun. Once the shift ended and the other men left, he was alone in the factory with a solitary guard standing watch. Teodor's skin prickled under the Nazi's stare.

The emptiness of this place, of his own heart overwhelmed him. Where was God when he needed him most? Probably sleeping, certainly not watching over his children.

Children he had stolen from them. Would this crushing pain ever ease? *God, help us.*

But no thunder rolled, no shaft of light split the darkness, no angel descended from the heavens.

He was alone. And fighting for his life, one the guard would likely snuff out at some point in the coming hours. No one could stay awake for five days.

A time or two, Teodor caught himself nodding off, jerking awake as his chin touched his chest. To keep sleep at bay, he allowed his mind to whir like a mower in the grain field. There was only one thing he could do in this situation. During the long hours, he perfected the plans for sabotaging the machines.

And just when they would do it.

❧

Natia wiped the sweat from her brow as she worked over the kitchen stove, boiling pierogi for dinner. With meat in short supply, the potato-and-cheese dumplings would be filling. She tucked her loose hair behind her ear to keep it out of her eyes.

Pan Fromm would be home soon. For the time being, Elfriede played with Dominik in the living room, keeping him content as she sang little songs and clapped his hands. He didn't care that an alley cat being attacked sounded better than Elfriede.

But what if he whimpered while *Pan* Fromm was home? What if he cried again tonight? Was sitting here, waiting for him, crazy? Maybe Natia should take Dominik and run. Run where? To the woods? *Pan* Fromm would bring his German shepherds and hunt her down.

And he would show them no mercy. Elfriede couldn't hold him off forever.

Natia shivered. She stared at the whitewashed ceiling above her, the one that reminded her of clouds. "Oh God, how can I do this? How can I keep Dominik safe? I don't know if I have the strength to keep going. I can't run. I can't fight. What can I do? Tell me, I beg you, tell me."

Her answer came in the squeak of the front door. Heavy footfalls. Then *Pan* Fromm's bass voice reverberated throughout the house. But it wasn't hard or angry like last night. Instead, it was light and his words were rapid.

Elfriede squealed. Natia peeked through the doorway to see *Pan* Fromm lifting his wife around the waist and swinging her in a circle, kissing her face the entire time. Then he set her down with a gentleness Natia had never seen from him.

When he approached the kitchen, she ducked back to the stove.

Pan Fromm stood in the doorway, leaning against the jamb. "My, my. What a lovely picture." He righted himself without uncrossing his arms, his eyes warm for a change. "There is a stack of books on the piano. Box them up and mail them to the address on the slip of paper in the top book. A friend of mine has a son who broke his leg and has a long confinement ahead of him. Without his Hitler Youth activities, he will be bored. I thought the books might cheer him. He's a good boy, much like I would want my son to be." A wistful sigh crossed his lips.

"And I have some good news. My father-in-law has come through for me at last. He is sending a delegation from Berlin to inspect the plant. If they bring him a favorable review, he will buy me a better commission in Germany."

Germany? And if that happened, would she be expected to go with them? Or …

To keep her hands from shaking, she wiped them on the white apron covering her full black skirt.

"To that end, I'm hosting a dinner party next week. Some high-ranking SS men are coming to tour our operation, to see what a fine job we're doing. This may be a little outpost on the edge of the world, but I intend to show them we aren't backwater. I've tasted your food, and I've heard you sing. Quite beautiful. I want you to entertain us."

"Sing?"

"Yes, sing. Not a lullaby, of course, but a few rousing, patriotic German tunes. Lively ones that will put the men in good humor. I have no doubt you will enchant them."

"But I don't speak German."

"*Pani* Fromm can teach you a few songs."

With Elfriede's tone deafness, how would Natia ever get the tune right?

"And, of course, you shall cook for us."

"Cook?"

"What are you, a parrot? That's what I said. You will cook. But none of your basic, plain Polish dishes. You will cook the finest of German cuisine. Schnitzel and sauerbraten, and a Black Forest cake that will make them think they died and went to heaven. Can you handle that simple task?"

"I don't know how to make any of that. I've ever only cooked the food my mother taught me."

"Then read a cookbook. *Pani* Fromm has several."

"I don't speak German."

"The woman who lived here before us left a collection. All in Polish, I believe. Before you came, I flipped through them. One has several German recipes. That should suffice. Unless you have more objections?"

Natia swayed back and forth. Her tongue stuck to the roof of her mouth. "*Nie.*"

Except that she couldn't read.

Chapter Sixteen

*N*atia stared at the spines of the cookbooks on the shelf above the stove. Polish, German, Japanese. The language they were written in didn't matter. Not one made sense to her. Though she'd attended the village school, she never could decipher the strange markings on the page. They blurred together until her eyes burned. At last, the teacher stopped trying to force her to learn.

Two days. That was all she had until the inspectors arrived for the dinner party. Important men. And if she failed to please either them or *Pan* Fromm? She shivered. *Nie*, she had to do this to protect Dominik.

All the German dishes he mentioned to her, she'd never heard of. She didn't even remember what he said anymore. How was she going to pull this off? She plopped onto the kitchen chair and covered her face.

Dominik gurgled and cooed as he knelt on all fours and rocked on the blanket on the floor beside her. The one light in this dark, dismal place. The one thing that kept Natia going. Teodor hadn't answered her song all week. The barracks sat dark and empty when she went by, no matter how early in the morning. Instead, the buzz of machines greeted her.

The Germans must be working the prisoners extra hard in anticipation of their visitors.

She glanced at the baby. Dominik grinned, one tooth poking through his bottom gum. So far, teething hadn't bothered him. So far.

Natia sighed. "Well, then, there is only one thing I can do."

She swooped Dominik from the floor and kissed his cheek. "Are you ready for an adventure?" She wrapped the growing boy in several warm blankets. She'd unraveled her own blue mittens to knit a cap for him. She popped it on his head and tied the string under his chin.

Elfriede had gone to her room to rest, so Natia hurried out before she woke. Today, she didn't even bother to head to the factory. Teodor wouldn't be there. She rushed to the center of town, by Chopin's statue, averting her eyes from the composer's likeness and the blood-stained stones. Instead, she headed to the butcher shop.

"*Pani* Rzeźnikowa, hello, are you here?"

A red-haired man Natia hadn't met before stepped to the counter. "Can I help you?"

"I need to speak to *Pani* Rzeźnikowa."

"She's not here. Is there something I can get for you? Though we are out of meat for the day."

"What? *Nie. Nie*, I need her. Now." This man wouldn't be able to help her, couldn't solve her problem. "When will she be back?"

"Not for a while, I suspect. Her husband passed away last night. His bad heart gave out."

Natia clutched the wooden counter. "Oh, that's horrible." Even though Teodor was still alive as far as she knew, she also understood the depths of despair that must be gripping *Pani* Rzeźnikowa.

"He hadn't been well for a while."

"I'm so sorry. Please, if you see her, convey my sympathy. I'm Natia Palinska." Dominik fussed, and she patted his back as she stumbled from the shop.

What a terrible blow to that wonderful woman. How was she going to cope without her husband? From what she had told Natia, they had been married for many, many years.

She kissed Dominik's cold, round cheek as she left the town square. "Now what am I going to do? How am I going to cook for these men? And sing for them?" Though she pinched the bridge of her nose, two big tears rolled down her face. Once they let loose, a stream of them followed.

She stopped in front of the many-windowed factory building, smoke pouring from the two stacks on either side of it. Clinging to Dominik, she sunk to her knees. "Oh, Teodor, Teodor. I need you. Why won't you answer? Can't you hear me?"

Only the blowing of a whistle replied.

Chopin's requiem "Poland's Dirge" sprang to her lips. The slow, mournful, minor key allowed the tune to weep along with her in both the words and the music.

> *By the storm they breasted,*
> *Every leaf is wrested,*
> *Now a birdling only*
> *In the tree sings lonely:*

Her voice cracked, and she cleared her throat.

> *O native land! Thy furrows*
> *Native blood doth redden,*
> *Woeful are thy sorrows,*
> *By foes thou art downtrodden.*

The wind tugged at her hair. Dominik whimpered. "I don't know what I'm going to do." She whispered her words to the empty heavens. "God, aren't you listening to me? Where are you when I need you?"

Top-heavy with Dominik in her arms, she tottered to her feet. She had nowhere else to go but to the Fromms. The onion-domed church spire, its cross reaching to the sky, beckoned her to come and rest, but without a priest, the doors remained locked.

She entered the Fromms' home through the back door, unwrapped a fussy Dominik from the blankets, and settled him on a quilt on the floor.

"Where you go?"

Natia gasped. "You startled me."

"Where you go?" Elfriede frowned.

"Out."

Elfriede approached her. Touched her face, caked with dried tears. "You sad."

Natia turned away.

Elfriede spun her back around, her blue eyes soft. "Why you sad?"

"*Pani* Rzeźnikowa's husband died."

"Oh no. She sad too. Such a good lady. Very, very sad thing." Elfriede shook her head, her hair in rolls around her face and hanging loose in the back.

"And men are coming."

"*Ja, ja.* Two days." Elfriede's countenance shifted, and she all but beamed.

"I have to cook."

"Good food. German food."

"*Nie.* I don't know." Natia gestured at the row of worthless cookbooks.

"Ah. I help." Elfriede scanned the books, pulled one down, and handed it to Natia. "Here."

Natia took the volume, the book heavy in her hands. She flipped the pages. "I don't know."

Elfriede furrowed her brows. "*Nie.* It's Polish."

"I. Don't. Know." Natia slammed the book on the table, sending Dominik into a wail.

"You don't know?"

Natia shook her head. "*Nie.* None of it. I can't read any of it."

"But you cook."

Natia pointed to her head. She'd watched her mother and memorized her recipes. But none of them were German, only simple Polish fare. Pierogi. Cabbage and peas. Borscht.

Her employer grinned. "I help."

"How?"

"You see."

Natia exhaled, long and slow. She'd witnessed Elfriede's clumsy attempts in the kitchen. There was no way she'd be able to save Natia.

∾

One day to go before the inspectors from Berlin arrived. Butterflies flitted in Elfriede's stomach, more than you'd find in an Alpine meadow. Erich had informed her these were very important men. He had to make a good impression. If he did, *Vater* promised him a promotion and a better position somewhere in Germany.

And now, she had a chance to help him find favor with these officials, including Herr Eisinger, the man whose wife had eight children for the Führer. She had to prove herself a worthy German officer's wife. Tomorrow, she would play the part to perfection.

Imagine, Natia couldn't read. She'd never met anyone who couldn't pick up a book and glean either information or entertainment from it. Maybe Erich was right. The Poles were much more ignorant than the Germans.

On the other hand, she enjoyed helping Natia. Right now, she sat at the kitchen table, jiggling Dominik on her knee while the baby gnawed on a piece of dry toast. Natia worked at the counter.

"Next?"

Elfriede glanced over the recipe for the Black Forest cake. "Flour. Two cups of flour."

Some of the German words were similar enough to the Polish ones that Natia understood what she said. Others, like this one, weren't. "What? I don't understand."

"Flour." She scraped her chair back, balanced Dominik on her hip, and opened the cupboard. To host this party, they had been allowed extra rations. Of course, the food labels were in Polish, which Elfriede couldn't read, but by opening the packages and tasting the contents, she found what she wanted. "Stir it in." She mimed what Natia needed to do.

The bigger problem came to Natia's singing. If she couldn't read Polish, she certainly couldn't read German. As Natia pitted the cherries, Elfriede sang the songs line by line. Her voice wasn't the best. In fact, Erich commanded that she not sing in his presence. Still, Natia was talented enough to figure out the melody. The words were another problem. Elfriede started with the first line of *"Panzerlied"* once again. *"Ob's stürmt oder schneit, ob die Sonne uns lacht."*

Natia stilled and focused on Elfriede as she sang. *"Ob's stut oder schnell."* She huffed. "That's wrong."

Elfriede chuckled, something she hadn't done since the night Dominik cried. *"Nie, nie.* Like this." With painstaking care, she modeled the line syllable by syllable.

Natia repeated, this time with the right words.

"Tak. That's good." She clapped, and Dominik, now sitting on a blanket in the middle of the room, imitated her. "Baby happy."

"Tak, he's a good baby."

Elfriede leaned over to kiss Dominik's forehead. An almost overpowering odor backed her away. "Dirty baby." And soiled diapers gave her gagging fits.

Natia directed her to the counter. "Here. You do it." She gave the batter a stir, then handed the spoon to Elfriede, stepping away and motioning for Elfriede to take her place.

She pulled the spoon through the flour and eggs. "Good?"

Natia shook her head. She took the spoon back and gave the batter a vigorous beating.

This time, Elfriede's efforts won Natia's approval. "Good, good. You do it." She scooped up Dominik and disappeared upstairs.

Nein, Erich was wrong. Natia and the other Poles weren't stupid or lazy or even ignorant. In many ways, Natia was smarter than she was, even though she couldn't read.

In another time, another place, another circumstance, they might have been friends. And Elfriede surely could use one.

Pawel hurried down the quiet street in the direction of the factory. Funny how Fromm almost killed him one minute, and the next, he was calling for him because he needed his services and expertise.

He entered through the main door. Fräulein Wurtz, a petite, red-haired woman, sat at the desk, clacking away on her typewriter. In the distance a phone rang and someone shrieked. "I'll be right with you."

"I'm the doctor."

She whipped her attention to him. "Of course. We've been waiting for you."

"Where is the injured patient?"

"Right through here." She led the way into a back office and opened the door. A young boy, no more than eight, sat on a chair holding a bloody rag around his hand, snot pouring from his nose as he screamed and sobbed.

Pawel's stomach clenched, threatening to expel his small breakfast. He hated being called to tend to children. Boys and girls who should be enjoying life, not working in squalid conditions.

A commotion sounded from the office. "I have to see the boy. Let me in. I have to talk to him."

The secretary almost shrieked her reply. "You can't. Get back to work or I will call *Untersturmführer* Fromm."

The door banged open. A scrawny man rushed in and knelt beside the boy. "Zygmunt, is that you? Is it really you?"

The child screeched. "My finger! My finger!"

"Zygmunt, listen to me. It's Teodor. Praise the Lord that we found you. Natia is here in town, living with a German family. She's going to be so happy."

The boy's wails lessened. "Teodor?"

Pawel turned to the prisoner with dark bags under his eyes and slurred speech. "You know this boy?"

"He's my wife's brother. Her family came with us on the train, but we had no idea what happened to them."

"You can catch up later. Right now, I need to care for him."
He turned to Zygmunt. "Let's look at that." The child screamed
as Pawel unwrapped the towel from around his hand. All color
drained from the boy's face.

"Hold on now. Take a deep breath. Don't faint."

Pawel unwrapped the last bit of bandage. Blood gushed everywhere. Zygmunt's left middle finger was missing.

The man behind him gasped and fell to his knees. "Oh,
Zygmunt, Zygmunt."

Pawel's heart clenched. What an awful way to locate your
family. "What is your name?"

"Teodor Palinski. I sneaked out during a bathroom break to
check on the boy. Word got around that a child had been hurt.
When I heard his description, I just knew, and I had to see for
myself."

Zygmunt pressed his bloody hand tight to his chest. "*Nie, nie.*
Don't let anyone touch me."

Pan Palinski rubbed Zygmunt's back. "Don't worry. The
doctor is here now. He'll make it better."

"I want *Tata.*"

His brother-in-law paled. "He's here?"

The child shook his head. "I haven't seen him since the train."

Pan Palinski's voice remained calm. "For now, you'll have to
put up with me."

"I need to take him to my office for stitches. Can you carry
him?"

In answer, Teodor lifted Zygmunt from the chair with a great
deal of care. "You'll be just fine. I'll make sure."

They exited the room and hurried to the front office where
Pawel paused just a moment to speak to the secretary. "I have to
take the boy to my exam room. And *Pan* Palinski is coming along."

"You can't whisk them out of here without permission."

The slamming of the door behind them cut off the rest of her
words.

Zygmunt continued his high-pitched wailing as they hustled away from the factory and toward Pawel's residence. He led the way to his exam room. "Put the boy on the table."

Pan Palinski did as ordered.

And Zygmunt passed out.

Chapter Seventeen

Teodor rubbed his gritty eyes and opened them as the doctor whipped the last stitch into place in Zygmunt's hand where his finger had been. Terrible as this was for Zygmunt, it provided Teodor a tiny bit of sleep. Still, the world around him spun. "Is the boy going to survive?"

The doctor nodded. "He should, barring any kind of infection."

"Conditions at the factory are not sterile. Far from it. Dirt, vermin, and disease are too common."

"And they have children running the drill presses?"

"*Nie*. Not running them. Mostly sweeping up, carrying the pieces from station to station. But we've been working long hours this week, getting ready for the inspectors. Could be they put him on the machine. Or he might have been playing around. You know how children are." Or how they used to be. Acid ate at Teodor's stomach.

His eyes burned seeing Zygmunt this way. He had always been somewhat of a mischief maker, but not a bad boy. Just a boy. One who liked to laugh, to run, to play.

If only Natia could see him. She'd had so much loss in her life. To be able to give this back to her would mean so much.

"That's why they don't have any business being near the factory. Let's move him upstairs to the bedroom."

Teodor lifted the boy, little more than a feather in his arms, and carried him up the steep steps to a simple room with a wrought-iron bed, a painting of Jesus above it.

"And he's your brother-in-law?"

"My wife has helped raise him since her mother died shortly after his birth."

The doctor gazed at Teodor. "When was the last time you had a full night's sleep?"

"I don't remember. What day is it?"

"What are they doing to you in there?"

"Whatever they please."

"And where is his sister, your wife?" The doctor pulled a quilt over Zygmunt's thin shoulders.

Some of the feeling returned to his numb heart. "She works for *Untersturmführer* Fromm."

The doctor stepped back, almost knocking over a small bedside table and a glass of water. "Your wife is *Pani* Palinska?"

"You know her?"

"I've met her several times."

"How is she? Can you arrange for me to see her? And for her to see her brother?" Teodor's heart danced. Maybe he could be close to her, maybe even touch her. That would be enough. Even if the guard shot him tonight, it would be enough.

The doctor gave an almost-imperceptible nod. "For her own protection, my wife has had to leave. I would do anything to be with her, so I understand. Your wife is a strong, brave woman. You should be proud of her."

Teodor's throat constricted. "I've always known and admired that about her."

"Stay here with the boy. I'll fetch her."

This was Teodor's chance. Perhaps the three of them could escape. Partisans lived in the forests. They would survive there until the end of the war. It would be hard, but if they were together, it would be worth it.

A pounding sounded from the door downstairs. "Open up, open up." Germans.

And just like that, any hope he might have had for escaping vanished like a dream when one awakened.

"I have to let them in."

Teodor shrugged his assent, even as the doctor took off down the stairs.

Within seconds, three lower-ranking enlisted soldiers, two bars on their collars, all carrying weapons, marched in. They grabbed Teodor and pinned his arms behind his back.

"What is the meaning of this?"

"We have come to return you to the factory. You left without authorization."

Like they would have given him any. "I had every intention of returning." He swallowed the lie. "This boy needed immediate medical attention. By the time I got permission to leave, he might have died."

"We'll see what *Untersturmführer* Fromm has to say." They dragged him toward the staircase.

The doctor stepped in front of them. "Wait a minute. My wife isn't here, and I need a nurse to watch the boy. Let *Pan* Palinski stay while I fetch her. I'll return in less than five minutes."

The big, burly guards glanced at each other, at Teodor and the doctor, and back to each other. The one with a slight lisp answered. "Five minutes. Not one more."

The guards released their hold on Teodor. He rubbed his sore wrists, then pulled a small, tufted chair to Zygmunt's bedside. The boy took steady, even breaths.

Bitterness filled Teodor's mouth. He'd been close, so very close to seeing Natia, and maybe even escaping this miserable place with her and her brother. She was all that held him here.

He gazed at Zygmunt's peaceful face, a fair-colored curl flowing across his forehead. Poor child. While it was one thing to miss your wife, it was quite another to be eight years old and without either parent. Even if they hadn't been able to run away, it would have been good for Zygmunt and Natia to see each other.

The little alarm clock on the bedside table ticked away the

minutes. True to his word, the doctor returned within the allotted allowance.

Teodor turned.

And there, in the doorway, stood Natia.

Time stopped.

The doctor peered at him over her shoulder, a word of warning in his hard stare. Teodor clamped his lips shut. But he couldn't look away. Here she was, his wife, in front of him just a couple of meters.

She'd lost more weight since the last time they'd been close. But her green eyes still sparkled. A dimple appeared in her cheek as a wide smile broke across her face. Her dark hair hung in waves. He itched to touch it, to run the silky length of it across his fingertips.

Teodor stood and motioned for her to sit. She scooted past him. On purpose, he didn't give her the room he should have. Instead, she brushed against him.

The ache in his chest expanded.

❧

For an eternal moment, Natia stood in the doorway and stared at her husband, still unable to believe what Dr. Bosco had told her. Teodor. At his house. Close enough to touch. To whisper to.

And not only Teodor, but also Zygmunt. She must be dreaming. The beauty of this moment was too much to be reality.

Teodor stood, his blue coveralls hanging on his thin frame. He sported a good amount of light-brown stubble on his chin and cheeks. His hair hung over his collar. His blue eyes were red, and dark half-moons hung underneath them. The poor man was exhausted.

But he pushed back a laugh.

Always laughing, he was.

Still her Teodor.

He motioned for her to take the seat beside the bed where her brother lay. She slid by her husband, brushing against his chest as he didn't leave enough room for her. Heat rushed through her body, a long-forgotten sensation of love and desire for him.

She dipped her head and dropped into the chair, still warm from his presence. Pretending to be the nurse, she held Zygmunt's hand and examined the bandages. Was he taller than she had remembered, or had time erased her recollection? Like Teodor, Zygmunt's fair hair was longer. And his hands were calloused, no longer the hands of a child. Not even the hands of a farm child anymore. Oh, the sweet boy. To suffer so much at such a young age.

Why, God, why?

She turned to Teodor. He blinked several times. He knew. He understood. His hand grazed her shoulder as he moved to the side. He was here for her.

She leaned over Zygmunt but used the song swelling inside to speak to Teodor. The words came out soft and pained at first.

> *When for a moment thou dost speak, my darling,*
> *'Tis like the music of angelic voices calling,*
> *Mute is my joy that I may be so near thee.*

As she continued singing, the notes reaching and soaring with her, the warble left her voice. The room paled, and only Teodor stood beside her.

> *Hark'ning, and hoping that thou may persevere,*
> *Naught else desiring, forever, forever,*
> *But so to hear thee, still to hear thee.*

The melody covered them for a moment. The guard broke the magical spell. "That's enough. The nurse has arrived. Time for you to go back to work." They grabbed Teodor by the elbows. She gasped.

They led him through the door.

She scraped back the chair. "*Dziękuję Ci,* for all you did for the boy. Take care. Please, take care." She couldn't keep the pleading from her voice.

He glanced over his shoulder at her, pursed his lips as if he kissed her, and then mouthed *I love you.*

She mouthed the words back. Over and over until he disappeared downstairs and the door banged shut. Tears streamed down her cheeks. She turned to the doctor. "*Dziękuję Ci.*" She could say no more.

He flashed her a sad smile. "When I found out who they were, I had to bring you here. I knew it would mean the world to you."

"It does."

"Then why do you grieve?"

She wiped her face, though fresh tears rushed in to wet it. "Will I ever see him again? To touch him as I did just now? This might have been the last time. I may never hold him in my arms. I may never sleep beside him through the night. There have been too many good-byes in my life. Was this another one?"

Dr. Bosco knelt beside her. "None of us has assurance of tomorrow, war or no war. All we can do is place our lives in God's hands and live them to the fullest."

"But how can I live that way when I'm so empty inside?"

"My dear girl, just allow the Lord to fill what is missing in your heart."

His words penetrated her ears, but not her inmost being. To be complete, she needed Teodor. Needed him more than she needed food or water.

And she needed Zygmunt.

She shook her head. Right now, she had to focus on today, on getting through the next forty-eight hours. "May I stay with my brother until your wife returns?"

"My wife won't be back anytime soon."

His meaning was clear. "Oh. You understand."

"But you do need to return to the Fromms. They'll miss you."

"*Pan* Fromm is entertaining the visiting dignitaries, so there is cooking and cleaning to be done. And he wants me to sing." She gazed at the boy sleeping off the trauma of his ordeal.

With a tenderness she'd learned from her mother, she brushed a lock of hair from Zygmunt's eyes. "And what about him? We can't allow him to return to that awful place. It's bad enough for my husband. Teodor is grown. Zygmunt is nothing more than a little boy. He has no one else. He needs me. Please, help me to help him."

"The Nazis know where he is. If he suddenly disappeared, they would hunt for him until they found him and killed him."

Dr. Bosco didn't have to finish that thought. Saving Zygmunt would cost him his life. But what kind of life did he have in that factory? Did he have any chance for survival? How long until something else terrible happened?

"Please, I beg you. Do you have children?"

The doctor nodded. "I had a son."

"Then you understand my need to get my brother out of there. I'm the closest thing he has to a mother. I would not be doing my duty if I allowed those monsters to lay their hands on him again."

He swallowed. "I'll do what I can."

She turned to him. "*Dziękuję Ci* for giving me this moment with my husband and my brother. I will lock it in my heart and hold it there forever. Never will I forget the kindness you've shown us." She stood on her tiptoes and kissed his cheek.

A few minutes later, she ambled in the direction of the Fromms' home. Her breath hung in puffs in front of her. The cottages along the route huddled together, closed against the winter's chill. A chill that ran deep into her bones.

❧

Leaning over the injured boy, Pawel clasped his hands together. *Children, Lord? Has this world gone so crazy that children are now hunted like animals? Treated no better than machines?*

The child slept peacefully. He would survive. For now, anyway. Once he returned to the factory, it was anyone's guess how long he would live. There had to be a way for Pawel to help him. Protect him like *Pani* Palinska had begged him.

He rubbed his furrowed forehead. Up to this point, he hadn't participated in anything more nefarious than forging documents. Dangerous enough in itself. But spiriting away a child from a prison camp escalated his involvement in the underground to a new level.

What would Antonina say? Her image appeared before him like a picture show. In the softness of her gaze, he caught the empathy she would have for Zygmunt. And then she would narrow her eyes, a mother's fierceness in them. Willing to do anything to protect one of God's precious children. Like she would have protected Józef if she had the chance, even though he was a young man when he was ripped from them.

Her likeness faded. *Tak*, he would have to help this boy. But how? The Germans knew he was here. If he disappeared, Pawel would be the first one blamed. And if they discovered he was *Pani* Palinska's brother, she would be next.

His heart pounded and the throbbing in his ears matched it. *Nie*, wait, that was the door. An insistent, persistent knock. Pawel shoved back his chair and went to answer it.

Pan Fromm stood on the porch step, then strode into Pawel's home, his hands behind his back, the angles of his face hard, his eyes cold. Without warning, he spun on his heel. "Where is the boy?"

"Sleeping in the upstairs bedroom."

"Wake him and bring him here. He needs to return to work."

"Impossible. The child just lost a finger. His body must heal, and the wound must be kept clean. He'll stay here for at least a week." Pawel swallowed hard at his bold words.

Pan Fromm spoke through clenched teeth. "Perhaps you didn't understand me. The boy is returning to the factory with me. Now. I didn't ask for your personal or professional opinion. I'm a busy man. Bring him to me this instant." Fromm's voice rose until his words rang in Pawel's ears.

"I object. Chances are he won't survive."

"That's not my concern." Fromm waved away Pawel as if he swatted a fly. "He is a prisoner, not a boy to be coddled."

"Coddled?" Pawel's head might just explode. "He's eight."

Fromm struck Pawel across the cheek, his jaw shifting. "I will not tolerate impertinence. The child is plenty old enough to work. Get him. Now." Fromm reached for the weapon in the holster on his hip.

What choice was left? Pawel lifted his glasses and rubbed his forehead, then climbed the stairs, taking as much time as he dared. While the precious seconds wouldn't ensure Zygmunt's survival, Pawel had to do whatever he could to delay the boy's return to the factory, even if it was only a minute or two.

Pawel woke the sleepy child and helped him down the steps. "I don't feel good, Doctor." Zygmunt's face was whiter than any winter's snow.

Blood loss. Nothing Pawel could do about it. They reached the front hall, Zygmunt swaying on his feet. He collapsed into a pile on the floor.

Fromm scooped him up and carried him from the house.

Chapter Eighteen

The world swam around Teodor as he pulled the drill press down and the bit ate through the metal piece. The whirring of the machine lulled him until he nodded off, awakening a second later with a jerk as a gun was cocked next to his ear.

"Wake up."

He bolted upright. His tongue was thick.

The Nazi remained expressionless as he backed away. He should have shot Teodor, like Fromm had shot his fellow prisoner. Why hadn't he? Did this one possess an ounce of mercy?

Today the inspectors were expected. The day the Germans anticipated showing off how well the factory ran, how well the laborers worked, how much they helped the fatherland.

The day Teodor planned his most dangerous sabotage. If he could remember what he was going to do. If he could pull it off without falling over.

A movement out of the corner of Teodor's eye caught his attention. *Untersturmführer* Fromm led three black-uniformed SS officers onto the factory floor. Teodor returned his attention to his work. His heart pounded. He finished the piece and dropped it in the box, glimpsing the German quartet leaning over one of the presses.

A whistle blared, startling Teodor out of his stupor. As soon as it quieted, so did all the machines in the area. Lunch. Time for some lukewarm broth and a break for their aching necks.

"Achtung." *Untersturmführer* Fromm's bellow stopped the men

in their tracks. "Get back to work." The way he narrowed his eyes and set his jaw silenced them all.

The foursome resumed their inspection of the department.

Jerzy leaned over. "Now what?"

Teodor shrugged even as his stomach dropped. His thought had been to pour the dirt into the workings of the big machine in the middle of the room while the men were eating. As it was, the time was tight. He didn't want to be missed. Now Fromm disrupted his plans before he even put them into motion.

If he wanted to go through with the scheme, he would have to do it with Fromm and his cast of characters still in the room.

He couldn't wait until later in the day. If he did, the inspectors might be gone. For the shutdown to have maximum effect, he needed to gum up the works while the Germans were still here.

"Palinski."

He jumped at the sound of Fromm's voice in his ear. "*Tak*."

"Show these men your dexterity with a drill press." He turned and spoke to his comrades before returning his attention to Teodor. "I told them you were a leader in the shop. They are eager to see your skills."

Teodor swiped his damp hands on his dark-blue work coveralls and picked up an undrilled metal piece. He drew in a breath as he set the template into place and pulled the lever that drove down the bit. "That's all there is to it."

One of the officers, his black uniform pressed to perfection, his pants ballooning from the top of his boots, stepped forward, his broken Polish halting at best. "We have wrong pieces come from here."

Teodor's heart revved up more. "Wrong pieces?"

The man, much smaller and wirier than Fromm, said a few words in German.

With a gleam in his eyes, Fromm translated. "They don't fit. The holes are drilled wrong. This is a repeated mistake, on about 5 percent of what comes from this department."

Teodor swallowed hard. Had they caught him? He crossed his arms, mostly so they wouldn't see his hands shaking. He needed an excuse. Fast. If only his sleep-deprived mind would work. "Sometimes the template slips. It's impossible to detect with the eye, but it could render the piece unusable in its application."

Fromm relayed the message.

The man slammed his fist into his palm and bellowed. Teodor didn't need a translation. The sabotage was doing its work.

Fromm turned to Teodor. "This is unacceptable. And I'm holding you, as the leader of this group of pigs, responsible. Clean up these mistakes."

"With all due respect, the men are exhausted. With little sleep come small mistakes."

"This has been happening for weeks." A vein bulged on Fromm's neck. "Long before we upped the quota. I will not listen to excuses. The work must be done properly. We can't waste materials. See to it that there are no more improperly drilled holes, or you will think this place is a palace compared to where you end up."

Fromm stomped off, the three visitors trailing him.

A line of sweat worked its way down Teodor's spine as he resumed his drilling. He concentrated on slowing his breathing. After several minutes, his heart rate returned to normal.

Jerzy bent down to pick up another piece. "Too bad your plan won't work today."

"*Nie*, I'm going through with it."

Jerzy widened his eyes. "You are?"

Teodor motioned for him to be silent. They worked for several more minutes. All the time, Teodor watched the group of Nazis make their way around the room. Soon, they would be in a position with their backs to the machine he intended to disable.

He couldn't afford a single mistake, or Fromm would have a reason to make good on his threats.

The Germans moved to the far corner of the room and circled a man. They focused their attention on him.

Careful not to scrape his stool back, Teodor came to his feet. Ducking behind his coworkers, all the while hushing them, he zipped to the largest machine in the room. Earlier this morning, he had informed the operator of the plan. Keeping the overseers in his line of vision, he dug into his pocket for the dirt while the operator opened the oil line.

Teodor poured in the soil. Nothing happened.

The operator nodded, and a lazy smile crossed his face.

Teodor scurried in the direction of his drill press.

"Palinski, *halten sie.*"

Fromm.

He froze.

"What are you doing away from your station? Did I not direct everyone to stay put during the inspection?"

"I had to use the lavatory. There were no other guards to ask, and you were busy."

Fromm reached him in four giant strides. "Step out of line again ..."

At his low, slow words, the hair on Teodor's arms stood straight. Fromm didn't need to finish his threat.

And with that, the big machine screeched to a halt.

❧

Teodor rocked on the ocean, an ocean he had never seen, with black water and black sky all around. The wind whipped his hair, his shirt, his pants, so hard that he bent sideways. A piercing cry reached him, but he couldn't understand it.

And the rocking, the motion tossing him to and fro, never stopped.

"Palinski, wake up."

He jerked to consciousness and sat, almost bumping his head on the bunk above him. Sweat bathed his entire body. He'd fallen asleep as soon as the machine ground to a halt and the foreman had let the men retire early. "What ... what is going on?" He rubbed his eyes.

Untersturmführer Fromm wrenched Teodor's arms behind his back. "Let's go."

Teodor writhed and struggled to stay on his feet. "Where are you taking me?"

"*Schnell.*" Fromm led him from the room. A sudden iciness chilled Teodor's damp skin. He staggered.

His turn to be interrogated. Again.

Fromm pushed him into the wooden chair in a corner of the office. The Nazi paced in front of him, cracking his knuckles. "We know what you did."

Teodor crinkled his forehead. "What are you talking about?"

Fromm reached behind his desk and pulled out a whip. Teodor had never even used one on his stubborn oxen.

Crack. The whip struck the desk. "Next time, I will strike your back. It will go easier for you if you confess. We will get the truth out of you, no matter what it takes. You were responsible for the machine shutting down, weren't you?"

"*Nie.*"

Fromm jerked him to his feet and shoved Teodor against the wall. "You embarrassed me in front of my superiors, made me look incompetent. My father-in-law will never recommend me for a promotion now. And it's all your fault. Because of you, my career is ruined."

The whip met his back. He bit back a yelp as tears sprang to his eyes. He swallowed.

"You sabotaged the machine."

"*Nie.*"

Crack.

"And you are the reason the pieces sent to Germany do not fit. You lead this group, telling them to make mistakes."

"*Nie.*"

Crack. Teodor gripped the concrete block wall with everything he had. Pain shot from his back to every part of his body.

"You are nothing but a dirty Pole. A vile swine. If you tell me the truth, I may let you live. Were you involved in this sabotage?"

"*Nie.*"

Crack. Teodor's knees trembled, and he locked them to keep from slumping to the floor. Something warm and sticky trickled down his back.

"Why do you continue in your lies? Do you not know that I hold your life in my hand? I have no reason to keep you alive. There are plenty more where you came from. The sooner we are rid of you, the better for Germany."

Teodor slouched against the cool wall.

Fromm pulled him upright. "This is your last chance. The last time I will ask. What was your role in the sabotage?"

"None."

Crack. "Wrong answer. I warned you." *Smack. Smack. Smack.*

Teodor choked on his own scream. He fell to the cold hardwood floor. Darkness niggled at the edge of his vision.

Fromm stood over him, a sneer lifting his Hitler-like mustache. "You wife is a beautiful woman. You love her, don't you?"

This was a ploy to get him to admit to his guilt. How could he live if they touched her?

"You're devoted to her. You would do anything in the world for her. Wouldn't you?"

Fromm made a circuit of the room before returning to hover over Teodor. "Just as I hold your life in my hands, I hold hers. I control what happens to her. And what doesn't."

Bile rose in Teodor's throat.

"What a pity for such a pure, innocent woman to be sullied. Or tortured. Or killed. You wouldn't want that to happen, would you?"

Could he take that chance? *God, what can I do to save her?*

Fromm was right. He would do anything to ensure that nothing happened to his beautiful, beloved Natia.

Fromm slapped the whip against his palm. "I'm running out of patience, Palinski. Don't think your death will be fast and easy, for it will not. And don't believe hers will be either."

Every muscle in his body tensed. He couldn't draw a deep breath.

He clutched his chest, the same way Mama had when the Nazis had ransacked their house for the fun of it. And Teodor had stood by and done nothing.

Natia's song broke into his consciousness. All else faded. She was there, in his mind's eye, her chestnut hair drifting over her shoulder as she came to him. Sang to him. Loved him.

Hark'ning, and hoping that thou may persevere,
Naught else desiring, forever, forever.

If he didn't confess, if he didn't say the words, Fromm would silence her song.

"I did it."

♪♫♪

Chapter Nineteen

Elfriede flounced into the kitchen dressed in a grass-green chiffon gown, diamonds sparkling in her ears and on her wrists, a pair of black patent-leather peep-toes on her feet. Her hair, usually rolled all around, hung down tonight, soft waves cascading over her shoulder.

Meanwhile, a stray curl found its way into Natia's eyes as she labored over the stove on the sauerbraten and wiener schnitzel. She still wore her black Polish peasant work dress.

The vinegary odor of the food burned her nose. She wouldn't have been able to eat any of it, even if she'd been allowed.

"Smells good." Elfriede spun in a circle like a gleeful child on Christmas morning. She pranced to the stove and lifted the pot lid. She dipped her spoon in the sauce, raised a thin eyebrow, and squashed her eyes shut. "*Nie*. Salt. You see." She held out the spoon for Natia.

Her reaction matched Elfriede's. The dish needed more salt. She remedied that situation while Elfriede tasted the other dishes. "Good, good. Ready?"

Natia glanced into the dining room. Elfriede's best Dresden china sparkled on the table, sprays of pink, purple, blue, and yellow flowers painted along the rim. Candlelight from the tapers in the candelabra bathed the room and shone off the polished silver. Then she gazed at her sauce-stained apron and pushed the hair out of her face.

"Come with me." Elfriede disappeared into her bedroom.

Natia kissed Dominik's soft cheek as he slumbered in a large box stuffed with blankets on the kitchen floor. "You be a good boy while I'm gone." The baby smiled in his sleep.

Zygmunt had done the same thing. Was he even alive? Dr. Bosco told her how the Germans took him back to the factory not long after she left. He'd had no time to help her brother.

With all her might she pushed those thoughts away. Tonight she had to concentrate on surviving.

With halting steps, Natia crossed the threshold to the Fromms' room. "Do you need help?"

"*Nie.* I help you." Elfriede held up a simple black evening gown. "For you to sing."

"For me?"

She nodded. "Beautiful, *nie?*"

"*Tak*, it is." At Elfriede's insistence she slipped the creation over her head. Never in her life had she worn such a dress. The plain gown hung on her thin frame, but the softness of the velvet spoke of its quality. At the hip sat a large, red rose. Even on her wedding day, she had not worn anything so fine. "I can't."

"You must. Erich say you must look good."

"My shoes." She motioned to her ankle-high black boots.

Elfriede pulled a pair of red pumps from the bottom of the wardrobe. "Here."

Natia widened her eyes. She had never worn anything like them ever. "I'll change after dinner."

"After dinner, that's good." Elfriede laid the gown over her pink chenille bedspread.

Natia turned to go.

"*Nein.* Sit down." Elfriede pointed to a bench in front of a vanity mirror. "I do your hair."

"But dinner—"

"It will be fine." Before Natia could object, Elfriede grabbed a silver-handled brush and drew it through Natia's tresses. Over and over. She relaxed her shoulders. The ministrations carried her back to before the war. Teodor combed her hair like this after she lost each of the babies. And even further back in time, her mother brushed the knots out every night before bed. So gentle.

At the memories, tears clogged her throat. She had even combed Helena's hair this same way. What had become of her sister?

Elfriede set the brush aside and worked on rolling Natia's hair much like she did her own. After she secured each pin in place, she swiped a little pink lipstick across Natia's lips. "There. You beautiful now."

Natia stared at herself in the mirror. The new hairstyle was nice, rather flattering and becoming. But there was no hiding the fright in her eyes. She hurried upstairs to her room to don a fresh apron before she flew down to put the finishing touches on the meal.

Before she had given everything a final stir, *Pan* Fromm and his mates arrived.

Dear Lord, please help me make it through this night.

He entered the kitchen. "Is everything ready?"

"*Tak*, it is. Elfriede has tasted everything and approved." She said the words more to assure herself than him.

"She wouldn't know a good piece of veal from a bad one."

Natia's stomach flopped. But at least the butcher gave her a decent piece of meat. Of that, she could be sure. "Everything will be delicious. Trust me."

"I don't trust any Pole for anything. Why, this afternoon, one of the machines broke down. Dirt in the oil line. Strange, don't you think?"

Why was he telling her this? "I know nothing about machines. Even on the farm, we used animal power. We didn't have a tractor for the plowing or harvesting."

"Even stranger was that I caught your husband near the machine, far from his usual work station, just about the time the incident occurred."

Her breath caught. "What are you saying?"

"Nothing. Nothing at all. Just mentioning the coincidence."

She wiped the sweat from her hands and lifted the lid from one of the pots. "If you don't want me to make a mess of dinner or to miss a note when I sing, then please, don't make me nervous. Let me do my job."

He leaned over her shoulder and whispered, "And you had better do it right. Stellar. Perhaps you can atone for his sins." His breath tickled her neck.

She shivered, despite the heat in the room, then slid sideways, away from him, and retrieved a serving dish from the china cabinet. Dominik, now awake, giggled as he sat in his box, playing with a couple of spoons Natia had given him.

"I've taken care of the problem of your husband."

Crash. The platter dropped from her hands and shattered on the floor.

Pan Fromm slapped her across the face.

Dominik wailed as Natia inched away from *Pan* Fromm, her cheek still stinging. The gravy bubbled over on the stove, an acrid burning odor filling the room.

He hissed, "Shut up the kid and finish dinner." He marched from the room.

Natia picked up the baby. She couldn't sing to quiet him. Her eyes stung with unshed tears. But she wouldn't cry. She wouldn't let that man see how he humiliated her.

She pulled the gravy off the burner. Balancing a still-whimpering Dominik on her hip, she stirred the pot. There was enough salvageable that it wouldn't ruin dinner.

Elfriede floated in. The instant she spied Natia and the mess on the floor, she bit her lip. "What happened?"

Why bother to tell her the truth? She believed her husband to be a good man. If she told her he hit his slave, it wouldn't matter one way or the other. It wouldn't change her mind about him. She jiggled Dominik, who stopped crying. "Nothing. We have to get dinner on the table."

Elfriede went for a broom.

"*Nie*. You go there." She pointed to the dining room. "Sit down. Talk to the men. I'll bring the food in a moment."

"What about baby?"

"He'll be fine. The platter breaking startled him. He can play while I work." But if he started to whimper . . .

Elfriede shrugged and left for the dining room.

"Now, you be a good boy and play with your spoons." Natia smiled and Dominik flashed a grin as she set him on his blanket.

She plated the food and, balancing two dishes, brought them to the spread. Three German officers sat at the table, silver eagles, iron crosses, and colorful ribbons bedecking their dark uniforms. They studied her as she moved about the room, dishing out schnitzel and sauerbraten. They chattered in German, their attention fixed on her.

At least she couldn't understand their words. All the better. She poked between two of them to refill their water glasses. A little bit, she understood. *Pretty. Pole.*

Ouch. She squeaked, jumped backward, spilling some of the water. Heat rushed into her face. One pinched her where a man should never touch a woman who was not his wife.

Pan Fromm scowled at her. She swallowed the stream of words that begged to flow from her mouth. Elfriede chatted with the very handsome man next to her, either oblivious to the incident or choosing to ignore it.

The group ate and drank with gusto. She scurried in and out of the kitchen, each time avoiding the man who pinched her.

"More beer." *Pan* Fromm held up his cup. He had already had three glasses. How much more did he need? The man she avoided also held up his stein. For sure, he shouldn't have more. She returned from the kitchen with several new bottles and refilled the tankards.

Her feet ached. Her back cried in pain. A tendril of hair escaped its pins and caressed her cheek. How much more of this could she stand? Already, they were almost out of food.

She returned to the dining room and huddled in the corner. At long last, *Pan* Fromm backed away from the table and set his napkin on his plate. She moved forward to clear the plates.

Elfriede motioned her to her side. "You take this away." She pointed at her place setting. "Then you sing. Wash later."

Natia nodded even though her stomach jumped like a spring calf. What if she forgot the words? Or sang them wrong? How could she force the lyrics through her lips? Elfriede told her they were patriotic German songs.

If she dared, she would choose a Polish lament. But *Pan* Fromm would understand. So, she would act like a trained monkey and perform what would please them.

She cleared the table in short order and stacked the dishes in the sink. What a mess. Dominik rubbed his eyes and yawned. He held his hands up for her. "Oh, sweet little one. How nice that you want me, but what an inconvenient time." She picked up the sleepy child, who nestled into her shoulder.

"Here, I take him."

Natia spun around. Elfriede stood in the doorway.

"I hold him. You sing. He sit with me."

Who knew what *Pan* Fromm would think of the arrangement, but that was on Elfriede. So long as Dominik didn't fuss. Natia kissed his curly, dark head. "Be good for *Pani* Fromm."

"Come. You put on your dress and sing."

Natia closed and locked the door to the Fromms' bedroom and slipped the velvet creation over her head. Soft. Gentle. Almost like Teodor's touch.

She entered the living room, the stares of everyone on her. But they didn't weigh her down. They didn't suffocate her. Or drive the song away.

She drew in a deep breath and imagined herself sitting on the rise behind their house, overlooking the green countryside, sunset streaking the sky with pink and purple. Teodor sat beside her. She nestled into his embrace, breathed in his clean scent, like that of fresh air and pure water. Together, they dreamed of the future God would give them. Of the children they would raise. Of the work they would do. Of the love they would enjoy.

As she opened her mouth to sing, she captured each of those vignettes of her life. She hugged them close, clinging to them, drawing on them as the strange-tasting words rolled off her tongue.

Tonight, she sang for Teodor, as he had been, strong and confident as he'd worked in the fields. She sang for each of the children they'd left resting in the ground beneath the big oak tree. She sang for Poland, her beloved homeland.

Those may not have been the words the Germans in the room heard. But they were the words her heart sang.

The last note of the final piece reverberated through the room. Teodor, their children, their farm faded into the mist. Instead, four Nazi officers rendered polite applause.

Elfriede rose to her feet clapping even as she held Dominik. "Brava. Brava."

Dominik slapped his tiny hands together.

All three of the SS men glanced at the child. The one who pinched her glared hard at him. He spoke and gestured for Elfriede to hand him the baby.

Natia rushed to Elfriede's side. "I will take him away so he doesn't bother you." She snatched Dominik.

"*Halten sie.*" The man continued, but Natia only caught one word.

Jude.

Jew.

Chapter Twenty

Elfriede's insides turned to pudding at the single word her husband's guest uttered. *Jew.* She jumped from the davenport, clutching Dominik against her chest. This precious, precious child was no Jew. "What are you talking about? *Ja,* he is Polish, but he is not a Jew. Isn't that right, Natia?"

Their servant stood stock-still, her face white as a cloud against the borrowed black dress. *Nein, nein,* it couldn't be so. Not this child she loved. Natia wouldn't do that to her.

Within a couple of heartbeats, Natia's face flooded with color. Righteous indignation. "*Nein, nein Jude.* Papers."

Elfriede used her Polish to speak to Natia. "Take Dominik. Get papers. Now. Go."

Natia fled the room. Erich frowned in her direction, his face reddening as much as Natia's as he lifted his angular chin. But Elfriede wouldn't let him take away this child who had become as dear to her as her own life. Not like he had almost done before. "What is the meaning of this, Erich?"

He laughed. Forced, if you asked her. "I am sure *Obersturmführer* Obermann didn't mean anything by it. Dominik does have dark looks."

"Not uncommon in this area of the world."

"Let's talk about this in the kitchen, shall we? Gentlemen, enjoy another glass of schnapps." He steered her to the back of the house.

Rinsed dishes towered over the sink, teetering like the Leaning Tower of Pisa. Coffee bubbled on the back of the stove, the warmth of it easing the tension in Elfriede's shoulders. "I won't have that man insulting me in my home."

"I would remind you that I am entertaining very important people. Keep your voice down, and don't speak to me that way in front of them. This is not like you. I thought you understood what this night meant to me. To us. I'm trying to impress them so your *Vater* will promote me and send me back to the fatherland. I thought you wished to leave here."

"What I wish is not to be questioned about a child I'm allowing to live in my home."

He growled his next words. "*Nein*, my dear, you aren't allowing the child to live here. I am. And if I discover he is indeed Jewish, mark my words, that Polish girl who brought him here will be very sorry. Above all, I had better not find out that you knew about this, or you will be just as sorry. You should be worried about producing an Aryan child for the fatherland."

"Dominik has a Polish birth certificate. If that isn't proof, what is?"

"All kinds of papers are forged these days."

"A doctor would never do such a thing."

"Oh, I have no doubt there are plenty who would. I know of one for sure."

The tenor of his voice sent shivers skittering across her midsection. Not Dr. Bosco. He'd been nothing but kind. He wouldn't do such a thing.

Natia clomped down the stairs and into the kitchen, waving a piece of paper. "Here." She thrust it into Erich's hand and spoke to him in Polish about Dominik not being Jewish.

He studied it, and Elfriede stood on her tiptoes and peeked over his shoulder. A corner of the certificate was missing, and it was creased and water stained. "This is real, Erich. The woman who brought Dominik here had it in her coat pocket. She was wet, so the paper would have gotten crinkled."

He turned to her and crossed his arms. "Did you take the paper from her coat yourself?"

"*Nein*. The doctor brought it over later. He said he found it as he was preparing the body for burial."

"Then this is no proof." Erich moved to the coal stove and opened the door.

"Don't." Elfriede intercepted him and snatched the birth certificate out of his hand at the very last second.

He barreled at her. She sidestepped, but not fast enough. He pushed her toward the stove. Out of instinct, she braced herself with her free hand. A searing pain sizzled up her arm.

"*Untersturmführer* Fromm, is all well?" The officer, the one who had made an advance at Natia, hovered in the doorway. "I am sorely disappointed in the way you run your factory and your home. And if this is a Jewish child, there will be dire consequences to you."

"*Nein*, the boy is Polish. He has a birth certificate."

"But he has the look."

"He is Frau Palinska's nephew. And I had her vetted before I allowed her to stay here. No Jewish blood, I assure you."

"Are you calling me a liar?"

Erich straightened his shoulders. "Not at all. If I even suspected the child of being Jewish, I would dispose of him and the woman immediately. Never would I allow them under my roof. Dark looks don't necessarily mean Jewishness. Slav, *ja*, but not Jew, I assure you. Let's have another drink and forget about this incident." The two men left the room.

Elfriede clutched her burned hand. Tears bounded down her cheeks, matching those racing down Dominik's.

Natia balanced the baby on her hip and examined the injury. "Stay here." Elfriede didn't catch the rest of what she said, but she left the room.

Elfriede slouched into one of the kitchen chairs. She stared at the angry red line on her palm, now blistering. But the true ache was in her chest. What kind of man had she married? To do this to her and march out of the room like nothing was wrong. His job was more important than her.

Deep down, she'd known the truth all along. *Vater* had been thrilled when she first brought Erich home. At last, she had done something that pleased *Vater*. So she spent more time with Erich. They danced together. She touched her cheek where he had first kissed her under the moonlight. They enjoyed picnics and picture shows. He took her everywhere and presented her as *Oberführer* Ausburg's daughter.

Not Elfriede. But *Oberführer* Ausburg's daughter. The only daughter of a high-ranking Nazi officer who could give Erich the upward mobility and prestige he so desired.

And then ...

"Here. Let me see it again." Natia returned to the room, Dominik still on her hip, a bottle of tincture and a pile of gauze in her hands. She set the sleepy baby in the box and knelt beside Elfriede.

When Natia applied the salve, Elfriede sucked in her breath at the stinging in her palm.

"I'm sorry this happened."

"I am sorry. You sing so nice."

"*Dziękuję Ci.*" Natia's lips twitched, like she wanted to say more.

A loud laugh streamed in from the living room. Elfriede bent close to Natia. "Erich is bad." Her chest squeezed.

Natia touched her cheek and murmured words she didn't understand. "You will be fine."

"How? Erich hurt people."

Natia nodded in the direction of the living room entrance. "Not now. We'll talk later, when he is gone." With all the gentleness of a mother, she bandaged Elfriede's hand.

"Dominik not Jewish?"

Natia shook her head.

All this over an innocent child. Not a Jewish infant. The paper proved otherwise. Erich was wrong. An honorable doctor wouldn't forge a birth certificate. How did the paper get so weatherworn if it wasn't in the woman's pocket? That was the only explanation that made sense.

At least, the only one Elfriede allowed herself to believe tonight. There were other hard-enough truths to swallow.

The dark dampness of the prison cell seeped into Teodor's bones. The cold, the mustiness, had become part of his very being. No matter how long he lived, he would never be dry or warm again.

He huddled in the corner, the weight of aloneness pressing on him. For three weeks he hadn't seen or heard another soul, except when he was taken out and beaten. Was he all alone in an evil world?

Oh, Natia, Natia. The echo of her music filled the hollow places. The lullaby she had crooned on the hill overlooking their house. The love songs she whispered to him as they lay together in bed. The hymn she sang on the train. What was it again?

His foggy brain refused to bring the words to mind. But the melody of it buoyed him. Through parched, cracked lips, he attempted to hum a few measures. His vocal chords vibrated, resonating deep inside. Only he heard the music. He and God. Maybe, out in the world somewhere, Natia heard him singing too. Felt him with her in a way only two who had become one flesh understood.

If he could just remember the words.

He rested against the chilly wall, wincing at the welts and bruises on his back. No window brought in sunshine. Just a sliver of light from underneath and around the heavy iron door. Was it dawn or dusk? Midnight or midday? Who knew?

Did God even see him? Was he out there? Teodor dozed. The world of reality and the world of dreams merged. Natia was beside him. A smile lit her face. She laughed, twirled, sang. So very, very beautiful. And his. That the Lord would give her to him was beyond belief. Teodor reached out for her.

She vanished.

"*Nie. Nie.* Come back to me, my love."

"Shut up in there." The first words spoken to him since he had arrived. He would cry if he had the moisture in his body to produce tears.

He scratched at the fleas and lice that bit him. They were his only companions. As a boy, he had heard of flea circuses. Perhaps he could train some of these insects to amuse himself.

He slept more, awakening with a jolt. Why did he have to return to consciousness? Slumber brought a respite, a release from this torture.

A key scraped in the lock. That must be what woke him. The door creaked open on rusty hinges. A guard entered, dressed in the clothing of the Gestapo, a belt around his gray-green coat, tall, polished black boots on his feet. He pulled Teodor to a standing position and dragged him from the cell.

Another beating awaited him.

The muscular guard squeezed Teodor's upper arm harder.

Maybe he was going to his death? The thought was more appealing than any other, save for release.

The guard pulled open another heavy door and pushed Teodor outside. His pulse accelerated. He took in a long, low drag of fresh air.

Just at the edge of the horizon, the sun put on a show of red, yellow, and orange. Never in his life had he witnessed such a spectacular sight. Rising or setting, it didn't matter. He would spend his last moments on earth enjoying the dazzling beauty of God's glory.

A glory he would soon behold with his very eyes.

Leaving Natia was his only regret.

"Strip."

Teodor turned to his captor. "What?" Maybe the man's Polish was poor.

"Strip. Everything off. *Schnell.*"

Humiliation and more humiliation. Even in death the Nazis refused their fellow human beings dignity. He complied with the order. A brisk winter wind bit his bare flesh. He tried to cover his shame, but the guard tied his hands behind his back.

Then he pushed Teodor forward, the flashlight casting a warm glow in the bitter night. A shiver coursed through him. The beam of light rested on a deep, old metal washtub. "Sit."

What a strange request. What was going on? Maybe this was just another vision. Another dream. But then the guard kicked him on his bare rear end. The pain of the jackboots meeting his flesh was too real.

To avoid another kick, Teodor stepped into the tub and sat. His buttocks met the cold tin. He shuddered and stretched out his legs. He could just manage to peer over the edge of the tub.

"This is what we do to Polish pigs like you." An instant later, the coldest water he'd ever felt engulfed him.

Chapter Twenty-One

*N*atia hugged Dominik tighter and pulled his blue knit cap over his ears as they left the house in the direction of the factory. Since the night of the party, she kept the baby out of *Pan* Fromm's sight as much as possible.

Her head still rang with his accusation. Jew. The officer saw right through their ruse. Dominik's coloring was dark enough to arouse suspicion. And the circumstances of his arrival on the Fromms' doorstep were shady enough to cast doubt on his identity.

Their only saving grace had been the man's threat against *Pan* Fromm.

If he hadn't been afraid for his own life, she might be in one of those awful camps *Pani* Rzeźnikowa had told her the rumors about. Auschwitz. Mauthausen.

A shudder wracked her.

Natia hurried down the street. A cold wind tore at her. Darkness was drawing in. For the past few weeks, Elfriede had retired to her room, the shades drawn, refusing most food. Tonight, however, she requested some beef soup. With any luck, *Pani* Rzeźnikowa would have a bone so Natia could make the broth. Elfriede had dropped too much weight.

A presence pressed on her, like someone followed her. She stopped and listened. The town lay silent, awaiting curfew. But still, someone's gaze pierced her like pinpricks on her skin. She spun around. There was no one. The road in front of the factory was empty.

She must be imagining things, was maybe even going crazy.

Shaking away the feeling, Natia gazed at the now-familiar rows of windows blinking in the factory facade. She had never come this late. Would Teodor be in the barracks? Or was he working? The drone of the machines, the smoke from the stack never lessened except for Sundays. That was the only day the place sat quiet.

She had to try. Had to see if he would answer.

> *When he leaves me, how lonely,*
> > *Do I long for him only!*
> *Was a sweetheart e'er so fine?*
> *And the sweetheart, he is mine!*
> *Was a sweetheart e'er so fine?*
> *And the sweetheart, he is mine!*

Only the hum of machinery and the call of a whistle inside the plant answered her. Not Teodor. Weeks had passed since he'd returned her song. For a long moment, she stared at the window where he had once appeared.

But not tonight.

Not any of the days or nights she'd come since the party. Where could he be? Even if his shift had changed, she'd tried so many different times of day, she was bound to have found one when he was in the barracks.

Was he ill? Had he been injured? Possibly, but why would that keep him from her?

Was he . . .?

Nie, nie, nie. She squeezed Dominik, fought down the rush of tears, and forced her lungs to breathe. There had to be another explanation. He was fine. Still in the factory, working hard, surviving, just as she was, until the heavenly Father would reunite them.

That's what she sang. That's why she told him to hang on. He would do that for her. He would do everything he needed to do to make it back to her.

He must still be at work. That had to be the reason he didn't reply. The Nazis must be slaving them close to twenty-four hours a day. Her poor husband. When this horror ended and they returned to their sweet farm, she would prepare a large meal for him with pierogi, tripe soup, and *karpatka*. Fill him up. She would rub his back and his feet. Would pamper him until the memory of this nightmare faded.

She could almost taste the sweetness of the potato and onion in the pierogi and the silky creaminess of the cream cake. Not only would she do it for him, but she would do it for the rest of her family.

Her family. Where was Zygmunt? How was he doing? Had his hand healed? And what about the others? Had they heard her song? Were they elsewhere in the bowels of this dungeon?

The dream of being reunited spurred her on to *Pani* Rzeźnikowa's place. She was just drawing the blackout shades when Natia arrived. She cracked the door. "What can I do for you so late?"

"I'm sorry to be a bother. Do you have a beef bone? *Pani* Fromm has been ill but is now asking for some soup. I don't have anything in the house for stock."

"Come in, and I'll see what I can do. And such a chilly night to be out with the child. It's warmer in here, though I have banked the fire. At least you can get out of the wind."

Natia embraced the older woman. "How are you doing?"

"Lonely. This place isn't the same without my husband, like all the life has been sucked out of it." *Pani* Rzeźnikowa's eyes shimmered, but she swallowed and controlled her grief.

Would Natia be able to do so in a similar situation? "I understand."

"My son comes to help out with the butchering, but it's not the same."

"How can you endure the loss?"

"With God's help. He's here with me, even in the loneliest times, upholding me. Taking care of me."

Mama always said God took care of them, and *Pani* Rzeźnikowa believed the same. Could Natia? Even though he had stolen her children?

"I dream of the day Karol and I will walk the streets of gold in heaven together."

"And I dream of the day Teodor and I walk the streets of Piosenka together with Dominik." She kissed his cool cheek. "How would you like that, little one?"

Pani Rzeźnikowa raised a single gray eyebrow, all traces of wistfulness gone. "You are going to keep the child?"

"Where else would he go? We don't know who his mother was. Most of his family probably is gone somewhere or ..."

"How will your husband react?"

"He has always wanted a house full of kids. He's seen Dominik. He'll be thrilled. One more to put around our table." And not in their graveyard, Lord willing.

"I was thinking more about *Pani* Fromm. Won't she want to keep Dominik? She and *Pan* Fromm don't have children either."

Natia shook her head, more to clear that thought from her brain than to dismiss *Pani* Rzeźnikowa's idea. "He would never take him. His looks are too Slovak. Not nearly Aryan enough. They couldn't Germanize him, like is known to happen with some Polish children." One small blessing. Some parents had their little ones ripped away to be taken to Germany, made to be the children of Aryan parents.

Pani Rzeźnikowa touched Natia's chin. "I am sorry to make you sad. I want you to be prepared, that is all."

"That's not why I'm sad."

"What is it then? You're so anxious."

"I hate to pour my troubles on top of yours."

"The Lord tells us to bear each other's burdens."

Mama would have agreed. Natia leaned against the wall. "Teodor didn't answer me again tonight. I've sung to him almost every day for the past three weeks, and he hasn't replied. He's always sung back to me. Even a little bit. Where is he? What is going on with him?"

Pani Rzeźnikowa took Dominik in her arms and drew Natia in an embrace. She breathed in the unique scent of meat and soap and mother. How long had it been since a woman had cared about her like this? Natia trembled from head to toe. "Why? Why is God allowing this? I don't understand, but I want it to stop. Just to wake up in the morning and find out this was a horrible nightmare."

"We all feel like that from time to time. But this is no dream. The Lord is testing us."

"Couldn't he have tested us in our own homes? In fact, he did test me by taking my babies from me. So why this?"

"I can't answer that. Only the good Lord knows. But all of this is within his will. Even my Karol's death. We must surrender ourselves to him."

Natia pushed out of *Pani* Rzeźnikowa's embrace. "I cannot believe that he would will this."

"If he didn't, then he's not in control of the world. And I couldn't live in a world like that. Only that thought sustains me in my loss."

"Take a look around. Does it appear like he's in control?"

"To our mortal eyes, it may not seem so. But he is."

On this point, Natia couldn't agree with *Pani* Rzeźnikowa. This just couldn't be God's eternal plan for her life.

❧

Bone-rattling shivers rocked Teodor, stirring the icy water surrounding him. The guard stood over him, no doubt to make sure he wouldn't climb out. A long greatcoat covered the Nazi. He pulled down the flaps from his hat. Thick gloves warmed his fingers.

Teodor couldn't control the quivering. His feet and hands went numb long ago. His brain too. There was only cold, ice, and more cold.

Natia appeared beside him once again. She smoothed back his hair and kissed his forehead. "I'm here, *moje serce*. All will be well. I promise. Don't leave me. Please, don't leave me."

He didn't leave. She did.

He couldn't stop the chattering of his teeth long enough to call out to her. *Come back! Come back!* She didn't listen.

A heavy drowsiness descended, pushing him farther into the water. He shook his head. *Nie*, he had to remain awake. To sleep would be to die. He wouldn't give his captors that satisfaction. What he needed to do was think. Maybe the fleas and lice on him and his clothes were freezing to death.

Not that kind of thinking. Beautiful thinking. About the future. The days when this nightmare would end, and he would be with Natia once more. On frigid winter nights, they would snuggle together under their quilt, her body warming his. She would hold him close, so close her heart would beat against his chest.

When spring came, they would take picnics outside, the bright Polish sunshine baking their skin. They would lie on a blanket and stare at the cloudless blue sky. Several children would play in the grass beside them. Laughter, singing, love. What a wonderful life they would have, little ones bringing them the greatest joy. The longing tore at his heart.

And then, when they were very, very old, they would sit together in front of the fire, the logs crackling in the hearth, the heat of the flames radiating to them. They would hold hands as their grandchildren clambered onto their laps, kissing them with sticky, sweet lips.

His shivering slowed.

"Wake up, no sleeping allowed." With his rifle, the guard banged on the metal tub, rousing Teodor. The present crashed like a wave around him.

Oh, God, when will it end? Take me home now, Lord. But Natia …

That hymn. He needed the words. The melody swelled, the

notes reverberating in his bones, but the words remained frozen in the recesses of his mind. He had to think of that day in the train, his wife beside him. So small, so fragile in his arms.

He hummed the tune, making as little noise as possible. No need to rile up the guard. The first phrase, and the second. Something about God helping. Our Savior. Wait, wait, wasn't that it? He sang the hymn.

> *God, my Lord, my strength,*
> *My place of hiding, and confiding,*
> *In all needs by night and day;*
> *Though foes surround me,*
> *And Satan mark his prey,*
> *God shall have his way.*

Yes, foes certainly surrounded him. He gazed at the guard, who clutched his weapon and stared straight ahead. He must have drawn the short straw to stand here and watch Teodor. Did he have family at home? A wife and children he tried to take care of and protect?

What a thought. Maybe this man was nothing more than a husband and a father watching out for those he loved.

What could have brought him to this place?

Through chattering teeth, Teodor sang with gusto.

> *Christ in me, and I am freed*
> *For living and forgiving,*
> *Heart of flesh for lifeless stone,*
> *Now bold to serve him,*
> *Now cheered his love to own,*
> *Never more alone.*

Rifle still in hand, the Nazi spun a quarter of a turn. He parted his lips and furrowed his brow. Maybe he knew the hymn, recognized the tune. Whatever the case, he didn't stop Teodor from singing. He started the next verse.

> *Up, weak knees and spirit bowed in sorrow!*
> *No tomorrow shall arise to beat you down;*

By the second line, the soldier blended his bass voice with Teodor's tenor. Though the language was different, the thought was the same. Teodor stopped and gulped. Could it be the song touched the guard's heart? The German nodded for Teodor to continue. Together, they sang the rest of the song.

God goes before you and angels all around;
On your head a crown.

For several minutes after they sang the last word, the world lay silent. Not a person stirring, an animal calling, a breeze blowing.

Teodor didn't breathe.

Neither did the guard. But his facial features softened, and his shoulders relaxed. He shifted his weight from one foot to the other, then turned to Teodor. "That was my mother's favorite hymn."

"My wife's too."

"Every day, she sang it as she worked. Whether she hung laundry on the line or baked bread or swept the floors, those words were on her lips. And what a beautiful voice she had."

"Natia's rivals the angels' chorus."

"What am I supposed to do?" The guard whispered the words.

Teodor allowed the question to hang in the air.

"'Christ in me ... Heart of flesh for lifeless stone ... Now bold to serve him.'" He took two steps in Teodor's direction. Then he stooped and set down his firearm. He slid off his coat, held it out, and turned his back. "Get out."

For a moment, Teodor couldn't move.

The man hissed, "Get out now."

Teodor sprang into action, climbing from the tub. The soldier untied Teodor's hands, and he slipped the coat over his bare body. Compassion. Dignity. Almost too much to believe. A miracle. Perhaps God was watching out for him after all.

The man turned to him. "I'm *Hauptmann* Maas. Call me Wilm. I have to take you back to your cell, but I will bring you a hot cup of coffee. And get you warmer clothes. I'll ask to interrogate you from now on."

Teodor couldn't force his mouth to move so he could speak. Kindness from the most unlikely source.

Wilm led him into the building and down the dingy hall and slid the coat from Teodor's shoulders. "We must be careful. Act the part. Both our lives are on the line."

Teodor shivered once again.

♪♫♪

Chapter Twenty-Two

A grimness settled over the Fromm household, much like the turbulent weather outside. This darkness was a physical presence, clouding them, covering them. Natia pulled her sweater tighter as she rolled out the egg noodles.

Christmas had come and gone without joy. Only *Pan* Fromm had exhibited much holiday spirit, and that might be due to the quantity of rum and eggnog he consumed.

Dominik crawled around the kitchen, over to Natia, and held on to her leg to stand. He bounced and giggled. She clapped the flour from her hands and picked up the little boy. "What is it, my sweet? Would you like a rye husk?"

Dominik babbled in reply.

"Very well, then, since you asked so nicely." Natia went to the cupboard and got out a piece of dried bread.

From down the hall, Elfriede's bell tinkled. These days, she seldom left her room. She wore Natia out with her constant demands. "Come on. Let's go find out what she wants." With the baby in her arms, Natia entered the darkened room, the blackout shades pulled down, the bed unmade, the white-and-blue quilt in a lump at the edge of the mattress.

"There you are. I want cup of coffee." Elfriede's blonde hair hung in greasy strands around her face. How long had it been since she'd washed and combed it? Her cheekbones jutted from her thin face.

"And I'll get you something to eat. Then, after lunch, I'll wash your hair and get you dressed. Get out of bed and start living."

"Why you so mean?"

"Mean? Hardly. I've done everything you've asked and more. All these weeks, I've held my tongue. But not anymore. You are in this bedroom, away from your husband, away from the world. No life."

"My life not good."

Natia closed the door and set Dominik on the floor to eat his rusk. "Maybe not. But you can't give up. You must keep going. It's what I tell myself every day."

"Why? My husband is bad man. He does not love me. He does not love anyone. Only himself. What happens to me? Why is he so bad?"

Natia sat on the bed beside Elfriede. She held her bony hand. "I don't know the answers. I have questions too. How could the world have gotten so topsy-turvy? The opposite of as it should be? We have to survive. That's all I know. I promised my husband that. I promised myself that. And now, I've promised Dominik." Elfriede probably understood few of her words. "You must live."

"But how? Why?"

"Day by day. I don't know if my husband is dead or alive. If he's alive, I have no idea where he is." Her heart clenched. She couldn't allow herself to think the worst. If she started believing that, she would drop to the floor in a puddle and never get up. To get out of bed each morning, she had to cling to that sliver of hope that Teodor was alive somewhere.

"You have love. Your husband loves you. I have nothing."

True, Natia wouldn't trade places with Elfriede for anything in the world. At the very least, she had known genuine, passionate love for a few years.

"Go away. Leave me alone. Let me die."

"*Nie.*" Natia shot to her feet. "I won't let you."

Dominik crawled to the bed and pulled himself to a standing position. A brief smile flashed across Elfriede's oval face. Natia picked up the child and placed him in Elfriede's lap. She kissed the baby's dimpled cheek and murmured to him in German.

Natia's stomach flipped. She'd done what she could to keep Elfriede from getting attached to Dominik. If she fell too much in love with the child, Natia stood to lose him. Another little one would be ripped from her arms. Even though she told *Pani* Rzeźnikowa that she didn't believe *Pan* Fromm would allow the child to become part of his family, the truth remained that if Elfriede truly wanted Dominik, there might be nothing Natia could do to prevent it.

Natia's breath came in short spurts, because on the other hand, she couldn't allow Elfriede to shrivel like an old woman without hope. Dominik cheered her, brought her out of her depression, if even for a few moments. Natia left to prepare some lunch, Elfriede and Dominik playing on the bed.

Two hours later, Elfriede sat in a chair in the living room, her hair brushed and loose around her shoulders, Dominik dozing on her lap.

"Do you feel better?"

"*Tak*. Good not to be in bed. But what about Erich?"

"What about him?"

"I am scared of him. Scared for you. And Dominik." Elfriede kissed the boy's forehead.

"I can take care of myself. And him." But could she? How long before *Pan* Fromm deduced the truth. Then what? Natia shuddered and pushed the thought to the back of her mind. Mama would say, *"Hidden from the eyes, out of the heart."* And Mama wasn't one to worry about anything. Natia swallowed. How difficult that had become.

She returned to the kitchen to start dinner. Even the German officers now had a tough time getting food. She had very little meat for tonight's meal. The flour in the tin was running low.

The front door banged open. Heavy footfalls crossed the living room.

Elfriede spoke to her husband in German, words Natia still didn't understand.

Pan Fromm answered her in his native tongue. His tone was harsh. Hard. Angrier than ever.

He stomped into the kitchen and strode in her direction. "There you are." He slapped her, and her eyes stung with tears. "You swine, you scum of the earth. I should do away with you and your husband right now."

Natia backed away until she hit the wall.

"You and your kind are the rottenest, the lowest of all people, no better than the Jews. The world will be a better place without you." He raised his hand to strike her.

She slumped to the floor. How had she angered him? "*Nie*, please, I didn't do anything." She covered her head. "Don't hurt me."

"Just what I don't want. A sniveling, whining, begging pig."

Mama would say, "*Mądry Polak po szkodzie.*" Smart Pole after the damage is done.

"You sicken me. Don't tell me you don't know what is going on. I've followed you to the factory. For weeks now. Yes, I know how you stop and sing. And I'm not so foolish as to miss the message in your words. What kind of code are you sending?

"All along, I thought your husband was responsible for the sabotage. He confessed. I punished him. But maybe it was you telling him what to do. Spying on me. Passing on my secrets."

"I did no such thing. Only sang to my husband words of love."

"Have you ever heard of Auschwitz?"

Natia froze. Was he going to send her there? Was that how he had punished Teodor?

❧

At the sound of her husband's voice reverberating throughout the house, Elfriede set Dominik on the rug. The child screamed. Elfriede ignored him and rushed into the kitchen.

Erich stood over Natia, who huddled in the corner. He raised his hand, about to strike her.

Elfriede dove forward, between Erich and Natia. "Stop it, Erich. Don't hurt her."

"What are you doing? She is a spy. Machines break down. Pieces are milled wrong. I blamed it on her husband, until I realized that when she sings to him she's passing my secrets."

"That's nothing but your wild imagination." The blood whooshed in her ears. "She doesn't know about your work. She doesn't speak German. She can't even read."

"Don't let her fool you. She can pretend she doesn't understand, but she does. A little infiltrator, that's what she is. Worming her way into our house to bring the fatherland to its knees. I won't allow it. This time, not the factory but the extermination camp."

"You're drunk. Don't come near me unless you're stone-cold sober. I picked her out of the crowd when she first arrived. She didn't have anything to do with coming here, couldn't have known that I decided to bring her into our home. Don't delude yourself with your fantasies."

He leaned closer to her and whispered in her ear, "You are deluded, my dear. That woman will ruin us."

Shivers raced down her arms. "I will keep her with me in the house. How is that for a compromise? And don't speak of anything war related here. I don't need to know." She didn't want to know, especially about those death camps. "Don't send her away. You'll see things better in the morning when your head is clearer." She pushed against his shoulders, and he stumbled backward.

"Fine." He pointed at her, his finger like an arrow to pierce her heart. "But she is not to go anywhere near that factory ever again. If I catch her outside of these walls, I will kill you both. Since you want to stick up for a Jew-loving, filthy, swine Pole, you can share her fate."

He staggered out of the kitchen. A few moments later, the bedroom door slammed shut.

Chapter Twenty-Three

Summer 1944

Teodor lay on the straw-filled pallet in the stifling infirmary at the factory and stared at the water-stained ceiling. Wilm had been true to his word. For months, he had brought him extra rations. The torture stopped. But the loneliness didn't. And Wilm could do nothing about the prison conditions. Sleep, that blessed relief, came hard. Broken men screamed day and night. If you could tell what time it was. Almost impossible. And the pests. There was no way Wilm could eradicate them.

Teodor wiped away the sweat that trickled down his temple and along his jawline. Without warning, he found himself released and back at the factory. Wilm had done what he could. He had saved Teodor's life. But he couldn't, or wouldn't, free him.

This place was either freezing or roasting. No happy medium. And most of the summer stretched in front of them.

He scratched at one of the many red marks on his arms. Fleas, lice, who knew what else. And the reason he lay in this oven of a room. Quarantine. They didn't want him back at work enough to risk spreading the typhus those bugs brought.

So here he was, alone again.

But maybe Natia would come. Perhaps he would hear her voice and get to answer her and let her know he was alive. She must have been frantic all these months when she didn't get any response.

A soft knock came at the door. "*Pan* Palinski?"

Teodor sat up. The voice was familiar. Polish. "Come in."

Dr. Bosco stepped inside and closed the door. "It's good to see you again."

Teodor stood and shook the man's hand like a well pump. "I can't tell you how wonderful it is to see anyone, much less a kind face."

"For a man who has been in prison, you're looking well."

Teodor stepped toward the doctor and spoke so only he could hear. "A kind guard took pity on me, brought me extra rations, and saw to it that my torture stopped."

"Torture?"

"How is my wife? Do you see her or hear from her?"

"From time to time, but not much lately. They must be well, because they haven't sent for me."

Teodor's arms broke out in gooseflesh. "It's enough to know she is alive. She will come to me then, at some point."

"I assume so. Now to get down to business. They brought me in to make sure you don't have typhus."

"I figured that was why. As eager as they are to be rid of us, it's curious the Germans are so concerned about the disease."

Pawel snapped open his black doctor's bag, took out a thermometer, and placed it under Teodor's tongue. "That they are. And for good reason. I heard that an outbreak at another camp decimated their workforce. They had to shut down the plant for several days until those remaining alive recovered enough to resume their duties. That's the reason they segregate the Russians, who often bring the illness with them." He withdrew the thermometer. "Your temperature is normal."

"I can tell you I'm healthy."

Pawel held up a finger for silence as he took out his stethoscope and listened to Teodor's heart and lungs. "Everything sounds good."

The doctor leaned close to examine Teodor's ear. "Did you know the Russians are knocking on the door of the prewar Polish border and that the British and Americans are in France?"

"Wilm whispered something along those lines to me. So it is true?"

"Germany will be squeezed in the middle until she is forced to surrender. If all goes well, it shouldn't be too many more months until the Soviets march into town. Hold on a little while more. The war is almost over."

Could he? Could any of them? The war might not end soon enough. "Could you do me a favor?"

∽

Summer's heat pressed on Natia as she sat on the narrow mattress in the tiny attic. Dominik toddled around the room, chattering and carrying a rag doll she had sewn. His damp curls clung to his sweaty forehead.

If there were space, Natia would pace like the caged tigers at circuses she'd heard about. Because that was what she was. The Fromms might as well have chained her to the bed for all the freedom she had. Months had passed since she last left the house. Not even a minute of sunshine bathed her skin.

Should she run away? Take Dominik, get as far from this place as possible, and wait for the war to end? She would, if it was only her life on the line. If *Pan* Fromm had only threatened her, she would have been gone long ago. When peace came, she would find Teodor.

If he was alive. With everything inside of her, she worked to bring his face to mind. The sound of his voice. The softness of his touch.

She failed. Was that because he had left her forever? Another good-bye she hadn't been able to say? She squished her eyes shut to force away the thought. But it popped up again, over and over.

Elfriede had shared with her what her husband told her. The Russians were advancing. If they got too close, he was going to send her to their chalet in Germany. Worry had edged Elfriede's words, because the Americans were also progressing from the west.

The war was coming to an end. Perhaps the Soviets were nearing their small village and their farm. Natia could go home and wait for Teodor there.

But then Elfriede reminded her of *Pan* Fromm's threat. How he would kill them both if Natia left the house. Had he really said that, or did she fabricate it so Natia would stay? Truth was a difficult commodity to come by these days.

What should she do? What *could* she do?

And if she left, would she be giving up any chance of finding her family? Months had passed since she had word of Zygmunt, and over a year since she had seen *Tata* and Helena.

Dominik grabbed Natia's hairbrush from the end of the bed and put it in his mouth.

"*Nie, nie.*" She took it back. "That's not for you. You play with your baby." She handed Dominik the rag doll.

"Natia?" Elfriede stood on the other side of the door.

"Come in."

Elfriede entered and sat on the floor. She tugged on her hands and bit her lip. "It is hot in here."

"Very hot."

"You can sleep downstairs."

And relinquish her privacy for the cooler living room couch? Never. *Pan* Fromm used the spare bedroom for an office, and sometimes he slept in there. Here, at least, she could lock the door and rest well at night. "*Nie, dziękuję Ci.* I'm fine. The summer doesn't last too long."

Elfriede crossed and uncrossed her legs. "What is wrong?"

Natia furrowed her brow and shook her head.

"You are not happy. You do not sing. You work and not smile."

How did she explain to her that grief drew the song from her lips, the song from her heart, the song from the very depths of her soul? That her being was as dry as the Russian steppes in summer. Elfriede's people had stolen Natia's home, her family, and every speck of joy. "I can't go outside. I can't sing to my husband. I won't be happy until I see Teodor and the rest of my family. Until I can go outside. Hear the birds. Feel the grass between my toes."

"I don't know what to say. I want you happy. I want you to sing."

To find her happiness again, God needed to restore to her everything he had snatched from her.

"I like you here."

"I miss my home."

"That, I understand. But what can I do? Erich, he will not let you go. And if you go, they bring you back maybe. Or somewhere else."

That speech was the most Polish Elfriede had ever spoken. And the truth. "I want to know my husband is alive. He might be dead." Her stomach clenched. *Nie*, he couldn't be gone. She would know it, would feel it in the very depths of her soul. She clung to the rope of hope hanging over the yawning chasm of despair, praying she didn't fall even though her hands were raw and bloody. "I don't know where he is."

Elfriede side hugged Natia. "This war is hard, *nie*? How can we understand? You are nice. I like you. I help you. But what can we do?"

"My mother always quoted Psalm 30 verses 4 and 5."

"Wait. I get my Bible." Elfriede clomped down the stairs and back up a moment later, her red, leather-bound Bible in her hand. She flipped the pages and found the passage. Though the words were different, the sentiment was the same. Elfriede read while Natia recited. "'Sing unto the Lord, O ye saints of his, and give thanks at the remembrance of his holiness. For his anger endureth but a moment; in his favour is life: weeping may endure for a night, but joy cometh in the morning.'"

Natia gasped for air, her chest swelling. Two very different people in very different circumstances but bound by this common faith. Sharing the same words in different languages. The beauty and the pain of it. What might they have been in another time and place?

Elfriede rested her Bible on her lap and caressed the page. "So you sing, and we give thanks. What we do." She bowed her head, and Natia followed suit. "Thank you, God, for helping us. We don't know what to do. Natia want her husband. My husband is bad. But you are good. You show us."

Natia worked to control her emotions so she could speak. "You know how much I miss Teodor, Lord. I don't know if he's dead or alive. Somehow, Father, let me know where he is and how he is. Give us strength to do what we have to do."

The little alarm clock on the table beside the bed *tick-tocked* away the minutes as they sat without saying a word, each lost in their own prayers. While the verses promised joy, that sensation didn't flood Natia's heart.

"Hello? *Pani* Fromm? *Pani* Palinska? Is anyone home?"

Natia bolted upright. Dr. Bosco? What did he want?

♪♫♪

Chapter Twenty-Four

After several failed attempts at knocking, Pawel cracked open the Fromms' front door and called inside. "*Pani* Fromm? *Pani* Palinska? Is anyone home?"

A little stirring sounded from upstairs, and a few minutes later, the women entered the living room. They both smiled at him, a little sad, a little weak, but smiles nonetheless. *Pani* Fromm waved him in, Dominik in her arms. "Welcome, Dr. Bosco. The baby is not sick. Why you come?"

"We're all well." Natia glanced around the room. Was she looking for someone?

"Is *Pan* Fromm home?"

"*Nie*. My husband works. Natia, we have coffee."

Pani Palinska turned to fetch the refreshments.

"Wait. I need to speak to you, *Pani* Palinska." He doffed his felt fedora and swallowed. "Alone, if I may."

Pani Fromm bit the inside of her cheek. "I don't know. What you have to talk about?"

He couldn't tell *Pani* Palinska his news in front of the German woman, especially since her husband ran the factory. *Nie*, this was for her ears only. "A personal medical matter."

"I don't understand."

"About her."

"Fine. I take Dominik to kitchen. But you don't say anything bad." *Pani* Fromm scuttled into the next room. Not far enough away for his tastes, but it would have to do.

"Please, can we sit down?"

Pani Palinska gestured for him to take a place on the couch and positioned herself in the flowered wing chair across from him. "What do you need to speak to me about? I've been fine, as fine as one can be in these times."

"You're thinner than the last time I saw you."

"I could say the same of you." She pursed her lips. No use in pursuing that line of questioning anymore. Everyone experienced low food rations. That's how it was, with the Russians pressing in from one side and the Allies from the other.

"I need to speak quietly, so *Pani* Fromm doesn't hear us. Her husband summoned me to the factory this morning to treat a patient. That patient was your husband."

She covered her wide-open mouth. "He's alive?"

"When was the last time you heard from him?"

"Before Christmas. I thought, I thought ... You said he was a patient. What's wrong?"

"He spent the last six months in prison. While I tried to get him to tell me about the ordeal, he didn't say much. I imagine it was horrific. He's thin, but not as thin as you would expect. A kind guard took pity on him and fed him." He almost told her about the torture, but she didn't need to know.

"He's ill?"

"*Nie*. He's healthy, much to my surprise. Covered in flea and lice bites, but not sick, by God's grace alone."

"Then why did they send for you?"

"The Germans fear an outbreak of typhus, like the one the Russians brought."

She slumped against the back of the chair, closed her eyes, and moved her lips. No doubt sending up a prayer of thanksgiving.

"He told me to tell you that he misses you and loves you."

Dishes clanked in the kitchen. "You want coffee?"

"*Nie, dziękuję Ci, Pani* Fromm. We're fine." Pawel returned his attention to the woman in front of him. Her hands shook as she finger-combed her dark, loose hair.

"I want to see him."

"I'm sure you do, but it's impossible. I don't know how long they'll hold him in quarantine before they release him to the floor. If I take you to him, you put not only yourself at risk, but him."

"I can't go sing to him anymore."

"Why not?"

She brushed her cheek. "*Pan* Fromm has forbidden me from leaving the house, ever, under any circumstance. If I do, he will kill not only me, but also *Pani* Fromm. How can I disobey when another woman's life depends on my absolute obedience?"

A pain struck behind Pawel's eyes, his temple pounding. "What has he done to you?"

"Nothing." She studied her hands.

"There is something."

Elfriede popped into the room. "I go upstairs. Dominik spill milk on his pants."

Natia straightened. "*Nie*, I will change him in a few minutes. Can you get coffee?"

Pani Fromm nodded and returned to the kitchen.

"She doesn't know?" Pawel trembled.

Natia shook her head. "I can't trust her. Look at who her husband is. I always change Dominik. But one of these days, I'm afraid she'll discover his secret."

"What will you do then?"

"Not much. I just pray and pray." Natia leaned forward. "*Pan* Fromm believes I'm sending secret messages to Teodor. Is that why they took him to prison? He was gone so long. Since the inspectors were here."

"He's been involved in some sabotage."

"Sabotage?" She almost shrieked.

"Keep your voice down. You should be very proud of your husband. He's a leader in the camp, and he's doing his part to make sure this war ends soon. He wants to get back to you as much as you want to get back to him, I assure you."

She stood, crushing the corner of her apron in her fist. "He is taking crazy chances. Tell me the truth. He could have died in that prison, *nie*?"

How much should he tell her? For the act of sabotage, which he admitted to, the Nazis should have executed him. Another act of God's mercy. "He didn't. That is the important part to remember."

"If you see him again, tell him to be safe. To live until this is over."

If any of them survived, it would be by God's grace, and only by his grace.

❧

Elfriede held to Dominik's hand as they came from the bakery and approached the grocer's shop. The child babbled and laughed as they went along. Such a joy.

She rubbed her flat stomach. No baby grew in her womb. And maybe it was better this way. To have Erich for a *Vater* was not a good thing for a little one. The nights when Erich was drunk or in a foul mood, in other words, most nights, were hard on Dominik. He would either hide behind her skirts or Natia's. He would whimper but had learned not to cry.

That didn't halt the slicing pain through her heart. Would the hurt of losing her baby ever go away? Would a night ever come that she didn't cry herself to sleep? Erich called her a failure, and that was what she was. *Vater* was disappointed in her because she couldn't produce a son. Erich was disappointed in her because she didn't produce the coveted promotions.

She squeezed Dominik's hand, her one ray of light in this dark and disturbing world. What would happen to them when the war ended? The Russians were nearing. Soon, they would have to let their prisoners go and would return to Germany. Would she lose Dominik? *Nein*, she couldn't. The pain would be too great to bear. Then again, Erich already hated the boy. Her husband would never allow the child to stay.

She peered at him as he stopped to pick up a pebble.

"*Nein*, you don't want to eat that. *Nein*."

Dominik dropped it.

The cloudless sky smiled on Elfriede, the sun warming her chilled arms. Red and yellow and orange flowers danced in window boxes. A gaggle of geese honked as they careened overhead.

Hard to believe that just a few hundred kilometers away, a war raged. For today, it was enough to enjoy the beauty of the town. Tomorrow and its cares and sorrows would arrive soon enough.

They passed a house with a picket fence surrounding the front yard, a patch of cucumbers and beets and beans filling the narrow space between the home and the street. Dominik cried.

"Hush, now." But when she looked at him to wipe away his tears, Dominik's face was dry. In fact, he flashed Elfriede a toothy grin. There came the cry again. If not Dominik, then who? She gazed around. The street remained empty. She peered over the fence.

A scrawny, filthy child, not more than eight or nine, huddled in a ball in the corner of the garden. Poor thing must be lost. "What are you doing?"

Tears washed ditches in the dirt on the child's face and snot poured from his nose. His light-colored hair lay matted to his head. He curled up ever tighter.

"What is wrong?" Elfriede opened the gate.

The boy screeched. "Go away."

She approached, her steps tiny and hesitant. "I not hurt you."

The boy sprang up, then collapsed. He held up his hands as if to shield himself. Dominik reached out to him.

"What is your name?"

He turned his back to her and covered his head.

"I not hurt you."

He tugged himself lower.

"What is wrong? Where you come from?" This wasn't a lost child. He couldn't stand. Perhaps he broke his leg. "I can help you. My name is Elfriede. I'm a nice lady. My friend, we can get a doctor."

She touched his bony shoulder, and he flinched. For a long time, she crouched beside him in the squash patch as he sniveled, then quieted. No sooner did he sneak a peek at her when a group of soldiers rounded the corner. He gasped and then hid his face.

Her mouth went dry. He feared them. But she wouldn't let them find him. She turned and sat on him, spreading her red polka-dot skirt over his bony frame. She didn't press down, but just touched his back, then released Dominik.

"*Guten abend*." One of the officers tipped his hat to her.

She avoided his gaze, staring at the ground, holding her breath.

"Ah, another Pole who thinks she's better than us. We should teach her a lesson." This one's voice had barely changed.

"Not now. We need to hurry, before *Untersturmführer* Fromm has our hides for being late again."

She didn't release her breath until they were long gone. Then it rushed out in one large gust. Should she laugh or cry?

The boy stirred, and she rose and helped him to his feet. "See, I good lady. I take care of you." She handed him her handkerchief edged with pink embroidery and nodded at him. He wiped his face.

Not until then did she glance at his chest. A yellow diamond with a *P* was sewn onto his shirt.

Nein, it couldn't be. That patch was for Polish laborers. Natia wore one. But this was just a child. A young boy. "Where you come from?"

He shook his head. She didn't need his answer to know. She grasped him by the hand. "Turn shirt." She motioned for what she wanted him to do. He obeyed.

"Now, we hurry." She pulled him out of the garden, through the gate, and onto the street. The heels of her brown oxfords clicked on the cobblestones as they scampered toward her house.

They created a spectacle, but if they didn't hurry, more soldiers might turn the corner and spot them.

The two blocks might as well have been two hundred kilometers. Would the house never get closer? Dominik got heavier with each step. With one last mighty push, they stumbled through the kitchen door and into the house.

Natia turned from stirring the borscht on the old black stove. "What? Who is this?" She waved the spoon in the air.

"A Polish child. A worker."

Natia's eyes widened, and her mouth opened. She slumped to the floor, trembling all over.

Elfriede went to her, shaking her by the shoulder. "What wrong?"

"That's not just any Polish boy."

♪♪♪

Chapter Twenty-Five

The scrawny, bony boy standing in the kitchen, right in front of Natia, was none other than Zygmunt. "This child is my brother. He's been held at the factory for eighteen months."

Elfriede shook her head. "It can't be true."

"About a year ago, Dr. Bosco brought me to see him at his office. Zygmunt had lost one of his fingers."

Zygmunt peered at Natia, his green eyes large. "Is it really you?"

Her vocal chords refused to work. Instead, she gestured for him to come to her, and they held each other for a long time, there on the floor, tears pouring down both of their faces. Just the sight of him stole the breath from her lungs. She tried not to blink lest he disappear, nothing more than a vision.

Elfriede brought them a glass of water, which Natia shared with her brother. "What happened?"

"I found him. He was hiding. In a garden. What could I do? So, I bring him here."

The only part of him that sparked recognition in Natia was his missing finger. That and his blond hair. Otherwise, he didn't resemble the child she'd helped to raise. He'd grown so gaunt, his eyes so hollow. "Do you remember seeing me when you were at the doctor's office?"

"*Nie*, but Teodor was there. I was happy even though my hand hurt. He told me you were living with some Germans."

She nodded even as a cold lump settled in the pit of her stomach. He couldn't stay here. *Pan* Fromm likely knew him. And if he found Zygmunt, neither he nor Natia would survive. "*Pani* Fromm, do you feel up to dishing out some soup for him?"

Elfriede nodded.

"I'll start heating the bath water."

With orders to follow, Elfriede perked up and got to work, fussing over Zygmunt, ladling his bowl full until it almost overflowed. "Not so much, or he'll get sick. Like Dominik when he was a baby."

Elfriede's cheeks pinked, but she returned a portion of the soup to the pot. By the time he downed the borscht, Natia had the bath ready, the water very warm. She helped him pull off his coveralls, little more than a thin rag by this time. His ribs and collarbone jutted out. She gasped, her pulse pounding at the injustice her brother had suffered. "What have they done to you?" If a child was in this condition, what about Teodor?

With Dominik on her hip, Elfriede entered the bathroom. "Is there anything ..."

Natia forced herself to smile at Zygmunt so as not to frighten him. "Can you manage everything else on your own? If so, we'll leave you to your bath in private."

"I can do it."

"Be sure to scrub well. The soap doesn't have the pleasantest smell, but it will get you good and clean."

He laughed, the sound as beautiful as water rushing over the rocks in the creek. "You always used to say that to me."

"Mama always told me the same thing." Oh, how wonderful to be near to someone who knew the same people she did, to have this connection to her former life. She had to tear herself away from him as she backed out of the room.

Elfriede covered her mouth with one hand. "Did you see him? He is very skinny. And very dirty."

"I saw." Natia fisted her hands to prevent herself from spewing out her venom on Elfriede. She wasn't to blame just because of her nationality. Her husband was another matter. "*Pan* Fromm oversees the factory."

Elfriede blanched like an apple stripped of its peel. "I know." She leaned against the rose-papered wall. "How can he do it? Look at what he does to little children. They do nothing to him. They were not bad. They should play. But *nie*, they work and work. What does Erich do to them?"

"I don't know. What an awful life."

Elfriede gazed at her. "I help him. He run away from the factory."

"*Tak.*"

"They will look for him. But not here. They think he would not be here. But Erich cannot know. He would—"

"How are we going to do that?"

"I don't know." Elfriede rubbed her forehead, her hands still shaking. "Dr. Bosco? He come when Dominik come. He help you. Maybe he help again?"

As much as Natia's heart cried out for Zygmunt to stay, pulling it off would be impossible. But perhaps the doctor could give them a hand. "You'll have to ring for him."

"Of course." Elfriede left to make the call.

Natia knocked on the bathroom door. "How are you doing?"

"This is great. I've never been so happy to take a bath in my life."

She chuckled. Spoken like a true boy. *Pan* Fromm hadn't completely broken him. "If you finish up now, Dr. Bosco will come and look at you."

"*Nie.* He'll send me back. He did once before." Water sloshed inside the bathroom, like he was climbing from the tub.

"He couldn't help it. The guards came to get you before he could rescue you. But we won't let that happen this time. He's a good man, someone we can trust. Don't worry. We're going to make sure you stay safe. You'll never have to return to the factory.

That, I promise." No matter how hard the promise would be to keep.

❧

On Teodor's second day back at the factory, *Untersturmführer* Fromm wandered over, his hands clasped behind his back. "Well, well. I didn't think I'd ever see you again. After all, you admitted your guilt. Why you survived, I'll never know. Had it been up to me, you wouldn't have. And I'm not going to make your time here pleasant or easy. Don't expect to hear your wife's songs."

Teodor bit the inside of his cheek. If he blurted out the caustic thoughts that danced on the end of his tongue, he'd be back in prison faster than the blitzkrieg.

The shift dragged on. Not much different than solitary confinement, except here he could see his fellow prisoners. He still couldn't talk to them.

Jerzy slipped from his stool, a coughing fit wracking his body. He made his way toward Fromm. The man gazed around the room, never moving his head. Jerzy stopped in front of him, his back to Teodor. Jerzy leaned in to speak to Fromm. Good luck getting out of here to get a drink of water.

Fromm narrowed his eyes. He threw wide gestures as he spoke to Jerzy. *Nie*, nothing had changed.

But then, Fromm smiled.

At Jerzy.

What was going on?

After a few minutes, he returned to his workstation. Teodor rubbed the back of his neck, the heat of the guards' stares boring into his skin. Jerzy leaned over and whispered something to him, but he blocked out his friend's words.

How interesting that on multiple occasions since returning to the factory, Teodor had caught him speaking with *Untersturmführer* Fromm, smiling and chuckling with him, altogether too chummy. Jerzy knew too much. And was too willing to share it.

"Hey." Jerzy threw a piece of paper at Teodor, making ignoring him impossible.

Teodor leaned over, picked up the crumpled bit of stationery, and tucked it into his pocket. He didn't think of it again until several hours later when *Untersturmführer* Fromm took him off the drill press and had him lugging boxes up and down the stairs from the factory floor to the train. At least he managed to escape the looks of his fellow prisoners. Especially Jerzy.

He paused for a minute on the stair landing between the second and third floors, the air warm and close but quiet, and read the note Jerzy had tossed in his direction. "Meet me in the lavatory at midnight."

The last thing he needed was for any of the Nazis to discover a note like this in his possession. He marched down the last two flights of the stairs, exited the building, and swallowed the small piece of paper.

He wouldn't go. Deep in the pit of his stomach, something didn't sit right. He couldn't identify it, but the nagging feeling refused to leave him.

The problem was, later that night, exhausted as he was, he couldn't fall asleep. He lay in the darkness, staring at the ceiling, as coughs gave way to snores. What should he do? What if Jerzy wasn't in cahoots with Fromm? Maybe prison had turned Teodor paranoid.

The bunk below him creaked, as did the floorboards beneath Jerzy's feet as he made his way to the restroom. Though he shouldn't, he really shouldn't, a few minutes later, Teodor also left his bed and bumped his way through the maze of bunks to the bathroom. "Please explain why you want to meet under cover of darkness."

"Why are you avoiding me?"

"Prison wasn't a trip to the seashore. I don't care to return."

"I can't blame you. But that doesn't explain your strange behavior since you've been back."

"How about your strange behavior?" Teodor's voice rang in the small space.

"Be quiet. Do you want the guards to hear?"

"That's what you want. Isn't that why you called me here?"

"What are you talking about?"

Teodor leaned against the wall. "You know very well."

He almost heard Jerzy shrug. "*Nie,* I don't."

"Since I've been gone, you've made friends with Fromm."

"That's ridiculous."

"Is it, now? I'm not so sure. You go and talk to him several times throughout the shift. And there's only one reason I can think that might be."

"Enlighten me." Jerzy coughed.

Teodor waited until the spasm passed. "You're snitching."

"You're out of your mind."

By now Teodor's eyes had adjusted to the dim light. He stood chest to chest with Jerzy and pushed him until his back was against the wall. "Tell me why you would turn on your friends, your comrades, your country."

"I'm doing no such thing." Jerzy's voice trembled.

"Oh, but you are. If I wasn't convinced before, I'm convinced now. You're the worst kind of harlot. One who sells his soul for what? A little bit of rest? Or a piece of bread? What is it? What was your price?"

"You are a fool." Jerzy jabbed him in the shoulder.

"You are a much bigger fool. I pity you. How can you sleep with yourself at night? How dare you call yourself a Pole? You are a *Volksdeutsche.* Selling out your Polishness for what?" Teodor spat on Jerzy's shoes.

He spun on his heel and stumbled back to bed. Sold out by a man he'd known for a good part of his life. One he had trusted. Jerzy had even worked with him, getting the dirt to gum up the machine.

Of course. That's how Fromm had found out he was the guilty

party. Jerzy's tattling got him sent to prison in the first place. Teodor's breaths came in rapid gasps.

Jerzy was right. He was a fool. A fool for ever trusting him or anyone in this miserable place.

Teodor's entire body ached. He tossed and turned, unable to find a comfortable position. The thin sheet and worn blanket tangled around his legs.

And though Teodor dozed for no more than a few minutes at a time the entire night, Jerzy never came to bed.

❧

Pawel drew his light jacket tighter. Though it was August and the weather was more than pleasant, a chill coursed through him. He hurried through the darkening streets toward the Fromm home.

Pani Fromm had not divulged much information over the phone, just that he needed to hurry. He'd heard worry and maybe a bit of fright in her voice. After the last time he spoke to *Pani* Palinska, what might he find? Had *Pan* Fromm hurt one of them? Or the baby? If only the women would let him take Dominik somewhere else. He had contacts throughout the country, places where the child might be safer.

Not that anywhere was safe these days. He'd heard rumblings from some of his contacts in Warsaw. Something about fighting in the streets. Not between Soviets and Germans, but a popular uprising. Everyday citizens, ready to throw off Nazi rule.

If only Antonina could be here where he could keep an eye on her, watch over her, keep her safe. Who knew what was going on to the north?

No sooner had he breathed a prayer for his wife, he arrived at the little pink house and rapped on the carved-wood front door. Low voices emanated from inside, and footsteps hurried to meet him. *Pani* Fromm answered, her blonde hair disheveled, her eyes red rimmed. "Come in, and hurry." She pulled him over the threshold and slammed the door shut behind him.

"What is this about?" He removed his fedora.

She reached to take his cap. "I was out today, walking home. I hear this crying. So small. I look down and see a boy. The soldiers came, but I hid him. Then I take him home. He works at the camp. His bones . . . Come, I show you."

He followed her to where *Pani* Palinska combed a little boy's wet hair. What there was of his hair anyway. His back was to Pawel. His rib and shoulder bones stuck out from underneath his almost-translucent skin. "Hello."

They both turned. *Pani* Palinska's eyes were bright, but she clenched her jaw. The boy scooted behind her. "Thank you for coming. My brother has escaped from the factory, and we need your help."

He peeked behind her to address the child and glanced at the boy's right hand. "Zygmunt?" He'd changed so much, grown so thin, that Pawel hadn't recognized him. "Well, we meet again. Can I look at you? I want to see how big and strong and healthy you are."

He nodded, his green eyes large in his gaunt face.

"*Pani* Palinska, would you get him a glass of warm milk please?"

She left the room to fulfill his request. He turned back to Zygmunt. "Did you run away?"

The boy bit his lip and stared at the ocher floor.

"You can tell me. See, I'm Polish, like you. I won't hurt you. Remember how I took care of you when you lost your finger? Let me help you."

"I ran away because I don't like the people there. I don't understand them, and I'm hungry. Please, can I stay with Natia?"

The words stuck in Pawel's throat. There was no way the boy could remain here. As soon as Fromm saw Zygmunt and discovered his relationship to *Pani* Palinska, there would be no stopping the Nazi's wrath. And he might not limit it to the Poles in his house.

Pawel faced Zygmunt again and smiled, just for the child's sake. "Let's get you strong and healthy." Pawel performed a brief examination. Though thin and malnourished, Zygmunt didn't have any other obvious diseases or conditions. "You're in good shape. Shall we go see if your sister has that milk?"

They made their way to the kitchen where *Pani* Palinska flashed them a tentative grin and poured the warm milk into a cup. *Pani* Fromm patted the wooden chair beside her at the small table. "You sit by me."

"Actually, Zygmunt, could you take your cup into the living room? If you don't mind, I'd like to speak with these two ladies for just a moment."

He took his mug and left.

Pawel crossed his legs and rubbed his chin. "He can't stay here."

Pani Palinska sighed. "I know. *Pan* Fromm is probably on the lookout for him. We can't let him find Zygmunt. Or discover his connection to me." She wiped a stray tear from her sunken cheek. "Much as I hate to send him away, I see no other alternative. There is nowhere to hide him."

"Agreed."

She spoke fast and low, probably so *Pani* Fromm couldn't understand them. "I know you're involved with underground activities, things to help people in trouble. We need help for Zygmunt. A safe place for him. A place where he can wait out the rest of the war and not have to worry about being sent back to the camp. And a place where I can find him when this is over."

He wiped his damp hands on his tan pants. If someone had been able to help Józef, wouldn't he have wanted them to? Even though it might mean another visit from Fromm, he had to do what he could.

He cleared his throat and spoke just as fast and low. "I have a contact in Warsaw. Even if he can't keep Zygmunt, he'll know of a place where he can stay. Next week, I have to go there, so I can get him some papers and take him with me."

"You'll help us?" Natia slowed her words and clasped her hands together.

"You'll have to explain to him why he can't stay."

"Just tearing away another piece of my heart. But you'll take him?"

"I will." A dangerous trip just got riskier.

Chapter Twenty-Six

Darkness spread its dense blanket over the village. *Pan* Fromm would be home soon. Natia stared at her brother, here in front of her. If she could only take him in her arms and hold him close forever. To lose him again would be as painful as losing one of her own children.

But keeping him here would be signing his death sentence. All of theirs. He had to leave. Now. Even though the pain was as real as a knife to the stomach, as the adult she had to control herself. She gazed at her brother. "Would you like more milk?"

"*Tak*. That was good."

Once he had a second full glass and she was settled in her seat again, she touched his hand, loath to ever release her grasp, loath to ever release him. "I never want to be parted from you."

His green eyes lit up. "Does that mean I can stay? Please, Natia, don't send me back to that horrible place. I was all alone. You weren't there. And a nice lady gave me these." He reached into his pocket and pulled out the handkerchiefs she'd sewn for her father and sister.

Her breath hitched, and she went cold all over.

"She said they had died." Fat tears raced down Zygmunt's face.

"*Nie, nie.*" If she refused to let her heart believe it, then it couldn't be true.

"I saw Helena. She was so still. So cold. I covered her with a blanket, but she didn't wake up. The lady told me she was living with Jesus and so was *Tata*."

Natia crumpled the pieces of fabric in her hand. How much would God take from her? Was no one going to be left?

"I love you, Natia. I miss you. Please, can't I stay?"

How she longed to hang on to this boy. She wiped the moisture from her face. Upsetting Zygmunt wouldn't help. Later she could mourn. Now she had to tell him he was going to lose her too. "*Nie*, you have to go."

"But ..." His chin quivered.

"Just for a little while. The war is going to end soon, and I promise we'll be together once more. It's not safe here. *Pan* Fromm lives in this house."

Her brother's face turned whiter than she'd ever managed to bleach the sheets. "You live with him?"

"I'm his servant."

"Can't you hide me? I'll be very quiet. He'll never know I'm here."

She stroked his cheek. "That's too dangerous. If he found you here ... Look, all you have to wear are your blue coveralls. But let's not talk about that. For now, let's enjoy being together."

"What's going to happen to me? Do I have to go back to that awful place?"

"Never. Dr. Bosco is taking you to Warsaw." She tried to smile but failed. "Imagine that. You'll get to see the big city."

"I miss *Tata* and Helena. I don't want to go away from you too. Please, Natia, don't send me away."

"I don't want you to go either, but this is the only way for you to be safe. If anything happened to you ..." A strangled sob cut off her words. After several deep breaths, she regained control. "Can you be brave for me?" If only she possessed a measure of the bravado she showed him.

"I don't want to be."

"But you must. We all must."

He nodded, his usual grin hidden. The work, this life, these deaths, had stolen his youth and innocence. Something he would never recapture, even if the war ended today. Her heart broke a little more.

"We'll only be apart for a short time. I promise."

Zygmunt rose from his chair, came to Natia, knelt beside her, his head in her lap, and they both wept.

At least she had the chance to tell him good-bye. She'd never gotten to say those words to *Tata* or Helena. Always, it was good-bye. And you never knew when it would be your final one.

❧

The front door slammed shut, startling Natia as she stirred the thin soup on the stove. *Pan* Fromm marched into the kitchen and whacked the wooden spoon from her hand.

She stepped backward.

"A child disappeared from the plant today. And I come to find out he's your brother. Zygmunt Gorecki. Isn't that correct?"

"Zygmunt?" She couldn't keep the tremor from her voice.

"Don't play dumb. You had a hand in this. I know you did. I've had enough. For too long I've been lenient with you because of Elfriede. But no more. I have a special place in mind for you. Get the child and your things."

God, nie. Don't let him take me to one of those extermination camps. Dominik and I wouldn't survive.

"Now."

On trembling legs, she climbed the stairs. As she packed her one spare skirt and Dominik's few clothes, she clung to him. "Don't worry. I won't let him hurt you. God, protect us. Please, I beg you. Don't let anything happen to us."

She took as long as she dared to finish the chore. Once she couldn't delay any longer, she stumbled downstairs, her entire body numb. Was her heart still beating?

Pan Fromm met her at the bottom step and grabbed her by

her shoulder, almost crushing her bones under his grasp. He pulled Dominik from her arms, then marched them through the front door.

Dizziness and nausea washed over her. The world spun and her knees buckled.

❧

Elfriede raced after her husband, out the front door and into the yard, her breathing rapid. "Stop it. Erich, don't. Don't take Dominik from me. This isn't right."

Natia stumbled, and Elfriede rushed forward, reaching them.

He growled and pushed her shoulder to move her out of the way. "What do you know about right and wrong? You duped me into marrying you by getting pregnant, but you can't bear a child. No children for the fatherland. Thanks to you, I'm a disgrace." He turned to Natia. "And thanks to her, I'm looked down upon and scorned by both those under me and my superiors. Your *Vater* detests me. I'll never get that promotion to Berlin. We'll never get out of this outpost on the edge of nowhere."

The sting of his words bit into Elfriede's heart. "This isn't about me. Or us. It's about you and what you're doing."

"Out of my way. I warned you she would ruin us. Since she's come, we've had nothing but trouble. I should have never brought her here. Never should have allowed this Jew baby in my house. That's a wrong I intend to correct."

"Dominik isn't Jewish. Please. You'll rip my heart open." Already, it was raw and gaping.

Erich struck her across the mouth. "Shut up. Or I'll do to you what I'm about to do to her."

The metallic flavor of blood stung her tongue, and her stomach plunged like an elevator without a cable. "Do to me whatever you want. But don't hurt Dominik. Or Natia. I need them, Erich. If you love me, you won't take them from me."

Wriggling in Erich's arms, Dominik screeched. He couldn't, wouldn't harm the child. Would he?

Trembling from head to toe, Elfriede reached for Dominik. "Give him to me. Let me take care of him." She wrenched him from Erich's hold.

Leading with her free shoulder, she shoved her way between Erich and Natia. He released his grip. Elfriede spun around and handed Dominik to Natia. "Take him inside. Go."

Natia grabbed the baby and bolted.

Elfriede released a pent-up breath and forced her voice to remain cold and even. "If you love me, you'll keep him here for me. Or *Vater* will hear about how you're treating me. I promise you, he will. And then instead of missing out on a promotion, you'll find yourself demoted to an infantryman in the Wehrmacht."

Elfriede's stomach jumped around in her middle like Dominik on the living room couch. But the threat was enough to make Erich back off. With a hard glare, he marched down the street, probably to indulge in some Polish vodka.

❧

Rivulets of rain raced down the kitchen window. Natia watched as the smaller droplets combined to make larger ones, the sky weeping with her. Would this captivity never end? Would she ever sleep without fear? When would *Pan* Fromm make good on his threat? These past several days had been their own form of torture.

"What you doing?"

She jumped and spun around. "Elfriede. I didn't hear you."

"I'm sorry. Dominik sleeps. I come for some coffee."

"I'm just peering out the window, wishing I could go home, to my babies, to the land I love. I miss my family, and I long for my husband. I need to see him. Not in a few weeks or months. I need to be with him now, especially now. You understand, don't you?"

"You miss Teodor. But that love, I do not know."

Natia grasped Elfriede by both hands. "To not love your husband with all of your heart? That, I can't understand. He is my song."

"You know Erich. He is not a nice man. He hurts people. How can I love him?"

"I thought you did. Why did you marry him?"

Elfriede sighed.

"Sit at the table and let me get you coffee. Then, we'll talk." Natia poured them each a steaming cup of the ersatz brew. With no sugar or milk, she had to almost hold her nose to drink the bitter liquid. But it filled the stomach. As the Fromms' rations dwindled, so did Natia's.

She scraped back a chair and positioned herself across from Elfriede. "We have lived and worked together for more than a year. At first, I didn't like you. But now, you're my friend. If I may be allowed to call you that."

"Your friend? I like that. But we cannot let Erich know. He would not like. He does not like Poles."

Natia nodded.

"Erich look so nice. So, how do you say?"

"Handsome."

"*Tak*, handsome. He is strong and smart. He thinks I'm pretty. So, we go together to cinema, to cafe, all over. My *Vater*, he likes him. A good Nazi, he says. You must marry him. Erich will take good care of you. Together you will make pure babies for the fatherland. That is what good German girls do."

"So you got married because your father wanted you to?"

"*Tak*. And I was going to have a baby. Erich was proud. He love me, says I am good German woman."

Natia reached over and patted her hands. "You don't have to say more."

"He get very angry when our baby die. And more angry when no more babies come. I did not love him. I don't now. But forever,

I must be with him. Why did God take my baby? Was I bad? God angry too?"

"*Nie*. You listen to me." Natia handed Elfriede a handkerchief, even though her own eyes streamed with tears. Pain ripped through her midsection as it did each time she lost a child. "For a long time, I thought that's why God took my children. Because I was not good enough."

Oh, those endless, dark days. Days of trying so hard to be good enough to deserve a child. One who lived. She did everything the doctor and the pastor told her to do.

And it wasn't enough. God wrenched each of her precious children from her womb. And the stabbing wound in her heart throbbed. Because what she wanted more than anything in the world was the one thing she couldn't have.

Her arms, Teodor's cradle, their home remained empty. The roundness of other women's bellies, the sweet melody of other children's laughter, the powdery fragrance of other infants' skin taunted her. Why couldn't she have what everyone else had?

Time had smoothed the jagged edges of the hurt. But nothing, not even Dominik, would ever take it away.

She drew in several ragged breaths so she could speak. "But God didn't take our children from us because we had done something bad."

"Then why?" Elfriede peered up at Natia, her full lips trembling, her teary blue eyes shimmering with unanswered questions.

"I don't know. I can't tell you." The one answer that would satisfy her longing, God withheld from her. Would she ever understand why he denied her the joy of giving Teodor a child?

But in front of her was a woman who understood her pain. This bonded them, formed them into a sisterhood that those allowed to be mothers would never understand. Only someone who had lost the way they lost could feel the same burning ache. And maybe, just maybe they could help each other.

"This is not a good time to have a child. What would have happened to my babies if Teodor and I were in the prison camp? Would they have been in there too?"

"*Nie*." Elfriede twisted the hem of her pink blouse. "Maybe. I don't know."

"I don't either. But that's what I think. It's best they aren't in this world suffering. *Tak*, my soul hurts when I remember them." The tears came even harder and faster, her sorrow cascading from her. "What would they look like? Like Teodor? Like me? Would they follow him in the fields or help me in the kitchen? What am I missing by not having them in my life?" A sob burst from her lips.

"All the words, I don't know, but I know your heart."

"But my children aren't hungry. They aren't cold or afraid. They aren't in pain. Or lonely. What more could I wish for them? How selfish to want them here, in this world, where people hurt others with so little regard." Even though their absence brought the tears that soaked her pillow every night.

Elfriede slid her chair next to Natia and drew her into a sideways embrace. "Dominik makes us mothers."

"He is my joy." But *Pani* Rzeźnikowa's words rang in her head. What would happen to Dominik after the war? Would Elfriede keep him? They couldn't divide him in half.

"You are good friend." Elfriede wiped her nose and flashed Natia a shaky smile. "You understand. I will help you see your husband."

"How?" Elfriede had never been to the factory or shown any interest in going. She would never be able to get Natia in there to spend a moment with Teodor.

"We will think of a way."

♪♫♪

Chapter Twenty-Seven

*E*lfriede's heart fluttered under her ribs like a caged bird. Here she was, marching Natia down the street in the middle of the day, right toward the factory where Erich worked. She couldn't get more brazen. Where had this gumption come from?

For her new friend, she would do anything. Natia understood the deep, aching longing that consumed her day and night. She was the first woman Elfriede found who knew what it was like to hold her still, lifeless child. And who knew that pain in the very depths of her being, who understood that pain would never cease.

To thank Natia for such a special kinship, Elfriede would risk her husband's ire.

She turned to Natia and nodded. She plodded behind, her head down against the wind that blew tendrils of brown hair into her face, her embroidered black shawl around her shoulders. Dominik nestled into Natia's shoulder. Elfriede smiled and kept moving forward.

The factory loomed before her, its smokestacks rising high into the sky, almost as if they could reach the fluffy white clouds floating overhead. Exhaust poured from the stacks. Her stomach churned. She shouldn't have eaten the toast Natia prepared for breakfast. It might not stay inside.

Nein, she promised to do this. She squared her shoulders and flung open the door to the factory's offices. Fräulein Wurtz sat behind a metal desk, plunking away at a typewriter. She didn't so much as glance up. "Can I help you?"

"I want to see my husband."

Now the red-haired secretary did tear her concentration from her work. "Frau Fromm. Your husband is busy."

"Tell him his wife is here on an urgent matter."

She patted her hair, rolled in the latest fashion, and sniffed. "Fine. But you can deal with his anger. He told me he wasn't to be disturbed."

"Disturb him." Elfriede's knees quaked under her brown speckled skirt.

Natia repositioned Dominik on her hip and leaned over to whisper to Elfriede. "Maybe this wasn't a good idea. We'll make him mad. Then I'll never see Teodor."

"Don't worry." But she couldn't stop the swarm of butterflies that battered the inside of her belly.

Within minutes of Fräulein Wurtz entering Erich's office, he stormed through the door. "What is the meaning of this? What is so urgent that you take me away from important business? I was on the phone with Berlin. I don't have time for your foolishness."

Elfriede smoothed down her skirt. "You have never shown me your office."

"That's your important business? You're nothing more than an addle-brained simpleton. Worthless. And what is she doing here? I forbade her from stepping outside. Ever."

"A friend sent a large package from home. It's heavy, and I couldn't carry it alone. You don't want me to hurt myself, do you? That's why I needed her to come with me."

"You are wasting my time. Go home."

"Fine. I'll send her to the post to get the package and straight home. But I'm not leaving until you show me your office. Please? I have no idea what it looks like in here." He wasn't cooperating like she'd thought he would.

"Out of the question. You aren't to leave her to wander the streets alone. Get out of my sight. Now. Both of you. I have to call Berlin back and try to explain what was more important than them." Erich turned on his heel, back into his office, and slammed the door.

Elfriede slumped and sighed. So much for her grand plan. "Come on. Let's go."

Natia gave her a half smile. Together, they turned and left the building. "*Dziękuję Ci* for trying."

"But you didn't see him."

"You tried. That was nice of you. *Pan* Fromm wasn't going to leave me alone."

"*Nie*. It was a bad idea." What had she been thinking? She didn't have the brains to come up with a simple plan so Natia could visit her husband.

"Most wives don't see them. That's fine." But her features sagged. She closed her eyes for a second before opening them again.

They continued their walk along the outside of the factory. Another idea struck Elfriede. "You sing for him."

"He might be working."

"Just try."

Natia handed Dominik to Elfriede and stood under the middle window in the long line of panes in the factory walls.

Elfriede didn't understand the words that Natia sang, but the rising and falling of the notes, the passion in Natia's voice, the glow of her face spoke of her love for her husband.

Oh, to have such a love. Something Elfriede would never know. Without the care of a husband or a child, her heart would remain empty forever.

She kissed Dominik's cheek. Here was someone who loved her. He drove away a small piece of her longing. The child was the only good thing in her life.

One she would cling to no matter what.

❧

Natia stood beneath Teodor's window. Would he be in the barracks in the middle of the day? Most likely not. Still, she had a chance, slim as it was. A chance to sing to him, to share her heart with him. To hear his reply.

Thro' the dewy valley murmuring brooks meand'ring,
Bells a-tinkling gaily, tell where herds are wand'ring,
Bright the sun is glowing, green are wood and meadow,
All around o'erflowing, life in sun and shadow,
I alone am lonely, mourning heavyhearted,
For the days that only all too soon departed.

Her heart almost burst from her chest. How much longer could she stand this?

She stood, peering at that window for the longest time. Dominik chattered behind her. Minutes ticked away. Natia's neck stiffened.

But no answer came.

A cold wind blew through her soul. She fell to her knees. "Why, God? Why? I can't do this anymore."

Dominik whimpered. Elfriede touched her shoulder. "I am sorry. We should not have come."

"I can't do this. Don't you see, Lord? I can't do this. Without them, what good am I? I don't have anyone to sing for. My children, my husband, my parents, my siblings, all gone. Have you turned your back on the entire world?" A low keening replaced the music on her lips.

For a long while, she crouched on the road and mourned for all she'd lost. For all that would never be returned to her. For all the crosses that marked the graves of loved ones.

"What is that racket?"

Pan Fromm.

Somewhere deep inside Natia, a dam burst. She stood and faced him. "Where are they?" She screeched the words and fought to keep from flinging herself at him. "Where are my father and sister? I want to see their graves."

"What are you talking about?"

"My father and sister are dead. And you killed them." She pointed at the monster before her.

Pan Fromm reached out and choked her.

Elfriede shouted at her husband and wrestled him away.

He spat on the ground. "Go home. Right now. Don't ever come back."

Elfriede grabbed Dominik and Natia, and they ran.

Teodor's legs ached and his arms burned as he reached the top of the stairs. Long ago he'd lost count of how many times he traversed these steps. Heavy boxes weighing him down as he carried them to the train, fatigue pressing on him as he climbed for more.

More parts headed for Germany to feed their voracious war machine. When would it end? Rumors floated like chaff in the wind. But could he believe any of them? He picked up several more boxes, stumbled downstairs and outside, and peered at the eastern sky, as if he might see the Russians pouring over the hill. But nothing. A few birds twittered in the trees, somewhere in the distance children played and laughed, and the train whistle carried across the kilometers.

He needed to hurry if he was to get everything downstairs in time. He stopped for a moment to catch his breath.

"What's wrong?"

Jerzy.

"Nothing." Teodor headed inside the building.

"Wait. You don't look well."

"You're one to talk." Though, as Teodor studied him, something struck him. Jerzy, still thin, no longer bore the hollow cheeks and vacant eyes as the other prisoners. "He's giving you food."

"He's releasing me next week."

"I wouldn't count on that scoundrel."

"He is. I've signed the *Volksdeutsche* agreement."

"Why? Why turn your back on your country now? It's only

a matter of months before there will be no more Germans in Poland. Our land will belong to us once again. You'll be forced to leave, branded as a traitor."

"If the rumors are true. They might be nothing more than hopes on the breeze. Today they are here, tomorrow they have vanished."

"I choose to believe them. The guards are nervous, jumping at the slightest provocation. *Nie*, the Russians are on the doorstep. I feel it in my bones."

"Or that might be fatigue. Whatever the case, you'll still be here and I'll be home, in my wife's arms."

Teodor bit the inside of his cheek. Oh, to have Natia hold him. To be home.

"You can have it too. You can go back to your farm."

"*Nie.*"

"Just go to *Untersturmführer* Fromm. Talk to him. Tell him you're ready to sign the agreement. He'll punch your ticket to Piosenka."

Home. The word flowed over him like a melody. Peace and quiet. Love and laughter. Work and rest.

"Get her out of this place. Take your wife and resume the life you had before."

Life before. They'd worked hard. They didn't have much, but they had each other. In those days, they didn't appreciate it. Now they would. And perhaps this time, the Lord would give them a child. Even just one. What joy would be theirs if the Lord fulfilled that request. Teodor might burst from the thought alone. The pull of their little town, their friends, their church tugged at him. Every fiber in his being told him to sign the paper.

For Natia's sake. So she would be free from worry, so she would be healthy and happy. Could he pick up the pen and sign it for her?

"Do it, Teodor. We'll ride the train together."

Should he?

Maybe. He could force his fingers to pick up the pen, to scratch his name on the paper.

It was well enough for Jerzy to sign, to pass secrets to *Untersturmführer* Fromm. More than likely, he wouldn't survive the winter either way. He might as well go home and kiss his wife and children once more. A final good-bye.

Teodor hefted two more boxes loaded with parts and picked his way down the stairs. The world spun around him. He closed his eyes but kept going. The train whistle blew louder.

Next week he could be on a homeward-bound train. But was his comfort worth betraying his country?

He stepped outside, his almost soleless boots crunching on the gravel as he staggered toward the tracks. Out there, somewhere, was home.

Home.

But what kind of home would he have if he signed the paper?

And then a haunting sound met him. A song. Natia?

I alone am lonely, mourning heavyhearted,
For the days that only all too soon departed.

Her sweet, honey-like voice was too unique to be confused. It was his Natia, singing for him. The words broke off. There was more, but she didn't sing it.

"Get going, Palinski. This isn't a holiday." The guard jabbed Teodor with the butt of his gun, hard enough to push the breath from his lungs, to bruise his ribs. *Tak*, the Russians were near. These days, even a brief pause in work brought swift retribution.

He shuffled forward. Sobbing. That's what he heard. Heart-wrenching, soul-clenching. *Nie, sweet love, don't cry so.* What could he do to take her pain away?

Her wails tore at him. Wails so much like his mother's when the Nazis came in 1939. Sobs that haunted him.

He'd never forget that day. "Open up, open up. We demand entrance, or we will break down the door." The harsh voices of the Nazis had spoken his beautiful native tongue.

Mama reached for him and clung to his arm. "Don't let them in. I'm afraid. Afraid they will take you, and I will never see you again. What would I do without you, my beloved son?"

Teodor freed himself from her grasp. "You heard them, Mama. They will enter one way or another. Let them come. We have nothing to hide."

"Just you."

"They'll see I need to take care of you and won't separate us." He gazed at the tiny woman beside him, once strong and vivacious, now bent with age and sorrow. Her face was pale, so very pale. A line of sweat dotted her upper lip.

The Nazis entered.

Their jackboots sounded on the wood plank floors.

Teodor froze, unable to move, unable to breathe, unable to think. The soldiers paused in front of him.

Mama clutched her chest and slumped against him.

And like that, she was gone. Forever.

A heart attack. If only he had fought them. Kept them out in the first place. Done something to protect his fragile mother.

And then he'd allowed the Nazis to separate him from Natia. But he could still protect her.

"Go home. Don't ever return here." *Untersturmführer* Fromm's screech jolted him back to reality. His voice traveled from the same direction as Natia's weeping. She lived with that, with him, every day.

What was more important to him? His wife or his country?

What an impossible choice.

♪♫♪

Chapter Twenty-Eight

The train chugged to a stop at a station on the outskirts of Warsaw. Pawel, Zygmunt still at his side, made his way to the city to find a safe place for the boy. While he was here, he would check on his contact. Some time had passed since he'd heard from him.

"End of the line. Everyone disembark." The German soldier, a metal helmet on his head and a rifle in his hand, marched up the aisle, repeating his announcement.

Pawel halted him. "Why do we need to get off here? This isn't my stop."

"This is all the farther we can go. Your countrymen decided to make trouble. Don't worry. We'll deal with it and restore peace in short order." The Nazi moved on, calling out again.

Pawel had heard about the uprising. The city was under siege. Students, the underground, everyday citizens took up arms and fought the Nazis. But it was brutal. Scores of lives were lost. Left with no choice, Pawel and Zygmunt followed the soldier up the aisle, down the steps, and into the station. A few people milled about, but not many. The place didn't bustle as usual.

Pawel clutched Zygmunt's small hand, his new identification papers stashed in the knapsack on his back. "What are we going to do if this wasn't your stop?"

Pawel turned to the boy and gave him what he hoped was a confident smile. "We'll have to walk. And what a beautiful day it is. After you've been cooped inside that factory, you'll enjoy it."

Zygmunt gave a single nod and plodded beside Pawel.

They exited the station onto the street, Pawel pulling up his collar and pushing his fedora farther onto his head. Danger lurked on every corner. He tugged Zygmunt closer and patted his coat where he kept his work papers in the inside pocket. If any soldier stopped him, he could produce those and avoid arrest. That was the hope, anyway, though work papers were no guarantee of safe passage. Now, not only for himself, but also for Zygmunt, he had to remain vigilant. Whatever it took, he would keep the boy from being forced to return to the camp.

Every few meters, Pawel glanced over his shoulder. Was someone following them? Getting ready to spring up behind them? *Nie*, the road remained empty save for a few women scurrying to market.

He picked up his pace, Zygmunt scurrying behind. He forced his steps to carry them in the direction of the center of the city. Not too far and signs of the uprising appeared. A burned-out building here and there. An abandoned barricade where citizens had opposed soldiers. Bloodstains on the street.

Zygmunt tugged on his coat. "What's happening?"

"Just keep your head down and keep walking."

Pawel turned the corner, and the scene changed. Groups of young men and women gathered near one of the government buildings, tables and chairs and chests of drawers holding back the Nazis. A tense quiet hung over the area. He pulled Zygmunt to his side and held him fast.

A young man with brown hair and tired blue eyes approached them. "What are you doing here, old man? And with a kid. Do you want to join us?"

"I'm here to meet a colleague."

"It's not safe. So many have already died. And now the Germans are pushing us back. I don't know how much longer we can hold out."

"Did you ever have a chance?"

"We did, until the Soviets decided not to come to our aid. We did the hard work for them, opened the door, but they sat on their hands and refused to help. Why, I don't understand. Trust me, the Russians are no friends of ours. But if you aren't here to help, to give your life for the cause, go home." The man ran off to join his compatriots.

Pawel continued, but this time he took to the alleys and the back ways, hidden in the shadows, away from Nazi eyes. Over the years, he'd traveled to Warsaw plenty of times to attend conferences and learn new techniques in medical care, so he had a fair idea of where to go.

The putrid odor of death and destruction hung in the air. He came to a street he needed to cross. German soldiers stood to his left, Polish citizens to his right. The bloated body of a teenage boy lay in the gap between the two.

He gagged and covered his mouth. Zygmunt whimpered. What had become of the human race?

Pawel turned on his heel and marched in the opposite direction until he came to another cross street and another alley.

Shouts and shots rang out. A battle, right on the streets of Warsaw. His breath hitched. He grabbed Zygmunt, squeezing his four-fingered hand, and ran. They popped out on another street. Several German soldiers surrounded a group of young men, beating some of them, herding them into olive-colored, canvas-covered trucks. Screams blended with the odor of petrol and burning tires.

Zygmunt's own cries joined theirs. Pawel covered his mouth and dragged him in the opposite direction. If only he could also block the sight from the boy's eyes, a sight neither of them would forget.

Back the way they came. Down another street. Into another alley.

Where were they? Nothing appeared familiar.

Out to another street. A group of women scurried down the thoroughfare, their shopping bags banging against their legs as a gaggle of Nazis chased them. One fell. The German yanked her up by her light-brown hair. She screeched.

Pawel motioned for Zygmunt to stay put as he raced into the intersection. "*Halten sie*! Stop it. Leave her be!"

The other soldiers didn't break off their pursuit, but the one dropped the woman to the ground and turned his attention to Pawel. The woman scooted backward, away from the melee. "Get out of here, old man." The pale-faced soldier approached him.

Heat streaked through Pawel's body. "What do you want with her?"

"This is none of your business."

"When you harm a woman, an innocent one, it is."

The soldier moved forward two more steps. "If you know what's good for you, you'll scat."

"Leave her alone."

Pain shot down his neck.

Blackness consumed him.

&

Teodor couldn't eat, couldn't sleep, couldn't think. *Nie*, he could think. He couldn't stop thinking. About Natia. Her song. Her crying. Her life with *Untersturmführer* Fromm.

He tossed on his less-than-comfortable bunk and scratched at the fleas that bit him. What was she enduring? What was that monster doing to her? In all the songs she had sung for him, she had never been as sorrowful as she had been today. Lonely? *Tak*. But now, more than that.

Broken.

He covered his head with the thin pillow to block out the sounds of snoring and coughing. The physical conditions took their toll on the men. Their bodies were shutting down. This suffering wasn't limited to the flesh but extended to their hearts and souls. The degradation of the human spirit.

How he loved to hear Natia sing. Any song except that one. Not the melody of hopelessness and despair.

But he had a choice. He could improve her existence.

Then again, Jerzy hadn't promised that Natia would go free. Only him. If he signed that paper, he might do so for no good purpose. If his fellow countrymen found out, his signature on that page could cost him everything. Including his wife.

"You're deep in thought."

Teodor jumped. "You startled me, Jerzy."

"What's on your mind?"

"You know."

"My tempting offer?"

"Keep your voice down. Do you want everyone to hear?" Teodor glanced around the room, most of the men slumbering away the Sabbath, their one and only time of rest. A small group held a simple worship service. Otherwise, no acknowledgment of God.

"Most of them are half dead anyway."

Like Jerzy himself. "They can't all sign the agreement. The Germans would have no one to work for them."

"They're running low on supplies. The choke hold around the Nazis' neck is tightening. They can no longer get food or raw materials. What are they going to do with us?"

"Perhaps they'll let us go home soon."

"Not a chance." Jerzy shook his head. "Do you think they want the Allies finding out what they've been up to? They'll kill us first."

"If I would do it—"

"You're going to?"

"I said *if*. If I sign, it would only be for Natia's sake. I would need assurance that she would be able to leave with me."

"Why wouldn't Fromm let her go?"

"You make it sound like he's sure to comply."

"If he says he's going to do it, he will."

Teodor punched his flat, flea-ridden pillow. "Don't bet on a German. You're out of your mind if you think he's going to keep a promise."

"Then talk to him first thing tomorrow. Do you have anything to lose?"

~

The sun had yet to clear the horizon the following day when Teodor shuffled down the hall to *Untersturmführer* Fromm's office. Teodor's heart galloped far in front of him. This was crazy. He must have lost his mind. That was it. The lack of food and sleep had clouded his judgment. He wasn't thinking straight to even entertain the idea of signing the paper.

But here he stood in front of Fromm's office door, his name in big gold letters on the plaque screwed into the wood. *Plant manager.*

The secretary was absent, so Teodor drew in a deep breath and wiped his sweaty hands on his pants before he knocked.

"Come."

He entered, the plushness of the office taking him aback. Fromm sat his well-muscled frame in an oversized leather desk chair situated behind an expansive oak desk. An exquisite Oriental rug of rich blues, reds, and greens softened Teodor's footfalls as he crossed the room.

Fromm tilted backward in his chair and puffed on a cigarette. "Well, what a surprise. Then again, maybe not so much. After my agreement with your friend, I thought you might show up. Looks like prison knocked some sense into you."

Teodor almost ran out of the office. But Natia's sad, sweet song rang in his head. He kept himself planted in place. "Is it true Jerzy is headed home?"

"To whatever might be left after the Russians have been through."

"The Soviets are that far west?"

Fromm wiped the smirk from his face and schooled his features to reveal no emotion whatsoever. But not before he'd tipped his hand. The Nazi sat forward. "What do you want? This isn't a coffee klatch. Get to your point or get out."

"What did he have to do to get released?"

"Just sign the *Volksdeutsche* paper."

"Excuse me if I'm skeptical. This late in the war, you're still providing the option for Poles to turn German? That doesn't make sense."

"Because you have no sense." Fromm tapped his cigarette on the edge of the ashtray, glowing embers falling in a flurry into the metal receptacle. "The war is not over. We have not surrendered, nor do we intend to. Whatever rumors you hear to the contrary are just that. Trust me, if we were going to lose the war, if we had to leave this place, we wouldn't keep one of you alive." The sneer returned to his lips.

A chill skittered down Teodor's spine. That was one promise Fromm was sure to keep. "If I sign the agreement, do I have your word that you will not only release me, but also my wife?"

"Why would I do such a thing? She's handy to have around." His blue eyes glinted in the harsh office light.

Teodor fisted his hands and spoke through clenched teeth. "You stay away from her."

"You are in no position to make threats."

"You'll be sorry you ever touched her."

"I'm inclined to withdraw my offer."

Teodor forced himself to relax. "If I sign, my wife comes too."

Fromm tilted his head. "Very well."

"In writing. Put the agreement on paper."

Fromm withdraw a pen from his drawer, scratched out a note, and signed it. "Are you satisfied? Are you ready to become a loyal German citizen?"

Was he? Could he do this? He stared at the paper. All he had to do was move the pen across the page. Scribble. A couple of black marks, and it would be over.

His Poland. His beloved home. His heart cried. Would it ever be the same, or would it be a desolate wasteland forever? Yet so many had shed their blood for it. Given their lives so he could be free. Could he turn his back on the land that had birthed him, fed him, sustained him? Then again, Fromm had broken Natia.

Teodor closed his mind to what that man might be doing to her. If he dwelled on it, he'd kill Fromm for sure. Without a weapon.

She needed the fresh air of home. Needed their children on the hill. Needed him.

For her, he would do anything. Anything to ease her hurt, take away her pain, make her whole again.

Even if it tore him in two.

"I'll sign."

♩♪♩♪

Chapter Twenty-Nine

*P*awel's brain drummed a mighty beat inside his aching head. His eyelids refused his command to open. He moaned.

"Shh, don't try to move. You've been unconscious for several days." A young male voice answered his groan. Pawel didn't recognize it.

He struggled again to open his eyes. This time, he managed to slide the left one open to a slit. Darkness draped the room, though a single candle on a table in the corner attempted to chase it away, lighting a portrait of the Black Madonna of Częstochowa. "What happened?" The sound of his own voice sent shards of pain piercing his skull.

"You're safe."

Safe? Why wouldn't he be? Wait, he was on a train. Had there been an accident? "Injured?"

"That soldier wasn't happy with you."

Soldier. A Nazi in an olive-drab uniform, a creased cap on his head. How did the train fit in? What was going on? "Where am I?"

"Warsaw." The thin young man with the pointed nose blinked a few times in the dim light.

"Warsaw." He let the word wash over him. Warsaw. That was right. But why was he here?

Zygmunt. It had something to do with the boy.

"Don't you remember?"

"It's fuzzy."

"You argued with a Nazi soldier about a woman."

The woman's face flashed in front of his eyes. Light-brown

hair. Big sapphire-blue eyes. High cheekbones. Similar in many ways to Antonina. "Is she hurt?"

"She managed to get away, thanks to you. You took quite a risk."

"I couldn't let him harm her."

"Well, you're both fine."

"You helped?"

"No one should treat another human being the way the Germans treat us. The Lord sent me to the right place at the right time."

"Where is Zygmunt?"

"Right here." The boy's voice came from near the foot of the bed.

An attempt to see him sent pain coursing through Pawel's brain. He puffed out a breath. "Are you hurt?"

"*Nie*, I'm fine."

The stranger hovered over Pawel. "He had a bit of a fright, that's all. Nothing a child should have to see."

The boy had seen far too much in his few years. If Pawel would never forget, what kind of nightmares would Zygmunt have?

"Where are you from? You don't speak city Polish."

"Pieśń Nabożna, south of Kraków, near the Czechoslovakian border. I must be going." Pawel sat up, the world spinning around him.

"Not so fast. You got conked on the head."

"I'll be fine." He needed to leave. His contact waited.

"You can't. It's the middle of the night. There's a curfew. And a battle's raging." The young man pointed to the darkened window.

Pawel rubbed his temple. "Where are we?"

"Give me your contact's address."

His stomach lurched. What did he know about this kid? Maybe it wasn't safe to give him that information. For himself, it wouldn't matter so much. But others depended on him. "What is your name?"

"It's best you not know. And the same for me. Suffice it to say that I'm a member of the Polish underground, fighting to free our homeland from tyranny."

"How do I know that?"

"Would I have saved you from that soldier if I wasn't?"

The pounding in his head muddied his thoughts. "I don't know."

"You can trust me. If you want to get somewhere, you'll have to give me the address. You shouldn't even be here. At any moment, they could round you up and send you to Auschwitz. Or, if you're lucky, they'll shoot you."

"I know too much about those camps." Places where people like Zygmunt and Teodor and Natia struggled to survive.

"Then you know you don't want to go there."

"I'm a physician. They should have sent me to a camp or shot me when they first invaded the country." Like they had his son.

The young man stroked his chin, only a few light hairs gracing it. "I'll take you out of the melee, but not until morning. It's late. I'll bring you something to eat and drink." He left the room, the door clicking shut behind him.

His green eyes wide, Zygmunt sat on the bed beside him. "I thought they were going to kill you."

Pawel chuckled, though light exploded behind his eyes. "My head's too hard. But they didn't hurt you?"

The child shook his head. "I hid in the alley until the man came to help you. I—I was scared you would go away and leave me like *Tata* and Helena did."

"We're going to be fine. I promised your sister. I'll make sure you're safe."

From the street below came shouts and gunshots. Pawel, though his legs shook, stood, shuffled to the window, and drew aside the blackout curtain. Fires turned the night sky blood red. Tension sucked the oxygen from the air. The uprising was just about out of steam. Would the young men like his rescuer even survive what was to come next?

Pawel leaned against the windowpane, the coolness of the glass welcome relief against his warm skin.

The young man returned, his breathing rapid. "We have to leave. Right now. I think we've been found out."

❧

A week. Seven days had passed since Teodor turned his back on all he loved and signed that paper. And still, Fromm held Natia and him as captives. His slaves.

Fire burned in Teodor's chest. He had done it for nothing. In the end, he hadn't saved himself. He hadn't saved Natia. And he certainly hadn't saved his country.

What more could he have done?

A Bible verse he had memorized as a child sprang to mind: *"Give us help from trouble: for vain is the help of man."* And how true. He was helpless. He couldn't protect his family.

Shoulders slumped, he sat on one of the long benches in the room that served as the dining hall, though it lacked tables. Why did you need a place to set your bowl when that's all you had to eat? If possible, the thin, watery gruel had become even thinner and more watery. The mealy potatoes that had once appeared no longer floated in the liquid. Little conversation swirled in the room. The men didn't have the energy to speak. All they had to live on were their dreams and the rumors that floated in from the Eastern front.

Just as Teodor dropped his spoon into his empty bowl, Fromm marched into the room. This was the man he had been foolish enough to believe would grant him his freedom. Instead, he had stolen what little Teodor had left.

He clenched his fists as he rose from the bench and stomped in Fromm's direction. Teodor came toe to toe with the man, even though he had to peer up to stare into his cold blue eyes. "You made me a promise." Teodor's words were little more than a hiss.

Fromm smirked. "I've never met more gullible people in my

life. You came here thinking you could best me. But you were wrong, weren't you?"

Teodor crossed his arms and ground his teeth.

"Weren't you?"

Teodor tightened every muscle in his body so he wouldn't rain punches on the man like he itched to.

"All along, I held the trump card. I have your wife. And for her, I made you dance like a circus dog. In the end, I came out the victor. Like always."

"I have a paper."

"You foolish, foolish toad." Fromm leaned over Teodor and forced him to take two steps backward. "Fromm giveth and Fromm taketh away."

"What about my wife? At least honor that part of our agreement. Show yourself to be a man of honor."

"I have more honor in a single strand of hair than you have in your entire body. You quivering, sniveling pig. You will never, never have your wife back. That is one vow I will keep." Fromm spun and strode from the room, his chin high and his shoulders back.

Teodor deflated. He covered his face and rubbed his temples. Fromm was right. He had won. Teodor never stood a chance against such a powerful and evil man. And once again, he had failed someone dearer to him than his own life. He thumped onto the nearest bench.

Without a word spoken, the men in the room filed past Teodor. Each glared at him on the way out. They had heard the conversation and figured out what Teodor had done. How long until they spewed their wrath on him?

Once the room emptied, Jerzy came and sat beside him. "Don't let him get to you. We tried our best. Fromm may have scored, but deep inside I believe we will be the eventual winners."

Teodor may have believed that at one time, but he didn't any longer. As long as Fromm held Natia, he had the upper hand.

And there was nothing Teodor could do about it.

Chapter Thirty

The bunk creaked under Teodor as he lay down after yet another long shift. He scrubbed his face. He had no way to protect his wife, to keep her safe from that monster she shared a home with.

"Hey, Palinski, I heard something interesting." Lech, once beefy but now scrawny with a long red beard, approached Teodor's bunk.

Teodor swallowed hard and worked to keep his hands from trembling. "You know how word spreads. If every rumor proved to be true, we would have been home years ago."

"But this one I heard myself." Lech straightened himself to his full height, cleared his throat, and spoke in a much-too-loud voice. "I hear you signed the *Volksdeutsche* paper. That you turned traitor."

Teodor sprang from the bed, hands fisted. "You heard wrong."

"There's no use denying it. We all know it."

"No one is more patriotic than me." Teodor struggled to keep the warble from his voice. His gut clenched, loosened, and clenched again. He might be sick.

Umph. Pain radiated throughout his midsection. Lech had punched him. Teodor sputtered and staggered backward. "What was that for?"

"For selling your soul to the devil. May you be very happy spending eternity with him."

Teodor righted himself, but Lech landed another quick punch to his gut. Before he could straighten, a horde of men descended on him, raining blows.

He fell to the floor. He deserved this. And more. He'd prostituted himself to Fromm and to Germany. For what? Nothing. He sat here. Helpless. Natia remained under that despot's roof.

God, why? Why have you forsaken me?

"Be still, and know that I am God."

The voice wasn't audible, but it was clear.

"Be still, and know that I am God."

The punches and kicks continued. His fighting, his striving, had been for naught. Who could help him? Not himself. Not Jerzy or Fromm. Only God.

He just needed to be still and let God do his work.

So much energy wasted.

If he had trusted God, he never would have signed the paper. If only he had realized that sooner.

What was done was done. He couldn't go back and redo the past.

Lord, I'm going to see you in a few minutes. I could not take care of my mother. I cannot take care of Natia. I never have been able to. Into your hands I commit her. And myself.

❧

Zygmunt clung to Pawel as the two of them followed the young man through the maze of tunnels and sewers underneath Warsaw. At the pace the man set, Pawel's head swam and the pounding pain in his temples matched the pounding of their feet.

Beside him, Zygmunt panted, young and weak from lack of food. "I can't go anymore."

Their rescuer didn't take the time to turn around. "We can't stop. The Nazis were in the neighborhood, searching the houses. When they find what I was hiding . . ."

"That's enough." Zygmunt didn't need to hear more. "We'll do our best to keep up." Pawel panted, shaky from the blow to his head. "Where are we going?"

"I can't tell you."

Pawel didn't expect any other answer. They had followed the man for what must have been hours.

"My feet are wet. And it smells," Zygmunt cried.

The sewers weren't pretty places. The poor kid. His nightmare never ended. "We have to stop. Surely they couldn't have followed us this far."

"Do you want to take that chance?"

The protest died on Pawel's tongue.

"We're almost there. Just a little farther."

The cold darkness of the tunnel seeped deep into Pawel's bones. Zygmunt must be miserable. He had no fat for insulation. For just a moment, Pawel stopped. "Climb on my back. I'll carry you."

Zygmunt wiped away his tears and scrambled onto Pawel. Though his arms burned and legs trembled after a short while, Pawel plodded onward.

When his legs refused to go one step farther, their leader stopped in front of a small door in the brick wall. "This is the place. We're on the edge of the city now, away from the trouble. You and the child will be safe."

Chapter Thirty-One

Late Fall 1944

Up in the chilly and dingy attic room, Natia rocked Dominik as he slept. A very hot, very sick Dominik. He barked a cough, his chest rattling. His breaths were short and shallow. The lullaby died on her lips. How could she sing when her heart broke?

She stretched her aching back but didn't stop rocking. Dominik might awaken if she did. The best thing for him now was sleep, the only thing left to her after she'd tried everything to break the fever. Even with caring for Helena and Zygmunt's illnesses, Natia hadn't encountered this before.

He'd gotten sick so fast. He went down for his nap healthy and woke up ill. What should she do? If Mama were here, she could guide Natia. But she wasn't. Her turn to be the mother had come, and she couldn't do it. Sure, she had managed to keep Zygmunt and Helena clean, fed, and going to school, but they were both healthy children. Never more than a cold or slight upset stomach.

Nothing like this. Not a fever that burned the back of her hands when she touched Dominik's forehead.

And Elfriede was out shopping. With so little food available, she had to get up early and stand in line with the other housewives to purchase enough for them to eat. Even though she was German, it didn't matter. They all had to make sacrifices for the great cause.

Natia was alone.

She stared at the phone on the wall, the black box a mystery to her. They never had money for such luxuries. Though she had watched Elfriede use the contraption, she had never done so herself. She trembled as she lifted the receiver from its hook.

The operator answered and put Natia through to Dr. Bosco. But his extension rang and rang. Now what?

Dominik stirred, then opened his dark, glassy eyes, let out a weak whimper, and snuggled his burning little body against her.

She paced the floor with this dear child she loved as much, maybe even more, than her own sweet babies on the hill. If God stole him from her, it would steal the very breath from her body.

Because someone could only stand so much loss in life. Natia had reached her limit.

The front door clicked open and shut. Elfriede, home from her shopping trip at last. Natia laid Dominik on the mattress. In her haste to get down the stairs, she stumbled on the last step and caught herself on the banister. She almost tumbled into Elfriede's arms. "You have to get the doctor."

Elfriede unwrapped the blue scarf from around her neck. "I don't understand. You talk fast."

Natia pulled in a few deep breaths. "Get the doctor. Dominik is sick."

The small smile that had played on Elfriede's lips disappeared. "He not sick before."

"I know. Please, go find Dr. Bosco. I tried to call him, but he didn't answer."

Elfriede wrapped her scarf around herself again and turned away as *Pani* Rzeźnikowa rounded the corner from the living room. Natia's head spun. Perhaps she was getting sick.

The older woman patted Natia's arm. *Nie*, her appearance had to be more than a vision.

Pani Rzeźnikowa shook her gray head. "Oh my dear, let's see what we can do."

"Why are you here?"

"*Pani* Fromm invited me for tea as thanks for some beef I got her."

Natia stepped into her embrace and sobbed, wetting *Pani* Rzeźnikowa's blue dress. "I'm so scared. I don't even know what medicine to give him because I can't read the labels. At home, the medicines were lined up so I knew what they were. Here, they are nothing but a jumble. What a terrible mother I am. God knew that so he took away my babies."

With her siblings, she'd had her father's help. But on her own, she was useless. At long last, she had the answer to the question why God kept her from being a mother.

Because she wasn't capable of being one.

Pani Rzeźnikowa allowed Natia to cry herself out. When nothing more than hiccups remained, she handed Natia a clean handkerchief. "Let's see how Dominik is. I'll put the water on to boil and be right up."

Within minutes *Pani* Rzeźnikowa climbed the stairs and bent over the mattress, feeling for fever with a gentle, experienced touch, much as Natia's mother had always done. "Poor little thing. Have you tried cold compresses?"

Natia nodded.

"That's good. His body is fighting the illness, so fever isn't an all-bad thing. How about cold syrup?"

"I don't know which bottle is which."

"You can always ask for help. There is no shame in that."

"I couldn't take him out in the rain. And Dr. Bosco never answered the phone. If I even called right. I've never used one before."

Pani Rzeźnikowa stood and smoothed Natia's hair. "You're doing well, especially under the circumstances."

"I'm not." She sat hard on the mattress and covered her face. She had no more tears. She'd spent them all.

The stuffing crunched as *Pani* Rzeźnikowa sat beside her. "Don't trouble yourself so. Mothering is hard. But you're managing. Your strength and resilience amaze me."

"I am the opposite of strong and resilient."

"God is giving you the daily grace to carry you through, just as he is giving it to me."

Natia peered at her friend. "You once told me that these circumstances are part of God's plan. How is that?"

"We don't always understand the Lord's ways. Sometimes we don't like what he is doing in our lives. Understanding what his plan is can be difficult and frightening. We wonder how a loving God can allow such awful things to happen. Questions come to our minds about his goodness and care for us."

"There is no joy or light in my life. How can God still be good? How can he be doing good things for me in this situation? When he rips my children from me?"

"Our problem lies not with God but with our perception of him." *Pani* Rzeźnikowa smiled and stroked Natia's cheek. Such a motherly gesture that Natia's heart ached. If only Mama had lived longer. "We look at our circumstances and see things as not good. But we don't see the picture clearly, as the Lord does. He knows what's going on. Things happen just the way he has planned they will. We aren't to find our joy and contentment in people or in our circumstances, but in him."

Natia stood and turned a circle in the room. "The world is so dark and silent right now. There is no joy. There are no songs to sing."

"Don't look to the things of this world to bring you joy. Only the Lord can give you a heart that is truly happy and at peace."

"Do you have it? The joy, I mean?"

"I'm not perfect. Like all people, I struggle. I miss Karol and wish he were with me. But this life and its troubles are temporary. In the end, if I rest in God, he'll bring me everlasting joy. And nothing can compare to that."

Natia stared out the window. On the quiet street below, two dark figures hustled through the drizzle in their direction. Elfriede was back with Dr. Bosco. "I'm scared. And lonely."

Pani Rzeźnikowa came up behind her and squeezed her shoulders. "All the more reason to rely on him."

Had she been trusting in the wrong people and in the wrong things? How wonderful to possess everlasting joy. That no matter your outward circumstances, your heart could be happy. What was the verse Mama repeated as she lay dying? *"Thou wilt shew me the path of life: in thy presence is fulness of joy; at thy right hand there are pleasures for evermore."*

But how did one get that joy? "It's not easy."

"*Nie,* it's not."

Natia scooped Dominik from the bed and carried him downstairs. "You'll be fine now, little one. The doctor is here. He'll make you better."

Dr. Bosco entered the home, shook out his wet coat, and handed it to *Pani* Rzeźnikowa, then took Dominik from Natia's arms. "Now, little man, what has been going on?"

Natia related Dominik's symptoms, and Dr. Bosco examined him. "Croup. That's why the cough resembles a bark. Some sugar and coal syrup. Do you have that, *Pani* Fromm?"

"I do."

"Good, here's how you administer it." He gave Natia the instructions as Elfriede went for the medicine.

Dr. Bosco and *Pani* Rzeźnikowa soon went their separate ways. Natia soaked a washcloth and went upstairs to Dominik. After stripping him down, she washed him in cool water to bring down the fever and sang to him, every song in her repertoire. He slept off and on, and she made several trips down the stairs and back up with cool cloths.

In between nursing Dominik, Natia put last night's leftover soup into a pot on the stove to heat.

"How is he doing?" Elfriede sat at the kitchen table, penning a letter.

"I think his fever is coming down."

"I help?"

"Just watch the soup. I'm going to feed him some the next time he wakes."

"I pray. Dominik will be fine."

Neither of them could bear to lose this child.

Natia returned upstairs to a whimpering boy. She picked him up and patted his back. "Do you need to be changed? Then I'll wash you down again and get you some warm soup. How does that sound?"

He nodded, and she laid him on the mattress to change him. Voices came from downstairs. *Pan* Fromm had returned home.

Just as she had Dominik's diaper off, the stair treads creaked. Where was the clean nappie? She couldn't find where she'd put it. The footsteps approached.

As she flung the blanket over Dominik, *Pan* Fromm entered the room. She could barely make out his words over the pounding of her heart. "My wife is not to be cooking dinner. That is *your* job. Get downstairs and get to work. This child has become too much of a distraction." He turned on his heel, then slammed the door behind him.

Natia released her pent-up breath. That was close. Much too close. The noose was tightening.

♪♪♪

Chapter Thirty-Two

January 1945

Teodor lugged another box of heavy parts to the train. The cold bit through his threadbare coat. Wet seeped through the thin soles of his shoes, and he shivered. He stopped on the landing as the world tilted in front of him.

If only he could do something—anything—to pay back the dogs who held him, his wife, and millions of other Poles captive. He fought to get his life back.

The one he'd signed away on that paper.

Jerzy stumbled after him. "If only we were home." He coughed. "Then again, I know what will happen if our families and our neighbors discover how we betrayed our country."

Teodor shivered. He knew too.

Jerzy sat on the step, his hands shaking. This man who had betrayed him. And coerced him into betraying his country.

Teodor fought to keep his voice low but couldn't keep the venom from it. "I prided myself on my love and my loyalty for my country. But because I listened to you, I threw that away. And for what? For nothing. It didn't help me or my wife. In fact, it turned out to be Fromm's own form of sabotage."

Jerzy clenched his fists. "Why blame this on me? You have a brain. I didn't force you to sign. You did it of your own will and volition. Stop trying to shove the fault down my throat."

Teodor leaned against the wall as if Jerzy had punched him in the stomach. He steepled his hands and touched his forehead. "Why? Why did I do it?" His voice broke.

"Because you love your wife even more than you love your country."

Teodor closed his eyes. "You're right. I do." As pain tightened in a band around his middle, he pressed his chest. "I do."

"What we did, we did for them. And only for them. It was a gamble that didn't pay off. But one I would take again in a heartbeat, if there were any chance, even the smallest glimmer of hope, of me getting home to my wife and my children before I die."

Teodor glanced up. "Don't talk like that."

"It's true. There's no time left to deny it. The tuberculosis is about to claim me. I haven't been a friend to you. I'll admit that, at times, I looked out for my own best interest and no one else's."

"In desperate times, when survival is a daily battle, sometimes that's what we do."

"Don't beat yourself up about signing. In hindsight, maybe it wasn't the best course of action. But isn't being with your wife better than anything?"

His wife was the best blessing the Lord had ever brought to him. But even touching her skin, laughing with her, sleeping beside her wasn't the ultimate joy and wasn't what was getting him through these difficult days and even more difficult nights.

It was the Lord.

Natia sang to him, but the Lord gave her the melody. Natia stood beside him, but the Lord never left him. Natia loved him, but the Lord sacrificed his Son for him.

The time had come to forgive. "I understand that you didn't do anything out of malicious intent. But you hurt me nonetheless."

"I know. I'm ashamed of my actions. In a way, I'm relieved Fromm didn't send me home."

"Why?"

"I would have had to tell my wife why I returned. To her, I wouldn't have been able to lie. And my actions would have crushed her."

"You'll see her again."

Jerzy shook his head, his hazel eyes shimmering. "I won't. I stopped kidding myself weeks ago. Even if liberation came tomorrow, I wouldn't survive the trip home. I hope you do. I want you to."

"When I get to Piosenka, I'll visit your wife and tell her what a fine man you were. How you fought to come home to her."

"That comforts me. Just don't tell her about the paper. Ever. Promise me?"

Teodor forced the words around the lump in his throat. "I promise."

೨

Dominik napped on a blanket at Natia's feet as she sat on the flowered chair in the corner of the living room, her knitting needles clacking away, Elfriede's embroidery floss *whishing* through the fabric. Natia watched the even rise and fall of the child's chest. No ill effects remained from the croup.

"What is for lunch?" Elfriede bit off the thread and chose another color from the basket beside her.

"A little soup and a slice of bread." They had nothing more. Each day Dominik's cheeks lost a measure of their baby-like roundness.

"You do good job with little food."

"*Dziękuję Ci.*"

The clock ticked away several minutes. In the distance came the banging of artillery. The Soviets knocked on their doorstep.

A couple of times this morning, Natia had caught Elfriede opening her mouth as if to speak, then shutting it right away. Whatever she wanted to tell Natia must be hard. Still, each time Elfriede did it, the knot in Natia's stomach tightened. "What do you want to say?"

Elfriede pricked her finger and stuck it in her mouth, then shook it out. "I'm sorry."

"What for?"

"For bringing you here. You should be with your husband."

"*Nie*. I would have liked to have been by his side, but I wouldn't have been your friend then. And I wouldn't have Dominik. So it wasn't all bad." Her heart ached for *Tata* and Helena, and she prayed almost every minute of every day for Zygmunt's safety, but God had brought blessings in the trials.

"You miss him."

"Of course. I will be very happy to be with him again." Soon. That day would be here soon. Each morning she awoke was one less day until Teodor held her close. The Soviets were nearby.

"What happens to me? When war is over?" Elfriede's hands trembled, and she set her embroidery to the side.

"What do you mean?"

"You have your husband. But mine? I do not know what will happen to him. Do I want him for husband?"

"Those answers, I cannot give you. But the joy of the Lord will be your strength."

"You say that. Why?"

"Because only the Lord could have carried us through this time. And he won't forsake us, no matter what lies before us."

"I don't understand."

In heaven, there wouldn't be a language barrier. She and Elfriede would sit down and have a nice, long chat then. "Happiness only comes from God."

"Ah." She smiled but furrowed her brow. "Happiness from God?"

"Even in the bad times." Even in the loss of her family. They were safe. They were experiencing everlasting joy. How could she want less for them? For herself? "My joy doesn't depend on what I have. Only on God." That's what *Pani* Rzeźnikowa meant. Joy only came through dependence on the Lord and him alone. Joy was forward looking, toward heaven. Would the pain of losing her children cease? *Nie,* but she could also find joy, even here, even now.

"That is hard."

Natia chuckled. "I'm just learning it myself. It's easy to forget."

"How can you be happy with bad things?"

"Because God loves me."

Elfriede scooted to the edge of the couch. "Even now, he loves you?"

"Always." *Tak*, always. She repeated that to herself. God always loved her. "He gave you to be my friend. And Dominik."

"I see. Even with bad, God is good. Then we are happy."

"That's the best way I've ever heard it put."

Silence fell over them once more, but not one of unease or tension. One of peace and contemplation.

What would happen to Elfriede after Germany fell? Would there be anything left of her country? *Pani* Rzeźnikowa brought stories of the Allies bombing Berlin day and night, ceaselessly, relentlessly. Nothing would exist but dust and rubble.

And *Pan* Fromm? Would the Allies hold the Nazis responsible for their war crimes?

At least Poland would be free. No more Soviets. No more Germans. Only Poles, living peaceful lives. She could almost feel the warm soil of their farm between her toes. The first thing she would do would be to climb the hill and sing her children a lullaby.

Dominik stirred and let out a good, strong wail. Natia picked him up. "Do your teeth hurt, little one? Let's go change your nappy, and I'll get you a cold spoon to chew on. How does that sound?"

The child cried all the harder, big tears rolling down his scrunched-up face.

Elfriede kissed his cheek. "I'll set the table while you change him."

"See there, Dominik. All will be well. A little soup in your tummy, and you'll feel better." Natia climbed the stairs to her attic room and laid Dominik on the mattress. "We'll have to hurry because it's chilly in here, don't you think?"

She pulled out a nappy and a pair of rubber pants, then set to stripping the little boy. He screamed as she worked and wriggled out of her grasp. "Come on. Let's get this over with so we can eat lunch."

But he ran to the other side of the room, still bawling.

"Dominik. Please let me get you dressed." She moved toward him, but he darted around her, as slippery as a Christmas carp. "You little stinker."

"*Nie, nie.*" He screeched at the top of his lungs, standing by the door, undressed from the waist down.

Natia glanced up.

Pan Fromm stood in the doorway, his face red, his eyes narrowed.

She ran to snatch Dominik before *Pan* Fromm discovered their secret.

"What is this?"

He knew.

♪♪♪

Chapter Thirty-Three

"What is this?"

At her husband's shouting, Elfriede raced into the tiny attic bedroom. His voice echoed in her ears.

"He's circumcised. A little Jew, right in my own home. Under my nose," he bellowed, almost shaking the rafters.

Natia clung to Dominik.

Jewish? That couldn't be right. Dominik couldn't be … Elfriede couldn't draw in a breath. How could Natia deceive her? Elfriede had come to care for the little boy, to love him almost as much as she would love her own child, had defended him and Natia.

Erich stepped in Natia's direction. Elfriede, with the element of surprise in her favor, pushed him to the side. "Stay away from Dominik. Don't come near him."

Erich whirled around and struck her across the cheek. "You knew there was a Jew in my house."

"He's a child, Erich." Her cheek stung but she held back the tears. No way would she give him the satisfaction of cowing her.

"A Jewish child. Filth. Her, I can understand. Dirt begets dirt. But you? I expected far better from you. How could you do this?"

"Please, calm down. Don't hurt us."

Dominik wailed.

"Hurt you?" He gave a chilly half laugh. "I'm going to kill you. All of you." He reached for his sidearm.

Elfriede's heart stopped beating. *Nein*, she couldn't let that happen. Couldn't allow Erich to harm the child, this innocent little love, no matter his ethnicity. She stepped forward and kicked her husband in the groin. "Run, Natia, run." Now her heartbeat thrummed in her ears.

Natia raced by a doubled-over Erich as she clung to Dominik.

Erich grabbed Elfriede by the ankle as she sprinted to get by him before he recovered from the kick. She tripped and fell on top of him and waited for the searing pain of a bullet.

"Leave me alone. Don't touch me. Get away from me." She kicked, bit, scratched. Did whatever she had to do to escape.

"You Jew-loving pig. You aren't fit to be called a German. How long have you known?"

As he huffed for breath, she scrambled to her feet. Once she had her balance, she kicked him once more, the heel of her oxford connecting with his temple.

As tears blurred her vision, she almost slid down the stairs, a shot firing behind her. Then she stumbled out the door and pushed Natia into the bright January day.

But where should they go?

And who was coming behind them?

Dominik wailed. Natia jiggled him. "Where?"

"I don't know."

"Dr. Bosco." The women chorused his name.

"*Schnell*." Elfriede pulled Natia by the wrist and dragged her down the street. She sang that lullaby as they sprinted as fast as the crying child allowed them. The music box-like tune calmed Dominik. Within moments he laughed and clapped his hands.

Natia tried to break off to go one way, but Elfriede held her fast. "*Nein*. We go around so Erich not come." She zigzagged through the little town, gasping for air. Any moment Erich was sure to appear around the corner. Or behind them. She glanced over her shoulder.

There he was. Two shots rang over their heads. Elfriede grasped Natia by the arm, and they sprinted. They cut through yards and down alleys until they couldn't draw in a deep breath.

Elfriede turned again. No sign of Erich. Somewhere, they had lost him.

There, up ahead, was the doctor's green cottage, a white fence surrounding the withered remains of last summer's garden. Elfriede peered left and right and behind her. Good, no one was about. She led Natia up the walk and pounded on the doctor's door.

He opened it, and she pushed her way by him. "Lock the door."

He complied with her order. "What is this? Why are you outside without a coat?"

Natia stepped forward and unwrapped her sweater from around Dominik's bare buttocks. "*Pan* Fromm came home while I was changing him."

The doctor rubbed the top of his almost-bald head. "So he knows."

Elfriede motioned for Natia to sit and then turned to the doctor. "What do we do now? Where do we go? Erich, he looks for us. He will kill us. Me too."

"We have nothing." Natia's voice warbled.

"Let me think." The man paced back and forth across his small but tidy living room. "I don't know where to bring you. The Soviets are advancing. Warsaw is no more, destroyed in the uprising. Kraków is about to fall. It's not safe there."

Elfriede's Polish failed her, either because Dr. Bosco and Natia spoke so fast or because she ran out of energy to follow the conversation. They bantered for a long while. In the meantime, she peeked through curtains. Any moment now Erich would figure out where they went. They couldn't stay here.

A movement caught the corner of her eye. Erich? *Nein*, just Herr Wójcik returning to his home. She closed the curtain.

Natia touched her shoulder. "*Pani* Fromm, you have a house in Germany?"

"*Tak*. Near Bremen. You want us to go there?"

Dr. Bosco nodded. "That's good. The Americans will be there soon. And then you'll be free."

"What if Erich finds? He will come."

The doctor switched to German. "He can't leave here. At least, not yet. He's still in charge of the factory. And I'm sure he won't want to explain to the authorities why his wife hid a Jewish child under his nose."

"You think we will be safe?"

"As safe as anywhere."

Natia kissed Dominik's forehead. "I don't want to leave Poland. Teodor is here. My babies are here. So is Zygmunt. You left him with those people in Warsaw. I have to get him. He's alone."

Of course, she wouldn't want to leave. And Elfriede couldn't blame her. "But I am German woman. I hear things. The Soviets are bad. Germans run away from Poland, away from Russians. Soon they come."

Natia paced the small room. "I can't leave my husband or my brother. I won't leave the country without them."

Elfriede's hands sweated. Natia was determined to stay. But Elfriede couldn't. If they parted ways, she might never see Dominik again. Never hear his laugh, feel his soft hands on her cheeks, smell his sweet baby scent. That would be too much to bear. "Fine. We will not go to Germany. We stay here. Go to her farm. But I must have Polish papers."

Natia plopped to the couch. "But Teodor. I need him. I won't leave Pieśń Nabożna without him."

What were they going to do? Any minute, Erich could burst through the door.

❧

Natia sat on Dr. Bosco's overstuffed couch, still clutching Dominik. "I won't go unless Teodor comes. I can't leave him. This, I refuse to do."

Elfriede widened her eyes larger than Natia had ever seen. "*Nie. Nie.* We go now. Erich will find us."

"How can you expect me to leave my husband?" Elfriede

didn't understand the bond she and Teodor shared. How could she expect Natia to go so far away? Never in their lives had they been more than a few kilometers apart.

Dr. Bosco sat beside her. "You need to be reasonable, *Pani* Palinska. For Dominik's sake, you need to leave as soon as possible. There's no time to waste."

Her stomach hardened. "Teodor." She swallowed her tears.

"I can see it's important to you that he come."

"Don't you think it would be wise for us to have a man with us? Someone who knows the way home?"

"You may be correct. I'll see what I can do."

"What if Erich comes?" Elfriede's voice warbled.

"You won't stay here. I have a small plot of land on the outskirts of Pieśń Nabożna. There isn't a home there but a little shed where I keep my tools. That's where you'll hide. Tonight I'll bring Teodor to you, and you can leave."

"Really?" Natia tingled all over. "I will see my husband tonight?" Her nightmare had turned into a dream. The best kind. But Dominik pinched her cheek and it stung, so she must be awake. "What about Zygmunt?"

"You'll have a surprise waiting for you when you get home."

"What?"

"I told you how I was beaten in Warsaw and saved by a young man. The man he took us to, the one who helped me out of the city, also helped Zygmunt. I received word earlier today. Your brother is in Piosenka, waiting for you."

"He's there already?" She bounced on the sofa. One less person to worry about and another reunion awaiting her. The time for good-bye had passed.

The doctor nodded. "And from what I understand, most anxious for your arrival."

"Imagine, Zygmunt safe and Teodor coming to me. I'll see my brother soon and my husband even sooner."

The doctor patted her hand. "If things go well, you will see him. This is dangerous, getting him out. Pray that nothing goes wrong."

～⌒～

Pawel closed the shed door and turned the key in the lock. He breathed in and released the air a little at a time. He had to be crazy to be involved in another scheme. This one to break a man out of the camp. One had tried to escape by jumping out of the third-floor window. Pawel treated his two broken legs, but according to Teodor, the man never returned to the factory.

He strolled along the side of the road as if on a little jaunt, even though the winter winds bit through his coat. He blew on his fingers to keep warm. All that he could spare, he'd given to the women so they wouldn't freeze until he returned.

Within a few minutes of arriving home, he packed his doctor's bag and turned to leave. Would he ever return? When would it be his turn to be arrested? Right now, he counted on the Germans having too many other things on their minds, namely the crumbling of their empire. Within days, Poland could well be on its way to complete liberation.

He touched the photo of his beautiful wife. Almost two years had gone by since he'd seen her. He ached to touch her, hold her, imbibe her scent. "Pray for me, my darling. I don't know how much longer I can escape their clutches." He touched his lips, then her lips in the photograph. "I'll see you later."

Whether the cold or his nerves got to him, he didn't know, but he came to the factory faster than usual. He entered through a side door and went straight to *Pan* Fromm's office.

"Can I help you?" The perky red-haired secretary drew a handful of files from her desk drawer and placed them in a box, one of many littering the room.

"I'm searching for *Untersturmführer* Fromm."

"He's not here. He went home for lunch but hasn't returned. I expected him some time ago. Would you like to wait?"

"*Nein*." In one way, it was better that Fromm was still out. That gave Pawel a little more leeway in the factory. On the other hand, it was a problem because that meant he continued to hunt for his wife. "I need to see Teodor Palinski."

"Let me call the floor and have him brought down."

"Can I wait in the infirmary?"

"Do as you please."

He jerked forward. Had she just said that? They must be ready to evacuate.

He made the rounds of his patients as he waited for Teodor, stopping by Jerzy's bed. "How are you doing?"

"Twice in one day, Doctor? I must really be sick." Jerzy coughed, and blood trickled from the side of his mouth.

The lung disease was taking its toll. "How are you feeling?"

"Very weak. Like I'm losing my grip on this world."

Pawel sat beside him. "You are."

"How long?"

"A day or two at the most."

Jerzy nodded and coughed again, clinging to the edge of the sheet. Some time passed before he caught his breath. "I hardly have the energy."

"I understand."

"Will you pray with me?"

"I'm not a priest."

"I just need someone to pray. There are things …"

Pawel bowed his head. "Dear Lord, please be near to your servant, Jerzy, as you usher him into your presence. Forgive all his sins through your Son, and cleanse him from all unrighteousness. Ease his pain and his suffering until the time he is with you. We ask this in Jesus' precious name. Amen."

"Amen. *Dziękuję Ci*."

Pawel almost answered that it was his pleasure. But it wasn't really. "You're welcome. I'll continue to pray for you. Just think. Your liberation is at hand."

"I'm looking forward to it."

"You summoned me?" Teodor stood at the end of Jerzy's bed. He grasped the top of the iron footboard, his knuckles white.

"I'll give you a few minutes alone with your friend. Then if you could meet me in the next room, I have something for you."

Teodor raised his eyebrows and bit his lip but nodded.

With his heart thudding and his hands shaking, Pawel slipped into the next room to await Teodor. His stomach bunched into knots even tighter than it had traveling to Warsaw during the uprising.

They were so close to freedom.

And even closer to death.

Chapter Thirty-Four

Teodor sat in the chair beside Jerzy's bed that Pawel had vacated. His friend's face matched the color of the snowy-white sheets his mother hung on the line every Monday. "You're going to get out of here, aren't you?"

"You know me." Jerzy coughed. "I'll do anything to leave. But you're going to make it."

"I think the Soviets are concentrating on the major cities. It might be a while before they get here."

"Don't worry. They will. Listen."

"*Tak?*"

"Tell my wife I love her."

"I will. I promise. As soon as I get back."

"Tell her only the good. That's how I want her to remember me."

Teodor nodded. "I will."

"Have you forgiven me?"

"I have. And I heard the doctor pray for you. I hope you have peace with the Lord."

"I do." Jerzy clasped Teodor's hand. "*Dzięki.*"

Teodor tried to smile but failed. "You're welcome." He got up and left without glancing backward. If he had, he would have lost all composure.

Pawel waited for him in the next room, an empty office. So some of the Germans had already been sent home. A sign of things to come, perhaps. "What did you want to see me about?"

"It's a long story, and one I don't have time to explain. Your wife, Fromm's wife, and the child are waiting for you outside of town. It's become necessary for them to flee. No matter what, Fromm can't find them. He'll kill them."

"Wait a minute. What did you say? Fleeing? Killing?" Teodor's pulse throbbed in his neck.

"Natia won't leave without you." He opened his black bag and drew out a set of his clothes, a coat, and a hat. "Put these on, pull the hat over your eyes, keep your head down, and walk out of here to the east, following the road behind the factory."

"And what about you?"

"Fromm is searching for the women. His secretary is too busy packing files to notice. I'll follow you a short while later. Walk slowly, so I can catch up with you. Hurry. There's no time to waste."

While Pawel turned his back, Teodor changed from his blue coveralls, the prison uniform, to Pawel's. They hung on him. Without the benefit of a belt, he would have to hold up the pants. For a moment, he stared at the *P* in a triangle on his discarded shirt. With the doctor's clothes on, a lightness enveloped him. That mark had weighed him down. Oh, to be free of it.

"Are you ready?"

Teodor pulled the brim of the fedora lower. "I am." His hands shook. Sweat trickled down his back despite the winter temperatures.

He made his way down the hall, struggling to keep a confident stride like Pawel's. If he hesitated, acted like he had something to hide, the Germans might stop him. He came to the office door where the secretary stood with her back to Teodor, pulling files out of the cabinet. She turned.

He screeched to a halt.

She waved at him and continued with her job.

He wiped his sweaty palms on his pants and turned the knob. Glanced around. Good, nobody about. He stepped out of the building and through the yard.

The guard. He had to open the gate. Pawel had a booming,

commanding voice. Teodor did not. He slouched more and turned his face away.

Without demanding identification, the guard unlocked the gate. Teodor sauntered through.

And tasted the sweetness of freedom in almost two years. How absolutely, utterly glorious. Words couldn't describe the euphoria. No one to tell him what to do or when to do it. No one to peer over his shoulder.

No one to make him afraid.

He gazed at the town, the people living normal lives just outside the walls of suffering. And then, *oomph*. He ran into something big and warm. Without lifting his head, he glanced up.

At a scowling, red-faced *Untersturmführer* Fromm gripping his gun. "Papers."

He gazed at the road, not daring to breathe, praying Fromm didn't recognize him. Having no identification to produce, he was headed right back to where he came from. *Nie,* somewhere worse. He lowered his voice. "I'm looking for the doctor. My wife is in labor. Ran out the door so fast, I didn't grab my papers."

"You'll need to come with me." Fromm grabbed Teodor by the upper arm. His knees softened, and he struggled to remain upright. To be so close to freedom and to Natia, only to have it end like this. He'd almost made it.

He peered over his shoulder. God bless him, here came Bosco. Teodor waved at him. "Pawel, there you are. I've been searching for you. My wife is in labor. We must hurry. I'm afraid there is something wrong with the baby." The trembling in Teodor's voice was real. He hadn't forgotten that day Andrzej died.

Dr. Bosco nodded. "You understand, *Pan* Fromm. There isn't a moment to lose."

By some miracle, Fromm lessened his grip on Teodor. Off in the distance, the blast of artillery broke the day's stillness. The Nazi unleashed Teodor and sprinted away.

Teodor sighed. "That was close."

"Too close." The unflappable Pawel had paled so the pallor of his face matched the grayness of his hair. "Let's get out of here."

"Where is Natia?"

"In a shed."

"How far?"

"Only about a kilometer. It won't be long until you're reunited."

"Reunited." Could it be true? For so many long nights, he'd dreamed of the day he could be with his Natia again. And here it was.

Before the war, a walk of a kilometer was easy. But now, always glancing over his shoulder to see if they were followed, he stumbled several times. Pawel caught him by the arm and held him upright. "I gave the women some bread and a little *schmaltz*. There's plenty there for you. Just hang on."

And then, up ahead, he spied the tiny building, probably just big enough to hold a few tools and a wheelbarrow.

And his wife.

Dried leaves from last fall crunched under his feet as he left the road and made his way to the outbuilding. He broke into a run.

❧

Shivers coursed through Natia as she huddled in the dark, dank shed awaiting Teodor's arrival. She held Dominik close and sang to him in a low, soft voice to keep him quiet.

> *A kitten sits on the fence,*
> *And he blinks.*
> *It's a very pretty song, and it's not long.*
> *Not long and not short, but just right,*
> *But just right.*
> *Come on, little kitten, sing again.*

Elfriede stirred beside her. "I'm cold. My toes and fingers."

They snuggled closer together. "They'll be here soon."

"Why you not tell me about Dominik?"

The question had been bound to come. "Are you angry? You

won't turn us in, will you?" Would she? Maybe to regain her husband's favor. To save herself from her countrymen.

"*Nie,* you are safe. I not tell anyone. Jew or not Jew doesn't matter. I love the boy. Like my own little baby."

The cold penetrated to Natia's bones. While it was good that Elfriede loved Dominik enough to keep his secret, perhaps she loved him too much. Enough to rip him from Natia's arms. And that, she couldn't allow.

She would die first.

Elfriede tugged the bright yellow-and-green quilt tighter around herself and sniffed. "You will take care of me and Dominik?"

"Teodor and I will look after you." And Dominik, of course. But he would stay with them forever.

Outside, leaves crunched under approaching boots. Was it them? Was her husband on the other side of the door? She handed Dominik to Elfriede and threw off the blanket, now warm all over. Her heart throbbed in her ears, the only thing she could hear.

A slit of light slipped into the building, growing wider and wider until the door stood open.

And with it, Teodor.

She squealed and rushed into his arms. He was thin and bony, but all hers. "*Moje serce.* Oh, Teodor. Teodor, *moje serce.*" She could find no other words to express this bursting of her heart.

He squeezed her to himself, his ribs like piano keys underneath her fingers. "Oh, Natia, how I've dreamed of you and longed for you. You are everything to me. I can't believe we're together."

Dr. Bosco shut the door behind him as he entered, extinguishing the light. "Keep the reunion quiet. We don't want Fromm to find us."

So Natia nestled into Teodor's shoulder and whispered, "For a long time, I thought I would never see you again."

"Every day, I fought to live so I could be with you. You kept me going."

"When you stopped answering me—"

"I was in prison."

"Dr. Bosco told me. But I thought I would die without you. You bring the song to my heart."

"I'm never going to leave you again, *moje słońce*." He bent down and gave her the longest, sweetest kiss she'd ever experienced, their hearts now pounding in unison.

Hard as it was, she broke away from her husband and peered over his shoulder at the doctor. "We will forever be in your debt. I can't believe he's here." She returned her attention to Teodor. "Are you real?"

In answer, he kissed her again. The caress of his lips against hers spoke of months of loneliness and longing. How well she understood. The seconds melded into minutes.

Dr. Bosco cleared his throat. "While I hate to break up the reunion, we can't stay. It's only a matter of time before Fromm figures out where to search."

Natia's mouth went dry. "How will we get home?"

"There's a farm down the road. They have a little cart and a donkey too stubborn for the Nazis to confiscate. We'll borrow it."

Teodor turned to face the doctor but didn't release his hold on her. "How will you explain?"

"I'll tell them I need it to make a call outside town. They might figure out the real reason, but they won't stop me. They're good people. Stay here, and I'll return soon. The situation to the east is chaotic. The Germans are headed west, as fast as possible. And you're headed behind the battle lines." He locked the door and left.

Teodor drew Natia to himself. She fit just right into his embrace. The Lord had created them to be like two puzzle pieces, put together to make one whole picture. "I'm sorry about your father and Helena."

For the first time since she learned of their deaths, she managed a small smile when thinking of them. "They are at peace."

Dominik toddled over and tugged on Natia's sweater. "Mama."

Teodor peered down. "Who is this little one?"

"This is the child I told you about. Dominik. He's Jewish. Elfriede and I have been hiding him since he came. That's why we must run. *Pan* Fromm figured out Dominik's secret."

She picked up the boy and held him between them. "He's a wonderful child. I love him, Teodor." She whispered to him so Elfriede wouldn't hear. "We have to take care of him and raise him as our own."

He leaned over and whispered, his breath tickling her neck, the hair on her arms standing up straight. "And we will."

Her insides glowed. "We're a family, Teodor."

"What about her?"

What about Elfriede? Would she try to keep the boy? Natia shook her head. Teodor would make sure Dominik stayed with them. For the first time in almost two long years, she relaxed. "That's *Pan* Fromm's wife. She's in danger as well."

"You're taking a German woman and a Jewish child with us?"

"You don't understand what we've been through together. Elfriede is a good woman who needs us." What if he refused to take them? She couldn't leave them behind. Wouldn't do it. Even if Elfriede wanted Dominik. Leaving her here to die would be wrong. But Teodor wasn't that kind of man. "You know this is what's right."

He nodded. "As long as I'm with you, everything will be fine."

"You're sure?"

"This is why I fell in love with you. Your love knows no limits. You care for the broken and downtrodden. I would expect no less."

The door swung open. Dr. Bosco motioned them from the shed. "We must hurry. The farmer's wife just came from town. The place is in an uproar. *Pan* Fromm is ..." He gazed at Elfriede. "Anyway, we have no time to lose. He's ransacking my house as we speak. When he finds the deed for the farm, he'll be here."

They weren't completely free yet. Much lay between them and their home.

Chapter Thirty-Five

Teodor hustled the women and the child out of the shed and to the wagon. They crowded into the small cart, shoulder to shoulder. The child fussed. Teodor took the reins and slapped the donkey's backside.

The animal hee-hawed but decided not to cooperate. On the next try, he flicked the reins over the donkey's rump. "Let's go. Come on, up with you."

But the animal had the audacity to turn around and stare at Teodor. They didn't have time for this. Fromm might be just steps behind them. Teodor hopped from the cart and took the donkey by the reins, pulling her until she moved her feet. "Couldn't your neighbor have had a fine young gelding?"

Dr. Bosco stood on the side of the road and chuckled. "They did. The Germans confiscated it within days of the invasion."

Teodor motioned for the doctor to take his place in the cart. "Aren't you coming? Your home is no longer safe."

"But it is my home. Where my wife will return to me, Lord willing, and soon, I hope. You understand. I cannot leave without her. Just as you would not be going anywhere unless your wife was by your side."

"What will you do?"

"Don't worry about me. I've lived here all my life. I can stay one step ahead of Fromm. But God go with you." Dr. Bosco peered around Teodor at the women in the cart. "With all of you."

Natia leaned over and swiped a tear from her eye. "You have been so good to us. We can never repay you."

"There is no need. Knowing you are safe is good enough for me."

"But will you be?" Natia's voice broke.

"God will take care of me."

Teodor clung to the donkey's reins. "Are you sure?"

"Positive. Now get going."

Teodor slapped the reins on the donkey's rump once more. At last the cart's wheels creaked and turned, and they plodded down the road, away from Pieśń Nabożna, away from the factory, and away from the doctor who had saved them.

Toward home.

Right now, he refused to think about what awaited them there. He had Natia. That's all he needed.

But he also had another woman and a child with them. A little one. A family. That's what Natia had called them. A child of their own. Wouldn't *Pani* Fromm want the boy? And wouldn't Natia's heart break into pieces when the German woman kept him for herself?

And his own heart? It would break too. They were so close to being a real family.

His head throbbed and he rubbed his temple. He swayed as the world spun around him.

Natia propped him upright. "That's enough. I'll take over. Get some bread and water."

His cheeks burned. "I'm sorry."

"Why? They've almost worked you to death."

"That was their goal. But I need to take care of you. You, Dominik, and *Pani* Fromm."

"You can best take care of us by taking care of yourself and getting your strength back." Natia's green eyes stood out in her hollow face.

"You haven't been eating well either."

"Better than you. There isn't much to go around for anyone these days. Not even the Germans." She glanced away.

She didn't tell him the truth. At least, not all of it. For now, he let it slide.

"Here." She reached inside a rucksack and produced a loaf of bread. One whole entire loaf. Small, but more than one piece. "Don't overeat."

Laughter burst unchecked from his lips. "That's not likely."

"I just got you back."

He rubbed her hand. "*Moje słońce*, don't be so serious. I'm not going to leave you. Not ever." But could he guarantee that? He glanced over his shoulder. *Nie*, he wouldn't rest until they crossed the lines into Soviet-held territory. Not until he walked onto his own farmland and stepped through the door to his home. By now, the Germans who took it must have fled.

His wife pulled him close, and he cuddled against her. How good to be back in her arms where he belonged. This day, the one he feared might never come, had arrived. That's what he needed to focus on. That, and getting them safely home.

A low rumble sounded ahead of them, the noise of many engines splitting the silent winter's night. Fromm had found them. He'd been bound to.

And he'd brought an entire battalion with him, judging by the noise of the approaching convoy. "We have to find cover."

Natia grasped the donkey's reins. "But where? There's nothing around." Her voice trembled.

He squeezed her. "There's a light ahead. See. And I can make out the shadow of a barn."

"We'll never get there before the trucks reach us."

Not with the donkey, that was for sure. Natia brought the animal to a halt. "We'll have to run. There's no time to waste."

Teodor scrambled down and reached back to assist *Pani* Fromm and Dominik. How would he be able to keep up with them when he could barely walk? He stumbled backward.

"This not work." *Pani* Fromm's words were steady. Even in the darkness, her blue eyes held a steely light.

"What other options do we have?"

"This not work. You go down there." The German woman pointed to the ditch beside the road. She must not have understood what they had been talking about.

"They'll see us. The baby will cry." Her plan was terrible.

"They not see you. I tell them I am going home. They help me and leave you alone."

The drone of engines approached, and the light in the distance flickered and went out. Making a dash for the safety of the barn was out of the question.

Pani Fromm motioned them away. "Go, go."

Natia handed him the baby, then turned to her slave master. They embraced far too long, sniffling back tears. What could Natia be thinking? She needed to take cover.

Paper-covered headlights swept around the curve in the road and gave off a dim light.

"Natia, now."

❧

Elfriede embraced Natia, holding her close for as long as she dared. What would she do without this woman in her life? This one who understood the deepest part of her soul?

She squeezed Natia, and the baby let out a squeal.

Dominik. She was about to lose him. But it had been inevitable. Keeping him had been an impossible dream. Not with Erich for a husband. And not once they knew the secret of Dominik's identity.

But without the boy, her life would be dark. Empty. Void.

She had to do this. Let him go for his own good. Give him the family she couldn't.

The pain in her heart stole her breath.

The rumble underneath their feet increased, tickling her soles.

If Erich wasn't among the approaching trucks, her plan would work. She had to do this for Dominik. And Natia.

Tears streaked down her cheeks as she rubbed Natia's bony back. "*Dzięki* for all you teach me. You are my friend. I not forget you. Ever."

Natia's own tears dampened Elfriede's cheek. "Good-bye, my friend, good-bye. God go with you. May he bless you and watch over you. *Dzięki* for helping me."

With a quick kiss on each of Elfriede's cheeks, Natia disappeared into the night, ripping Dominik away.

Elfriede wiped the moisture from her face as she climbed into the cart. *Please, Lord, keep Dominik quiet. Keep them all safe. And may Erich not be in any of those vehicles.*

The motorcade came ever closer. She licked her dry lips and swallowed hard. No doubt they would hear the thrumming of her heart in her chest.

Several trucks passed and a motorcycle, not even slowing to help what appeared to be a lone woman stranded at the side of the road at night. Then an automobile braked and halted beside her.

A lanky officer dressed in his olive-gray uniform stepped from the car. "Papers."

The world around Elfriede spun. Why hadn't she thought about that? With running out of the house, she hadn't grabbed any identification. Then again, it was best not to let this man know who her husband was.

Her husband, her hunter.

She stiffened her spine. If her voice didn't break, she could pull this off. "I am so thankful you stopped. Here I am, trying to get away from these awful Soviets, and all I could find was this donkey cart. And the animal has no intention of moving."

The man looked her in the eyes for the first time. "You are German?"

"*Ja*. Weeks ago, my husband warned me to leave, but I didn't want to be without him. By the time I heeded his advice, it was too late to get a train. Can you help me?"

"I will still need to see your papers."

In the darkness he wouldn't notice her bat her eyelashes, so instead she honeyed her voice. "I am Frau Eisinger." Elfriede used a name Erich had thrown around as a couple they should admire, a soldier loyal to the cause and a woman loyal to her husband. "There is no time to stand on formalities. I'm fleeing the Russians, as are you. All I want is to return to the fatherland and await the war's outcome. Surely you can help a fellow German, and a woman at that. Isn't that what a true German would do?"

"I shouldn't because we were told to be on the lookout for a woman accused of hiding Jews."

So Erich hadn't given up on finding her. "As you can see, I'm all alone. So very, very alone."

Dominik picked that moment to let out a squeak. Elfriede held her breath. Natia must have shushed him in record time because he didn't make another sound.

Just as Elfriede released the air from her lungs, the officer moved around the cart toward the group in the ditch.

"Just an old cat on its last legs. I heard it a few times while I waited for help. The poor thing won't last until morning." Would any of them? "No need to bother. I'm terribly cold. Could you please give me a ride to the next town?"

The soldier broke off his pursuit of the sound and returned to her side. "Get your things. I'll take you."

"I fled my home with no time to spare. I have nothing."

"Climb in, then."

With everything inside of her, Elfriede worked to avoid turning for one last good-bye to the people who had come to mean so much to her. The loss stabbed her with a physical pain, and she gasped.

She climbed inside the automobile, the warmth from the engine enveloping her. As she sank into the seat, she attempted to peer out the window. Nothing but blackness. Good. The rumble of engines faded in the distance. No more approached. The little group would be safe, and the donkey and cart would still be there for them to continue their journey.

As the soldier shifted into gear and pulled onto the roadway, Elfriede relaxed. *Dear Lord, please go with them. And with me too. Don't desert me.*

Because without him, she would be alone in the world.

Chapter Thirty-Six

Pawel sat at his desk, papers scattered across it. Fromm's work. Since Antonina had left, all the order had gone out of his life. Nothing was as it should be. He sighed. Antonina, his love. Where was she? As the Soviets closed in, more time passed between words from her.

When would he see her?

Teodor and Natia had been reunited. Ah, to witness such young love. He and his wife had once been that way. As the years passed, they had settled into their comfortable routine and taken each other for granted. At least he had.

But that would change once they were together, once he held her in his arms. He would thank her for each meal she cooked and tell her how delicious it tasted. He would compliment her on how beautiful she looked, every day, no matter what. He would talk to her and never stop, because all too soon the time would come when there would be no more words.

Cherish her. That's what he would do. If only he could get her back. When she'd left, they hadn't thought about her return and how they would find each other. They hadn't counted on still being in German-occupied lands with a swath of Soviets between them.

Pawel groaned. Would life ever be the same?

How had it come to this? The grand plans he had at the beginning of the war, how he would fight the Germans who stole his son and make his only child proud, had been for naught. *Tak*, there had been a few he had aided, but not enough. Not nearly enough.

So many thousands, maybe even millions, of his countrymen lay cold in their graves, the Polish ground bathed by their blood. And his aid to them had been so small, so insignificant.

As he rose from the chair, it creaked. He straightened the papers on his desk, then turned and swiped a layer of dust from the books on the shelf behind him. He wandered into the bedroom and picked up the clothes that lay in a pile in the corner. When he opened the wardrobe to hang them, he caught a whiff of Antonina's scent. Though time had diminished the potency of the fragrance, the odor of jasmine tickled his nose.

He slammed the door.

In the kitchen he swept up the broken dishes from the tile floor and wiped the counters. Once he had the kitchen returned to order, he sat in the old brown armchair beside the front window and peered into the gathering darkness.

He would wait for whatever came next. His hands didn't tremble or sweat. When a man strode up the path to the house, Pawel went and opened the door before he knocked.

Pan Fromm's eyes glinted in the light streaming from the house, and he stood ramrod straight. "You've been expecting me."

"What do you want?" Pawel's words escaped on a sigh.

Fromm pushed by him. "Where are they?"

Pawel clamped his lips shut.

"Tell me now or face the consequences. You weren't delivering a baby; you were helping my wife escape with those Poles and that Jew. Where are they?"

Still, Pawel's heart didn't beat any faster than normal.

Fromm struck him across the cheek, and he stumbled backward. But better to hold on to his secret than tell Fromm what he knew. If he concealed the information, Fromm wouldn't kill him. Not until he learned his wife's location.

"I demand you tell me where they went. You were part of their escape." Fromm leaned in, his hot breath on Pawel's face. "I'll go so far as to say you were the mastermind. All this time, we allowed you to live because you were of use to us. But you were the brains of the entire operation, weren't you? *Weren't you?*"

Pawel remained statue still.

Fromm shoved Pawel into his chair, pulled his handgun from its holster, and waved it in circles. "Don't you dare move or I'll fire. They're here somewhere, and I'm going to find them. And then—" He blasted a shot into the ceiling, plaster raining on the tile floor.

The man had gone mad. Still clutching the pistol and aiming it somewhat in Pawel's direction, he pulled the cushions from the couch and overturned the end table. Then he grabbed Pawel and, with the barrel of the gun in his back, Fromm forced Pawel into his office.

"They're here. Where have you hidden them?" He swiped the books from the shelves and worked to move the bookcase. "This has to open. You've hidden them behind here. I know it. I can smell them."

Pawel choked back the laughter rising in his throat. Apparently Fromm didn't have the best nose.

Room by room they went like this, Fromm flashing the gun in Pawel's face as he ransacked the entire house for the second time today. And Pawel stood and watched without a tremor passing through his body. This absence of fear was strange. He should be terrified, but he wasn't. He had plenty to hide, and Fromm would find it if he conducted a less frantic search.

This sensation must be from God. There could be no other explanation. Pawel enveloped himself in it, a cocoon to protect himself from Fromm's craziness.

Maybe Józef experienced this peace too, as his life came to an end, right in this very room, with his mother and father as onlookers. How they had scrubbed the tiles to wash away his blood.

If Pawel could just be sure that his son had not been frightened. He closed his eyes and brought the horrific scene to mind once more. This time, as the events played out, he concentrated on his son's face.

Ah, the smile. He'd forgotten Józef's smile as the Nazi raised his gun.

A joy because he knew where he was going.

And now, Pawel could go to the same place with the same joy.

When Fromm turned up nothing in the last room, he stuck the pistol in Pawel's chest and pulled the trigger.

And there was Antonina again, her blonde hair swept away from her face, leaning over him, kissing him, then standing and smiling at him with that sweet smile she reserved only for him.

Welcoming him home.

<hr />

Natia covered Dominik's mouth to keep him from crying as the car carrying Elfriede pulled away. Beside her, Teodor shivered. Was he only cold, or did he fear what lay in front of them?

Silence fell. In winter no crickets sang, no frogs croaked. The world remained as still as death.

Time went by, maybe a few minutes or a few hours. However long, Natia's heart must have thudded a million times until Teodor moved beside her and rubbed her back. "That was close." He dared to give a low chuckle.

"I didn't understand all of what Elfriede said, but whatever it was, it worked. She saved our lives."

He pulled her to her feet, and she situated Dominik on her hip. His eyes wide, he stared at Teodor. Natia pointed at him. "That's *Tata*." How delicious the word.

Dominik nestled against Natia's neck and sucked on his thumb. "He'll get used to you. He's the sweetest boy." And hers. Theirs. No one would rip him from them now. Elfriede was on the run and didn't know where she would end up.

Standing there in the cold, moonless night, hunted by the Germans, Natia giggled, then laughed, then guffawed.

"I think you've gone crazy, *moje słońce*." Teodor's soft voice held a note of concern.

"He belongs to us. Don't you see? We have a son. A little boy all our own. He's not going to end up on the hill with the others. He's a real, living, breathing child. For all time, we'll be a family."

Teodor kissed her behind her ear, and a different kind of shiver shot through her. "I couldn't be happier than I am in this moment."

The Lord had restored her joy. But it wouldn't be complete until she stood on the land that belonged to them. She pulled her husband close. "Let's go home."

"I would love nothing more."

Natia scrambled out of the ditch, her legs burning by the time she reached the road. She turned to Teodor, who struggled on the incline. He wasn't the strong, virile man she had known and loved almost her entire life.

Once she had Dominik packed into the cart and covered with layers of blankets, she went to help her husband.

"How are we going to do this when I don't have the strength to get out of a ditch?" He stared at his feet, his shoes held together with rags tied around them.

How would they? Two half-starved people with a small child and only a vague idea of how to get home. The odds said they wouldn't make it. Dominik shifted in the cart. "Mama, Mama."

A well burst inside her. Their dream lay within reach. The farm, the two of them, and their child. "We haven't survived so long to give up now. This is not the Teodor I know. That man wouldn't let everything he wanted slip through his fingers. He wouldn't give up." She grasped him by the hand and pulled until he stood on the road. "That's the first step."

He caressed her cheek. "I should be the one taking care of you."

"Between the two of us, we'll find the strength we need. That's what marriage is about. I made vows too that day we were joined into one. Let's see if we can get this donkey moving so we both can ride for a while."

They climbed aboard, and Teodor snapped the reins on the animal's backside. She must have had enough of standing in the cold, because the cart creaked forward. Maybe not at the pace they would have liked, but in the right direction nonetheless.

"Do you know what got me through those long, awful days?"

A smile rose to her lips. "I think it was the same thing that kept me going."

"Each day, I listened for your song. When I heard it, I knew you were alive and well. I could close my eyes and pretend I was with you instead of inside that prison."

She snuggled against him as they plodded home. "Was it as horrible as I imagine?"

The donkey *clip-clopped* for a long while. The quiet almost suffocated her. Teodor cleared his throat. "It was bad, and I will never say anything else about it. We have all suffered. But that is in the past. Look at what we have in front of us. Many happy years, Lord willing."

She wouldn't force him to speak about his experiences. If it was better for him to forget, then he should lock those memories away where they wouldn't haunt him.

"Sing to me, *moje słońce*. Right now, I need to hear your voice."

She sang to him through that long night, until pink painted the bottom of the clouds.

Until the rattles and squeaks of another line of tanks drowned out her voice.

♪♫♪

Chapter Thirty-Seven

Only when the soldier had driven for about half an hour did Elfriede relax against the back of seat. By now she must have enough space between her and Erich. He wouldn't think to search this far away, believing her too stupid to be able to escape such a distance.

But what lay ahead? What should be her next step? *I don't know, Lord. Please show me.* "Where are you headed?"

The man, Otto, didn't break his concentration from the convoy of vehicles in front of him. "Just a short ways. The Russians are mounting an offensive. We're pulling back to regroup and make a stand. We won't allow them on German soil."

"Is there a train station?"

Otto slipped a cigarette from his shirt pocket and, with one hand on the steering wheel, lit it and puffed. "I imagine so. It makes sense to take us where we can get supplies. Though the Soviets are bombing the rail lines."

"Bombing? Then it isn't safe for me to travel by train."

"There's no way to travel that guarantees you're going to get where you're going."

"Then how am I supposed to return home?"

Otto shrugged. "You might be best taking your chances on the train."

Nein, that had been a silly thought. The conductors demanded payment and papers, neither of which she had. There had to be another way.

They continued their journey, and Elfriede dozed from time to time. Her hair had escaped from its rolls and pins, and with no comb or brush, she let the last of it down.

Her stomach roiled in her midsection, a wave of nausea crashing over her. "Pull over."

"I can't."

She heaved, fighting back the vomit.

Otto whipped to the side of the road and came to a screeching halt. She flung the door open and threw up right beside the car. Twice more she heaved, until her stomach emptied itself. The nausea didn't pass, but she had nothing left to expel. She reached behind her. "Do you have a handkerchief?"

He slapped a rough piece of cloth on her open palm, and she wiped her face. "*Danke.*"

"Are you okay?" His question didn't harbor a tone of care and concern, only irritation.

"I'm fine." No point in telling him otherwise. If she did, he might toss her out and leave her to fend for herself.

She clutched her stomach as they drove onward. How much longer could she hold on before she would have to make him stop again?

Behind them came a low, dull rumble that grew in strength and volume every second.

"Stop the car."

Instead Otto pressed on the accelerator, and they jolted forward.

"Stop! I'm going to be sick."

"Do you hear those Russian planes?"

The bile rose higher in her throat. "How do you know?"

"After all this time, I know the difference between German engines and Russian ones."

"They must be going to Berlin." Elfriede fought back the rising of her stomach.

"Too low. They probably have us in their sights. They must have seen the headlights."

She couldn't hold back the nausea any longer. Fearing messing up the inside of the auto, she cranked down the window, leaned over, and vomited.

The *ack-ack* of gunfire broke the stillness. Her heart raced, matching the rhythm of the shooting.

The car swerved. Otto pulled her inside. "Get down! Get down!"

Ahead of them, the earth exploded, showering dirt and rocks on the vehicle. She couldn't breathe.

As Otto tugged on her left hand, her right elbow hit the door handle. The door swung open. Another earth-rocking boom splayed dirt everywhere. He released his grip on her wrist. Once more, he jerked the wheel.

She worked to grasp something. Anything. But nothing presented itself.

She tumbled from the vehicle and rolled to the side of the road.

A whistle, louder than anything she'd ever heard, screeched above them. She covered her ears, then her head.

For a moment, there was silence. All the air rushed from her lungs.

Kaboom. Kaboom. Kaboom. Explosion followed explosion. Her ears rang. Hot air flowed over her, carrying with it the odor of fuel and burning rubber.

Elfriede heaved again. Nothing came out, but she couldn't control the vomiting.

When the buzzing in her head calmed, the screams of men replaced it. Shrieks of bombs and of dying soldiers. She couldn't discern which was which.

As suddenly as they had arrived, the Russian planes left. Shaking from head to toe, Elfriede didn't dare leave the safety of the ditch. She concentrated on inhaling deep, regular breaths and keeping her stomach from rebelling.

An eternity might have passed, or maybe only a few minutes. Time didn't matter. At last, though, she climbed from the ditch.

Nothing remained of the convoy. Russian bombs had wiped

out every truck and every car. Only smoldering hulls remained. And charred bodies.

She turned away from the horrific sight and, as she gagged, she covered her mouth and fell to her knees. Sobs wracked her.

What was she going to do? The attack had obliterated her only means of transportation. Where was she? There was nothing to give her a clue. Unless it was a large arrow pointing toward Berlin, it probably mattered very little.

"Oh God, help me! Are you there? Are you listening?"

Only the bitter, biting wind whipping through the bare trees gave her any answer.

What was she going to do? She had to come up with a plan, but the horror, the illness, the cold robbed her reasoning skills.

She paced in small circles to stay warm. Maybe she should start walking. But where would she go? How would she survive?

Dawn painted the sky pink and yellow. Time left her with only one option. She pulled her coat tighter and marched in the direction the vehicles had been traveling. The brisk movement kept her warm, and the upset in her stomach subsided.

From behind her came the ticking of an engine, and she turned to find a car speeding in her direction. She moved to the side of the road to avoid being run over.

But the auto slowed and stopped beside her. Though it bore no official marks, it must belong to a German. The average Polish citizen didn't have access to petrol. Right? Still, her hands dampened with sweat.

"*Dzień dobry.*" Though the fair-haired man at the wheel spoke to her in Polish, there was no denying his German accent.

She blew out a breath she didn't realize she'd been holding. "*Guten tag.*"

A smile crossed his face, and a dimple deepened in his right cheek. "Ah, you are German."

She trembled. Maybe it wasn't a good thing this man was a

fellow countryman. She was a hunted woman. Breaking her gaze with him, she marched away.

He inched the car forward to keep pace with her. "I'm Bernard Wimmer. And you are ...?"

There was no way she could outrun a car. Her only chance lay in continuing her earlier charade. "Frau Eisinger. My husband sent me out with the convoy back there. I ... I think I'm the only one who survived." The lump in her throat was not part of the act.

"You were in one of those vehicles?"

She nodded.

He opened the door and motioned for her to get in. She glanced over her shoulder. *Nein*, Erich didn't follow her. At this point she had nothing to lose. She wasn't going to survive without help. After flashing Bernard a small smile, she slid into the seat beside him.

She rubbed her hands together. "*Danke.*"

"How long have you been out there?"

"Most of the night. The Russians bombed us, and the convoy exploded. I managed to escape the car just before it burst into flames."

"God was watching out for you."

She turned her attention to him. His Aryan profile was strong, yet his mouth and green eyes held softness. How different he was from her husband. She twisted the wedding band on her finger. "*Ja*, he was. I don't know how I'm alive when everyone else is ..."

"Where are you headed?"

"Home."

He tipped his head and gave a three-note chuckle. "That much, I figured. We're all going there. Where is that for you?"

Could she trust him? She had no real reason to, but there was something about him, something she couldn't identify or articulate, but his words about God watching out for her relaxed her. They might be a ruse, but her gut told her they weren't. "Bremen.

Any assistance you could give me would be much appreciated. I have nothing left."

"Don't worry. I'll make sure you get on the first train we find headed west."

She bolted up straight in the seat. "Isn't that dangerous? Otto, the young man who was giving me a ride, said the Russians were bombing them."

Bernard frowned. "There is no safe travel these days. This is war. There are always risks. I'll do my best, but the rest we'll leave up to the Lord."

She nodded. Here was another person God put in her path to help her and to draw her closer to him.

"I'll do everything I can to return you to your home so your husband can locate you when he gets out."

"My husband ..." Elfriede stared out the window as the Polish countryside flashed by. She would miss this place and these people. Already an ache filled her heart. Where were Teodor and Natia? What about Dominik? She stifled a sob. Were they safe?

"What's wrong?"

She startled, almost having forgotten about the man at the steering wheel. "Nothing." How did she tell him that she wished her husband would be captured, that he deserved whatever punishment the Soviets meted out to him?

"I'm sure this is hard on you. Do you have any other family?"

"I was an only child, and my mother passed away some years ago. And my *vater,* I don't know what will become of him. If he's still alive, I'm sure the Americans or Russians will detain him."

"Any children?"

That loss cut more than anything. She loved Dominik, even if he was Jewish. If only she could be part of his life. Maybe Natia would tell him stories about her. Perhaps he would grow up knowing that he had one woman who gave him birth, another who raised him, and a third who loved him from afar.

Elfriede wiped away the tear that trickled down her cheek.

Bernard cleared his throat. "Are you okay?"

"Missing those I love."

"You'll be home soon."

Ja, home alone, because she would never live with her husband again. If their house still stood and Erich never returned, perhaps she would sell it. They had planned to fill it with children.

But she would buy a place with two bedrooms. One for her and one for Dominik, should he ever decide to visit.

Chapter Thirty-Eight

Teodor sat in the back of the cart as the line of tanks approached, the ground rumbling underneath their engines. Natia kept driving. Between the weakness and the fatigue, they would have never made it to the ditch. Besides, men in tanks weren't on the prowl for a couple of labor-camp escapees. They had put too many miles between themselves and Fromm. If he was going to find them, he would have done so by now.

At least, that's what Teodor counted on.

Dominik, his thumb in his mouth, climbed onto Teodor's lap and stared at the tanks. Teodor couldn't stop the grin that broke out on his lips. Oh, how nice to have a little one so close. The boy bounced, pointed, and clapped.

"Those are tanks." They could have fun together, the two of them. He could teach Dominik about farming and animals and fishing. All the things a boy needed to know. No wonder Natia had become attached to him. He was an easy child to love. Teodor had already fallen for him.

The first in the column approached and then squeaked by. More and more came, the sound of them roaring in their ears. Teodor caught himself holding his breath. Were they fleeing the Soviets or preparing for a battle? He and Natia didn't want to drive straight into a firefight. They might have to find another route home.

As each tank passed, Teodor studied them. While they resembled those from the beginning of the war, the ones that had rolled down the narrow lane through their quiet village, they had different markings. One sported a red star. Another had something written on the turret in Cyrillic.

Cyrillic. "Natia, we've done it. These are Soviets. We're out of German-held territory."

She turned to him, her green eyes large. "We are?" The words came out as a sigh.

"Do you know what this means?"

She shook her head, her dark curls bobbing.

"We're free, *moje słońce.* Free. No more Germans." He refused to spoil this moment with his fears about what Soviet occupation might be like. "The war is over."

"It's over?" She chuckled and then released a full belly laugh before dropping the donkey's reins and climbing into the back with them. She kissed him on the mouth, hard, full of passion and desire.

Teodor groaned. As soon as they got home, he would show her how much he loved her and how much he'd missed her.

When she broke away and he regained his breath, he tossed Dominik into the air, catching the giggling boy and pecking him on the cheek. "Your life is no longer in danger, little one. You can live without fear."

Dominik wriggled from his grasp and toddled to the cart's edge. "Look, look."

Natia patted the boy's head. "*Tak,* my dear, that's your freedom."

"Mama."

How beautiful to hear a child call his wife mother. He was an adorable boy with dark hair curling over his ears, long lashes framing his dark eyes.

Teodor's breath stuttered. If Natia was Mama, that made him *Tata.* For so long he'd prayed for a son. Now he had one, one who would come to know him and love him. "We'll wait here for a while. The Germans we saw last night must have been fleeing from this group. Who knows where they will engage. If we don't hear fighting from the town after a time, we can go there."

The donkey brayed and pawed the ground as Natia settled beside Teodor and snuggled against him. "I can hardly believe it. After all these years, those Nazis are gone. We'll get our farm back, our lives back. And it will be better than ever."

He couldn't crush his wife's optimism, wouldn't do that for the world. But life wouldn't be the same. The Soviets were here now, and deep in the pit of his stomach, something told him they weren't leaving soon. What would that mean for them and their little farm?

There was also the matter of the *Volksdeutsche* paper he had signed. If anyone in the town discovered that piece of information, life might become very difficult.

He shook his head. No point in worrying about something that might or might not happen. For the moment he had everything he needed. If he and Natia, and now Dominik, were together, that was all that mattered. God would take care of the rest.

Right now, he would enjoy this moment with his family and treasure it forever.

❧

A sea of people surrounded Elfriede in the Berlin train station. Not just a sea of them, but a rolling, swirling tide. Some were women bustling to their jobs in other parts of the city. A normal day, except the Third Reich was crumbling. Others were soldiers on their way to the front, nothing more than boys barely old enough to shave or men stooped with age. And still others were warriors returning from the fighting, broken in both body and spirit.

The usual train ride of a few hours had taken several days. Bombed-out locomotives and cars littered the tracks. Unexpected stops stalled them for hours, and unreliable train schedules frustrated her progress.

Here she stood, the warmth of the station and the press of humanity sending surges of nausea through her gut. She pressed her hand to her belly and fought it off. This illness was strange.

The upset stomach only plagued her in the morning. If she had food in her, no small feat these days, she was fine.

Sickness in the morning? She allowed herself to consider the possibility. About six weeks had passed since her last cycle. And she and Erich had been together.

She trembled from head to toe. Could it be? Could it really be? No other explanation made sense. She touched the place below her stomach, a place where a most wondrous miracle was happening. After so much time, she was pregnant. No doctor needed to confirm it. She knew it as sure as she knew her name.

And now, Erich could never find them. Even if it meant she had to flee Germany, she would protect her child from his father at all costs.

She wouldn't be alone in the world. A cascade of tears chased away all her sorrow, all the hurt and pain she'd endured. There, in the middle of the Berlin station, she hugged herself and cried with joy.

"Don't worry, my little one. I'll find a safe place for us. I promise."

All she needed to do now was figure out which train to board. One away from the Russians, one away from Erich, one away from *Vater*. She would break free from them all. With no other family, she'd make a life for herself and her child. The money Bernard had given her out of the goodness of his heart would have to be enough.

Which of these trains would carry her to a safe location, one away from Erich and away from the bombing she'd heard about? Bremen wasn't safe, but was any German city?

Dresden? Munich? Cologne? Where should she go?

She licked her lips. Whichever train they called next would be the one she would board as long as it headed west. She would trust the decision to God. He knew much better than she did where she belonged.

"Frau Fromm, is that you? I can't believe I found you."

The voice struck a chord of familiarity, but Elfriede couldn't place it. She turned, searching for a face she recognized but didn't find any. Wait a minute. That red hair. Elfriede bit her lip. There was only one person she knew with hair that color.

Erich's secretary from Poland. How had she gotten here? How had she found her?

And where was Erich? She had to run. Now. She hadn't come this far for him to capture her.

Elfriede spun around and around. No sight of him. If she couldn't see him, perhaps he couldn't see her. There had to be a way out. But how? Where?

Here came Fräulein Wurtz. Erich had to be right behind her.

Though her legs shook, she pushed forward, her pulse racing. "Excuse me, excuse me, I have to get through. Please let me through. Out of my way, please. I'm in a hurry." Her voice rose in pitch, but the crowd refused to part. She was trapped. As soon as the woman reached her, Elfriede would be as good as dead. Even if Erich wasn't with her, she must know that Elfriede helped hide a Jewish child.

Just as a sliver of light shone in between the two people in front of her, Fräulein Wurtz grabbed her by the arm. "Where are you going? Didn't you hear me?"

Dizziness washed over Elfriede. "I'm sorry, but I must leave. I'm going to miss my train." She wrenched out of the woman's grasp and glanced over her shoulder. Any moment she would spy Erich staring at her with his icy blue gaze.

With everything inside of her, she pushed against the crowd in front of her. Fräulein Wurtz grabbed her again. Elfriede struggled against her. The woman's hair hung in disheveled knots around her pale face, dark half-moons under her green eyes. Her lips, devoid of their usual red coloring, were bruised and swollen.

A gasp escaped Elfriede before she could check it, and she stopped struggling. "What happened?" Had Erich done this to her?

"The Russians overtook us before we got away. They ... Well, I just can't say. It's the most awful thing that ever happened to me. Unspeakable. But I fled before they killed me. Or maybe they didn't want to. Maybe those soldiers just wanted to torture me."

"Hurry. Before Erich catches us." Elfriede turned to go.

"Your husband—"

Fräulein Wurtz's quiet words stopped Elfriede in her steps.

"He's not coming."

"I don't understand."

Fräulein Wurtz worried the hem on the sleeve of the light wool coat she wore over her tattered green dress. "He had been away from the factory for a long time. I had no idea where he'd gone. When he returned, his face was redder than I had ever seen it. He slammed his office door shut. I heard him smashing everything."

She wiped her dirty cheek. "All of the sudden, the Soviets were there. They marched right into the office without a word and grabbed your husband."

Elfriede's knees trembled. "Is he ...?"

"They took the officers outside. I heard shots."

Numbness spread upward from Elfriede's toes until she didn't feel anything. And that was wrong, wasn't it? When your husband died, weren't you supposed to be sad? Maybe angry? But not this. *Danke.* I appreciate you giving me the news. Will you be okay?"

"Someday, maybe."

Fräulein Wurtz didn't say anything about Dominik. She must not know. And the numbness that enveloped Elfriede gave way to a spreading warmth.

At last Fräulein Wurtz released her grip on Elfriede. "I have to catch my train. I was going to try to find you once things settled down to let you know. I can't believe I ran into you here."

"God's providence. Take care of yourself. I'll pray for you."

With that, Fräulein Wurtz melted into the crowd until Elfriede lost sight of her. She found a bench and sat down, rubbing her midsection. "Did you hear that, little one?" She whispered so only she and her child could hear the words. "We will be safe now. We can go home in peace. I don't know yet what I will tell you about your earthly *Vater*, but I will tell you that you have a heavenly *Vater* who loves you very much. He is watching out for us and taking care of us."

And right there, in the middle of the busy train station, Elfriede found her joy. She laughed.

Chapter Thirty-Nine

*D*ominik snuggled against Natia and whimpered as the donkey plodded along the road. Her throat burned from so much singing to keep the little boy happy. Even her tunes no longer kept him from complaining.

The trip wore on all of them. Dark bags hung from underneath Teodor's eyes. Her stomach growled and grumbled. With Dominik on her hip, she knelt next to her husband. "Teodor, there's a farm ahead. Dominik needs some milk, and we all need something in our stomachs."

He stroked her cheek. "You have been so good and uncomplaining."

"After all we've been through, this isn't anything to whine about. But with each turn of the wheel, I get more anxious for home."

Teodor nodded. "Won't it feel good to be in Piosenka again, warm and snug and secure?"

She sighed. When would that be a reality?

Teodor guided the donkey and cart into the farmyard. Before he climbed down to ask for provisions, a woman stepped outside and waved her apron at them. "Get out of here. We've had enough beggars. There is no food here."

Natia pointed to Dominik. "Just a little milk for the baby."

"*Nie.* Nothing for any of you. Leave now, or I will call my husband, and then there will be trouble. Go on."

Teodor took up the reins once more and pulled back into the

lane. "Don't worry, *moje słonce.* There will be another farm with kinder owners."

She leaned against him and closed her eyes. Just to sleep in a soft bed once more would be glorious.

Next thing she knew, Teodor was shaking her. "Look." He pointed to a little town on the horizon. "Do you know what that is?"

"I have no idea." She shifted Dominik who had fallen asleep in her lap.

"Look hard and remember."

She squinted, but none of the buildings, not even the church steeple, triggered a memory.

Wait a minute. That steeple, painted white with an onion dome just below the cross. She had seen it before. But where?

She gasped and trembled. "This is Śpiewka, where we left from on the train."

"We're almost home."

"Did you hear that, Dominik? You'll soon be there. And we'll see Zygmunt too." She kissed the top of the slumbering child's head. He stirred but didn't awaken.

As they drew closer, a tune built in her chest. Despite the rawness of her throat, she allowed the melody to pour from her lips.

> *God, my Lord, my strength,*
> *My place of hiding, and confiding,*
> *In all needs by night and day.*

Dominik blinked his eyes open, and Teodor joined the song.

> *Though foes surround me,*
> *And Satan mark his prey,*
> *God shall have his way.*

By the time they reached the town, Teodor and Natia sang the last verse together with Dominik's off-pitch cooing.

> *Up, weak knees and spirit bowed in sorrow!*
> *No tomorrow shall arise to beat you down;*
> *God goes before you and angels all around;*
> *On your head a crown.*

The final notes of the song drifted away on the breeze. Tomorrow would never beat them down again. Life would have challenges, that was sure. But together with the Lord, she and Teodor would face them.

Dominik patted her cheek. "Mama?"

"Mama is happy." Out of the darkest, hardest time of her life had come a new strength and the greatest joy of all. Could a heart burst with happiness?

The journey between the town and their little farm, only several kilometers, was the longest part of the trip. More and more, she recognized their surroundings. A farmhouse with a familiar red-painted door. A grove of trees. A little stream flowing despite the cold, a gaggle of geese still playing in the water.

The cart ascended a small hill. Natia grabbed tight to Teodor's hand, because on the other side of the ridge lay her heart and soul.

He turned to her. "Are you ready?"

She nodded, her windpipe almost closed off.

They crested the hill, and there before them lay their farm. The whitewashed exterior of their house gleamed in the sunlight, the steep-pitched thatched roof in good repair. Whatever Germans had lived here had taken care of the place. Another blessing.

"Dominik, see this? This is your new house. Your home, where we are going to live together as a family."

The little boy stared at the house, then back to Natia. "House?"

"*Tak*, Dominik." Teodor gestured wide. "Our house and our barn and our land."

"Hurry up, Teodor, I can't wait any longer."

He urged the donkey forward. Never had an animal plodded so. She caught sight of the home she'd grown up in and the land beyond it. *Tata* and Helena would never return here. That piece of her would always be missing. But they lived in a far, far better place. In a palace of gold. She whispered into the breeze, "I love you *Tata*, Mama, Helena. We'll always remember you."

A lifetime passed, and then they finally pulled up their drive.

Home. They were home.

Teodor swung Dominik to the ground and helped Natia down. Zygmunt raced from the house and into her arms. "Natia, I thought I'd never see you again."

"I promised we'd be together. And you'll stay with us for always."

"I'm so glad you're home."

"And I'm so happy to be here."

At last.

Every muscle in her body relaxed, and she released Zygmunt, then turned to Teodor. "There is one thing I want to do before I go inside."

"We'll come with you." He and Natia each took hold of one of Dominik's hands, Zygmunt following behind, and the group made their way to the top of the hill where three little crosses still stood.

Natia released her grip on Dominik and dropped to her knees, tracing each of the names. "Beata, Szymon, Andrzej. I promised I would come back, and I have. These long years, I have missed you. My heart has been here." She touched her lips and then each cross.

The pain, once raw and fresh, was now scarred and aching. "I prayed that God would spare each of you, and in his way, he did. You did not experience hunger or pain or fear. For that, I am grateful.

"But I never stopped loving you." She pulled Dominik close to her side. "This is your new brother. I wish you could have known him, that you could have grown up together. I can see you splashing in the brook and chasing each other around the fields.

"No matter how much I love him, that doesn't mean I love you less." She drew in a ragged breath and swiped at the cascade of tears. "Every one of you has a place in my heart, my children, my loves."

Teodor knelt beside her and wrapped her in an embrace. "They know."

"I will take all my love for them and shower it on Dominik."

"You are a wonderful mother. I love you more than anything."

"Sing, Mama." Dominik squirmed between Natia and Teodor.

Śpij maleczko moja mała, czas na ciebie już. Ja cię będę kołysała, a ty oczka zmruż. Luli luli luli luli luli luli lu Luli luli luli luli, a ty oczka zmruż.

The song for her children. The song her heart sang. The song of joy the Lord had given her.

Acknowledgments

When I sat at my computer and wrote the first words of this book, I never realized what an emotional ride it would be for me or how personal it would become. As Natia and Elfriede struggled with infertility and pregnancy loss, it ripped open raw spots in my heart I believed long healed over. But I'm grateful for this journey and to be able to share a bit of my heart with each of you.

I, too, suffered through years of infertility. I, too, suffered pregnancy loss. Often, I felt alone. Like no one understood. Like God would never grant me what I wanted most. The things that Natia and Elfriede experience and feel are the same things I experienced and felt.

For those of you going through similar experiences, please know you aren't alone. God is still with you. And he will see you through the pain. If you need someone to talk to who understands, please contact me at www.liztolsma.com.

Out of that dark time in my life, he brought me the joy of adoption, three children I love more than I ever thought possible. He gave me more than I ever dreamed and has blessed me beyond my wildest imagination. Today, though the pain is still real, I can say I'm grateful for those difficult times because my greatest joys came from them.

And the book wouldn't have come to fruition without the contributions of so many people. It wouldn't be the same without my own beloved children: Brian, Alyssa, and Jonalyn. How I longed and prayed for each of you. What was God's purpose in not granting me biological children? So I would have each of you to love.

Brian, you are a fine young man who, like Teodor, would do anything for his country. I love you for that. Thank you for making me a mother. You will never know what a great gift you have been to me.

Alyssa, I love you with my heart and soul. Your kind, gentle spirit is an inspiration to me. Thank you for all you do for me when I'm busy and under deadline. I'm so proud of the beautiful woman you have become. I can't believe you are mine. As you prepare to embark on life outside of the nest, may God go with you. I'll miss you.

Jonalyn, you will never understand the words in this book, yet you understand more about the human spirit and the will to survive than I ever will. Thank you for your patience with me and for just being you.

And to my husband, the father of these children the Lord blessed us with. Thank you for being such a leader in our home and such a man of God. Thank you for putting up with me when life gets crazy. I love you more than words can say, *moje serce.*

Thank you to the Pencildancers—Diana, Jen, and Angie— for cheering me on and keeping me on task. If I didn't have to report to you each Monday, I'm not sure this book would have ever gotten written. You are the best!

Many thanks to my amazing agent, Tamela Hancock Murray. Can you believe this is book number eleven for me? Without you, I would have never made it to one. Thank you for all you do for me.

I can't begin to thank the team at Gilead Publishing enough. I love working with you guys! Becky, Jordan, Dan, and Katelyn— you make a great team. Thank you for making me feel part of the family. And thank you for all the hard work you do on my behalf. You are great blessings in my life.

Thank you to my amazing editor, Julee Schwarzburg. I can't

say enough about the hard work you put into each book. Without your thoughtful suggestions and your gentle teaching, these stories wouldn't come to life the way they do. There is no one I would rather work with.

A special thanks to Dawn Cahill and Stephenie Hovland for help with finding the source of the hymn that appears throughout the book. You can see what an integral part of the story it became.

Dziękuję Ci to Maja Litwajtis for help with the Polish words in this book. It was fun working with you and sharing some of the Easter traditions our families have in common. Thank you to Pegg Thomas for putting us in touch with each other.

And thank you to all my readers. Over the years, I've enjoyed getting to know many of you. Thank you for taking these journeys with me. Sometimes the stories aren't the easiest to read, but they are necessary to tell. Thank you for your loyalty, for your wonderful reviews, and for your encouragement to keep writing!

♪♪♪
Notes

As the Germans fled Poland, the Soviets flooded the country. Life was not easy for those who survived the war. As Communism sought to wipe away the memory of the Germans, so much of the history from WWII in that part of the world has been lost. I spoke to a Polish woman who ran a local deli, and she confirmed that she was taught nothing about the war in school. It was something the people never spoke about.

Because of this, the exact number of *Polenlagers* (Polish labor camps) is unknown. Sources I consulted varied widely, from forty to four hundred. What is sure is that many Poles lost their lives during the occupation. Three million Polish Jews perished. Three million Polish Christians did also. I wrote this book to bring their story to light.

I took information I found on several different camps and rolled them into the one. Likewise, the town of Pieśń Nabożna is a compilation of several Polish towns near the Czech border.

The Germans did institute a policy of resettlement of Poles. Many Germans were displaced in places like Ukraine and had nowhere to live. The Nazis stole homes and farms from the Poles, gave them to these Germans, and sent the rightful owners away to prison camps.

I read an account of a couple of Polish women who served inside a German officer's home. They hid several Jews in the basement of this home, literally under the German's nose. This became the inspiration for Dominik's arrival. By the way, the Nazi never discovered the secret in his home.

You might wonder why Teodor's last name is Palinski and Natia's is Palinska. In Slavik languages such as Polish, Czech, and Russian, there are male and female endings of names. Palinski is the male version; Palinska is the female version. The set of rules is complicated, but that's the short answer.

Though I strive to make the history as accurate as possible, I am only human. My apologies for any historical errors contained within.

About the Author

Liz Tolsma's specialty is historical fiction—from WWII to prairie romance. Her debut novel was a finalist for the 2014 Selah and Carol Award. She prides herself in excellent storytelling, presenting accurate historical details, and creating persevering characters.

Liz is also a popular speaker on topics such as writing, marriage, living with courage, and adoption. She and her husband have adopted all their children internationally. Liz resides in semi-rural Wisconsin with her husband and two daughters; her son currently serves as a US Marine. Liz is a breast cancer survivor and lives her life to the fullest. In her free time, she enjoys reading, working in her large perennial garden, kayaking, and camping with her family. Visit her blog, *The Story behind the Story*, at www.liztolsma.com.

Connect with Liz!
Facebook: @liztolsma
Twitter: @liztolsma
Pinterest: @liztolsma
Instagram: @authorliztolsma

Coming Soon

The next stanza in the Music of Hope series

Visit us online for the latest updates:

www.liztolsma.com

www.gileadpublishing.com